LOVE'S SWEET TEMPTATION

His body turned, his amber eyes locked with her own, their intensity seeming to burn her. He lifted a large brown hand and stroked her chin, and she noted involuntarily the hair of his forearm and the black thicket at his chest. The fingers sent a shiver through Ermgarde's neck to her breasts, and she dropped the linen cloth. Her hand went to his cheek, caressing the growth of bristle on his square jaw.

Averting her eyes quickly, she anticipated his next request and scurried for the length of linen, holding it out to him whilst she looked away. He took it, and she could hear the water slap as he stepped from the tub. A tentative look found him standing before her with the linen secured about his hips, his gaze full of amusement.

"Shall I see to the removal of the tub, my lord?" she asked, hopefully, seeing it as a plausible excuse to leave him and collect her tattered senses.

"No. Methinks you could do with a bath yourself . . ."

THE BELOVED

Julia Wherlock

CHARTER BOOKS, NEW YORK

THE BELOVED

A Charter Book/published by arrangement with
the author

PRINTING HISTORY
Charter edition/March 1987

ISBN: 0-441-05383-1

Charter Books are published by The Berkley Publishing Group,
200 Madison Avenue, New York, New York 10016.
PRINTED IN THE UNITED STATES OF AMERICA

For Christopher

*And with grateful thanks
to Bristol City Museum.*

THE BELOVED

BOOK
One

One wore his mistress' garter, one her glove;
And he a lock of his dear lady's hair;
And he had colours, whom he did most love;
There was not one but did some favour wear;
And each one took it, on his happy speed,
To make it famous by some knightly deed.

— Michael Drayton (1563-1631)
  Ballad of Agincourt.

CHAPTER

1

WAUTER FITZSIMMONS'S DARK BROWS WERE DRAWN TOGETHER in scrutiny over intense, amber eyes. The wide mouth—its cruel lines muted by dust and the stubble of brown-black beard—showed the merest semblance of a smile. He was oblivious to all except the gentle roll of hills that sloped to meet the pale blue sky on all sides.

For several moments only he and the land existed; there was no gay jangle of horse harnesses, no chatter from his squire, no rumbling from baggage cart or ribald laughter from the men-at-arms in the rear of the column. He let out a contented breath. *His* now for as far as the eye could see, his demesne, the baronial lands of the Lord of Synford.

This was his reward, a mark of esteem and gratitude from England's new king. Wauter took it as his due. He'd served the new king and the old faithfully over the last decade, earning his spurs of knighthood many times over in those troubled years when Henry IV precariously held the throne, and his son battled against the Welsh under their formidable leader, Owen Glendower.

The fortunes of the mighty never ceased to amaze him—nor his own, come to that. He had been but fourteen years old when his father, Simon of Waverley, had sent him to Bolingbroke, Earl of Derby and Duke of Hereford, to learn the ways of gentlemen and mayhap prove worthy of the spurs and title of sir knight.

It had been an uphill struggle in those early years. He was a child without name or right to inherit when his father died. Those rights would go to his half-brother, Ralph, who had had the good fortune to be born on the right side of the blanket—the legitimate heir. Being a bastard taught him to bear the stupid slights of others, to curb his temper instead of fighting, each time his dubious parentage was brought forward for examination. Eventually, his honor was not so easily outraged.

It was Bolingbroke who had schooled him to ignore the snickers and whispers. He insisted that bastardry was by no means unusual, reminding Wauter that the first Norman king of England, William the Conqueror, had been born out of wedlock. Hadn't his own father, John of Gaunt, sired bastards aplenty by his mistress, Catherine of Swynford?

In the two years preceding the fifteenth century, when Wauter was just into his teens, Bolingbroke began to show signs of discontent. He and his sons, Henry, John and Humphrey, revolved around the court of Richard II, and they seemed happy to serve the king, just as John of Gaunt had done during Richard's minority. But whereas it might have pleased the old duke to serve the innocent child-monarch, there was no pleasure for his descendants and their allies to swear allegiance and pander to the wishes of the grown king. Felicitous words of friendship were feigned; Richard was unlikable to all but a few.

He was surrounded by sycophantic courtiers on whom he lavished favors, had been accused by the church of indulging in perverted vices and did nought to endear himself to the powerful lords of the land.

The king decided to be rid of such irritants. In 1398 the Duke of Gloucester was taken to Calais and held prisioner; his subsequent death was almost certainly murder. The Earl of Warwick was sent to the Isle of Man in perpetual banishment. The Earl of Arundel was executed on Tower Hill, whilst his brother, the Archbishop of Canterbury, was exiled for life. Only Henry Bolingbroke and Thomas Mowbray, Earl of Nottingham, remained.

Obviously they were uneasy, wondering why *their* outspokeness against Richard's rule had not been silenced along with the rest. And the anxiety could have done little but increase when Richard bestowed upon them the dukedoms of Hereford and Norfolk. Surely that wasn't the action of vengeful royalty.

Mowbray spoke of his unease to Henry, declaring that he knew the king sought their downfall, and the latter, feeling pressured from all sides to act, reported the conversation to his father. The aging Duke of Lancaster was still a staunch supporter of the king—perhaps out of habit—and advised Henry to confront Mowbray in the presence of the king.

Accused of talking treason, Mowbray strongly denied the charge. The king watched the two nervous men with hard-to-conceal amusement. Henry would not be called a liar, Mowbray could not back down from his denial. Eventually it was arranged that they would settle the matter in a trial of combat that September at Coventry. However, for whatever reasons, Richard was disinclined to let them fight it out on the field of honor and instead banished them both—Henry for ten years, Thomas for life.

They were just into a new year, four months of hard-to-swallow banishment across the Channel behind them, when news came of the death of John of Gaunt. Henry locked himself away, to feel his grief alone. But the morose mood quickly turned to one of thundering rage when he learnt that Richard had had the audacity to declare him banished for life and the duchy of Lancaster forfeit to the crown. That he wouldn't endure.

In May of 1399, Richard made his most monumental blunder of all in departing with an army for Ireland to put down the unrest.

Henry decided it was time to go home.

Their progress from Ravenspur to Pontefract was little like a campaign. Richard's ineffectual viceroy, the Duke of York, dithered in the south trying to muster resistance and, as Henry marched, his ranks were swollen by Lancastrian supporters from every region and the heads of two dynasties, the barons Percy and Neville. Never one to miss an opportunity, Bolingbroke would no longer be satisfied with the return of what was rightly his. The Duke of York, with a small royalist force, gave in to the inevitable and threw in his lot with Henry at Berkeley Castle, Gloucestershire, on the 27th of July. Richard, returning from Ireland on the same day, was gulled into believing that Bolingbroke was appeased by the return of his possessions. He allowed himself to fall into an ambush laid by the Duke of Northumberland's men at Flint.

Bolingbroke was master of England.

His claim to the throne went before Parliament—Richard having been coerced into abdication—and, although the claim was paper thin, Parliament had no objections. For the most part they were sick of Richard, so why not give Bolingbroke a try? After all, if he didn't suit, someone could always be found to replace *him*.

Richard came to a violent end at Pontefract Castle where he had been held prisoner. It was considered imprudent to leave a usurped king alive to make trouble in the future, so Bolingbroke became King Henry IV on Monday, the 13th of October, 1399. Hence, Wauter found himself serving a monarch instead of a duke.

Eventually Wauter became aware of the rhythm of the horse beneath him. The destrier exuded a feeling of pent-up energy, and Wauter had to pat the warhorse's thick, black-brown neck. "In a while, Rogue," he assured the beast.

Eyes blank to the verdant countryside, it was evident he had been deep in thought for some time. The view had completely changed. Before them on the road, nestled amongst copses and gentle hills where sheep grazed, was a village made up of a squat, Cotswold stone church surrounded by huddled groups of sagging, half-timbered cottages.

His squire, Robert de la Vallée, spurred his mount forward to parallel Lord Wauter. " 'Tis the hamlet of Dillbury, my lord. Do we make a call upon the priest?"

"Aye, why not, seeing as we pass through. But see that the hounds are kept securely leashed in the cart. Our welcome cannot be assured if they decide to have their sport with the geese and chickens in yonder street."

"I'll see to it, my lord," said Robert with a grin, wheeling his horse around and heading back to the cart that held Lord Wauter's personal effects, plus the dog handler, Knollys, and a pack of sleek greyhounds.

They crossed the ford that marked the boundary of the village proper and went leisurely up the main street. Wauter noted with satisfaction the Red Lion emblem of John of Gaunt swinging from the gable of the inn. It was evident which faction the community had supported during the troubled years. No White Harts of Richard II here.

Like so many villages that nestled upon the Wiltshire-Gloucestershire border just west of the Cotswold Ridge, where limestone showed through the grassy hills, Dillbury's inhabitants had taken to sheep farming.

Wauter would call Dillbury's bailiff to Synford as soon as he was settled and instruct the man on how he expected those first payments of rent and tythe to be made. As for the year and four months that the demesne of Synford had been without a lord—old de Witt having died without issue to carry on the line—Wauter would let that pass. What better way to gain the people's good will than to let them keep the meager sums they had made?

Those of the village who were not occupied in the fields came warily but curiously to the doors of their homes. Who was this man who rode down their street, glancing at all and yet seeming to look at no one? Men noted with trepidation the twenty or so men-at-arms who rode to the rear, eyeing their hardened faces and show of weaponry. The women's eyes were drawn to the leader, his giant's frame atop the ferocious looking beast disconcerting them. With ill-cut locks falling over dark, shadowed eyes, and dust-grained face showing a stubble of beard about his jaw, they likened him to a brown bear.

Beside him rode a youth who looked frail by comparison; the standard he had unfurled showed three gold crosses and one silver castle on a black field. The whole was divided by a sinister bend of red. They could guess at what that meant: a bastard. But whose?

Chickens and geese squawked away from the thudding hooves that sent up choking clouds of dust. Children either clung to their mothers' skirts in terror or, if they were older and less timid, they ran alongside the column of men, calling out with enthusiasm. A few of the men-at-arms could be seen to puff out their leather-jerkined chests under the admiring gaze of the youngsters.

The sun had gone and the single bell of the church tolled the faithful to vespers. Seeing the nobleman turn into the north street that led to the church, the curious villagers followed. Wauter looked back once and smiled cynically. This evening, at least, the priest was assured of a large congregation.

At the lychgate he dismounted, motioning for the soldier behind to take the destrier's reins. He stretched, flexing his muscles, and there were scant females watching who didn't sigh at the sight. Then, with Robert de la Vallée at his shoulder, he stepped through the recessed Norman doorway, still oblivious to the commotion he was causing.

Father Anshelm's heart lurched as he caught sight of the large, soldier-like figure looming in the aisle. Then an audible

sigh escaped him when the man moved from the shadows of
the rotund nave piers and revealed himself to be unarmed and
smiling. Coming forward from the chancel, the priests' eyes
widened as half the village seemed to spill in behind the
stranger.

"I had intended to make myself known to you in a quieter
manner, sir priest, but opportunity presented itself, for Dillbury is on our progress to Synford. I am named Wauter Fitz-
Simmons, the new lord of this demesne," explained the man.

"Ah, I see," Father Anshelm smiled in welcome. Not a rob-
ber baron, then, as he had first thought.

Behind them, the villagers who hadn't caught the full conversation begged of their neighbors, "Who? Who?"

"Wauter Fitz-something-or-other. Our new lord."

"Oh!" The word was full of speculation.

"I am pleased to welcome you, my lord. Will you stay for
vespers? Afterwards, if you need lodgings and supper, my
house is at your disposal. Our host at the Red Lion will look
after your men—I presume you travel with a retinue?"

"My men are outside. No, I'm afraid we cannot stay the
night. I am eager to see Synford and, if we press on, will be
there by dawn."

"I understand."

"But mayhap I could partake of a glass of wine after you
have conducted your service."

Anshelm nodded agreeably before going back to the chancel
with a swishing of cassock skirts.

The villagers, finding themselves achurch and unable to
escape without causing offense, mumbled through the sung
praises, their attention on Wauter and the squire.

During prayers Wauter let his eyes roam about the nave.
There were no pews—as was the norm in most churches at the
time—the infirm and sick sitting on the stone seats carved in
the walls. For the most part the people of Dillbury looked
healthy and adequately clothed. There were few infirm or
undernourished to be seen. How many potential men-at-arms
were among them? How many archers? Perhaps a contest
could be arranged between the villages of his demesne to ferret
out the best fighters.

The amber eyes returned to the two peasant girls who stood
at the front of the worshipers. He had noted them earlier—the
obvious faith of one and the dutiful compliance of the other.

They, along with a handful more, had been at the church on his arrival, not like the others. The youngest, with the makings of a nun, sang the songs joyfully, lifting her head and staring trancelike at the hammer beams above. The eldest, perhaps seventeen or so, followed the well-remembered words but without the same fervor. She, he could never visualize as a nun, and his own thoughts were becoming far from holy.

Her hair was midnight black, and in the pale light of the altar tapers the edges shone blue, like a raven's wing. Her face in profile was tanned gold, and her lips were full and dark, flashing white teeth that were without flaw. Oh, to plunder that mouth! Wauter felt his loins stir. He hadn't had a woman since leaving London, and that was nigh on a week ago—a lengthy period of abstinence for him!

He couldn't distinguish the color of her eyes, save that they seemed dark in the waning light. Their shape was incredibly round and dark lashes cast shadows upon her cheek. His eyes scanned her body from her coarse homespun tunic, which was laced across the full, high breasts, to the tattered hem at her calves which was cut short to show off tanned ankles and bare feet.

No wonder serf girls were forever getting themselves tumbled, if that was how they dressed, he thought. At court the ladies swathed themselves in tunics, houppelandes, mantles and surcoats, every inch right up to their ears concealed, even veiling their hair. His eyes lingered on the black, slightly waved tresses of the girl, noting where they ended at the swell of hips. He imagined the feel of something so luxurious.

Robert de la Vallée heard the husky current that had crept into his lord's praying and looked for the reason. Ah, so that was it. He knew the signs well. The wench would find herself on her back before the night was through, he was sure.

Ermgarde intercepted yet another bold stare from the Lord of Synford and looked away in confusion, stumbling suddenly over the words of the Gloria. Why did her heart beat as if to escape the confines of her breast? Seeing what was in his mind all too clearly behind the hungry stare, she should have known better, known the risks she was bringing upon herself. But she couldn't help it. He drew her eyes like a magnet, and the feelings that washed over her left her palms damp and her cheeks flushed.

The service was drawing to a close. She tried desperately to concentrate on what Father Anshelm was saying from the pulpit, but to no avail. The dark-haired one, emanating brute strength, had robbed her of all thought save of what it would be like to lay encircled in his arms. She shook herself with alarm. What was the matter with her? Fearfully, she realized her thoughts had never strayed down that path before.

"Ermgarde? Come, sister, you are in another world. Everyone is leaving."

"What? Oh yes, sorry, Maud, I was . . ." Ermgarde broke off lamely, not daring to continue further. Maud was too goodly to talk to on *that* subject. Tell her sister she had the urge to lie with a man!?

She looked to the door of the church, but he was already gone. They were quite alone. Could she have mistaken that look? She'd felt so sure, so certain of his peaked curiosity. But he couldn't have been, or at least not to the same degree as she because he had gone. The fire within her died to a smolder and Ermgarde went out into the cool twilight of the graveyard feeling cheated, and yet relieved at the removal of temptation.

CHAPTER

2

WAUTER TOOK A HURRIED YET COURTEOUS FAREWELL of Father Anshelm then went to join Robert, who stood waiting with the destrier at the foot of the priest's house.

"Which way did they go?"

Robert grinned wolfishly. "On the westerly track out of the village. My bet is their father keeps sheep, my lord."

"More than likely. Let's be off then; I've promised Rogue a gallop." Wauter gave a final salute of farewell to the priest who stood on the porch of his stout house and, wheeling his mount about, pounded down the street, Robert following in his dusty wake. The men-at-arms quickly erupted from the Red Lion at their summons, then the formidable looking band took the westerly track out of Dillbury.

Already intoxicated, the men-at-arms were ready for anything, their spirits leaping as the two figures came into view before them. So it was to be wenching! They knew this game of old; most agreeable.

"There they are, my lord," pointed out Robert, eagerly.

"Aye, I see them." Wauter kicked his mount into a full gallop and let out a chilling roar that was echoed by his men.

Ermgarde and Maud clung to each other in fear as they registered the thunder of hooves, followed by the male roar, as they walked home. Their eyes—rounder than ever, like cornered rabbits—shot back along the path. Instinctively they began to run. If they could reach the copse, perhaps they could lie low until the men rode away.

"Oh Mary, Mother of God!" shrieked Maud, hysterically, stumbling along in her terror.

Ermgarde was no less frightened, but a great deal more penitent. She had brought this down upon them by the blatant interest she had shown. God upon high was going to punish her in the most mean of manners for entertaining such sinful thoughts in His house. But she hadn't known. It had never seemed conceivable that the naive invitation she gave with her eyes would mean submitting to him *and* his men! Blessed saints, poor Maud! This would kill her, for she had never wished to be any man's save the Lord's.

They were running apace, the hooves sounding terrifyingly nearer behind them. Then Ermgarde floundered in a rut made by oxen, and fell down.

Maud stopped at the moan of pain and exasperation, turning back in order to help the elder sister to her feet. Ermgarde was strugging to get upright, testing her ankle frantically. It pained her but she would still run. She had to. The alternative was far worse than any sprain!

"Go on!" she screamed to her sister. "I'm right behind you. Whatever happens, don't come back. Run to father . . . get help."

Maud obeyed mindlessly. The group of horsemen bearing down upon them filled her with a strong sense of dread. Her sister was wiser, knew best. Maud always followed her instructions without argument, and the thought of those men. . . . Her stride lengthened; her pained lungs and a stitch in her side swept Ermgarde from mind. She knew only that she had to get away.

Ermgarde knew that they were closing, but her pace failed to quicken in response to the message from her brain. And when the dust rose and she was cut off by circling horses, the girl stopped and wrapped arms about her face in protection from the flailing hooves that threatened from all directions. Maud was too close, still in danger. She didn't dare scream her terror or her sister would try to aid her, and then neither would be saved.

Two riders took off after her sister. She moaned sickly, turning her fear-crazed eyes to the Lord of Synford, who had edged his imposing mount through the other riders. He hovered threateningly over her, his face hard and full of lust even in this poor light.

"Please, lord, I beg you, leave her be," pleaded Ermgarde, backing away from the massive hooves of the destrier that seemed itching to tread her into the ground. Her grandfather had told her how they were trained for warfare. They had no fear of the smell of blood like ordinary mounts, and in fact seemed savagely enlivened by it. They instinctively kicked at anything that fell before them—knight or fellow beast—with a bloodlust that equaled their riders'.

So intimidated was she by the destrier that Ermgarde was hardly aware the lord had called back his men.

"Back!" It was like an order to hunting hounds and the two responded not unlike curs, wheeling their mounts about obediently and riding to him with surly expressions.

He laughed derisively, feeling that they deserved some sort of explanation after being cheated. They had wanted the fleeing wench. "There would have been little fun in it, men, with her chanting prayers and saying Hail Mary's all the while beneath you."

They were inclined to disagree, but didn't dare to voice their disappointment. It wouldn't have been the first time they had tumbled some religiously minded female. Why, during the Welsh Campaign they'd sacked many a nunnery, and several of the men had pilfered beneath the habits of the good sisters. They still had this girl, though, with her veil of hair and lissome body. They began licking their lips, anticipating the spectacle of the other men enjoying her before their turn.

"Shall I quiet her down for you, my lord?" asked one swarthy, leather-clad figure, eagerly dismounting from his horse and advancing on Ermgarde.

"She looks subdued enough," observed the lord amusedly, watching her wary retreat before his man-at-arms. He wondered how easily she would surrender—whether she was used to a tumble or would give too much of a fight.

Ermgarde's shoulders seemed to sag, as if resigned to the inevitable as she was backed into the circle of horses. Her chin sank, swirling black tresses around her breasts, their lushness seeming too weighty for so delicately boned a face. The man's breathing grew rapid at the sight. Then, just as the man-at-arms would have grabbed her and forced her to the earth, the girl snatched his dagger from its sheath and slashed at the offending hands.

There were stupified gasps from the men and a rumble of appreciative laughter from the lord. They'd caught themselves a bitch with spirit. Now it was the soldier's turn to retreat, backing off with lacerated palms clenched under his armpits, his eyes pain-glazed and enraged.

"Come near me and I'll turn the blade upon myself. Get

what fun you can from a dead body!'' she sobbed, the wounding of the man sending her to the verge of hysterics. Not until that moment had she ever felt malice toward any human, but willingly she could have killed him. She looked around, crazed. They had her trapped within the circle. Horses' heads and leering faces blurred before her eyes. There was no escape.

Pain weakened her grasp on the hilt of the dagger, causing her to cry out and clench her wrist. She looked up into the closed, brow-shadowed eyes of the lord, knowing it was he who had disarmed her. He no longer seemed amused by her terror.

'' 'Twould be a pity and a waste to turn that knife upon yourself,'' he told her brusquely, leaning down from his mount in one assured movement and grasping her beneath the shoulders to hoist her onto the destrier. She settled in front of him, petrified into stillness.

"Me thinks the wench is shy and in need of privacy,'' he ventured laughingly for the benefit of his retinue. He coaxed the horse beneath him to back-step out of the circle in a pattern used to escape a dangerous military situation.

Well, if that didn't beat all! The men-at-arms looked at each other in growing discontent. He wasn't even going to give them the fun of watching!

Robert de la Vallée, as surprised by his master's actions as they, took control. "I suggest we repair to the village and find more willing amusement. Where should we meet you, lord?''

"Synford,'' called Wauter, his mind on the tiny waist encircled by his hand.

The May night had turned chill when Ermgarde was dropped to the ground beside a darkly running brook, the long grass reaching up to her knees and scratching her legs. For a moment she thought about fleeing into the dark and making her way cautiously to her father's house. But he must have sensed what was in her mind.

"I shouldn't bolt, if I were you. Old Rogue would like nothing better than to hunt you down.''

So she stood where he dropped her, stiff and angry. And afraid. They weren't far from the woods, she knew, having sensed their direction of travel in the dark, but no one was likely to discover them or try to effect her escape. There were no lights at windows, or smoke rising from chimneys; no friends near.

The short ride had thankfully ended quickly, for she had had to suffer the constant nearness of him, the vise-like grip as he clenched her to his chest, the male smell—horses, sweat and leather. Their overpowering presence hadn't allowed her time to think.

She sensed rather than saw him dismount and tether the horse to a sapling yew nearby. Then he was behind her, pulling her back against him urgently, wrapping his arms about her like a lusty bear and burying his face against the midnight shroud of her hair.

"Your name?" he asked, his mouth finding the lobe of her ear while a hand fanned downward from her waist, applying pressure against her belly so that her buttocks were pressed into his hard flanks and aroused manhood.

"Ermgarde, my lord," came the eventual reply, gasped out as the other hand traveled upward to her breasts. He fondled, then pulled at the laces that bound her bodice. He was making it difficult for her even to remember her name! Yet it was fear, surely, that set her thoughts into turmoil, not passion.

The smoldering sensation that had taken hold of her in the church had evaporated at the sight of him leading his retinue to hunt down Maud and herself. Now all she could think of was that he might force her and then hand her over to his men for their enjoyment.

The girl writhed in his grip, crying out in confusion. "Please, my lord, *don't*. Give me a moment that I might be calm. I was sorely frightened and cannot now respond to you."

He released her abruptly, snorting like some ill-tempered horse, and went to stand at the stream. Lord above, now the wench was crying! Trust him to pick a touchy one. His voice was cold and dismissive. "The men like the excitement of the chase, girl, and that was *all* I intended they should enjoy this night. You were for me, me alone. Get youself gone now, for I've lost interest in the whole business. And stop that damnable noise! Have you no conception of how it grates on my nerves? Heaven only knows why you should take on so. Your brazen invitation was obvious enough in the church. It's I who should feel vexed at having my time wasted."

Ermgarde settled into the grass, fixing her gaze on his impressive outline, not daring to speak. Silvered clouds sailed across the moon, leaving the sky clear and the gentle landscape bathed in pale light. For the first time the girl became aware of the chill in the air and rubbed her hands and bare feet.

Lord Wauter turned at the movement, evidently surprised to find her still there. "Haven't you gone yet?" he muttered, peering down at her, the bridge of his nose and cheek bones silvered by the night light.

She gave a meek, "No, my lord."

He snorted again. Kicking at the grass beneath his feet in consternation, Lord Wauter tried to make out the expression on her face. Nothing was clearly defined save the dark pools of her eyes and stubbornly pursed mouth. What was he to do with her, pray? Certainly not tumble her. Her earlier bout of tearfulness—which thankfully had ceased—had deadened his desire.

He looked at her hair, the dark shroud cascading to her hips. "How came you by such a name?"

" 'Tis French, my lord."

"I *know* that," he said shortly, with superior inflection. "That is why I asked."

"My father named me, lord, but 'twas my grandfather who first heard of it. He served as soldier under the Black Prince during the French Campaigns of the 1350's, and heard the name in a poem. Truly, 'tis Erm*e*ngarde, but everyone shortens it for the sake of convenience."

"Then you are named for one of the greatest patronesses of France, Ermengarde, Viscountess of Ventadorn," Wauter told her.

"I don't know about that, my lord."

" 'Tis a fact. She was the only Ermengarde of import and had poems written and sung in her honor by the troubadour, Bernart de Ventadorn. He was so besotted with love for the lady, he referred to her as Bel Vezer—his Lovely Vision."

"How wonderful to be so well loved. Do you know the poem, my lord?"

"Lines, not the whole. 'Tis performed at court sometimes."

Court. Oh, that magical word! "Are *you* often at court, lord? What is it like? Is it true that the lords and ladies dress in sable and ermine, and that the females shave their foreheads

and pluck out all their eyebrows?'' inquired Ermgarde, genuinely entranced.

"Yes.''

She pouted in ill-concealed disappointment. What sort of an
answer was that? He was being purposefully awkward, she
knew, determined that she shouldn't forget her place.

"Do you like the court, my lord?'' she ventured once more.

Wauter gazed down at the shadowy figure in exasperation
and wonder. God in heaven—but a short while ago she had
been wailing in terror, squirming from his grasp as if he'd
been afflicted with leprosy. Now here she was chattering away
like a hen in a coop! There was no sense to it. And, worse still,
he was allowing her to get away with it instead of sending her
home and putting an end to this travesty.

He sat down beside her, aware anew of the smell of meadow
and sheep that clung to her, drawing his knees to his chest and
clasping his arms about them. He watched the dark waters of
the brook as he spoke. "I like the court well enough for the
short periods of time that I am there. But mostly I'm cam-
paigning or, as now, come here to secure the lands that have
been given to me by the king."

"You know the king?'' She could only stare at Wauter in
wonder.

"We are acquainted."

"You don't look like a baron. That is, I think you are as a
baron should look, but *nothing* like Lord de Witt. He was a
drunken lecher. Father used to make me stay indoors whenever he journeyed to the village."

"You shouldn't speak of your betters thus," criticized
Wauter.

"But it was true, though, lord. No woman under forty was
safe."

"He had the right. Don't forget that."

"Father didn't. That is why I was always kept out of sight,
for I was just past twelve at the time."

Wauter's lip curled in distaste. For himself, he'd never
knowingly taken any girl under the age of sixteen! It was a
gentlemanly rule treasured in his mind, for by that age most
girls were already well experienced.

"And why aren't you married? Or are you? You must be
well past the wedding age."

"I've been *asked*, lord," Ermgarde told him, her pride surfacing. "But they were not the sort of fellows I'd like to have stayed with for life. And my parents don't mind the extra mouth, for I look after the sheep with Maud."

"Maud was the girl with you tonight?"

"Yes. I must thank you for sparing her. She wasn't born for an earthly existence. Her longing is for the church. But of course that's impossible. 'Tis only fine ladies who become nuns, and father couldn't afford to see her admitted to an order."

"How many brothers and sisters have you?"

"Seven. Eight by the autumn."

Wauter couldn't suppress a laugh. "Your parents must have a strong *affection* for each other."

"Oh, they have, lord. I think that is why I haven't wed. I'd have to feel something akin to what's between them."

"And what will your father do when he finds out you've been stolen away this night? Your sister has no doubt spluttered out her story and he likely thinks you raped, or worse. I can see it was a mistake ever looking at that pretty face of yours."

"Never fear, lord. He'll do nothing against you, I'm certain. He's well aware of the rights of a master over his vassels," assured Ermgarde, less certain in her own mind.

"I hope you're right. 'Twould be a shame if I had to punish him for forgetting those rights."

For several moments the girl was thoughtful, musing over the problem in her mind. *What* would her father do? She hugged herself coldly, becoming acutely aware of the man beside her now that silence enveloped them. She shivered, wishing those thick-set, leather-clad arms about her.

"I'm no longer frightened, lord," she told him, turning a little so that she could tentatively watch his reaction. There was none to speak of.

He said, simply, "Good," and rose to his feet to stretch like a Goliath.

In miserable indignation, Ermgarde followed suit, relacing the bodice of her tunic and watching as he untethered the horse and whispered to it. He showed more interest in that vicious beast than he did in her! He mounted. Was he going to ride off and leave her? Her heart beat a panicked tatoo.

"Come. 'Tis time to leave." He extended an arm to her.

Ermgarde approached warily, nearing the destrier with trepidation, a question marking her moon-bathed face.

"Go? Where? You're not taking me back to my father?" she asked, fearing for him.

"Nay, I'm not."

Her wrist was grasped, she was hoisted up behind him, the frail seams of her skirt tested as she found herself astride the horse's considerable rump. Her arms went about the man's impressive girth, clasping pleasurably at his belted waist. After a while her cheek came to rest against a shoulder blade.

Ermgarde didn't know where they were going; she didn't think to ask. That was neither here nor there. Of import only was the fact that she was with him.

CHAPTER

3

WAUTER REINED IN ROGUE and eyed the castle of Synford, which rose up before him. Not very grand, but wholly functional and stout to his eyes. A four-storey Norman keep loomed from within the walls; it was a basic rectangular structure with arched embrasures from the great hall level upward, its summit crowned with crenellated battlements.

This was the place to start the FitzSimmons dynasty.

He gently shook Ermgarde, who had been seated in front of him for many hours now, since that time at the black of night when he had felt her arms slacken about his waist, and had lifted her around to his front.

She roused slowly and with obvious reluctance, trying to burrow against his jerkin. Bemusement at her whereabouts gave way to a smile. "Good morn, my lord." The red mouth issued the formal greeting shyly, and she shifted uncomfortably, wondering how she came to be in his arms.

For several moments Wauter didn't speak. He was gazing back into those eyes, startled by their color. Violet orbs peered back, framed by thick, curling lashes. He dragged his gaze away, back to the castle, feeling idiotic in his obvious fascination. He'd fallen in love with a peasant!

"Let us go in," decided Wauter, eager to get behind those curtained walls and appraise himself closely of what henceforth was his. Rogue moved to the drawbridge, spurred by his master, his hooves clattering across the oaken structure beneath them.

In the ward lined with shadowed lean-tos, the chickens that pecked idly about were sent squawking in all directions by the horse. The lord was about to lower Ermgarde to the ground when an uncertain, wary voice called from behind.

"How can I help you, sir?"

The girl was dropped instantly, Wauter's hand drawing

forth sword from scabbard, Rogue wheeling around instinctively to face the owner of the voice.

The snorting horse and menacing sword of the rider filled the old man's eyes with fear. "Please, take pity on me! I mean no harm, really I don't!" he whined, in a rush of panic. "I wondered only who came. Few strangers pass through Synford."

Wauter sheathed his sword, glowering. "That was a foolish thing to do, old man. I don't like surprises."

Obsequious now, the wrinkled, gaunt-faced serf shuffled forward, then beamed Wauter a grin that revealed blackened stumps where teeth should have been. He kept a tight hold on the pitchfork he had picked up fearfully on spying the bear-like rider enter the ward. It wouldn't afford him much protection should the intruder prove to be unfriendly, but it comforted him nonetheless.

Wauter turned his eyes to Ermgarde, who crouched, a grimace on her face, at his horse's feet, rubbing that area of her anatomy which had come into harsh contact with the ground. She shot him a look of indignation as he dismounted, her pride wounded.

His annoyance at her for failing to understand his rough treatment was transferred to the cringing old man. His voice rasped as he inquired, "And *who* might you be?"

"If it pleases you, sir, I am one of the late baron's retainers. I come now and then to see that the drawbridge and suchlike are kept in working order. He charged me to do thus before his death."

"That is gratifying, my good man, though in future you shan't need to worry yourself with such things. I am the new lord here and my men follow behind."

"Our new lord? But . . . why . . . we've heard nothing of this . . . no word was sent. My apologies, my lord, that you should arrive to find the place thus"—his eyes wandered about the ward disparagingly—"and no one here to greet you. We would have put things in readiness."

"Nay, don't concern yourself. I had no mind to survey this place for the first time with hordes of curious villagers pressing about and causing a nuisance. If you would go now and have those who once served here assemble promptly, 'twill suit me fine."

"I'll see to it right away, my lord." The old man back-

stepped deferentially, his hooded eyes beholding the wench for
the first time. A beauty indeed, though obviously from peasant stock. Could it be that the new lord had the same appetites
as old de Witt? Martin the Carter harkened back nostalgically
to those days when his master had filled his castle with the
tastiest wenches in the county. Too bad he was now too en-
feebled for such strenuous play, for some lords could be
generous with their leavings.

Touring around, Wauter learned that food stores and a
water well were kept below ground. There were no torches
available and a closer inspection would have to wait. Ermgarde followed in the baron's wake; her presence no longer
seemed to register with him as he examined every nook and
cranny of the ground floor. He paused to admire the small,
neat chapel built into one corner among the supporting piers
of the keep. The fan vaulting of the ceiling showed breathtak-
ing workmanship, obviously of a later date than the cruder
Norman core. The rest of this floor would be given over to
sleeping and living quarters for his men, he decided, and it
would house the armory.

Wauter mounted the stairs next to the main door of the
keep, bounding up them two at a time, and was soon out of
Ermgarde's sight.

Following, she soon found him past the two lines of trestles,
benches and the supporting piers of the gallery, which gave the
hall a nave-like appearance. He sat lazily in an X-shaped chair,
woolen-hose-clad legs stretched out before him and crossed at
the ankles. His attention was held by a chicken that strutted
unperturbed up and down the table before him. Ermgarde
watched him, her heart taking up that irregular beat which was
becoming familiar at the sight of him.

The dark-shadowed eyes left the chicken and settled on her
as if he had just become aware of her standing inside the door.
The glow in his eyes warmed her, flushed her cheeks and made
her legs tremble.

" 'Tis a dismal mess. But once the servants have been put to
work and the walls strewn with a few tapestries and banners,
'twill look quite regal," he mused.

Ermgarde scanned the walls, imagining it all, seeing the
beautiful lords and their ladies sauntering along the gallery
against the blue light from Norman arched windows that were

decorated with perpendicular tracery. So grand, so fine—so unattainable.

"Let us explore further before the place is overrun with the curious come to gawk at their new lord." He rose from the chair and made his way behind the screen painted with red and black chevrons that separated hall from solar. His muscled agility left Ermgarde to envisage the powerful body beneath the jerkin belted snugly at the waist. His large proportions, the bulging thighs and biceps, bear-like girth, all gave her cause to be both captivated and nervous. She felt a yearning that ached for something, though she wasn't quite sure what.

Ermgarde reached the solar and took in the cozy feel of the room, noting the leaded window panes, the recently constructed fireplace and the canopy chimney bearing the de Witt coat-of-arms. Wauter was once more climbing, this time up an unobtrusive spiral staircase set into the corner, which was evidently for the sole use of the lord and immediate family.

For someone who had never before set foot inside the castle, the new baron was endowed with an uncanny sense of direction. On reaching the top of the stairs and waiting for Ermgarde—who wasn't used to spirals and clung to the walls dizzily before reaching him—he turned a sharp right and opened a door set into a gloomy recess.

"The lady's chamber," he told her without even looking in to assure himself it was indeed so.

"How did you know?"

"The Normans were predictable builders."

The corner chamber was quite empty, and the unadorned Cotswold stone walls lined with narrow arched windows heightened the effect. A cream light set the chamber in a mellow glow. It was pleasing to the eye and bright, and the glass recently installed at the windows would keep it relatively comfortable during the chill of winter.

"A little plain perhaps?" wondered Wauter, aloud, retreating back into the passage.

Ermgarde kept her peace. Having spent all her life in a hovel made primarily of clay, straw and rubble stone, she thought the chamber a prize. But it wasn't her place to make comment.

They moved down the corridor from the southeast chamber to the southwest, and even Ermgarde had no doubt that the next room they came to would be the lord's.

Wauter opened the door and glimpsed in, about to usher the girl forward, then abruptly barring her way with a burly arm. He placed his bulk in the doorway, blocking her view as he glanced about with amused surprise. So de Witt *had* been a lecher, and one with quite jaded tastes, if the decor was an accurate reflection of the man. Evidently the last lord of Synford had traveled to the East at some time, or had dealings with a merchant in Eastern artifacts. The wall tapestries and sculptures showed kohl-eyed women dressed in the gossamer-thin garments of those heathen countries, when they were dressed at all. Their postures left little to the imagination, most either copulating with masked, god-like figures or else reclined in seductive poses.

Wauter coughed, wondering what he was to do with such tasteless furnishings, and stepped back, pulling the door to him. "Nothing of interest in there. Let us move on to the gallery."

Ermgarde nodded readily, having glimpsed past the barrier of his body. She'd been shocked by what had met her eyes. Coupling she understood, but what those people in the silken threads were doing was something entirely different and disturbing to her virginal mind.

They reached the eighth arched window in the line of eleven that flanked the gallery and Wauter paused to stare out with pleasure on his new possessions. There were woodlands where he could hunt, flatlands running on either side of the stream where he could conduct arms practice. He was content, and, to top it all off, he'd found love.

Wauter had savored the courtly games of love and found them lacking after the initial amusement had worn off. There were few ladies at court, to his mind, who deserved the adoration that was heaped upon them by knights obsessed with the doctrines of chivalry.

Love. He'd professed it often enough in the lighthearted, dishonest manner that was the way of most courtiers when they sought a lady's favor. Now, here was the real thing. It couldn't be seen or appraised like some fine object, but it was there just the same, a tangible thing. And with each moment he spent with her, though few words passed between them, his certainty grew.

She was beside him, supposedly taking in the view of his northerly lands, though her thoughts were truly no more on the countryside than were his own. He sensed her awareness of him—as if she knew his mind, knew him more thoroughly than anyone had before. It was an eerie sensation.

Her small, work-roughened hand rested on the sill and his covered it on sudden impulse. She didn't flinch or draw away with false modesty. He slid his hand up her wrist to her elbow and she was pulled into his arms, feeling the length of him against her with a shock of desire. Her body curved itself to the muscled contour of his, her bare arms sliding around his neck serpentlike, so that her breasts were flattened to his chest.

His amber eyes glowed down at her and when he drew back his lips, he looked like a ravening wolf. Then he lowered his mouth over hers and Ermgarde moaned with the pleasure. Even on tiptoe, straining against his body, she couldn't seem to get close enough, to bring her body into contact with as much of him as she would have liked. Wauter came to her aid, a hand circling the curves of her buttocks to draw her up against him fully.

She felt the core of him, whimpering when his tongue explored her, her belly knotted with yearning. Her legs turned to water.

Ermgarde was set on her feet abruptly, staggering slightly in surprise. She looked up at him askance, wondering what she had done to offend, but his eyes were no longer on her. He stared over the carved stone ballustrade into the void below, his face portraying annoyance. Voices wrested Ermgarde's attention and she followed Wauter's line of vision. Their cocoon-like solitude was over.

"My lord? Lord, I have brought the servants as you required," called Martin Carter, at the head of a vastly assorted crowd, his gaze scanning the hall in search of his new master.

Lip curling in exasperation, Wauter muttered a curt acknowledgement of their presence.

CHAPTER

4

MINUTES AFTER THE OLD SERVANT burst into the hall, Lord Wauter's retinue clattered into the ward with much commotion and Ermgarde sought out Robert de la Vallée, as the lord's squire, to see if there was any assistance she might provide during so hectic a settling-in.

Robert, struck by her beauty, which was so more apparent in the daylight, could see immediately why Lord Wauter had ridden ahead to Synford for an entire night. It would take more than one night to tire of such a wench.

"Your name?" he asked, hefting sections of black metal armor from the baggage cart.

"Ermgarde, sir."

"Ermgarde? Rather grand for your like, is it not?" he opined haughtily. She might be the lord's temporary plaything, but he wished her to have no illusions about her place. "Very well, girl, you may take these lighter sections of plate up to the closet next to the lord's chamber. And when you've finished that, find someone to shift the bed from his chamber to the lady's and have the place made habitable. My lord has expressed a preference for that chamber until the furnishings can be altered in his own. By and by, as yet I am without the spurs of knighthood, so you shall forego calling me 'sir.' Master Robert will suffice."

"As you will, master Robert," agreed Ermgarde, finding his predilection for protocol amusing.

Soon the smith had chased the chickens from the forge and found tinder with which to start a fire. There was even a small amount of coal from the mines at Kingswood, near Bristol, to ensure a blaze over which he could fashion new hinges, brackets and anything else the carpenters might need to aid in repairs.

Lord Wauter's falconer looked over an outbuilding that he

thought might prove suitable for the castle mews, and the master of the hounds, Knollys, unleashed his yelping pack of greyhounds to wander and make themselves at home about the ward.

Within the keep the new lord was putting the erstwhile servants through a vigorous examination, dispatching those who wouldn't suit and assigning the remainder to their new duties.

Using the postern door to the keep and the back stairs to the bedchamber—as per instruction from an officious Robert de la Vallée—Ermgarde had quickly assembled all the lord's harnesses of armor in his closet. Then she marshalled two idle servants to move the baronial bed from its previous sumptuous location, to the plain but far more tasteful lady's chamber.

Other women brought up chests of linen and the lord's apparel and set about righting the room. They stuffed mattresses with fresh straw and covered them in new ticking and—whenever they could sneak a peep—scrutinized this low-ranking stranger in their midst.

Ermgarde left them to prepare the bed and clear away the dust, and started back down the stairs.

Robert de la Vallée was nowhere to be found and, after inquiring of several men-at-arms, she finally learned that he had taken off for the woods with a hunting party to find some game for the lord's table. It was dusk when the band returned displaying the conies, thrushes and larks that they had killed.

Robert, his cheeks pink with youthful exhilaration, threw the bloody rabbits at the serving girls who came from the kitchen and, steering his mount toward the stables, cast his eye upon the hovering Ermgarde.

"Master Robert, the lord's room is in readiness. What more would you have me do?"

He dismounted, the bells on the horse's bridle jingling, and set about removing the heavy, Hessian saddle. After some thought, he decided. "Have a tub taken up to the room. My lord is partial to a bath after a long journey. You can attend him."

Ermgarde colored to the roots of her hair.

Robert laughed. "What's brought the blush to your cheeks? Heavens, but peasants are prudes about such things! All great houses have someone to attend to the bathing of themselves and their guests; it's customary. And it's not as though you

have cause for embarrassment at the thought of seeing Lord
Wauter in all his naked glory. You did, after all, spend last
night—''

"But we didn't," Ermgarde hastily corrected him.

"You didn't? You mean he never . . . ?" Robert looked at
her, stupified.

She shook her head, shamed that he should know the lord
found her resistible.

"Good lord!" He set the saddle atop the wooden partition
that divided his stall from the next and gazed at her inquiringly. "Why didn't he?"

"I was frightened, and then he didn't seem inclined to."

"Well, I never!" Robert shook his head, bemused. "As for
the bath—you'll have to attend him. Everyone else is busy
enough as 'tis. No, I'll have no arguments. What's between
the lord and you is no concern of mine."

He turned his back on her, removing reins and bridle, and
Ermgarde glared at his fair head haloed by locks clipped
neatly just below the ears. If he wasn't her better she'd have
been tempted to box those arrogant ears just as she did her
younger brothers' when they vexed her. But one had to have
wary respect for Robert de la Vallée. She flounced out of the
stable and went in search of a servant who might know where
a tub could be found, growing more agitated with the passing
moments.

The Lord of Synford was as much surprised by the choice of
bath attendant as Ermgarde herself when he stepped into the
chamber, all urgent business seen to.

Ermgarde hovered uncertainly beside the coopered tub from
which an inviting cloud of scented steam rose, her eyes
downcast, her hair falling about her face and breasts. "My
lord, your squire bid me ready your bath," was all she could
think to say.

"Humph . . . thoughtful of him," said Wauter. He cast an
eye about the transformed chamber, which was now very
pleasing with its carved bed and furniture, as well as the
damask and brocade covers and hangings colored in a startling
gold and black. He began to unbutton the top of his jerkin,
then paused on an afterthought, looking directly at Ermgarde.
She looked fit to die of embarrassment and so pity took him.

"Go find my squire and instruct him to collect a change of

wardrobe from my closet along the passage. A houppelande, braise, tunic and hose—he'll know what to give you."

"Yes, my lord." Ermgarde scurried out, glad of the reprieve no matter how short. She loitered accordingly, but could only delay her return for so long. She knocked; he bade her enter.

"Put them there." A burly arm, brown tanned and sinewy, pointed to the bed.

She obeyed, sending up a prayer of thanks that he was already in the tub and wouldn't require undressing. Then she stared out the window at the blackness, waiting. To have become his on the spur of the moment was one thing, but this feared and yet desired closeness was unbearable. The tension was becoming torturous.

Why didn't he speak? Her body steadily grew more rigid as she listened to the splash of water behind her and his steady, rhythmical breathing. Eventually it was Ermgarde who spoke, fearing her nerves would snap if she didn't put an end to the situation. "Do you require anything else, my lord?" Her voice was tremulous.

There was a momentary pause before he ventured, "Wash my back, if you will."

She turned, keeping eyes rooted to the floor and knelt behind him, then took the square of linen and chunk of soap that he held out. As she washed she stared fixedly at the back of his head where brown-black locks curled untidily and wet at his nape.

Somehow the eyes strayed. He had an admirable back where the muscles rippled freely whenever he shifted position, and Ermgarde soaped each curve and sinew thoroughly, wondering over the powerful symmetry. His numerous scars only added to his overall appeal and the girl's hands moved unconsciously over them, familiarizing herself with the angry red or faint silver marks. She stopped washing, breath coming laboriously, a finger tracing one silver zig-zag down his spinal column.

His body turned, as did his head, and his amber eyes locked with her own, their intensity seeming to burn her. He lifted a large brown hand and stroked her chin, and she noted involuntarily the hair of his forearm and the black thicket at his chest. The fingers stroked the lobe of her ear, sending a shiver down through Ermgarde's neck to her breasts, and she dropped the

linen cloth, her hand going to his cheek, caressing the growth
of bristle on his square jaw.

Suddenly he seemed to shake himself free of the spell that
held them and, turning away, rose from the bath, presenting
Ermgarde with a picture of taut buttocks and sturdy legs, as
the water streamed down in rivulets.

Averting her eyes quickly, she anticipated his next request
and scurried for the length of linen with which to dry him,
holding it out to him whilst she looked away. He took it, and
she could hear water slap as he stepped from the tub. A tentative look found him standing before her with the linen secured
about his hips, his gaze full of amusement.

Would he dismiss her now? Surely it was the squire's duty to
see to the dressing of his lord? "Shall I see to the removal of
the tub, my lord?" she asked, hopefully, seeing it as a plausible excuse to leave him and collect her tattered senses.

"No. Methinks you could do with a bath yourself. You
stink of sheep!"

Ermgarde looked at him agape as he padded across to the
bed where his garments lay. "Me? Nay! I . . . I couldn't!" she
spluttered, staring at the water in horror.

"Why ever not?" he wanted to know, eyebrows lifted, waiting for some good reason that was hardly likely to be forth-
coming.

Take a bath! Was he mad? Did he expect her to undress
without a qualm? And then again there was another very good
reason for her reluctance: everyone knew that bathing was
unhealthy, liable to give any fool a chill from which they'd
never recover. Washing her hair and the skin that showed had
always seemed adequate for her and the rest of the family,
with perhaps a yearly immersion in the stream that ran
through Dillbury when the weather was fair. But she'd never
taken a bath. *No one did*.

"I can't, my lord. I'd catch cold and die," she uttered, fearfully.

"Nonsense. Bathing never harmed anyone. I've been doing
so all my life and I've never been in bad health. Now off with
that tunic and let's have no more of your idiocy."

The firmness of his tone jarred her. "But, my lord . . .
please."

"I'm going to find my squire and get a shave. If you're not

in that tub by the time I return, I'll undress you myself. Understood?''

Ermgarde eyed the spicy water with suspicion as the lord donned a pair of russet hose and shrugged his way into a loose undertunic. Turning from the bed he smiled at her look of distress, buckling his belt and running fingers through his wet locks. He went to the door, leaving her to come to a decision, but if she couldn't, he'd do so for her on his return. One way or another she *was* going to take a bath!

The alarmed girl didn't act until she heard him speaking to one of the men-at-arms in the passage on his return. Then, in a sudden rush of panic, she pulled the tunic over her head and leaped into the tub. Drawing a deep breath in apprehension, she sat down, hands flying to cover her breasts, which the water didn't quite reach. The door opened and he entered.

A crooked smile creased his face as he went to stand at one of the window embrasures, as she had done earlier, supposedly looking out.

Painfully aware of his presence, Ermgarde moved cautiously, relieved to find that the water was having no immediate ill effects. Picking up the soap and sniffing it, she rubbed it experimentally between her palms, wondering at the creamy lather. It smelled marvelous. She rubbed her knees, surprised to find that her skin was peachy-tan beneath the accumulated filth, and several shades lighter than she had thought. She washed one spot, then another curiously, eventually dampening her hair and soaping it into a lather.

She looked to where he stood, unnerved to find that he had ceased to browse over the view and was now watching her. Instinctively she sank lower until the water reached her neck.

"How do you find it?" he asked, the sight of her before she had sunk modestly leaving his voice husky. She had magnificent breasts; generous, with pert rosy nipples as dark as her lips.

" 'Tis not so bad, my lord." She wondered how she was going to get out of there with him standing watching. He was leaning nonchalantly on the sill, scrutinizing her.

Then, causing Ermgarde even more discomfort, he left the window and came to kneel behind her so that she was covered suddenly by his considerable shadow.

"I'll wash *your* back," he decided.

"I . . ." The lord wash her back? How could she say nay? Quickly she pulled the black tresses around to cover herself as best she could, bending a little as she felt the pressure of his hands going to work. Head bowed, she felt a crimson biush color her cheeks.

Wauter discarded the cloth, using his hands instead to run over her peachy flesh with a growing awareness of his urgent need for her. She felt good; his hands, slippery with soap, glided up about her neck and throat, touching earlobes and delicate jawline beneath the masses of hair. And down, following the soft lines of her shoulders and arms. He had to have her.

Ermgarde's eyes narrowed langourously at the sensual touch, her skin shivering, and again she experienced that aching knot of yearning in her belly. Even her embarrassment lessened as she came alive beneath his knowing touch.

He traced a trail of kisses from one shoulder to another. She turned with desire, wanting his lips on hers, her mind closed to all save the feel of him and her growing passion. Their lips met, and her dripping arms fastened about his neck even as he encompassed her waist in a crushing embrace.

Ermgarde was hoisted from the tub, his mouth against hers as he issued a growl of desire and transported her the short distance to the low, giant-proportioned bed. There he deposited her, pulling tunic over head and dropping hose before joining her.

She watched his hasty undressing with awed fascination, the sight of his naked body causing her to forget her own state momentarily. Her earlier imaginings had not been exaggerated. He was a proud man, a might frightening, too. His eyes devoured her face with its wide-eyed expression as his hands explored her, savoring breasts and belly, thighs and hips. Then his lips traveled the same course, teasing nipples and gliding down over navel, his tongue leaving a trail of fire.

Tentatively her fingers reached out to explore him in return —damp locks, bull neck and tautly muscled shoulders. The hair of his barrel chest was like wiry silk to her fingers, and the muscles rippled beneath her touch. She let her palms run lower, down over his flat belly and slim hips, though nervously avoiding that one area from whence his manhood sprang.

Wauter moved appreciatively under her ministerings, obviously delighting in her increased boldness, though surprised, too. Could this mean that she wasn't altogether ignorant of the rites of love? Virginal she appeared, and yet. . . . There was an eagerness in her that caused him some doubt. He'd had virgins before, girls glad to part with their virtue, yet even they put up a token resistance. Ermgarde showed no apprehension, false or otherwise.

He drew his body away from hers and looked hard into her face. Great luminous violet eyes looked back at him, clouding with passion, and at the same moment tiny fingers fastened about the shaft of his manhood. His eyes half closed with the pleasurable sensation and, dropping his mouth to hers, a hand delved for her own hidden softness. What did it matter after all whether she be pure or not? His wanting her hadn't lessened.

Had she better stop? He'd grown dangerously large to her mind as it was. Then he was exploring her and her grasp on his manhood became firmer, almost frantic, as her own feelings leaped out of control. Her other hand twined in his hair, tugging it, pulling him down closer as his tongue darted between her lips and the fingers stroked and probed delicately, causing her legs to go rigid and her body to writhe. He could see that she was more than ready.

She felt the tip of him pushing firmly between her thighs, glimpsed down and could see the black triangle of hair at his loins and that part of him which was striving to gain entry. She managed a nervous smile, the lusting look in his amber eyes making her shiver. Her hands reached up and clasped him behind the head, feeling the urge to consume those lips. A murmur of discomfort escaped her as her body's resistance gave way bit by bit and he pushed surely into her depths, his loins molding between her thighs.

Wauter's heart sang out. She *was* a virgin. His, only his— for now, and always. At last he allowed his mouth to come down to hers, kissing her with a savage joy, tongue ravaging and lips working until he had Ermgarde moaning.

The discomfort had gone as quickly as it came and now there was only pleasure, her body arching against his to fit him all the more. Her mind leaped every time he moved against her. She forgot his bearing and moaned his name, "Oh, Wauter . . . Wauter."

It sounded like a sigh, or a thirsty cry for a drink, and he grinned, thinking her beauty beyond imagining in those moments when her body lost all control and she looked up at him pleadingly, wanting to put an end to the exquisite torment he was inflicting. She was almost there, he could tell, her head lolling langourously from side to side, her eyes opaque, no longer focusing clearly on him.

She couldn't stop it. Whatever was building within her had passed beyond her control. She gave herself up to it, meeting his quickening thrusts and grasping at his taut buttocks to bring him into her further. And, finally, there it was, that explosive throbbing that sent shock waves through her. Her nails dug into his flesh and she cried out, half in terror, half in elation, believing naively that she couldn't survive something so shattering.

The throbbing died eventually and her breathing lost its gasping quality. She looked up at Wauter, taking in the almost pained look of concentration as he moved purposefully on, the air rushing down his nostrils, jaw clenched. He'd been so wonderful, so thoughtful. To lay with him and find such joy had surpassed her wildest dreams.

Ermgarde brought an arm up against his back, holding him close, drawing herself up against him and burying her face in the hollow of his neck. She kissed whatever flesh her lips contacted, tasting the sweat that had broken out over his body and finally finding his lips to kiss him in the manner he had used on her. Her tongue darted against lips, caressing him, her lips worked passionately and the Lord of Synford moaned in response, taking up a killing pace. His large hands grasped at her hips and, ramrod stiff, he slid into her depths for the final time, shuddering as he released his seed.

With a drawn-out sigh, he came to rest down the length of Ermgarde, his face nestling in the hollow of her neck where a pulse throbbed. He wrapped his arms around her and held her close.

He whispered amusedly, "There, now you smell only of me, not sheep. My sweat, my seed. You're mine, just as if I'd put my seal upon you."

"Willingly, lord, for I do love you," she answered honestly, seeing no reason to keep her feelings hidden.

"You too? Is it possible for two people to be smitten so quickly and completely? I've more years of experience, can compare rationally what I feel for you against past interludes, but what of you? You're only a child, not worldly wise. How can you be sure?'' he demanded, amazed to hear her say that his love was returned, wanting desperately to believe and yet doubting.

Ermgarde looked levelly into the intense, troubled eyes. "I'm sure of what's in my heart, lord. From the moment I saw you I wanted nothing but to be yours. No man has ever made me feel remotely like that. 'Tis love, I'm certain.''

"Then all will be well," he sighed, the burden of doubt lifting as he found her lips to kiss deeply.

The chamber door groaned open and Wauter's head shot round, his body quickly positioning itself so that the more intimate portions of Ermgarde were hidden. She shrank against him in embarrassment.

Robert de la Vallée froze in the doorway, the color draining away from his face as he took in the thunderous countenance of his lord; the silver goblets, which he carried upon a tray along with roasted chicken and a chalice, rattled noisily. He spluttered, "My lord, I beg your . . .''

"*Out*, Robert. Now!" roared Wauter, looking as if about to jump from the bed and give the squire a lesson in etiquette that he'd never forget. He couldn't, because Ermgarde would be left in the open, exposed to the gaze of the lad. Not that Robert showed any inclination to study Ermgarde's finer points at that moment, so acute was his terror. He'd never seen Lord Wauter angrier.

"I'm sorry . . . had no idea . . .''

"Out!"

Robert fled, the heavy door crashing closed behind him.

Wauter turned to Ermgarde and chuckled, "That should remind him of his station. Have to teach him some manners, too. Asking admittance to a chamber instead of barging in had better be the first lesson, don't you agree?''

" 'Twould save some red faces, lord," said Ermgarde, smiling now. He rose, nodding, and pulled on the russet hose. "In my haste to be rid of the lad I did forget to tell him to leave the tray. You're hungry, no doubt. I'll have food brought up for you. Eat, then rest, my love.''

She looked at him inquiringly. "And you?''

"I have business to attend to, messages to send. They will not wait.''

Ermgarde was still uncertain enough not to make demands and ask him to stay, her position far too precarious, but even so it was difficult to hide her disappointment.

With his undertunic replaced and a splendid crimson-and-black brocade houppelande donned over the top, Lord Wauter raised one of her small hands to his lips before departing the chamber, his touch sending a tingle up her arm.

CHAPTER

5

ERMGARDE STRUGGLED INTO HER DRESS and made for the hall. She was ravenous despite the hearty platter that had been brought up to her for supper, and was eager for another encounter with the man who had declared his feelings so unashamedly.

She had his love. Her heart swelled with the knowledge and yet she couldn't quite believe it. How could he love her? She was no great lady, not like the Ermengarde of Bernart de Ventadorn's verses. But he had sounded so sure of his own heart, she reminded herself in reassurance.

An air of doom fell over her just the same. He was a wealthy lord. She was a peasant who tended sheep. Such significant differences didn't make for a lasting future between them and she was realist enough to understand and accept it. It would be a case of cherishing him while she could, aware that one day his love would wane and she would be set aside.

The hall was a hive of activity, but there was no sign of the lord or his squire. The women were at the cooking pots, the aromas of slow cooking and their merry chatter testifying to their presence behind the screens. Others were cleaning methodically, setting down new rushes on the floor and seeing to the making of torches for the wall sconces. Martin Carter had set the few available male servants to hanging the lord's tapestries and banners.

Ermgarde found the lecherous old servant nothing short of obnoxious, but, as the new bailiff, he was the only one from whom she could gain knowledge of Wauter's whereabouts. So she forced herself into a half-smile in answer to his stumpy grin. "Where might I find Lord Wauter?"

"He be gone avisiting. Won't likely be back today," enlightened Martin, letting his eyes travel insolently down to her breasts.

"Mind your thoughts, you old toad. My lord wouldn't like the path on which they travel," she muttered low, determined he should see that she neither feared nor respected him.

"Mighty sure of yourself, aren't you? But the time'll come. . . . He won't always want you," he reminded her.

"But for the present, he does, and you would do well to remember it. Now tell me where he is."

"Like I said, gone visiting. To Berkeley. Mightn't be back till morn."

Ermgarde controlled her look of disappointment. "Then what about his squire?"

"He be abroad too, off to Dillbury on lord's business." Bending his knee in a highly mocking fashion, Martin made off down the hall, leaving Ermgarde to color uncomfortably, aware of the sniggers of those who had witnessed the little scene.

What business had been so important as to necessitate Lord Wauter leaving without so much as a word of farewell? More than likely, she surmised, he was already acquainted with Thomas FitzHarding, Lord of Berkeley, and had taken this opportunity to call on his nearest neighbor. Yes, that sounded most obvious, and yet she was piqued. It was only hours since their passionate union but already she yearned for him anew, resented his seemingly offhand behavior. It would be difficult to become resigned to such a lot.

Up in the gallery, where she had gone to observe the main gate and barbican—through which Wauter would emerge on homecoming—and to be out of the way of the other servants, Ermgarde let her eyes wander over the scattered dwellings of Synford.

There was no set village, but rather a network of narrow tracks off which the peasants homes were built. There was no church, the religious in the community traveling to Dillbury for spiritual guidance when they felt the need.

Her eyes wandered up from the barbican to the expanse of southerly hills where scattered copses broke the smooth line of horizon, imagining her lord hunting there against the dense greenery of elms, hounds snapping and snarling in his wake, retinue in attendance.

A hazy movement at the shadowed foot of a tree trunk caught her eye. Was it someone up there? The shape was distorted—its brown-green hue camouflaging it against the surround—so that she couldn't be certain of what she was looking at. Then the colors separated and she clearly distinguished three figures in the home-dyed tunics of peasants—two in brown, one in murky green. Ermgarde concentrated her gaze, becoming uneasy.

The figures remained stationary a few moments longer, evidently watching the goings-on at the castle, then they disappeared back into the trees. She bit a thumbnail nervously, almost certain that it was her father and elder brothers. Their appearance would bode no good.

For the rest of the day she kept returning to the windows of the gallery or solar to scan the countryside for any signs of her family, knowing they would make some move before long. She was virtually powerless to avert the inevitable catastrophe, but there was no further movement amongst the trees. She prayed her eye had been deceived by distance. The figures could have been the innocent forms of retainers from the castle who were spying out the reserves for future hunting. If only it *were* so.

With relief, she spotted Lord Wauter and his party approaching the gates in the twilight. No attack materialized as she had dreaded, and she could tell by their unhurried, orderly return that they had not been waylaid. Obviously her father—if it had been he—had had sense enough not to ambush so strong a body of men. But even so Ermgarde would not be at ease until her lover was safely in the ward and the gates shut securely behind him. She scurried down the back stairs, through the postern door into the ward.

She reached the ward near the gate at a run, silently cursing the men who were taking their own good time in raising the portcullis. Through the slowly rising grill she could see Wauter's party nearing the drawbridge.

Suddenly, though not altogether unexpectedly, shapes loomed up from the tall grass on either side of the track. Her father and brothers! Idiots! her mind screamed. Ermgarde shrieked through the arch of the gate, wanting to warn Wauter, fearful for her flesh and blood and what they had in mind. To raise arms against the lord was to die!

The man at the winch above the gate looked at her in bewilderment. Whatever was she screaming about? Then his brothers-at-arms shouted up frantically, echoing Ermgarde's urgency. "Get that damned thing up, you fool! Our lord is being attacked!"

Men burst from the gatehouse, crossbows and longbows in hand, and scurried beneath the portcullis as it rose laboriously. They hovered uncertainly on the drawbridge, not daring to loose an arrow or bolt lest they hit one of their own. They called back for the others to bring axes and swords—weapons of close combat.

The portcullis was up at last. Ermgarde could see clearly beyond, though she had no wish to and laced her fingers across her eyes while screaming at them to stop.

"No! For God's sake, no! Don't. . . ."

She ran forward, wresting her way through the men-at-arms who were converging on the seething group on the drawbridge. She could see Wauter hit out at her elder brother, Brodrick, with the flat of his sword, whilst the lad stabbed and sliced ineffectually at the other's shin and thigh with a vicious-looking dagger. Rider and mount turned in a defensive circle.

As Rogue maneuvered, flailing his hooves and gnashing his teeth, her father came into view among the other riders. He was growling and swearing as he tried to reach at least one of them with his dagger. The others seemed to be toying with him, in no mind to crush his skull with a mace or run him through, though they were presented with ample opportunity. Ermgarde could only surmise that Wauter had guessed their identity and had given the order to subdue rather than slay. The Lord of Synford looked highly annoyed by the incident, as if fighting against peasants was beneath his dignity. His face was a dark mass of stern angles in the torchlight.

Her younger brother, Rowen, flashed into view from behind the group of horses. He disappeared just as quickly with a howl of rage as he caught the heel of a man-at-arms boot and hurtled off balance into a dry ditch. He was seized swiftly by the soldiers and disarmed.

Jostled about, Ermgarde could hardly find the breath to shout, "Father! Brodrick, stop before harm is done!" But she doubted they heard her or even realized she was there. In any event they kept fighting, aware of the futility and yet too proud to acknowledge defeat. Even then, knowing *them* relatively safe and unlikely to sustain serious injury, she was terrified that they might still find an opening and strike at Wauter, so keenly did they seek revenge for her supposed abduction.

"I came here willingly, Father," she shouted uselessly, her voice mixing with a dozen cursing, shouting others.

Wauter lost his patience with Brodrick, especially when the lad succeeded in making an ugly slash down his leg and, aiming precisely with the flat of his sword, he caught the youth a blow to the back of the head that sent him sprawling to the ground.

Ermgarde made to go to him through the sea of shoving elbows and snarls, but she could make little headway. Brodrick was grasped by the arms and legs like a sack of flour and hefted across the drawbridge into the ward. He didn't look to be seriously hurt from what she could see.

"Now you!" snarled Wauter, turning Rogue about so he was looking down at Edward the sheep herder.

Her father roared in return, throwing himself at horse and rider in a frenzied last attempt to exact his deadly price, blade arcing through the air but making no contact. Wauter slammed a gauntleted fist down upon the other's wrist, rendering the fingers momentarily numb so that the dagger dropped to the ground. Ermgarde remembered how he had used that highly effectual tactic upon her. Then Wauter's sword passed to a man-at-arms for safe keeping and the Lord of Synford flung himself from the saddle, knocking Edward to the oaken planks of the drawbridge and landing heavily atop him. Her father grunted as the wind was knocked out of him painfully.

Someone grabbed Rogue's reins and the riders and foot soldiers fell back, forming a circle so that the combatants might have ample room.

The two bodies locked together, rolled and writhed on the floor. They looked like brawlers at an inn or two angry bears, her father in mossy green, and Wauter in brown-velvet cotehardie and tattered black hose. They seemed mindless to all save the need to knock the other senseless, and the air was filled with their grunts of exertion and growls of pain. It was an undignified spectacle.

Wauter just had the advantage, being several inches taller and broader, but Ermgarde's father was wiry and quick. Like a wolfhound against a greyhound. Yet it was inevitable to the enthusiastic watchers that their master would ultimately prove stronger.

When the faces of both had been reduced to blood and bruises, Wauter connected with a clenched fist that sent a shock wave through his arm and sent Edward gurgling blood and spitting out broken teeth. He lay in a daze on the ground, a fist rising reflexively then dropping to his side again as unconsciousness claimed him.

Ermgarde felt sick.

Wauter rose unsteadily to his feet and gestured for someone to carry the prone man within the keep. He felt his own mouth where a tooth wagged loosely, and frowned. Ermgarde looked at him with tremulous rage before rushing to her father's side, her eyes brimming with tears. His black mood grew. He felt jealous, almost wished that he'd been the one knocked unconscious so that she'd rush to *his* prone body! She ought to be grateful that he'd given them their lives, thankless bitch, instead of making him feel like an ogre. After all, *he* was the one who had been under attack!

He walked unsteadily between the gate towers, shrugging aside his men's admiring remarks, hose squelching inside his leather shoes where the blood had run and congealed. By the time he reached the prisoners he was feeling positively evil.

"Lock them down in the storeroom for the night," he thundered, "I can't think what to do with them now."

Ermgarde cast him a pleading look, the implications of that order terrifying her. But he ignored her.

She watched her father and brothers being manhandled through the door that led down into the storeroom. Edward's wounds looked far worse than they actually were and with luck he'd end up with only the loss of a few teeth and a broken nose. But what did Wauter intend to do with them? They'd struck at their lord and by rights they should die! Surely though, Lord Wauter, despite his justifiable anger, couldn't, wouldn't. . . !

She shut the door to the bedchamber behind them, afraid and yet unable to refrain from seeking assurance that he wouldn't do her family harm.

He slumped into an *X*-shaped chair and tore the hose away from his slashed leg with an exaggerated, dramatic movement, illustrating his anger, and Ermgarde fell to her knees before

him. Hardly daring to look into the bruised, swollen face, she
wrung her hands in a pleading gesture. "My lord, please, I beg
you on behalf of my foolish family: Spare them. What they
did was unpardonable, I know, and they deserve punishment.
But don't kill them for they were motivated out of love for
me. Surely you can understand that?"

Her eyes sought agreement in his as her hands, mechanically
and unbidden, tried to help him get free of the leggings. He
shoved her away with a snort, sending Ermgarde sprawling
onto the oaken planks of the floor.

"If there is one thing I detest above all else, 'tis a cringing,
fawning female! How far will you go, I wonder, in your crawl-
ings for their sakes? No, on second thought, I'd rather not
find out—'tis sickening. Get up off the floor!"

Pushing the hair from her eyes, the girl scrambled to her
feet, seething then, while Lord Wauter, schooling himself not
to limp, but grimacing with every stride, went to the sideboard
and extracted a small rosewood chest from one of the com-
partments. From this he took an embroidery needle and
thread.

Her limbs trembled with rage. Was this the man she had
loved without reserve but a night ago? At that moment she
wanted to fly at him brandishing teeth and nails, wipe away
the arrogant indifference on his face.

He was atop the bed now, bolsters propping him up, his
injured leg lying stiffly before him. The needle had been
threaded. His eyes behind swollen lids went to the silver
chalice and basin on another piece of furniture.

"Bring water and cleanse the wound. Who's to say that
whelp's rusty dagger might not cause it to fester. Then you'll
have to put in a few stitches, for the cut is deep," he told her,
critically examining the wound, eyes never once coming up to
glimpse her face.

She should have mustered some self-control, remembered
that her blood relations' lives hung in the balance, but all she
could call to mind was his cold efficiency. At that moment he
was detestable.

Ermgarde picked up the chalice; the freshly drawn water
was icy cold. At the bed she stopped, fixing her angry violet
eyes on him meaningfully before she flung the entire contents
over the wound.

He snorted and bellowed in rage, like a bull before a charge and, snatching out with a quick, powerful movement of his sword arm, grasped the hair at the nape of Ermgarde's neck.

For her effrontery she anticipated death or a flogging at the very least, and his eyes, flaming like coals as he wrenched her toward him, seemed to confirm this. Flung onto the bed with his hands going about her throat, she lunged at him with her nails in an attempt at self-preservation—for she felt like a sparrow pitching its strength against a hawk.

Her nails left a track across his cheeks as she added her own marks to those her father had dealt earlier, and she tried to find his eyes as the man above her tightened his grip about her throat.

At the point of choking, the pressures of his hands suddenly relaxed and Ermgarde gulped for air in painful gasps, amazed to find herself still alive. She was hoisted to a sitting position and the needle and thread pressed carelessly into her hand.

"Now see to the wound," he told her levelly, an icy threat following, "and never dare to display such bitchery before me again. You have been warned."

Aye, she marked well his words, her empty hand going tremulously to her bruised throat. A new respect of him checked her anger. She took his left leg in a left-handed grip and set to work, drawing the deep, gaping wound together and anchoring it with stitches more often reserved for her mother's blankets. If Lord Wauter felt any great discomfort, he showed no sign of it the few times she glanced up into his stoic, blanched face.

When it was done and Ermgarde had bitten through the thread, Wauter fell back atop the bed apparently relaxed, hands clasped behind his head. There was no tautening of facial muscles to betray the pain that he must feel, and the girl couldn't help a grudging admiration despite her ire. Where did his weakness lie, if any was to be found?

She looked awkwardly from the needle clasped in her hand to the half-clad figure beside her, taking some comfort from the fact that his anger seemed to have waned. He was greatly to be feared when in a rage and she would never provoke such an emotion in him again without good cause.

A calloused hand reached out and grasped her about the shoulder, pulling her gently but firmly to his side. She put up no resistance, and although she had sorely tested his patience, again she felt compelled to ask, "What will become of them, my lord?"

She heard him expel his breath in exasperation and inched closer to him, placating, resting her face upon his chest so that her hair cascaded over the skin of his loins, making him shiver.

He wouldn't be pressed into an answer that night to comfort her. With his hands running through her heavy tresses, he replied evasively, and in a manner that brooked no further discussion, "At this point in time I am sufficiently angered to be hard on your maniacal family should I confer punishment, so don't press me. The morn will be soon enough to deal with them."

Her anxiety lessened not at all at those uncompromising words and unconsciously she moved away from Wauter atop the bed, torn by her love for him and worry for her own. He made no move to keep her near him.

CHAPTER

6

ERMGARDE WAITED UNTIL the water bearers had filled the bath and had left before she slipped from the modesty-saving coverlet and shrugged out of her tunic. Those who remained scanned her body with eyes like hawks and eyebrows lifted. They exchanged smug nods of satisfaction as they took in the bruising that marred the beautiful throat. No more than she deserved, no doubt; she was an uppity wench.

She sought the waters like a haven from their prying eyes, immersing herself and sitting statuelike as they grudgingly soaped her body and washed her hair. When they'd finished bathing her, they swathed her in a length of soft linen, then they proceeded to rub her vigorously, taking delight, Ermgarde perceived, in being none too gentle.

Body glowing pink, they doused her liberally with lavender water that made her nose twitch with irritation. Then they dressed her in the tunic and fine stockings that had been acquired from only heaven knew where. Her eyes opened wide with wonder as a houppelande of brown and gold brocade was lowered over her head. The heavy garment, with a long, trailing hem and dagged sleeves, was stunning, the silk thread a pleasure to her fingers. She gaped from one sour-faced woman to the next, hoping that someone might explain the sumptuous garb.

One woman piped up indignantly. " 'Twas one of the lord's costumes. He roused us from our beds and made us work through the night altering it for you. But 'tis too fine for your like, if you ask me."

Wauter had ordered it made for her? That knowledge she imbibed with spirit and she fixed cold eyes on the woman. "Well I *don't* ask you, so hold your tongue."

The other snorted, her wimpled face turning florid, her lips compressing, but she refrained from further comment, shar-

46

ing an affronted look with the closest of her confederates.

When they had gone, still muttering as they hefted the tub between them, Ermgarde walked unsteadily about the chamber, trying not to trip over the trailing hem of the boldly-patterned brocade.

Why? she kept asking herself, wriggling her neck as if the black undertunic that rose to her ears would cut off her breath at any moment. She didn't dare to sit down lest she crush the fabric, so she made her way slowly—skirts not allowing for her usual energetic step—to one of the room's embrasures. There she tried to concentrate on the early-morning activity in the ward.

Her eyes lit instantly on the mounted figure of Robert de la Vallée, who entered the arched gatehouse next to a rider who looked less at home upon an ungainly mule. For what purpose had Father Anshelm been brought to the castle?

Ermgarde was further mystified when, later in the morning, she witnessed the arrival of Thomas FitzHarding, Lord of Berkeley, and his retinue. She had never set eyes on the man before, but she had no doubt that it was he because of the arms embroidered on the surcoats of his men. Everyone around the vale of Berkeley had seen the chevrons and crosses of his family coat-of-arms at one time or another. He was the most powerful landholder in the region, his lands stretching as far north as Gloucester and beyond, and as far south as Bristol.

Curiosity piqued, she would have liked to go down and find out from some talkative servant why so eminent a personage had come to call. But she had to forego the plan when she learned that Wauter had sent word—via a mumbling servant—that she was to remain in her chamber until sent for. In other words, she thought, I am a prisoner!

Her anxiety grew. Something was happening about her that Wauter obviously meant to keep secret until such time as he saw fit to enlighten her. Were the two visitors in truth judges who had been asked to sit with him at the trial of her father and brothers? Mayhap Father Anshelm had been asked to hear their last confession before they were put to death! She bit all her fingernails, worried to the point of physical sickness. What else could it mean? But why the gown? Did he intend to humiliate her by forcing her to attend the trial? If so, it would be hard to forgive him. Then again, how could the priest and lord have arrived so soon? Berkeley Castle and Dillbury were some way off and the attack by her family had only happened the previous evening. Surely messengers couldn't have been sent out and the two guests appear in answer so speedily? Her head spun with the possibilities.

Around noon, her speculating came to an end. Martin the Carter appeared, his attitude subtly changed for the better, the bold insolence gone from his gaze as he asked Ermgarde to follow him to the gallery.

She seated herself in the minstrels' section at the top of the hall, a comfortable, cushioned chair placed there specifically for her. Martin shrugged unhelpfully at her look of bewilderment before he shuffled away.

The high table below was empty, as was the long expanse to the main door of the hall and the stairwells. Whatever was going on?

There was a creaking directly below—perhaps the solar door opening—and then she could see Lord Wauter as he strode into view and took the largest chair at the high table. Simultaneously, the doors at the far end of the hall swung open and her father and brothers were herded in. Ermgarde's eyes darted back and forth between the motionless trio and lone figure. It was obvious that the Lord of Synford desired her to watch, though he cast not a glance over his shoulder in her direction.

Her father, standing protectively in front of his wary sons, snarled like some dog spoiling for a fight when the lord crooked his finger and beckoned them forward. They advanced, determined to show no fear, though their eyes cast about the shadows beneath the gallery and its supporting piers, expecting assassins to do their lord's bidding.

The fact that they spied no other human forms didn't lessen their unease. Then Rowen saw Ermgarde seated high up in the gallery behind Lord Wauter's chair. He paused, laying a hand on his father's sleeve. "Do you see her? Up there, look."

Edward's eyes traveled upward, and locked instantly with hers. Her pale face and violet eyes implored him to caution, while her hands wrung anxiously in the folds about her sumptuously garbed lap. He had never seen the girl more beautiful—or more terrified.

The lord rose from his seat and Edward's attention shot back to him malevolently. If only he had a dagger so that he might slit that defiler's throat before they hung him!

Wauter looked impressive and merciless as his gaze swept leisurely over the trio. Even in defeat they still managed to effect an air of uncompromising bravado that Wauter found irritating. It was all too evident where Ermgarde's willful streak came from when he looked at the swarthy, powerful build of her father. She had obviously inherited her darkness and charged vitality from him. Wauter's voice boomed at them from the high table. "You three did seek to harm me and in so doing have brought about my displeasure. By rights you should be dead, as perish all who would dare to lay hands of violence on their overlord. But this is my wedding day and so I refrain from having it marred by the shedding of blood or the stretching of your necks!"

The three males cast him a look of confusion, relief and no small measure of surprise. He'd spared them? No, surely not? Wasn't it just that he would delay their punishment until *after* this wedding of which he spoke? And who was he to marry?

The same question thundered through Ermgarde's brain. Who? But no, it couldn't be true! He'd spoken not one word to her about a marriage. And *why* should he? She had no need nor right to know; she was but a passing passion. It explained the arrival of Father Anshelm. But who was the bride? Why hadn't he prepared her for this shock? He professed to love her and yet already he would replace her with another—his wife! Ermgarde was stunned by his apparent cruelty. Had he planned it thus, this to be her punishment for taking her family's side?

He wouldn't look at her, though he must surely feel her eyes boring into his back, and his face in profile told her nothing. A hand went to her heart to quell the roar there, but even knowing he had spared her family wouldn't lessen the anguish his words had wrought. She couldn't endure the pain.

Then he was speaking again, his manner cold as he addressed her father. "Had you but come peaceably, shepherd, instead of seeking my demise on the wrongful assumption as to my intentions concerning your daughter, this morn you would have been greeted to my castle with all the cordiality reserved for the father of the bride. Your behavior, however, has made such a welcome forfeit."

Edward gulped in speechless disbelief, while behind him Rowen gave an audible moan as he recalled their hot-headed,

impetuous behavior. They'd tried to kill Lord Wauter; he'd
spared them and, if their senses weren't totally addled with
terror, he had just informed them that he intended to marry
Ermgarde! Blessed Virgin, what had they done? He glanced
sideways at Brodrick, who was likewise wearing a stupified
look.

Edward coughed, shuffling his feet uncomfortably, then
cast Wauter a less lethal look than before. His voice was
defensive, indignant. "But how were we to know what you
had in mind, lord? 'Tis not commonplace for one so noble of
birth to take to wife a peasant . . . my daughter. What were
we to think when you took her off? I'm surprised . . . nay,
amazed." He shook his head as if he still didn't believe the
other's words.

Ermgarde's already painfully beating heart had lurched to a
terrifying stop. *She* was to be his wife! That had been the most
unthinkable, yet, obvious answer and it had never entered her
head. There was no other!

Her eyes went down to Wauter. He was looking at her,
gauging her reaction with concealed amusement. It pleased
him to startle her into further silence, for obviously she hadn't
dreamed of such an outcome to this meeting. He noted the incredulous eyes, which were enormous against the shocked
pallor of her face and, with an inner feeling of satisfaction,
turned his attention back to the others.

"I had decided the morning after bringing your daughter
here that I would marry her and, accordingly, sent forth for
Father Anshelm to come perform the ceremony. 'Tis a pity
you were not at home when he called to inform you of my intentions. 'Twould have saved a great deal of unpleasantness."

Edward hunched his shoulders and kept his gaze on the
scrubbed boards of the floor where a greyhound dozed. How
could he have been expected to know, he reasoned with
himself. Blast it all! Now he'd probably turned the man
against him unto eternity. The lord *wants* to marry his girl?
Bed her, yes, ruin her as was his right, but *marry*. . . !

And what of the girl? He looked up at her thoughtfully. She
looked shocked. Was this what she wanted? Or was it that she
was too terrified to refuse, lest the lord change his mind concerning their fate?

"I would know how my daughter feels about this, lord," he
asked.

Wauter raised his eyebrows, turned to Ermgarde and inquired, "Well, what say you?"

" 'Tis what I want," she managed breathlessly, looking for something in Wauter's composed face. He smiled, confident of her answer, sure of himself.

Her father's brows rose in surprise. There was no doubt in his mind, after listening to her, that she was smitten, nay, besotted. He had never thought to see the day when his daughter made cow eyes at a man!

"*You* have no objection, I trust?" asked Wauter, frostily.

Edward shook his head with vehemence. "Oh nay, lord. So long as it is as my daughter wishes, I am content."

"I am glad to hear it. And, seeing as you are here, we might as well put you to good use. You can hand her over to me officially at the altar. Your sons may accompany me to the chapel, where we will await you."

Edward affected an awkward bow. He had regained consciousness after the fight and expected every hour that followed to be his last. Now he was going to a wedding!

Rowen and Brodrick followed on the lord's heels in bemused silence, and their father, looking up to Ermgarde as she rose in her shimmering gold gown, couldn't hold back his pleasure. "Let us be off to your wedding then, my girl, or rather, my Lady of Synford."

The impact of those words made Ermgarde's already unsteady legs wobble violently.

In the Great Tower at Windsor, King Henry smiled at the missive that had just arrived from Synford informing him of the baron's intention to wed. He wished the man well, having a long standing fondness for Wauter FitzSimmons, but even so he thought the man a fool. Women—bah! They'd never get him that way.

Politics was a different matter, however, and, even as he cast the missive onto an untidy pile of rolled parchments on his table, his mind was moving once more to familiar pastures —something he'd been thinking, dreaming, scheming over for some time.

France.

France was in the grip of civil war, had been ever since Charles VI's brother, the Duke of Orleans had been assassinated at the instigation of the Duke of Burgundy, during one of the monarch's bouts of insanity.

Henry found it gratifying to read dispatches that told of Armagnaques and Burgundians going at each other's throats. He had begun to see a way in which he might further divide and reap the benefits of the conflict.

A little negotiating mightn't go amiss. Mayhap he would side with Burgundy. Then again. . . . Perhaps Charles's supporters would pay him more to remain neutral and away from the fight. The possibilities were endless and tantalizing.

Smiling, he toyed with the ruby on his left index finger. Vainglorious, conceited some would say, but Henry wanted to prove to his people that England had made the right choice in accepting the son of a usurper as their king, instead of the earls of March whom Richard II had named to succeed him.

The Lancastrian pride demanded the return of the Angevin Empire, which had dwindled over the years until England held little in France beside Calais, the Brittany harbors and some land around Bordeaux. The Lancastrian ambition wanted more. France itself. And there would never be a better time.

CHAPTER

7

IT WAS DONE. A heavy gold ring, studded with rubies and enamelled in black, circled Ermgarde's finger shortly after Father Anshelm blessed the pair. Now he watched, in slight shock, as the Lord of Synford enfolded his lady and sealed their mutual bond with an empassioned kiss.

Then, while Wauter introduced a portly Thomas FitzHarding to his bride, the priest made his way to the Shepherds, beaming his habitual smile. "It must be pleasing to see the girl wed at last, Edward. And so well, too."

Edward didn't look convinced. He was still suspicious of the slightest movement made by the men-at-arms who stood about the lower portion of the chapel and guardroom where they had witnessed the marriage. And as yet he couldn't think of Wauter the Seducer as his son-by-marriage, not after wishing him dead but hours before.

" 'Tis too soon to tell," he muttered.

If Edward still had doubts, his sons did not. They found Lord Wauter inspiring and could see nothing disagreeable in being related by marriage to a baron. And he had made it plain as they accompanied him to the chapel that he bore no ill will over their earlier behavior. He had even praised the way they had come to the defense of their sister.

As the bride and groom led the way up to their solar amidst a hail of congratulations and the sudden noise of servants preparing for a feast, the two lads made their own plans for the future.

Brodrick was the eldest of the children at eighteen—a tall, sparsely fleshed youth, his hair black in the manner of the father and his eyes darkest brown. He would be Wauter's man, he decided, for surely a baron could always find a place for another devoted follower? Modesty forbade him to say so, but he was as good an archer as could be found in the width and breadth of England and already showed some skill as a fletcher of arrows.

Rowen's plans were of a more rustic nature. Brought up within the simple framework of country life, his interests centered around getting food for the table and clothes for his back. Just into his teens, he gave the outside world scant thought. He had two dogs—black-and-white, shaggy-coated curs, whose origins were rooted in the Welsh hills. When they were not employed in the tending of sheep, they would follow their master about his dubious business—poaching, tracking down quarry, retrieving. They weren't ideally suited to hunting, he had come to realize, since they tended to maul the caught game or, worse still, devour it before he could bring them into line and bag it. So he fixed his interest on the sleek-coated, sinewy hounds that roamed at will about the castle and ward. Wouldn't it be just *too* wonderful to work with such a pack?

Now, how was he to reach his aims? The obvious course, he decided, was to obtain his sister's ear. She had always had a soft spot for him, admiring his plump features and rosy cheeks. One woebegone look from him and she'd be won over, for sure.

Wauter's fingers tightened reassuringly over Ermgarde's hand on the table, a gesture she greatly appreciated. Before her at the high table were the soldiers and servants of Synford who bowed respectfully. They came in a long line according to rank, smiled and voiced their felicitations. The thought of trying to rule them made her mouth go dry with terror.

Without thinking ahead, knowing only that she wanted Wauter, she had gone breathlessly through the marriage vows like one who dreads that some beautiful dream will end. Those vows had been her immediate assurance of keeping him. Now, she fearfully began to realize what being the Lady of Synford would entail. Not only was she his, but the responsibilities of his lands had come partly to her. How was she to cope? By all the stars in heaven, she had no inkling of how to go about running a castle!

Momentarily she wished herself a shepherdess again, then the long brown fingers caressed her palm and she knew she wouldn't exchange this for anything. Wauter was hers. She could overcome any obstacles with that knowledge.

Homage paid, the servants began to serve the first course of the wedding feast, and the soldiers retreated to their posts. Ermgarde felt more at ease with the smaller number that remained. Her father and brothers sat at her left, and next to Wauter, on her right, were Thomas FitzHarding and Father Anshelm. Robert de la Vallée—who had not so much as batted an eye in response to the extraordinary events of the day —served them.

The Lord of Berkeley, jovial and florid after several swiftly downed drafts of wine, proposed the toasts and kept the mood gay. As the wine took increasing effect, so the toasts accumulated. Not only did the bride and groom have their health drunk to, but also Edward and his "fine looking sons," the king and the royal dukes; even Father Anshelm.

Dusk fell and at last Thomas was struggling for a good excuse to empty his goblet. Sluggishly, he raised the vessel aloft. "To a glorious reign."

The others echoed the toast and drank, Rowen giggling. He had never encountered Thomas's like before and found him amusing. Then Wauter took Ermgarde's hand and rose with her beside him. He had delayed in the interest of etiquette long enough, he decided; now, nothing more would keep him from taking his wife to bed.

"We bid you good evening, though pray don't leave my table until you are of a mind. I would have everyone happy this night."

"Oh, we quite understand, Waut, you devil," slurred Thomas, eyes glassy and mouth smiling with a knowing, lecherous twist.

Father Anshelm tut-tutted at the latter's reference to Satan and smiled fondly at the couple, cordially wishing them good night. Then again, he wondered, looking up into the lord's looming, dark presence, was Lord Thomas's lighthearted reference so far from the truth? The amber eyes of his host burned with an intense, almost dangerous passion as he took the girl by the arm. The priest was uncertain of the man, a hesitant hand going unconsciously to the heavy crucifix at his chest.

Wauter's gaze fell on his father-by-marriage. "Be my guest this night. In the morn I would like words with you and your sons."

Edward managed a nod. Was there some new treachery awaiting them with the dawn, he wondered. As the priest had sought comfort and reassurance from his cross, so Edward clasped all the firmer the knife with which he had been cutting meat.

Ermgarde was ushered impatiently into her chamber, Wauter shutting and barring the door behind him. He didn't intend to be disturbed that night. Ermgarde stood awkwardly at the spot to which he had propelled her. How strange it was to realize that this was *her* chamber. She stared mutely at the man divesting himself of houppelande and tunic, emerging only in hose with the muscles of his hair-matted chest and arms rippling. He grinned, then wrapped his arms about her, pulling her close so that she could feel his urgency, the hardness of him pressing against her belly.

After what had befallen her the last time she was closeted with him, Ermgarde had to admit that she was a little afraid. But her desire of him hadn't diminished. And there was nothing brutal about him now.

"Now, my lady. . . ." His voice was husky as he unbuckled the heavily embroidered girdle at her waist, loosening her houppelande.

Momentarily she gave herself up to his hands, allowing herself to be disrobed so that she stood before him in her tunic and stockinged feet. Then, as his words registered, the old fears returned.

"Oh, my lord, whatever have I done? Even wanting you as I did, it was idiocy to enter into this marriage. I'm no lady."

His eyes softened as he pulled the tunic over her head, her arms remaining raised in an enticing pose that made the perfection of her breasts more pronounced. "You weren't born one, that is all. You are now, to me."

"I'm frightened."

"What? With me at your side? Don't be so foolish," he chided.

Warm lips nuzzled the hollow of her neck, hands cupped and toyed gently at her breasts, and soon Ermgarde forgot her fears. She was lifted and deposited gently upon the bed, his lips never once leaving hers.

He drew away eventually, resting on his elbow to look down at her. "I would have you just as you are, and as for acting as chatelaine, I will teach you all you'll ever need to know."

His free hand stroked her slender throat, then circled

around her breasts where the nipples sprang to prominence beneath his knowing touch. Ermgarde sighed, limbs seeming suddenly weak yet hips straining up against his roused manhood. My, how she loved the feel of him.

Her hunger for him was bottomless and when he kissed her again, Ermgarde opened to him willingly, probing with her tongue even as he did, their breaths mingling, bodies melting against each other.

Her hips rubbed against him, her legs wrapped about him, and Wauter slowly entered her, savoring the enveloping warmth. He pushed on, wanting, it seemed, to find her very core, reluctant to pull back. Ermgarde began to move desperately, her passion already out of control. He laughed then and took up a steady rhythm, delighting in her unabashed need for him.

"Greedy wench," he teased.

She wrapped arms about him, relishing the tickling sensation of hair on his chest against her breasts. Her eyes watched him adoringly.

"Who can blame me?"

In answer he delved deeply within her, watching the look of ecstasy take over her face and her eyes cloud.

"According to Ermgarde, Master Edward, yours is a sizable brood. Have you made any plans about their futures?"

The shepherd looked back suspiciously at the lord. What was the man getting at now? Edward didn't like surprises, and he'd already suffered enough of them over the last few days. He shrugged his shoulders and cast the lord a glance that said any such plans were none of his business. His voice was gruff. "Why do you ask, my lord?"

" 'Tis just that I thought you might consent to the oldest of them coming to live at the castle," explained Wauter, pouring beer for the three, then resuming his seat next to Ermgarde.

She had wondered why he'd called this family meeting in the solar, away from the clatter and interruptions of the great hall, and now she cast her husband a surprised glance.

While Edward digested the suggestion and his sons exchanged a look of delight, Wauter continued, gesturing to the lads. "Take these two—they are of an age, show intelligence and a willingness to learn. If you could manage without their help, I should like to have them with me and teach them the ways that befit the brothers of a lady."

"Well, I don't know," Edward said noncommitally, wondering where the trap lay in the excellent suggestion. But his
boys, who felt bound to make their opinions known, couldn't
abide the thought of this opportunity slipping through their
fingers.

"Father, please say yes."

"*Please*," implored Rowen.

"I can learn soldiering."

"I can work with the hounds."

Wauter was pleased with their response and looked to Edward. The man managed to smile fleetingly at his sons. He was
going to lose them, sure enough, and it worried him, aroused
his protective instincts. Yet he couldn't say nay, deny them
this chance to climb the ladder from obscurity as Ermgarde
had done.

He nodded his head slightly. "Very well. I thank you, my
lord, for having made this generous offer. You may have my
sons and reshape them from their peasant molds—*if* 'tis possible."

The boys hugged him and there was an audible chuckle in
the man's depths as he tousled their hair.

"As for my daughters—you have Ermgarde already. Only
Maud and Alice are of an age to leave their mother. On returning home I shall put your offer to them."

"Good. My wife would like their company, I'm sure. She
needs someone more her own age and I'll not have her consorting overmuch with the servants. Perhaps, though, young
Maud should take the veil, as is her wish, rather than savor a
boisterous life here with us?"

"That's what she'd like, my lord, but I've not the means to
grant her wish. She will come, along with Alice, and be grateful for the privilege." As Ermgarde was the realist amongst his
children to some extent, so Maud was the dreamer. He'd long
ago lost patience with her. She spent her time telling a rosary
and smiling vaguely at those about her as if, he'd oft mused ir-
ritably, her wits were addled. The goodness and light that
emanated from her made him feel awkward. Castle life might
just force her out of her shell.

Edward departed after hesitantly shaking Wauter's extended hand and clasping each child to himself. Then the lord
dispatched his two new charges to separate quarters; Brodrick

to the guardroom where Robert de la Vallée would find him a sword to suit; Rowen to the kennels where he would be billeted with Knollys, the master of hounds.

Wauter permitted himself a smile, satisfied with his work. And Ermgarde nestled against him before the canopied fireplace of the solar, showing her appreciation with a lengthy, uninhibited kiss.

Finally her lips departed and she smiled up into the face whose features looked as though carved of granite. "That was a generous gesture. I shall like having my own about me."

"Just so. Though in truth I engineered it as a means of soothing relations between your father and myself, rather than affording you companionship."

Her smile turned to a grin. "Either way, it was pleasing."

CHAPTER
8

ALICE HAD NONE of the awkward shyness that afflicted poor Maud. She did not scurry away like a startled mouse should one of the lord's retainers seek words with her. On the contrary. From the day of her arrival she demanded and received the willing attention of every man in the castle. She ruled the ward with her swaying hips and seductive smile, a show of ankles and calves or a toss of uncovered locks assuring the men's continuous interest. They watched for her, anticipating and hailing her appearances with open ribaldry, eager to fall under her spell.

The Lady of Synford worried, concerned that Alice's escapades and ceaseless flirtations with the men might lead to trouble. Whatever would her father say if he could see the way Alice was facing womanhood? Ermgarde was glad that his visits to Synford were few and far between. And Wauter was no help. He seemed to find the precociousness of the girl amusing and would only issue token scoldings for her behavior after persistent nagging from his wife.

Eventually Ermgarde tired of arguing with her sister, especially when it left her looking like an overly prudish matron. She would just hope that Alice came through her dalliances unscathed.

As the summer gave way to autumn, Ermgarde found herself settling down to life at the castle with surprising ease. Her husband, as promised, schooled her in the domestic running of the household and, if the servants resented carrying out the orders of a former shepherdess, they were wise enough not to show it. The lord's love for her was obvious, as was hers for him, and accordingly they treaded warily, for none wished the baron's wrath. One out-of-place remark about her lowly background would have brought swift and merciless retribution.

It was hard to dislike Ermgarde, anyway. She was no ruthless matriarch, and spared them of the slaps and whippings that serfs had come to expect as their lot. They respected her, little knowing that her lack of corporal punishment stemmed from lack of confidence, rather than soft-heartedness or sense of justice.

Through the summer months, Wauter busied himself on a series of journeys to the villages of his demesne, appraising the men for their soldiering potential and making himself known in general. On Sundays he held archery contests and on Mondays he sat in judgement at the castle court, meting out justice and wisdom to erring or feuding serfs. He went hawking, hunting, even fishing, and set up sessions for arms practice and tilting. Life was busy, yet the pace was pleasantly slow.

Ermgarde plied her needle dutifully, spurred on in the disliked chore only by the fact that she was working on a surcoat for Wauter. Embroidering for him seemed to make the job worthwhile. The crosses on the dexter side denoted part of his father's coat-of-arms, the castle on the sinister, his own, and the telltale red bend through the middle declared to all his bastardry.

She looked across to Maud, who relished her sewing and lovingly embroidered yet another page marker for her psalter. She appeared to like life at the castle just so long as she could stay in or around the solar, but beyond that safe haven, Ermgarde knew, she felt threatened.

Ermgarde forced the silver thread for the argent castle through the eye of her needle and smiled to herself, lowering her head so that it would go undetected by the other, and savoring the habitual glow of thoughts about Wauter.

The great bear was hers—half tamed now by her love but still showing bouts of wildness that left her breathless—completely vanquished. Her hold over him was strong and her confidence grew in leaps and bounds. There was no doubt of his love. If she'd asked for the moon, Ermgarde didn't doubt that he'd strive to obtain it for her or kill himself in the attempt. But she wanted nothing save him. Her life was idyllic. Well, *almost*. There was still Alice.

Even now she was down below in the ward, having sniffed disgustedly at Maud's suggestion that she occupy herself with needlework. Ermgarde was resentful and would have liked to be out of doors, too, on so fine a day. *Could* have been, save for the backlog of work that kept her busy.

Ermgarde sighed heavily, wishing in part that the girl had never left the Shepherds. Her younger sister, Clare, would have made a far more suitable companion, having a personality that was midway between Alice's wildness and Maud's timidity. In truth, Clare had a nature not unlike her own.

Alice's vivacious giggles rang out piercingly as she approached the solar through the hall accompanied by Wauter's booming laughter, which sounded as though it originated in some deep well within him. The noise was vaguely irksome to her and she laid down the surcoat, annoyed that she had the pious Maud's company while Alice made merry with her husband.

They burst into the solar together, Alice's arm crooked through Wauter's. He was laughing even while he admonished her for her behavior down below and disentangled his arm to go sit on the arm of Ermgarde's heavily carved X-shaped chair.

" 'Twas provident that I came across this temptress when I did. She was in the guardroom, would you believe, with half the soldiery of the castle helping her to try on Robert's harness of plate."

Ermgarde frowned. "Alice! You know the guardroom is out of bounds."

" 'Twas only innocent amusement. The men enjoyed it, were very eager to help with the dressing."

"Doubtless," said Ermgarde, voice acid.

"She brightened a dull hour, and as for Robert—I fancy the lad thinks himself in love, the way he was to the fore of her avid admirers."

"Nonsense! Robert in love? Nay. Why, I've never so much as smiled at him. He's not for me, no matter that he's a squire and like as not will be a knight some day. I've already made up my mind as to whom I want."

Wauter was no longer listening. His eyes were running admiringly over the scarlet and black houppelande that his wife wore, lingering on the deep, sable-edge V that plunged between her breasts, affording him a tantalizing glimpse of creamy peaks. Ermgarde noted Alice's remarks, however, and was set wondering at the possible implications, especially when the girl's yearning hazel eyes focused on Wauter. Could it be that Alice was secretly harboring a passion for the man? His effect upon women was all too apparent. Ermgarde knew

that, for herself, just the sight of him was enough to kindle
sparks of passion. Was it inconceivable that he might not
unwittingly affect the sister in the same way?

Such problems she could well do without. She prayed that
intuition was wrong, hoped that if Alice was feeling anything
remotely unchaste for her brother-by-marriage, it turned out
to be a harmless case of infatuation that would die a natural
death.

If not? Then she would be sent home without further ado!
Ermgarde's decision was without hesitation. She smiled
automatically at her husband as he drew her hand to his lips
and kissed the fingers one by one. But her eyes were following
Alice.

Alice wore her hair uncovered despite her sister's persistent
reminders that a lady always veiled, if not wimpled, her hair
before any male who was not a close family member. Now she
tossed the hip-length tresses behind her back and came to sit at
the stool beside Maud's chair, casting a disparaging eye over
the other's needlework.

"I wonder that you haven't long since died of boredom,
dear Maud," she said, pulling the folds of her sage-green
houppelande more tightly down through the black girdle so
that her adolescent breasts swelled and pressed against the
square neckline.

Maud remained stoic, not deigning to reply. Her face
seemed to shrink down into the high collar of her dowdy gown,
like a tortoise seeking its shell. If Ermgarde's soul was in danger because of her blatant delight in earthly love, then Alice,
to Maud's mind, was well and truly damned. Maud could find
no redeeming characteristics in her younger sister. She always
thought of blackness when she looked at Alice. Though she
didn't know why, something behind the prettiness made her
tremble.

"I was thinking," said Wauter, running a hand over the
sausage-like braid that hung heavily down Ermgarde's back,
"it might be a good idea, if, after the noon repast, the men
and I went to the meadow for some arms practice."

"Is it really necessary? They seem lethal enough to me as
'tis. Or is there a campaign in the offing?" remarked his wife
uneasily.

"It's a possibility, love. Our king will not be long in coming
to a decision over France."

"Oh, Wauter, I'm feared to hear you say such. If he invades France you will go with him, won't you?"

He confirmed her worries with an emphatic nod. "What else could I do? I'm a soldier, his man to command. Surely you wouldn't expect me to stay at home? I'd miss you, *of course*, but I'd have to go. I'd be ashamed to plead other commitments, as some did when we fought against Owen Glendower—staying cozily safe behind the walls of their own castles, swearing that they could not, however much they desired, leave their dying grandmothers, ailing wives and children, or run the risk of having their castles sacked by mercenaries in their absence. I'd be loath to make such excuses."

This was what she had feared. He'd go when the call came, without a moment's hesitation and few regrets. And there was nothing she could do about it, save torture herself with worry in his absence, fret for him and pray he would come home whole.

Alice was enthused, taking an opposite view from her sister on the subject of war. "Would that *I* were a boy so that I could follow you. Such excitement! And I, poor female, must stay home and forego the pleasure. Some"—her eyes strayed to Ermgarde and a false smile touched her lips—"would tremble at the possibility and much rather stay safely in their tower rooms, but not I. War. . . . The thought makes my blood course the faster through my veins. It's not fair. I'd make as good a squire as Robert *and* be better company."

"And very fetching we know you'd look, Alice, in full harness," laughed Wauter, chucking her under the chin before his eyes were drawn back, full of love, to Ermgarde. "Don't be so gloomy. I'm not going to disappear this very moment. Will you come down to the meadow this afternoon and watch your brother and me work out?"

"Oh, *I'd* love to," Alice agreed readily, her eyes running over his magnificent, leather-clad body. The thought of seeing him fight filled her with an excitement difficult to disguise.

Ermgarde raised an inquiring eyebrow. Yes, she would *definitely* have to watch Alice. "Of course I'll come. I'd like to see for myself just what progress Brodrick is making."

Maud, as everyone had expected, declined to go with them and, red with embarrassment at having witnessed her sister Ermgarde and her brother-by-marriage exchange a thorough kiss, she cast down her eyes to the embroidery and said a prayer for them both.

Ermgarde took comfort in the luxuriant warmth of her sable cloak as a biting wind cut across the meadow. Her eyes took in all the combatants, but kept returning to Wauter and Brodrick, afraid lest one lose concentration and allow the other an opening. Their axes were blunted yet could still render a careless fellow unconscious.

Alice found only excitement in the spectacle, shrieking with delight when one of the men-at-arms delivered a wild blow with his flail and floored his opponent. The prone man was dragged from the field and had his split head instantly administered to with a dollop of hot pitch.

Ermgarde turned disgustedly back to her husband, nose twitching from the odor of shriveling hair and flesh. How anyone could *want* to spend an afternoon carrying on so, she couldn't imagine.

Another fell, this time sent off balance by a shield swung backward. The victim fortunately sustained nothing more than wounded dignity and an itching face after sprawling head first into a patch of stinging nettles.

There was no denying that Wauter was magnificent, and her heart swelled with pride. Even garbed in the same type of leather practice harness as his men, he dwarfed all by a head, and exhibited the widest pair of shoulders on display.

He laughed with obvious enjoyment, goading the infuriated Brodrick, who had not been able to score a single point, and dealt the lad's shield a blow with his axe that sent a visible shock wave back through the other's arm and brought a grimace of pain to his face.

"Enough!" cried Wauter, eventually.

Immediately the clang and clatter of metal faded away and the panting, sweating men-at-arms turned to their leader.

"Refreshments, me thinks," he decided, clapping his arm about Brodrick's shoulder and coming toward Ermgarde through the relieved throng. They wasted no time seeking out the servants who acted as cup bearers.

Wauter took two cups from a hovering servant and handed one to his former opponent, a few words of praise sending the lad happily on his way, then his eyes locked with Ermgarde's and their bottomless violet depths promised untold delights for the coming night; Brodrick and fighting were temporarily forgotten.

Catching his wife's hand, the lord drew it to his lips, unmindful of his sweaty state as he sensed that she bore it no mind. Somehow he was filled with a constant need to touch her, to steal kisses, however chaste in public, and almost smother her when they were alone. There had never been a hunger the likes of which he felt for her.

"You were kept entertained, I trust?"

Ermgarde pursed her lips. "If there were no wars men would invent them, me thinks, so that they could continue to have their fun."

Alice came to stand beside Wauter, sipping eagerly at her third cup of wine and licking her lips enticingly. "You were by far the most skillful on the field, Wauter, and certainly the handsomest. Can I loosen your harness for you, or mayhap hold your axe while you drink?"

He laughed, not above enjoying flattery and clasped an arm about the girl's shoulders as he had done with Brodrick moments before, squeezing her playfully. "I thank you for your consideration, Alice, but I have a squire to undertake such duties."

Alice made no attempt to wriggle free, her sister noted with a hardening expression. In fact, she snuggled closer and pouted when Wauter dropped his hand and concentrated on drinking his wine.

Ermgarde snapped angrily, "Alice, I think that cup had best be your last. Drunkness in females is most unbecoming."

Her husband raised an eyebrow. Why was Ermgarde constantly picking on the girl? There was undeniable friction between them. Perhaps Alice was a might wild, but then Ermgarde had shown herself a vixen on occasion, and had been forced into a more gentle guise only by her position. He liked the younger sister, found her friendly, and disliked the tension that his wife seemed to create.

Unwisely, he found himself trying to defend Alice, his wife's eyes burning so brightly that he immediately regretted it. "Surely a little drinking will do no harm? 'Twill only make her carefree, hardly drunk."

"She's becoming a killjoy, just like Maud," Alice declared in a grumble, looking to Wauter for support.

"Not quite *that* bad," Wauter laughed, trying to relieve the situation with a winning grin.

Ermgarde rose indignantly to her feet. "I'm *not* a killjoy! But someone must watch her morals. Alice needs no wine to make her carefree!" And with that she stamped away through the tall grass and nettles in a fury.

Wauter made as if to follow, but Alice grasped his forearm, thrilling at the touch of muscle and hair beneath her fingers. "I should leave her be, Wauter. 'Twas the sight of you fighting that has put her into such a mood. She is a typical, weak-spirited female when it comes to such things. Even with blunted weapons she was afraid for you. Give her time to calm down."

"Perhaps you're right." Women and their moods infuriated him.

Alice's grip tightened, her fingers seeking but finding no response from his flesh. "Maybe we could go to the wood and find some wildflowers for her?" she suggested, her eyes almost smoldering.

He roared with laughter, and pulled away. "I'd look an oaf carrying a posie to her, Alice, don't you think? That's not my way. Besides, the season for bluebells and primroses has long since passed."

He picked up his battle-axe and shield and started off, no further thought spared for the girl who swished her locks angrily and followed in his wake. But it wouldn't always be like that, she promised. He wouldn't always walk away from her, arrogantly dismissive. She would have him eventually, *and* the wealth and power that went with him. Ermgarde could keep her position as wife, for Alice didn't want anything so humdrum.

She would be his mistress, the pampered and coveted one who would share his moments of pleasure and glory. She'd be spared the tedious necessity of bearing children and acting as chatelaine. It would be she whom he took on his journeys, richly gowned and dripping jewels; she would wield the power.

For too long Ermgarde had been the bane of her life, the obstacle, the favored one, and Alice was not of a mind to live on hand-outs and cast-offs for very much longer.

Once she'd stolen Lord Wauter, as she'd had to steal a great many things from her sister in the past, she would make the unfortunate wife's life an utter misery.

It would be no more than the older sister, the much cherished first daughter of the Shepherds, deserved. God, how Alice hated her for all those years of handed-down rags, discarded and outgrown toys that Edward had so painstakingly carved in wood. Seldom could she recall there ever having been anything new for her—nothing that she had ever truly craved anyhow. Ermgarde's meagre possessions, however, had always been irksomely appealing and still were!

Virgin still she might be, but innocent she was not. She knew ways to please a man that Lord Wauter, let alone Ermgarde, had never dreamed of! She'd learned young, during secret meetings with the old lecher, de Witt, in the woods near Dillbury. He had given her pennies for the use of her eager hands upon his jaded body and she had realized then that the way to attain power was through the manipulation of men. Gaining experience and pleasure, she had made herself a tidy purse.

Lord Wauter was no lecher, but Alice didn't doubt that when she gave him an open invitation he would prove himself the wholly sexual male and rise *splendidly* to the occasion.

Her revenge would be sweet indeed.

CHAPTER

9

WAUTER MADE HIS WAY to Ermgarde's chamber, knowing that a bath would be readied for him there. As he walked, he unbuckled the straps that secured his leather jerkin. His right arm throbbed with the customary pain that came after hours of wielding a battle-axe, but that would soon disappear.

His dark features were pensive as he entered. What sort of mood would she be in now? He couldn't fathom what had brought on that bout of temper in the meadow.

She occupied an *X*-shaped chair in the weak light thrown by the arched window embrasure, mending his torn undertunic. Her violet eyes snapped up, then went back to the movements of irritated fingers upon material and needle.

"Your bath is readied," was all Ermgarde could say without letting her anger erupt again.

He snorted and yanked off the leather jerkin and sweat-stained tunic, then thrust a booted foot in Ermgarde's direction. "Lend a hand."

She answered the curtness with a glower and pulled off one muddy suede boot, then the other, before rinsing her hands in the tub and returning to her mending.

When Wauter pulled off his hose and stood before her proud in his nakedness he expected her to melt. She usually did, unable to resist a peep at his impressive form or make some saucy comment. His frown deepened as her head remained bowed, the raven tresses curtaining her expression. Pride wounded, he sought the water furiously, sloshing much over the sides.

"Damn it all, what ails you, woman? What have I done that you should act the shrew?" he thundered, unable to school himself against anger any longer.

The noise of horses' hooves and wooden wheels rumbling on the path beyond the castle walls broke Ermgarde's concentration. She discarded her sewing and leaned further toward the embrasure, half rising to catch a glimpse of the caravan that approached.

"Who comes?" Wauter forgot his former question, as curious as she.

"I don't know. There is a litter escorted by half a dozen mounted soldiers—but they wear no arms on their surcoats—and an ox cart carrying baggage . . . coffers, it would appear."

"Um, sounds familiar." Wauter had risen from the bath and, draping a length of linen carelessly about his loins, he padded to the window, dripping water as he peered through the ill-manufactured glass that distorted objects beyond. Even so, he knew who came.

"Trust Mother to come without sending word ahead. That one does love to put others into a flap with her appearances from nowhere."

"Your mother! Oh, lord above, Wauter! Is my gown befitting? Should I veil my hair? If only I'd known, had some warning. . . . Will she expect some sort of welcoming banquet? I'd better send out Rowen to bag some fare for the table, have Martin Carter—"

"My love, my love, be calm," he laughed. "Lady Margaret will expect or want nought but the normal fare of our table. As to how to greet her—be natural and you will win another heart. Now, please, hurry and help me dress or she'll no doubt come bursting in here and find me in the altogether, a sight to which she hasn't been privy since I was a tender age."

Wauter's attempt at humor did little to calm his wife and she sped about the chamber in a dither of activity, fetching fresh hose, tunic and cotehardie, then nigh bullied him into the clothes.

"Why has she come, do you think? Do you often see her?"

"We keep in touch, ofttimes happening to be at court together. As to why she comes—I expect she has heard of my marriage and wants to congratulate the woman who managed to put the fetters on me."

Wauter was finally dressed, Ermgarde running her comb through his wet, unruly locks when there was a knock at the door and one of the servants entered. "My lord," said the girl, "a Lady Margaret Parfrey awaits you below in the solar."

He nodded. "Have wine brought there. We are on our way down."

Ermgarde's hand was taken and patted reassuringly as Wauter led the way downstairs. The girl's mental picture of Lady Margaret had been colored by Wauter's mention of his mother and her dealings with Simon of Waverley. She expected to encounter a frail, aged beauty who had never recovered from her shame of bearing a bastard, a quiet creature whose face was furrowed by penitence; a martyr to the lustful cravings of man.

The Lady Margaret who strode forward and gave her son a bear hug couldn't have been further from those imaginings. She was garbed quietly enough, her black houppelande, white starched wimple and grey veil giving her the look of an abbess. But an inner vitality shone through. Her hearty chuckle matched Wauter's in volume, and the shapely body that reached to his shoulders was possessed of an ageless agility.

She slapped him on the back and, placing her hands on her hips, laughed wickedly. "So you finally got caught! You'll never know the extent of my delight when the king gave me the news on my arrival at court. I just had to come and see for myself."

Then her eyes went to Ermgarde, taking the girl in with an appraising sweep of brown eyes that missed nothing. She smiled warmly, much to the latter's relief. "Well, you look sturdy enough; good childbearing stock, I'd guess, and downright fetching too. 'Tis plain why marriage has at last appealed to him. Your name?"

"Ermgarde, my lady." Automatically she dropped into a curtsy—a conditioned reflex of respect for her betters—and her eyes were cast down in weakness.

"Enough of that," decided Lady Margaret, though she was well pleased by the gesture and the girl's pleasant nature. A strong hand grasped Ermgarde about the elbow and encouraged her to her feet, the plump face, surrounded by the flawless white of her wimple, beaming a hearty grin.

Ermgarde managed a somewhat nervous smile as she was steered to a chair and her mother-by-marriage plunked herself down nearby so that she could watch the other clearly.

The wine arrived and Wauter poured, watching his wife who looked vaguely intimidated. His mother had that effect on strangers, but it would soon pass.

Lady Margaret drained the cup and held it out for a refill.
"Tell me about yourself, Ermgarde. With a name like that you
are mayhap part French? There was nothing in Wauter's
missive to the king about your background and the court is
buzzing with speculation. Is your father a knight or squire? Or
mayhap he's in no way involved with military service? That
would make a refreshing change. The lords of Waverley and
the Parfreys are, or were, fighters to a man."

Ermgarde squirmed uncomfortably and tried to avoid
Wauter's amused face lest she glower. "My lady, my origins
are very humble, I'm afraid. My father was a shepherd and so
was I, until your son took me for his wife," she mumbled.

There was a delighted squeal from the older woman. "Oh,
how splendid! Wauter, only you would dare to do something
like this. Truly you are your mother's son to so swim against
the tide of convention."

"Mother, please don't make it sound as if I married
Ermgarde only to outrage others. I love her."

She nodded musingly. "I believe you do and that pleases me
no end. FitzSimmons the Bastard and the Sheepgirl—'tis like
the material for one of those courtly romances Chretien de
Troyes was so fond of writing."

Wauter laughed. "You are an incurable romantic."

"I make no apologies for that, either. After all, my level-
headed son, 'twas romance that brought you into being,"
pointed out his mother.

"Well met," he conceded. "And for that romance, which
heralded my coming, I thank you. I now have good cause to be
thankful for my birth."

Ermgarde felt the warmth of his smile upon her and returned it, their love a tangible thing.

"Lord, what a mooning pair!" cried Lady Margaret, mockingly. "And you have the nerve to accuse *me* of being a romantic, you lovesick swain? Look at yourself!"

Her son pressed for the court news and, more importantly,
of the king.

She was cynical. "The court is much as it ever is—formal
and chivalrous to the naked eye and just a might licentious
underneath. There are the usual family feuds, the same old intrigues. De la Mare's daughter has been sent home in disgrace
after getting herself pregnant and being in the silly position of

not knowing which of her lovers was the father. As for Henry—his growing piety is something to behold. Me thinks he's after the nomination for pope! In truth, he's little like the youth who was once your companion; shies away now from the females about him as if they were the creatures of Satan, and cloisters himself constantly with those prayer-mumbling Benedictines of his.''

"Are there any rumors of war?''

"There is whispering, though nothing substantial. No one knows what is in the king's mind. Humphrey believes that his brother may well negotiate with the Armagnacs, forcing them to outbid their rivals for English support or neutrality. It would be just like him to play one faction against the other and enjoy it all immensely. But as for war—not this year; nor the next, to my mind.''

Lady Margaret took a deep draft from her cup, then leaned toward her son. "Heavens, I almost forgot the most important piece of news: Henry has freed the Earl of March!''

"Freed him?''

"Aye, threat though he be, as the son of Dirty Dick's acknowledged heir, the king in his wisdom has decided to end his imprisonment.''

It took Ermgarde several moments of deep thought before she concluded that Dirty Dick was the lady's nickname for dead King Richard.

"Henry must indeed feel secure in his kingship to do such a thing,'' Wauter commented.

"More than that. He has also restored the man's estates to him. Either Henry is a fool—which is exceedingly unlikely—or a genius. Me thinks he seeks to ingratiate himself further to his people by such actions. There's no doubting but that it was a popular decision with the commonality. Let us hope that he doesn't have cause to regret it, that March will be content with freedom and nurture no designs upon the throne, which he could rightly claim as his own.''

"Aye, for even if March should not hold such ambitions, there are always those who would try to press a man into such a position for their own ends, use him as a puppet-king. I pray the king keeps March close to him and therefore safe from the politics of others.''

"Amen.''

Ermgarde put down her cup and rose to her feet. "Such talk

is above my head, I fear. So I shall leave you awhile and go see to the preparations for supper. The evening meal will give you a chance to meet my brothers and sisters.''

"How nice to be surrounded by your own. Life within a castle can be lonely for a woman, so no doubt you are glad of your sisters' presence.''

Ermgarde nodded, certain that were she to answer, her doubts and cynicism would appear in her voice. In truth, her sisters were not much company at all!

The meal progressed well, Lady Margaret eating and drinking like a man and sighing appreciatively when she'd had her fill. "Um . . . most tasty, and the cider, commendable. Is it your own brew, Wauter?''

He tossed a mutton bone beyond the high table where the dogs awaited. "I don't know, Mother, You'd have to ask Ermgarde. She is in charge of the household.''

Ermgarde couldn't swallow her food fast enough and Alice stepped in. "I made the cider, my lady, as my sister has enough duties already to burden her. One so inexperienced with the running of a castle cannot be expected to cater for every need of her lord. Not at the outset. So I help out where I'm able, with the little things that make life more pleasant for us all. It is, I believe, the little things that make all the difference.''

"Quite so,'' agreed Lady Margaret, smiling, though she'd lifted her eyebrows and fixed her gaze on Ermgarde quizzically. "Such a helpful sister must be invaluable?''

Ermgarde was dutifully loyal. "Alice is very helpful.''

"I wish only to please,'' said Alice, sweetly, clicking her fingers at a tardy servant in admonishment. "You've allowed Lord Wauter's cup to run empty. That just will not do. Sister, you must be daydreaming to allow for such a thing.''

Ermgarde bristled but held her tongue, noting how unimpressed her mother-by-marriage was by Alice's performance. "I am suitably chastened, Alice. Call Jasper, why don't you? He can play recorder while you sing for us. I'm sure Lady Margaret would like to enjoy yet another of your talents.''

"As you wish,'' Alice readily agreed, instructing a servant to collect the novice minstrel, who was doubtless eating his fill in the kitchen at the far end of the hall.

"Ermgarde has a fine voice, too,'' Wauter said with a loving glance, "but she is shy of displaying it in public and will sing only for me, in the privacy of the solar.''

"But might you not, just this once, be tempted to sing for us all in a duet with your sister?'' coaxed his mother.

"I fear not. Alice enjoys the public performance as I do not,'' Ermgarde said politely, feeling a blush spread up her neck.

Alice smiled, leaving her seat to join Jasper Verny on the floor before the high table. Because of Ermgarde's modesty, Alice would have everyone's attention and she fully intended to exploit the opportunity.

She stood, flinging her chestnut tresses behind her so that none of her curves were obscured beneath the snug-fitting gown of russet velvet. Not letting her eyes dwell too long on Wauter as she sang the simple ballad composed by her accompanist, she strayed back often to smile when he was watching, or turn stony when he committed the unforgivable lapse of conversing with his wife. She didn't spare a glance for Lady Margaret. The woman was unimportant, to her mind. But Lady Margaret had been watching her closely.

"Your sister doth positively glow under the gaze of so many men,'' she commented to Ermgarde as she sipped her cup of cider.

"She's of an age where she likes to exercise her power over us,'' Wauter joked.

"Then let us pray she causes no grief to herself or others during this period of change.''

Ermgarde looked at the older woman closely, seeing a look in the healthy features that caused her to wonder. Could it be that Lady Margaret saw the same thing she saw when she looked at Alice?

Alice finished her song and sank into a graceful curtsy, then took the hand that Jasper extended and rose to the noisy acclaim of the men-at-arms. There was a smile for the sergeant and an alluring eyelid flutter for Robert de la Vallée—who sighed—before she left the entranced recorder player and moved across to the high table with a studied sway of her hips. She paused before Wauter.

Politely, he was attentive as she ceased her entertaining, beaming a dazzling smile that had a devastating effect upon Alice.

"Well done, Alice. Very sweet.''

"Thank you, my lord. I'm glad you liked it,'' she breathed,

looking coy yet with body poised calculatingly.

"You have an appealing voice," complimented Lady Margaret.

"Jasper's compositions improve daily," continued Wauter, oblivious to her charming ways.

"I think she deserves some token by way of reward," enthused Robert, shouting from a lower table.

"A reward is it?" Wauter considered.

Alice's eyes gleamed.

Ermgarde and Wauter's mother watched the proceedings with quiet interest.

"Then what shall it be, Alice?" asked Wauter jovially. "No king's ransom, mind you, for I am not rich beyond your wildest imaginings. Ask for something simple and I'll strive to grant it."

"I ask for nought but a kiss."

Wauter's amber eyes widened in surprise. "A kiss? Is that *all*? Why not the ring from my little finger instead? 'Tis of value and will last far longer."

"Nay, I have named my price, lord," she cooed. "Now I charge you to pay it."

How innocent it all appeared, how spontaneous and unplanned, though Ermgarde was not amused as Wauter rose to pay his dues. Merrily, he took Alice in a firm, bear-like grip about the shoulders and gave her a smacking kiss on the cheek. Ermgarde positively seethed when her sister wriggled herself into position to give Wauter a lingering lip-to-lip kiss to the accompanying cheer from the men in the hall, her slender arms coiled about his neck like a snake.

CHAPTER

10

"YOUR MOTHER IS . . . UM . . . *extraordinary*," decided Ermgarde, sliding under the golden coverlet fortified now by a fox-fur quilt to keep out the autumn chill.

"Even that seems an inadequate description," mumbled Wauter, peeling off his hose quickly and joining her.

Immediately their bodies moved to one another, seeking warmth as their arms and legs entwined and their senses became aroused at the contact.

"Ah, there's nothing like a wife on a cold night," sighed Wauter, burying his face into the warmth of Ermgarde's nape and smelling the sweetness of her hair. "Now that we're alone once more, will you tell me what it is that ails you?"

Her hand fell away from the muscled hip she had been stroking as the image of Alice surfaced. She rolled onto her back, the light from the single taper showing her perturbed face. " 'Tis Alice. Men can be so blind about such things, but I've been watching her. I think mayhap she believes herself in love with you."

"What!" He rose on an elbow, looking down at her, not certain whether she jested or not. "Nay! Whatever put that crazed notion into your head?"

"I'm sure of it. Think. Before you dismiss this as idiocy, think about the way she trails behind you, hangs on your every word, makes good use of any excuse to touch you. And as for that kiss this evening. . . ! I could have strangled her! I don't want to believe it myself and hope that it's merely a fleeting infatuation. Who can blame her, after all, for mooning after you? I know only too well what she see's in you, for they are the selfsame things that attracted me. But I'm worried."

"Oh, Ermgarde, are you certain this thing isn't in your head? I know she follows me about, but even so I'm doubtful there's anything unchaste in her mind. 'Tis nought but a touch

of hero worship, like Rowen is apt to exhibit. You worry needlessly.''

"Lord, you must be blind! She wants you, I tell you! I can
see it in her eyes. And I'm possessive enough not to want
things going any further. Mayhap if you guard your affection
and cease unwittingly to bolster her hopes of requited love,
this thing will peter out with no harm done.''

"Very well, I shall mark your words and be on my guard
with her in future.''

"That is as well, because should this state of affairs continue, I'd have no other alternative but to send her home,''
said Ermgarde decisively.

"What a ruthless female you are,'' he said in amusement.
He drew her into his arms, Alice dismissed as easily as ever
from his thoughts.

"To assure my exclusiveness in your heart I can be without
mercy to any who would threaten it. Loving you as I do, my
jealousy against such is hard to control.''

Wauter pulled her atop of him, shivering at the touch of her
firm breasts against his broad chest, forcing a knee up between
her thighs so that she was open to the exploration of his hands.

She trembled, and leaned into the hardness of him. He
groaned at the pleasure, straining upward, his mouth seeking
her breasts, then lips, as he felt Ermgarde guide his manhood
to her softness and move with exquisite slowness down over
the length of him.

"Show me how much you love me,'' he challenged.

And she smiled assuredly, biting at his shoulder and ear as
she rode him like a stallion.

Beyond the postern door of the keep was the castle garden,
cultivated during the spring and summer by the gardeners
after the neglect following the death of Baron de Witt. A lattice fence overgrown with ill-tended brier roses and honey-
suckle ran around the garden. It was here that Ermgarde and
Lady Margaret strolled when life within the stout walls became oppressive, sometimes accompanied by Maud, though it
was evident that the younger sister did not approve of the
courtly dame and often found excuses to be elsewhere.

Lady Margaret was not ignorant of Maud's feelings and had
spoken on the subject one afternoon when they happened to
be alone—Maud having gone to one of the outlying crofts to

administer a herbal potion to a peasant weak and delirious from the poison of an adder bite.

"Maud doesn't approve of me, I fear," she said as if thinking out loud, weeding out a withered rose from the lattice work and tossing it away. "Has she always been so pious?"

"Always. Do not take her disapproval to heart, though. It falls upon us all and you are not being singled out in any way," Ermgarde giggled.

"I had noticed. Poor Wauter has only to kiss you publicly to bring a look of outrage to her eyes."

They strolled on, along the grassy path that bordered the cabbages, both smiling mildly.

After Ermgarde's initial feeling of intimidation had worn away, she had found it easy to like Wauter's mother. Lady Margaret was plain spoken, with few lady-like affectations, and her lively warmth made her the ideal confidante and companion, as her sisters never could have been. Mayhap it was her devilish way of speaking candidly of her past and her overpowering presence that offended Maud's piety, yet these were the traits Ermgarde found most charming.

There was little left to know about the lady. She seemed pleased to tell of her love for Simon of Waverley, knowing Ermgarde would understand, and display no disapproval.

She had been the only child of Ralph Parfrey, her mother dying in childbirth, and although the lord had married again, he never had another child, and certainly no male heir to inherit.

At Ralph's death, Richard II had seen to it that the family's Shropshire estates reverted to the crown—in other words, himself, and that on whim he would grant it to whichever of his sycophantic courtiers most pleased him at that time. Homeless, dowryless, Margaret had then to rely on the generosity of that selfsame king to keep her from beggary.

She lived at court as lady-in-waiting to Richard's French wife, Isabelle, who, irony of ironies, was dispatched back to her homeland in 1400 after Bolingbroke usurped the throne, minus *her* dowry.

Margaret had not gone unnoticed by Simon, but newly wed and still trying hard to be a dutiful husband to the sweet-natured girl whom he'd married for political reasons at the urging of his parents, he strove to keep his growing desire in check.

Eventually, though, the presence of one upon the other became torturous and too much to bear and they became secret lovers, keeping trysts at Windsor and Westminster Hall right under the noses of king and queen.

Then the inevitable happened and the king was furious when he learned she was pregnant. He demanded to know who the father was, threatened her with imprisonment and other dire consequences if she kept mum. She flatly refused, saying it would do no good to name him, he being wed to another.

The king fumed, the queen refused to have her as a lady-in-waiting any longer and the court waited gleefully for Richard's answer to so delicate a problem. But he couldn't even banish her from court, having relieved her of her home and lands!

Margaret became worried, fearing that she would be given to the first willing male who came to the king's attention, whether noble or lowly born, old or infirm. But Bolingbroke, Simon's true master, was watching over her, and, anticipating the warped king's mind, had Simon steal her away from the court. He wanted her placed under the wing of John of Gaunt, Duke of Lancaster, Bolingbroke's father—or, more precisely, under the gentle care of John's mistress, the beautiful Catherine of Swynford.

Both women had one thing in common: They openly defied the conventions of public opinion by proudly producing bastards. Catherine had been John's mistress for many years, having set her seal on his heart long before his political marriage to Blanche of Lancaster. Had her father been higher placed, he might have married her, but Blanche meant wealth and more power and, like his son, John's ambitions came first.

Margaret produced a son, Wauter, her pride dampened somewhat when Simon's wife herself became pregnant shortly thereafter, dashing the mistresses hopes once and for all of becoming his wife.

But despite the lack of husband, or mayhap even because of it, she had been content to watch Wauter grow to resemble his father.

Lady Margaret paused and seated herself upon the stone bench that had been carved into the foot of the curtain wall, signaling Ermgarde to occupy the spot beside her.

"I've been thinking. This may sound as if I'm trying to be rid of Maud because she disapproves of me, but in truth I think it would be to her choosing also. I know an abbess who presides over a Magdalen nunnery to the north of Bristol, and, with some persuasion, I think I could make her agreeable to taking your sister as a novice. What do you think?"

Ermgarde laughed, unable to control herself. "I'm wondering how a woman with your disreputable character could possibly know a nun!"

"Oh, do be serious!" cried the older woman with mock severity.

"Very well. I think it would be a splendid idea."

Margaret then cast her eyes to the cabbages as if reluctant to look the other in the eye, her face sobering. "Now that we've solved the problem of the saintly Maud, what about that other sister of yours?"

"Alice?" Ermgarde felt growing anxiety. Had Lady Margaret noticed something that had been lost upon herself? Her younger sister had shown no new evidence of flirtation with Wauter, mild or otherwise, and Ermgarde had taken heart. A girlish infatuation soon over and done with, she had concluded. But she couldn't be so sure.

Margaret framed her words carefully. "Dear Ermgarde, I don't know what it is, 'tis nothing I can put my finger on, but I feel wary of her. She has your wildness, and yet it is not tempered by a kind nature. I've been watching her watching us. You, me, Maud and Wauter, *especially* Wauter, as if she's gauging us, waiting for her chance to . . . Lord, I don't know. These sound like the drivelings of a senile old woman. I hesitate to suggest you send her home, but . . . I'm sure your mother would appreciate the help, what with the new baby having arrived and all."

Had Ermgarde imagined the pleading note in the other's voice? She looked into Margaret's face, which mirrored her own troubled thoughts, seeing the wisdom yet still reluctant. "I feel some of your anxiety concerning Alice, yet how can I send her home? She has done nothing to warrant such cold dismissal on my part."

"Let us pray it remains so."

CHAPTER

11

ALICE WATCHED FROM BEHIND one of the rotund piers that supported the fan-vaulting in the keep chapel. Supposedly she had gone there to pray, but her thoughts weren't upon God.

Through the low arch that separated chapel from guardroom, she could watch Wauter as he oiled his sword and dagger and fell into conversation with Robert de la Vallée. Her breath grew labored at the sight of him talking. He had one foot planted on a stool and an elbow supported on his knee. No other in the castle could boast a body like that; the long legs with sturdy thighs, every muscle accentuated by the tight-fitting hose, the bulge of his manhood riveting her eyes.

Over the past few weeks she had schooled herself to behave because she'd feared that Ermgarde was suspicious, but the sight of him now was more than she could bear. She threw caution to the wind and decided to indulge her need to hear the husky voice that sent chills down her backbone. If not, she'd surely go mad.

"Good afternoon to you, my lord, Robert." She nodded to each in turn, but ignored the interested gaze of the youth, to approach her would-be lover. Would he notice her gown? She breathed deeply, forcing the peaks to further prominence beneath the mulberry velvet, the most beguiling of smiles touching her mouth.

Wauter's soldiering talk ceased and he smiled at her, absently. "Hello, Alice. Been praying, have you? Let us hope then that you'll not become as prickly and pious as Maud."

"Oh, nay, my lord," she laughed, touching his hand as it clasped the jeweled hilt of his sword. "You need have no qualms about that. I sought the quiet of the chapel merely to think."

His smile had faded, she noted with perplexity, and his amber eyes had focused on her pale hand which rested on his own.

Wauter withdrew his hand swiftly, Ermgarde's warning coming to mind. He coughed awkwardly as he intercepted Robert's frown. "Alice, I would talk with you, alone," he told her sternly, leading the way from the guardroom, his forceful grip about her wrist sending a shiver of anticipation through her. Did he read her mind?

Robert watched their exit with a sickening feeling. Damn his master! He loved him, respected him as a soldier, yet damn him he did for playing the lecher. Wasn't the beautiful Ermgarde enough? Did he have to have Alice too?

She wondered momentarily why he didn't take her to some cozy chamber upstairs, thinking that it would be fitting to lose her virginity upon a soft mattress, perhaps even in her sister's bed! Yet whatever was his liking, she would be glad to comply.

Their hasty passage stopped at the door of the half-timbered stable and Wauter pulled her inside, looking about to ascertain their privacy. Rogue snorted at his master's entrance, while the other stalled horses showed a like mild curiosity.

Alice stood before him, chestnut hair falling enticingly about her breasts, her eyes watching him closely. Lord, what a predicament! His wife was right and Alice's moist-lipped smile confirmed her warning. Now it was up to him—though he'd rather have been a hundred miles away than face an awkward, embarrassing situation like this.

"Hurmph. . . . Alice, such a duty sits ill with me, but I perceive that it is high time to make some things plain between us."

"Oh, I wholeheartedly agree," she breathed, stepping forward until he gestured her to stop.

"I think . . . *Lord*, how can I put it? Alice, I pray you're not harboring any unchaste feelings toward me. If you are, I beg you to turn your attention elsewhere. 'Twould injure your sister terribly to know that you look on me as anything more than a brother. And I don't want to hurt her."

Her features radically altered, running the gamut from delight to disbelief and pain. "What? You mean you will not take me as your mistress? No, surely you don't mean that! I love you, Wauter, truly, and I'll share you. I'm not greedy. You can keep your relationship with me secret. If you'd rather Ermgarde didn't know, I'll understand and never do anything to betray my feelings. But don't shun what I want desperately to give, I beg you!"

"Christ! You're nought but a child! Whatever has put this idea in your head? If you feel anything for me 'tis only infatuation, and nothing but ill could come if I succumbed to your charms. I'm sorry, Alice, but I don't have any feelings for you and I can only think of you as a sister."

"Nay, don't say it! 'Tis not infatuation but *love* I feel. Take me here, now, and I shall prove my feelings. I've had no other man, nor want any save you."

Wauter shook his head, pushing her off when Alice would have clung to his neck and kissed him.

"Don't, Alice! You demean yourself by begging for favors."

"I don't care. I'll get down on my knees and grovel if only you'll bed me."

And she did just that, kneeling at his feet in supplication, and taking the neckline of her houppelande in both hands.

Wauter's eyes widened in surprise as she rent the material and suddenly her breasts, then navel and finally her triangle of chestnut curls suddenly became exposed to his reluctant gaze. She peeled back the remaining cloth from her shoulders, leaving no contour uncovered. Her smile was one of certainty. *How* could he resist her now?

Wauter felt the unwanted stirring in his loins and took a deep breath in order to marshal his resources and tear his eyes away from her nakedness to return to the less enticing features of her face.

"Cover yourself immediately," he thundered, his face colored by anger and painfully controlled lust. "You do act worse than a harlot, Alice, and lose my sympathy for your plight into the bargain."

Sobbing now at his rejection, the girl pulled the gown about her and bowed in dejection.

"We will say no more of this incident and pray that it goes unreported by others," Wauter told her, striding to the door. He needed to escape the inviting body that would oh-so-willingly-entrap him if his willpower lapsed even momentarily. "And in future you will conduct yourself as the perfect lady when in my presence or I shall have no alternative but to see you sent packing. You understand?"

"Aye, I understand, and I'll be good," she sobbed brokenly still on her knees. "Just don't send me away. If I could not see you again I know I would die."

His parting remark was softened somewhat with pity. "Nay, you'll not die. I fell in and out of love a dozen times at your age and thought it the end of the world each time. You'll get over this soon enough."

Alice's face was humorless as she allowed Robert to lift her from her mount and set her down in the shadow of the trees on the hill. He tethered the horses while she scrutinized the castle at twilight before dropping into the grass and finding a tender new blade to chew upon.

Robert was pleased at his good fortune, for, after days of cold rebuffal, Alice had finally given in to his cajoling and agreed to ride with him. Perhaps this night he might steal a kiss? Or was that too forward and likely to cool her down again? Best to first see which way the wind blew.

He seated himself beside her, surprised by her abandoned pose; lying back like a wanton, skirts riding up to show off saffron-wool-stockinged legs to the knee. But why was he surprised? Hadn't he seen her go willingly to the stable with Lord Wauter? Whatever had spurred her to chase the master was not apparent now. Alice no longer sought him out, Robert had noticed with a rekindling of hope, and, although her eyes might covet him from afar, she did nothing by word or deed to betray her feelings. Mightn't he still win her with the kindness and ardor that Lord Wauter could not provide?

He reclined on an elbow and spun a lock of her hair around his fingers. "You are the most fair of creatures, Alice. Your hair is like costly silk, your eyes like woodland in the rain."

She laughed in his face. "For God's sake, Robert, don't seek my favors with platitudes like every other swain within the castle walls! If 'tis a kiss you want, take it, but be done with romantics."

Lord, but she possessed a cutting tongue! He wanted nothing *but* to kiss her, of course, but her detached attitude, as if she cared little one way or t'other, irked him. Unconsciously, he pouted.

She slammed her eyes shut. "Don't play the petulant child. We both know why we are here. Why waste time mouthing sweet words that owe nothing to sincerity? Come now, kiss me."

"But I meant those words. I do love thee above all others."

"I'm sure you do, my sweet," she said dismissively, her

voice sounding bored as she laced her fingers at the back of his neck and pulled him toward her.

Robert moaned, losing himself instantly to her power, and savoring the mouth that toyed lazily under his own, his manhood becoming erect as she urged his body atop her own.

Oh bliss! To have all of her at his fingertips when he had dreamed of nothing but a kiss!

"Alice . . . Alice. . . ." he breathed against her lips, intoxicated, a hand groping down the bodice of her gown. He trembled as he explored her firm breasts.

She freed her mouth from him. " 'Tis too cold to disrobe, but you have my permission to lift my skirts."

He followed her instructions in a daze of wondrous disbelief, a lump rising in his throat as he uncovered her pale limbs. She opened her legs for him without the slightest show of modesty, tugging at his hose impatiently as he knelt over, transfixed.

"Do hurry, or 'twill be a frozen morsel you savor," she snapped, hoping it would not be as painful this first time as she had heard.

Wauter wanted her. Of course he did, for wasn't she beautiful? 'Twas only his regard for that simpering Ermgarde that had stealed him against her, for she'd seen the desire in his eyes that day in the barn, sure enough. She would make him jealous by flaunting her lovers and bring him to her willingly. She *would* have him in the end. Wauter, wealth and position.

Robert's mouth was on hers again and she only tolerated the contact by pretending he was Wauter. But it didn't work. There was no comparison between this callow youth and the goliath of a man who would crush her with his delicious weight.

Her maidenhead resisted only slightly, and then Robert was riding her with abandoned excitement she couldn't share, while the ostentatious gold chain he wore about his neck chafed her breasts mercilessly.

She was his: Alice, his dream of earthly delight. Below him, enveloping him. Ye gods! He shuddered and exploded at the thought, collapsing upon her with a whimper of pleasure.

She pushed him away, his usefulness over. Her voice cutting as she came to her feet. "Me thinks you'd best take some lessons in bedding a wench, Robert. You did perform like a virgin!''

He pulled up his hose in mortification. "In truth, Alice, I was. Next time I shall endeavor to please you.''

"Next time? There might be; then again, there might not. Mayhap if I had some trinket of yours I'd feel more favorably disposed. How about that chain about your neck? It would make a worthy token of our mutual regard.''

Robert hesitated. It had cost him a year's hard service for his lord, but then he looked into those limpid hazel eyes and acquiesced. If proof of his love she needed. . . . He lifted it over his head and presented it to her, bowing slightly, like a courtly knight paying homage.

"Thank you, Robert," she said coolly, as if it were nothing more than her due. "We should get back to the castle now.''

She declined his help and mounted her mare, wincing at the twinge of discomfort. Thank heaven he had been so wound up in the pleasure of losing his own virginity that he hadn't noticed she'd lost hers. How possessive he might become if he knew he'd taken that prize!

They rode back to the castle in silence, Alice allowing one kiss on the cheek at the stables, though giving the impression that she did so under sufferance. Robert retired to the guardroom, experiencing none of the elation that should have been his on such a night.

CHAPTER

12

As SUMMER APPROACHED, the FitzSimmonses received and accepted an invitation to Lord Thomas's estate in the Vale of Berkeley. Robert could be left, Wauter decided, to protect their home should the unlikely need arise.

Ermgarde was excited at the thought of noble company, and saw the visit as an opportunity to practice the manners that Lady Margaret had patiently taught her. Lord Thomas would forgive her any blunders of etiquette that might ensue, she felt sure.

But the visit proved a disappointment to her. Though Wauter seemed to enjoy the dull suppers, the men's talk of war and the days spent tilting in his hosts' yard, Ermgarde was left to endure the company of lacklustre noblewomen. Worse, it rained for the duration of their stay, locking her within the chill walls.

Berkeley was beautiful, there was no denying. It was set upon an emerald meadowland where a brook threaded a lazy path and a quaint church marked the field beyond the curtain wall. But Ermgarde felt continually chilly, and Thomas did little to alleviate it with his delightful tales of yore.

She was told the castle history upon her arrival, Thomas leading the way through an elaborate twelfth-century door into the keep. He then ushered her up worn stone steps, above which sally holes and arrow slits had been built to discourage unwelcomed guests with missiles, hot oil and, if need be, the contents of chamber pots!

"I'm the fourth Thomas to hold the title, you see, and this one,"—he slapped an arm about the shoulders of a youth who walked in a gauche manner beside him—"will be the fifth. Anyhow, the third Thomas was lord here when a suitable prison was needed for Edward II back in 1327. Edward was as unpopular as Richard II, perhaps even to a greater degree, because he was—how shall I say it—*contrary* in his earthly desires."

Ermgarde had looked bemused.

Her husband drew her aside and whispered a clearer explanation.

"Oh!" She blushed profusely, avoiding Thomas's amused chuckle as he led the way toward a chamber off the main room, the interior of which could be plainly seen through a grilled, window-like aperture.

But Ermgarde wasn't listening to Thomas now, having encountered an ominous odor that made concentration impossible. Should she make some comment? Or might that be impolite? The subject was most certainly indelicate! But, oh dear, the stench! She put a sleeve to her nostrils.

"Thomas gave over the castle for a while so that it might be the king's prison, and it was in this room that Edward was kept until his subsequent assassination."

Ermgarde went forward with morbid curiosity to look over the cell, a sleeve still to her nose. The interior was a disappointment, and certainly not what she would have expected from a royal prison. A stout table, chair and several religious artifacts lined the walls. Nothing to say a king had ever been there.

Lord Thomas looked suddenly solicitous. "Oh, forgive me, Lady Ermgarde, I've grown so accustomed to the nauseous air in this room that I forget the sensitive noses of others. Shall we move on?"

"Yes, please. But where does it come from, my lord?" she asked, dubiously.

"There." He pointed to a hole in the stonework of the floor behind them. " 'Tis the dungeon."

Ermgarde had drawn back from it warily, crooking her arm in Wauter's and seeking the comfort of his nearness.

"Aye, 'tis best not to get too close. The well runs down for nigh on thirty feet and the matter at the bottom would be a most unwelcome cushion were you to fall."

"And dare I ask what is down there?"

"Nothing of recent addition, yet even so the stench persists. In years past it was a charnel well, or a dumping hole for dead beasts. The occasional live prisoner was thrown down there too, to die horribly of asphyxiation and feed the fumes of putrefaction."

What with the stench and the vile history, Ermgarde felt her stomach turn. "I wish I hadn't asked."

"The well was kept stocked while the king resided here, but to everyone's chagrin he remained unharmed by the vapors and had to be dispatched by other means. If you're curious, I think it best you ask your husband, for even I'd be sorely embarrassed to tell you."

They left the room, to Ermgarde's relief, and she whispered, "What could possibly bring a blush to Thomas's cheeks?"

Wauter was as uncomfortable as Thomas and cursed the man silently for having piqued her curiosity. "The king being, um . . . perverted in his desires, his murderers dispatched him to the next world with a red-hot poker thrust . . . thrust . . . Oh hell, use your imagination!"

Ermgarde did, and shivered in revulsion.

The last evening before their return to Synford, Thomas staged an elaborate feast in the great hall, depleting his pantry reserves and making free with the Mediterranean wines that he'd acquired from a Bristol merchant. For his friend Wauter and the beautiful Ermgarde, only the best was good enough, and he wished them to depart with fond memories.

The hall was filled to overflowing when Ermgarde entered on her husband's arm, aware of the open admiration beamed her way. None could deny her beauty and grace, and throughout the evening she felt herself under constant surveillance from admiring eyes, taking no small measure of confidence in it. One had to be exceptional indeed to steal the attention away from her husband and host!

The night progressed with ease, the festivities from the lower tables increasing in volume as oft-emptied goblets were refilled to the brim. The candlelight half concealed the antics of the castle soldiers, but now and then an indignant squeal from a serving wench and the ribald laughter of her assailant reached Ermgarde.

"More wine, my lady?"

She smiled at Thomas's squire, who acted as their butler, finding his attentiveness charming.

"I thank you."

He lingered over his pouring, his eyes running over her in ill-concealed pleasure, taking in the valley between her opulent breasts, and breathing in the hint of perfume that floated from

beneath her golden veil. His flesh tingled as he imagined the
body beneath the cream brocade. The mantle of raven hair
was hidden from view yet glowed darkly, giving a tantalizing
glimpse of its splendor.

A low rumble of curses startled the squire and made him
straighten guiltily from his perusal.

"Keep your eyes on your task, lad, or I shall be forced to
teach you better manners."

Ermgarde felt herself shrink down fearfully into her chair,
worried for the squire.

He tried lamely to excuse himself, "I beg you pardon, my
lord. I never meant—"

"Enough. She is beautiful, I know, but she is *mine*. Never
forget the fact again."

"Of course, my lord." The squire hurried off to a safe
perch a few feet away.

Ermgarde sighed in relief, chiding herself for having smiled
in the first place. But then, she hadn't known it would have
such a devastating effect. Her gaze was sheepish as it moved
from goblet to husband, but she could only guess at his mood
since he was conversing with Lord Berkeley once again.

Much later, and feeling excluded by her husband's and
host's preoccupation with war talk, Ermgarde rose a trifle
dizzy from her seat. The full-bodied wine was beginning to
have its effect. "Lord Thomas, the repast was most excellent
and the wine . . . um . . . *devious*, I think is the appropriate
word. Now, with your permission, though, I should like to
retire. The hour grows late."

"Of course, sweet lady, of course. I bid you a good night
and pray you will not take umbrage if I detain your lord a
while longer? I seldom have a chance to air my views to someone I admire and respect as a friend."

Wauter grunted at the compliment, deigning to cast his wife
but a fleeting glance as her chair was removed by a servant.
She left through the arched doorway to the left of the high
table.

So he was still annoyed with her then, she mused. Well, in
that case perhaps it was just as well Thomas sought his company a while longer. With luck he wouldn't gain their bed until
the early hours, and staggering in drunk, he would spare her
his ire.

This wasn't the first time he'd shown some mild outrage at

other men's interest in her, and she doubted it to be the last. Back at Synford in the summer, one unfortunate stable boy had made the mistake of staring overlong at her ankle when helping her mount her mare for a morning's hunt. A cuff about the ear, delivered out of the blue by Wauter, was his swift punishment. It also served to warn any, who watched open-mouthed and with trepidation, that they could expect the same or worse if they challenged his ownership.

And even she, innocent of any crime, had not seen out that day unscathed. Her posterior had smarted the whole night through after being administered to by the palm of his large hand. What an indignity that had been!

She awoke with a start a while later. Drunken guffaws filled the chamber, bringing her to a warily upright position. The chamber door was open and Thomas and Wauter clung together, bouncing from one side of the portal to the other as they tried to make an entry.

"Ssh, or yoush'll wake her," warned the rotund of the two.

"I meansh to do so directly I gainsh my bed, anyhow," Wauter told him, this talk bringing a throaty chuckle from the other.

Her husband's eyes lighted upon her first, followed by those of his host who swayed and clutched more surely to Wauter's girth.

"Shweetheart," breathed Wauter.

"Ah!" Thomas gasped in finally spotting her. "There you ish'en."

Ermgarde couldn't see their faces since the only light in the vicinity came from the passageway. But she sensed that both men were leering and, accordingly, she pulled the bedcovers up to her chin.

"Shall I help yoush beshtween sh'covers?" offered Thomas, hoping for another glimpse of those satiny-smooth shoulders.

"I ca'manage." Though his brain was clouded, Wauter discerned the suggestive note in the other's slurrings and his jealousy was immediately galvanized.

Spinning his host about, he shoved him haphazardly out into the passage, then found the edge of the door with his boot and slammed it before Thomas could seek reentry. A string of disjointed profanities followed, to which Wauter called a cheery "Nighty-nighty"; then the lumbering tread of Thomas's retreat sounded.

"Indulshant I may be to my friends, but yoush mine alone." His head-on collapse upon the bed made the structure shudder, then he writhed about like a grounded whale. "Ermshgarde, lend a hand," he pleaded, getting slowly nowhere with his undressing.

She couldn't help but laugh, relieved now that she perceived he was in a jovial frame of mind and looked unlikely to be a menace.

"Drunken sot," she said, voice mildly chiding as she knelt over him in the darkness and unfastened the heavy, jewel-encrusted belt that drew in his houppelande at the waist. The rich and heavy garment itself presented more of a problem, its voluminous folds turning her efforts into a nightmare.

In his stupor Wauter had the impression that he was suffocating, and thrashed about as Ermgarde tried to drag the garment over his head.

"Argh. . . . Help!"

"Do be still!" she ordered impatiently, frowning down at him when at last the houppelande came free of his leaden bulk and he calmed down.

He lay prone and uncooperative as Ermgarde removed his final articles—boots, hose and tunic—and the only sounds to rise from his lips were throaty chuckles when his wife inadvertently tickled his more sensitive areas.

Now that she had him undressed, the next problem was how to get him from the foot to the top of the bed. She could expect little help from him! She encircled his chest with her arms and tried dragging him across the bed, but her hair became trapped beneath her knees, defeating her efforts. " 'Twould serve you right if I did leave you where you lay, you useless specimen! And *stop* that infernal laughter!"

Her fingers were tickling again and Wauter squirmed helplessly, thoroughly hindering her attempts. Then when her hair brought her up short once more and she fell upon him, his body responded to the closeness of her warm flesh and nipples against his furred chest in a surprising manner, considering his condition.

His hands began to grasp and stroke, and he paid no heed to his wife's exasperated cry as he somehow managed to find his

way atop of her, forgetful of taking his weight upon his
elbows until her pained struggles reminded him. He raised
himself, head swooping to her breasts where he nibbled and
teased, a hand sliding down over the taut belly to find that soft
place she offered eagerly to his questing fingers.

The hardness of him against her belly was like a signal that
never failed to trigger something within Ermgarde. She responded instantly to him, forgot her exasperation of moments
before and sought now only to accommodate and help her
slightly befuddled lover reach their mutual goal.

She molded herself against him, straining her hips enticingly
upon the hardness at his groin, fingers probing between their
bodies to stroke the sensitive flesh of belly and loins. There
was a drunken grunt of pleasure, then a badly aimed kiss on
Ermgarde's nose instead of her lips, and she gave in to a fit of
giggles that stopped only when he thrust into her, her mind
traveling then upon a well-remembered erotic path.

His legs straddled her, drawing her limbs together, tightening her about his manhood to make sensation rule supreme.
Ermgarde gasped at each thrust, not sure how she endured
such a battering of flesh and senses, yet savoring the climb to
realms of sensuality beyond belief. Toward the end, when his
driving became relentless and both had lost their reason completely, she drew more surely together her thighs and whim-
pered through the final throes of passion.

Robert de la Vallée watched incensed, every fiber of his
body trembling with rage as his love laughed at the joke made
by another man, then voiced no protest when he patted her
rump familiarly.

Why was she doing it to him? Was she immune to the suffering she caused him? First the Lord of Synford, then
himself, now all the knaves within these walls seemed to be
sampling her favors!

He threw down the harness he had been polishing and
strode into the strong light from the shadows of the stable, his
fair hair, bleached by the elements, making a startling cap of
gold about his thunderous face.

Cast her eyes in the kennel lad's direction, would she? Not
while he drew breath! Enough was enough.

Rowen was also watching Alice, an eyebrow raised disap-
provingly as he struggled to keep the new pair of wolfhounds

under control. Their leashes bit into the palm of his hand as they playfully pulled him along. He was annoyed, not so much by his sister's action as by the lack of help from his fellow kennel lad. Why anyone would prefer chasing girls to the company of two such fine canine specimens was quite beyond him.

The dog handler, Entwhistle, was as powerfully built as the would-be knight, but he possessed none of the other's fighting skills. So when he received a couple of viciously aimed blows to the stomach, he doubled over and fell moaning into the dust of the ward.

Alice watched the jealous outburst dispassionately, the merest hint of annoyance on her features. She cast the groveling figure, who was attempting to rise, a withering glance full of contempt. So easy a victim underlined her own suspicions as to his undeveloped masculinity. Maybe he wasn't such a good bed companion after all.

"How tiresome of you, Robert," she hissed, aware now of the interest the incident had awakened among the men-at-arms in the ward.

He contemplated her, his face flushed with anger. She had the look of some biblical harlot, her mouth painted red and her body draped with jewelry. Each ring, bracelet and necklace—his among them—was the price some male had paid for bedding her, and she wore them all like trophies, a veritable treasury around her neck alone.

"Whatever has happened to your sense? Why are you doing this to me? I love you, Alice. Surely you must realize that? Am I so lacking and ineligible that you must give cheaply to others that which I would take in honor and pride?"

"Then you are a fool, dear Robert," she said, kicking at the kennel lad's grasping hands as he sought to use her skirts as a hoist. "Why pay so heavy a price when you can, for a small token of appreciation, have me virtually for free?"

"Disgusting!" He could no longer reign in his ire and unleashed it by punching the unfortunate lad who'd just gained his feet.

The force of the blow sent the youth sprawling a good two yards before he hit dirt again, Robert's knuckles smarting from the contact. Still unsatisfied, he straddled his prey and began banging the other's head upon the hard-baked ground.

The dogs strained at their leashes, smelling blood. Everyone, save Rowen reigning in the animals, seemed hypnotized by the spectacle and he debated with himself what to do. Clearly Robert had to be stopped before he killed the senseless youth beneath him.

He'd spotted Lord Wauter earlier at the barbican gate. Gambling, he shouted and prayed that the man was still within the ward and in earshot. "My lord, my lord, come quickly!"

Wauter sat with the blacksmith, his admiration as great as it had been at twelve years of age, when he had first witnessed the art of mailmaking. Yet, even above the noisy clanging of hammer upon anvil, he heard the frantic cry of young Rowen and slid from his perch atop the work bench.

Emerging into the sunlight, he was met by the excited barking of hounds and a group of his men-at-arms riveted by some spectacle. He strode forward, pushing his way through the throng until he came upon what held them spellbound.

"Robert!" his voice boomed, but the young man appeared deaf to all but the prone figure he straddled and punched. Growling with annoyance, Wauter caught his squire by the neck of his cotehardie and dragged him away.

"What are you about?" he demanded.

Robert seemed aware of Wauter's presence for the first time and he staggered backwards, his eyes falling on the kennel lad with a startled gasp. "Oh my God! I did not mean. . . . He was too familiar with Alice. I meant to teach him a lesson. I . . . I lost control."

"Lost control? You almost murdered him!" Wauter cried. Then, grasping the other's shoulders, he ordered two gawking men-at-arms to carry the unfortunate recipient of Robert's ire into the guardroom. "Tend him as best you can. I shall be there presently."

" 'Twas an unprovoked attack," said Alice, quickly, seeking to extricate herself from any blame. "I was in no need of protection and Entwhistle certainly didn't need so harsh a lesson. Why, the poor lad was only seeking to keep me amused."

Remembering her forwardness in the stable on that other occasion, Wauter wasn't wholly convinced. Neither was he totally blind to her behavior with the men under his command. "Henceforth, Alice, you will stay away from the wards and guardroom, and take your recreation to the garden like your sister and Lady Margaret. Now, get you gone to their feminine company."

Coldly dismissed, she glared at him for a moment, her lips

tightening stubbornly as if tempted to refuse. But then she seemed to think twice. She'd come through this irritating episode rather smoothly and it would prove imprudent to act rashly all of a sudden. Best to remain the innocent party, she decided. One happy happenstance that brought a triumphant lightness to her step was the knowledge that Lord Wauter now realized others found her attractive enough to fight over. Before long he might realize what he was missing and succumb to her charms. She winked lasciviously at the guard as she passed and entered the keep without a care.

Wauter tousled Rowen's hair and thanked the lad for his summons, then led Robert to the deserted interior of the woodshed.

"This will not happen again, do you hear me?" The Lord of Synford thrust the other against a neatly stacked pile of logs, his massive form dwarfing Robert as he poked a finger at his squire's chest to underscore his point.

Feeling threatened, Robert inched further against the wood, nodding in affirmation.

"I know not what is between you and Alice, but I counsel you to leave well alone. That one is trouble."

Even in his reasonable fear, the squire couldn't remain silent. "Or is it because you covet her yourself that you warn me off? I saw the pair of you go into the stable that day and she emerge sometime later with her gown rent!"

"Why, you impudent cur!" Wauter's arm pressed against the throat of the other and his eyes blazed murderously.

The young man choked beneath the steely pressure. "I love her. Can you say the same? 'Tis you who spoiled her so that she cares not now with whom she lays! Don't you dare to lecture *me*!"

"I've never touched her and I pray you listen well. My own wife warned me that the girl bore me an unbrotherly affection and to be on my guard. Thankfully, it did turn out, for what Ermgarde said was true. That day at the barn she offered herself—though I took her there only to talk sense into her, make the girl see that she held no place in my heart, and when I refused her she ripped the clothes from her own body in an attempt to entice me. But don't look to me as the stealer of her virginity, Robert."

Wauter's anger lessened as the squire wept openly. Thank God his own love was not the torturous kind. How would he have reacted to Ermgarde's entertaining half the males within the castle? Entwhistle would most certainly have been dead, and the rest of her savorers, too!

Robert was in agony. He had long believed that Alice had been bedded by the lord and he had come to terms with the supposed fact because of the man's superior rank and physical allure. What woman, after all, didn't sigh after the baron? But now, to be told that Wauter had had no hand in her deflowering was just another blow. If not Wauter, then who? Who else had the faithless bitch panted for? Who else had been there before him? God, he couldn't endure this!

"Who?" he cried in anguish and slid down the woodpile, the scraping of his skin against rough bark as nothing compared to his sore, bleeding heart. "Who?"

Wauter shrugged, standing back from the crumpled form. "I have no idea. What I do know is that you need to be free of her for a while. Perhaps then your pain will lessen and you'll be able to face her rejection without further violence. Away from her you may forget her, or see her as she really is."

"I know what she is. Still, I love her."

"Then you have my sympathy, for 'tis a hopeless love. I think you should spend some time in the king's household. Harry has a way of overlooking us, isolated as we are in the country. Mayhap 'tis time we reminded him of our existence, Robert. A knighthood is more than likely if you catch his eye and make yourself useful."

"I'd rather remain, my lord. But if 'tis your wish that I go. . . ."

Wauter extended his hand and hefted the young man to his feet. "I don't want you to go, Robert, but I think it would be best all 'round. You must be able to look at this business objectively, and that I doubt you can do with Alice so close by. Go to Harry for a while, until things are sorted out in your mind. Whenever you wish to return, your place at my side will be waiting. And mayhap," he hugged the youth, "you will fill it as Sir Robert, then. Think how prestigious that would be for me?"

A weak smile was all that Wauter received by way of reply.

How convenient that French Charles, surfacing momentarily from lunacy, should declare himself for Armagnac, vow Burgundy a traitor and bar him from Paris. Henry couldn't have asked for more, yet he got it.

The previous year the Duke of Bourbon had made a raid into English Aquitaine and defeated an Anglo-Gascon force at Soubise, returning to Paris to be feted for his gallant deeds and become the hero of the high-born ladies. Now Henry would use that raid to advantage, crying that he was an innocent victim who was but seeking recompense for the wrong done to him.

John of Bedford was the first to become party to the king's plans, and as he listened he wondered if power wasn't unhinging his usually sensible brother.

"But how can you be serious?" he scoffed. "Demanding the return of the Angevin Empire, I can understand. Even the unpaid ransom for their old King John is a legitimate claim. But the duchy of Normandy, half of Provence, the hand of the French king's daughter plus a dowry of two million French crowns, *and* the French crown itself?! Ha! I ask you, Harry, can you imagine Charles, mad as he is, giving in to demands like those? After all, dear fellow, it was only a piffling raid into English territory, not a seizure of *all* our lands."

"Correct, brother, correct." Henry put an arm about his brother's shoulders and spoke conspiratorially, making a show of looking about the chamber as if the walls of Windsor had grown ears. When next he spoke it was with relish and a note of bravado. "*But* don't you see, I *know* they won't entertain such demands. That's what I'm counting on. I foresee negotiations bogged down in deadlock for some months, which will, of course, leave me no choice but to declare war upon them to take back what's rightfully mine!"

John could only wonder proudly at the deviousness of the other's mind.

CHAPTER

13

MAUD WAS DISPATCHED willingly—and with heartfelt thanks to Lady Margaret—to the Magdalen nunnery at Bristol. She was escorted by six of the most somber men-at-arms that Wauter could muster among his garrison. They would see to her safety and ensure that she arrived in an untouched state.

It was only after her departure that Lady Margaret unveiled some surprising information about the order.

"What do you mean?" Ermgarde asked, delighting in the freedom to speak plainly now without offending anyone's ears.

"The Magdalen houses were originally established to correct fallen women, to help them see the error of their ways and turn them into prized servants of the Almighty." A wickedly mischievous smile creased her face.

"Lady Margaret, you jest, surely?" The girl couldn't help but laugh, even while she looked scandalized. "Nuns are supposed to be virginal and pure of mind."

"Most are, my dear, and I think we can safely say Maud won't find herself reciting a rosary amongst too many former whores, even if I cannot vouch for the purity of *all* of them. But as to what I said about the establishing of the order—that was quite correct."

"Tarnished handmaidens," mused Ermgarde aloud, finding the revelation amusing.

"Oh, Ermgarde, in some things you are as naive as your sister. In no way has the church ever sought to curb prostitution, nor do they particularly want to. Most hold with St. Augustine's beliefs that if you took away such women, then the innocents would fall prey to the lusts of men."

The young girl listened, amazed, her picture of an uncorrupt church crumbling to dust. She'd been aware that priests took mistresses and fathered children, and that the Holy

Fathers in Rome (numbering three at the moment) were more involved in Vatican politics than in spiritual well-being. But they also condoned the selling of women's favors!

Margaret smiled at Ermgarde's surprise. "Don't fret about her. The experience will do her nothing but good. Let her see the church and its many flaws, learn to accept that women may give their bodies yet still return their love of God. 'Tis time, I think, that she learned to temper her proud right-eousness with a measure of compassion for those of us who have erred and who appear soiled in her eyes."

"You may be right. And, knowing Maud, she will like as not rise above any unpleasantry and drag her new sisters, will-ingly or not, up with her," said Ermgarde, paying heed to Margaret's words that had quietened any qualms she had been feeling.

Henry's frame seemed to shrink further into the folds of his sable mantle as William of Colchester, Westminster's abbot, led him beyond the high altar of the great church. He shivered, wrapped his arms about his chilled body and struggled to keep from stamping his booted feet to set his circulation going. He must show reverence for his illustrious forebearers, whose bodies were sealed into ornate sepulchres of alabaster, granite and limestone.

"You are free to supervise your underlings," said Henry dismissively to Colchester, as he left the gold and crimson of the altar behind and found the quietness of the royal chantries where the light from a hundred tapers was at pains to reach.

The abbot bowed and retreated.

Again there was that chill rippling down his spine, but the king told himself he was merely cold. He had no fear of others long dead. Nay, after all this was the day of the dead and the cortege that now approached the gate of London excited no trepidation in him. What Henry felt was obligation to the re-mains beneath the fine stone effigies, a need to do goodly deeds in this life so that he could rest here among them with-out feeling inferior. Vainglorious to the end.

He passed Henry III, Edmund Crouchback and Eleanor of Castile, and felt awed by the majesty of this company. He came to the semicircle of lesser, yet still noble kings, pausing over the carved likeness of his great-grandfather, Edward III and his great-grandmother, Philippa of Hainault, thoughts deep until he focused them on the occupier of the space behind the high altar.

Edward the Confessor had lain in this place of honor since before the Norman Conquest of 1066, his circular and diamond carved sepulchre from pre-Norman days looking out of place and vaguely quaint.

It was to this king that Henry knelt momentarily, seeking strength like a supplicant and vowing to restore the other's isle to its former greatness. The young king wrapped his black mantle about him and sat in the coronation chair, taking up the sword and shield that had belonged to his great-grandfather, and eyeing the weapons that had seen service at Crecy. The great victories over the French at Poitiers and Crecy had not been his, but he had never tired of hearing of them. Might he not someday command the same reverence that his great-grandfather enjoyed? This sword, battered and ragged-edged though it was, now served as the state sword, carried at coronations and cherished like some holy relic. Would his own accoutrements eventually find their way into this abbey?

"Sire, the cortege is approaching the abbey," said Colchester, after giving a nervous cough to attract the king's attention.

Henry rose and replaced the sword and shield, noting Colchester's faintly disapproving look and telling him brusquely, "They belonged to my great-grandfather," as if no further explanation were necessary.

They made their way to the nave in silence, and no sooner arrived when the doors were opened and the cortege entered, the place filling with pall bearers and a respectfully subdued court.

This day they had come to inter Richard II in Westminster Abbey as was his right. He had been removed from his former lowly resting place at Kings Langley, where he'd been buried after his assassination.

Henry wished he held a handkerchief when the casket passed him on its journey to the high altar, for his uncle stank in a way that permeated the air despite his supposedly sealed container.

Duty has been done, and, more importantly, seen to be done, thought Henry as he watched Colchester gesture the congregation to genuflect for the prayers and Mass. Richard II has been returned to his proper place. Now who could look upon me as ought but the magnanimous, all-compassionate king?

Ermgarde sighed over her work. It seemed never-ending. But Rogue needed a caparison to replace the old one, which was tattered and discolored from countless jousts and melees.

If she sighed at the task, then Alice positively snorted her displeasure, jabbing needle through silk as if it were a mortal enemy.

At last the elder sister looked up, her patience wearing thin as she witnessed the agitation of the other. "Why don't you go take a walk in the garden? You could keep Lady Margaret company while she picks the last of the blackcurrants."

"I've no desire for her company, sister, if you don't mind," she said curtly as she dropped her sewing and went to stand at the embrasure to stare wistfully. Wauter was in the ward, muscled body bare about the waist, since he had stripped in the humidity of the late summer day to practice swordplay with two men-at-arms. Aye, he was worth two men any day, as his finely tuned body executed moves effortlessly. Damn the man for denying her and then unmercifully seeing to it that she had few opportunities to find pleasure elsewhere. She knew that to watch him was to fire her desire for him, but she couldn't draw her eyes away from the window. He held her spellbound, drew her thoughts until her world was centered around him, her consuming goal to have him in her bed.

Ermgarde was watching her, wondering what fermented behind those hazel eyes. It was evident that something troubled her, had for some time. In fact, she had been in this disquieting mood ever since Robert had left for Windsor. Could it be that she now regretted her rejection of him and yearned for his presence?

"Alice, why were you so cold toward the squire de la Vallée? I do not wholly understand your attitude. He was handsome, was he not? Destined for at least a knighthood, and it was so obvious that he adored you."

Alice gave a bored shrug of her shoulders, her back still facing her elder sister. "I just didn't love him. Would you rather I had given him false hope? To my mind that would have been far crueler than being rebuffed."

"No, of course not, if there was no hope for him. But did

you need to be quite so harsh in your treatment? Firmness should be tempered with kindness."

Alice spun around, eyes flaming anger in a way that made Ermgarde shrink away.

"Don't lecture me! I will not stomach the court of one when I know with certainty whom I want! I'll have no substitute."

"Then who do you love, Alice? Speak his name and I shall see Wauter about arranging a marriage. I wouldn't stand in the way of your happiness." Ermgarde was earnest, her eyes wide with expectancy as she waited for the name of Alice's chosen one.

Alice's laugh was piercing, shattering the last fragments of calm that Ermgarde possessed. "Tell *you*? Ha! Can't you guess, dear sister? You say you wouldn't stand in the way of my happiness, but you do, *you do*!"

Dumbstruck by the outburst, Ermgarde watched the girl storm from the chamber, those words leaving her completely puzzled. She stood in the way?

Seconds later Wauter breezed in, waving a piece of rolled parchment at her. "We've been invited to Warwick."

"Indeed?"

"Aye, for a whole month of tourneys and feasting. The idea appeals to me. What say you?"

"Accept then. 'Tis about time I met the earl in the flesh, though his missives have given me some hint as to his character."

" 'Tis settled then; we'll leave within the fortnight. 'Tis some time since I've had the pleasure of testing arms against the earl. Hmm, have to check my harness and lances. Now where did Robert put my battle-axe and flail? Not my practice ones—those are purely for ceremonial occasions. Trust the lad to go lovesick now of all times. I've no squire. What about Brodrick? Mightn't the responsibility be too much for him just yet, though?"

Ermgarde was deaf to Wauter's thoughtful musings. She was wondering if her gowns were suitable, thinking perhaps that she might have to have more fashioned in a hurry. Would there be enough time to bring in a dressmaker, furrier and shoemaker? Perish the thought that she'd shame Wauter by appearing at his side like some graceless bumpkin!

"I've nothing fitting for such company. I can't possibly go or I'll disgrace you."

He laughed at her mortification, grasping Ermgarde about the waist and pulling her hard against him. A hand roved over her buttocks. "If you wore a hairshirt or a corn sack you'd still have everyone gaping in adoration. Don't worry, the clothes you possess will do well enough. Besides, should you put on too much of a display, I shall no doubt spend the entire month fighting off rivals, and that would never do. I have to keep my strength for jousting."

Ermgarde's hands strayed playfully over his hose. They tugged at his waist and uncovered enough flesh to allow for some enticing exploration. "I pray you'll save enough energy for the evenings too, my lord."

"I can always find the strength for you, my beloved." His strong hand grasped her wrist and forced her palm downwards to the part of him that her nearness had aroused.

"Not now, Wauter. Someone might come in," she protested, though made no move to stop him when he began to pull up the skirts of her houppelande.

He seated himself and pulled her astride him, hands twining in her hair to bring her close for a teasing kiss. "Should I hear the footsteps of anyone approaching, I'll simply bellow for them to be off. Who would dare to disobey?"

Who indeed? She gave herself up to his kisses and artful hands, ready for him when he eased himself into her, making Ermgarde squirm delightedly above him.

Alice's approach was naturally soft and she was about to lift the latch and enter when giggles and heavy sighing reached her through the door. She stopped in her tracks, her face going first ashen, then florid with rage. The bastard was taking Ermgarde, there, in the solar! *No!* It should be me!

Her ear pressed against the planking of the door, listening in anguish to every word of love, every grunt of exertion and sigh of increasing fulfillment. Horrible! Disgusting! Yet she couldn't move away.

With her eyes closed, she imagined what was happening behind that door and obliterated her sister's body from her mind, replacing it with her own. Oh yes, she could feel him, working within her, calling her name as she gave herself without restraint. "Alice . . . Alice . . ." like a sigh from his determined lips. She trapped a hand between her trembling thighs, stroking in unison to the sounds beyond the door, her breath as belabored as theirs.

CHAPTER

14

WARWICK CASTLE STOOD ON THE BANKS of the River Avon, the most centrally situated castle in England.

The entourage from Synford approached from the west meadows, took the bridge across the river, then crossed the deep, dry moat that encircled the imposing structure. A great barbican gate straddled the moat, its oaken doors and double portcullis making the advance of an enemy nigh on impossible. No wonder Warwick had remained untaken since its fall to Simon de Montfort during the baron's war with Henry III, and then had only succumbed because an assault was launched upon its weaker curtain wall.

Their train had been announced, for they had scarcely passed through the gatehouse before the ward bustled with noble people as well as the customary men-at-arms and servants. From the half-timbered buildings that offered shelter about the curtain wall emerged sumptuously attired courtiers, surcoated pages and an army of lackeys.

Ermgarde was surprised by the size of the welcoming party and reigned in her mount nervously alongside Rogue, who was taking a path toward the largest of the buildings where a crowd had gathered on the grass.

A wiry-framed man, his features finely marked and his forehead high, stepped forward ahead of the others, hugging Wauter the instant he slid from the saddle. The man's small mouth broadened into a grin. "So here you are at last, then. 'Tis good to see you again. I spy your accoutrements." His eyes fixed on the cart that carried Wauter's knightly paraphernalia. "Good, good. 'Tis a while since I've tried out against you. Mayhap this time I shall find the upper hand."

Her husband laughed derisively. "You can try." Then Warwick was at Ermgarde's side with upraised hands to assist her from the palfrey, unable to resist holding her a while longer than need be before planting her feet on the ground.

Her violet gossamer veil was lifted momentarily by the breeze in the ward, disclosing her features and her no-less-startling violet eyes. Warwick sighed.

Grasping her hand and lowering himself reverently to a knee, the earl kissed her palm and fingers, his voice grave as his eyes danced merrily. "Now all comes clear. Who would not marry Goddess of Love, Venus herself, if the chance were his? Dame, I am your slave."

She smiled prettily, but was lost to say something quite so gracious in return.

Warwick was on his feet again, his houppelande of mid-blue and silver no less spectacular than her golden-girdled gown of violet-and-cream brocade. He took her hand and ushered her into the crowd. Wauter brought up the rear, his light greetings bringing a warm response from the crowd before they spotted the beautiful Ermgarde.

"By all the saints! Where did you find her, Waut?"

"At her prayers," he answered, truthfully.

"Some devils have all the luck!"

Ermgarde moved from one group to the next, trying to remember the barrage of names, faces, trying to keep her nerves at bay. The women were wary and formal, save for a few who were beauties themselves and saw Ermgarde as no great threat. The males, to a man, let their eyes rove over the exquisite creature with unveiled interest.

Humphrey of Gloucester looked enraptured as he took her hand and helped Ermgarde to her feet after the curtsy, seeming reluctant to loosen his grip. He placed his lips to her fingers and there they lingered as he breathed, "Incomparable," his bobbed, fair locks caressing her flesh.

Wauter was at her side forthwith, warning her humorously, "Beware of this ducal imp, wife. His brother, the king, doth despair of him and no lady is quite safe from his deceiving show of innocence."

Gloucester gave a rascalish smile, denying nothing, as if he was not displeased by his reputation.

Still flustered by the ardent kiss and the pressure of the duke's hand, Ermgarde was at a loss for some witty remark, and instead said simply, "I shall mark well your words, husband."

Richard Beauchamp, Earl of Warwick, resumed his role as

host. "Now, I think a modest repast is in order. Then, this afternoon what say you all to a tour of the tiltyard—give the lists an inspection before the joust on the morrow?"

The men cried out enthusiastically; their ladies nodded dutifully in agreement.

The modest repast in the great hall was anything but, consisting as it did of six courses, each enhanced by a different wine. At the foot of the hall, minstrels chorused songs as the guests ate, many of their songs in the French tongue of their origin, so that Ermgarde could only guess at their meaning.

"They play well," she commented, finding that she was too excited to eat. She picked delicately at the roasted capon on her silver platter, as Lady Margaret had instructed.

"And so they should, with Pent Trumper and Wauter Haliday amongst them, minstrels to the king. I dare say Gloucester spirited them away from his brother's court for this occasion."

Seated on the other side of the trestle with his lady, Lord Camoys leaned toward Wauter, inquiring in a low voice that was meant for no one else's ears, "Has the Duke of Gloucester enlightened you yet as to the latest steps the king has taken concerning his grievance with France?"

Wauter shook his head, biting into the chunk of pheasant speared on the tip of his knife.

"Harry had increased his demands upon the French. We all know that these negotiations have been something of a pointless exercise, but now, and the best news possible, Waut, I'm sure you'll agree, he's given the signal to start mustering. It will go out officially to his dukes and earls within the next couple of days. The French Campaign is within sight, me thinks."

Wauter's interest had grown throughout the disclosures, Ermgarde noted uneasily. She didn't like this talk of war. Lady Camoys bestowed upon her a sympathetic smile, as much as to say, "you must bear it and learn to be strong like the rest of us."

Wauter mused gleefully, "A chevauchee into France, do you think, Thomas?"

"That is my bet. But what of you, Waut? Will you be glad to join us this time? Newly wed and with such a vision of a wife, I could understand your reluctance. Some will be staying to keep secure the Welsh and Scottish borders, and I don't doubt that Bedford would smile upon loyal supporters should Henry decide to leave the governing of England to him while elsewhere.''

"Nay! Stay at home? Tom, what can you be thinking? I'm a soldier, 'tis my life. Ermgarde understands that. Don't you, sweetheart?" Wauter's hand covered her own atop the table and he looked for the expected confirmation upon her face.

It was some moments before she resigned herself to the fact that no protest on her part would have the power to keep him home. "England is suffering from boredom, I believe, and 'twill only take the word 'war' bandied about the countryside for every duke, earl, knight and yeoman to stop what he is doing and head for battle! That is my opinion, my lords.''

Wauter and Thomas looked at her sternly, wondering how a female had managed to come so close to the truth, and Lady Camoys looked astounded by the outburst. Where had the girl got such notions from? Why, nobody *liked* making war. How could they? This proposed campaign was to do with principles, to teach that horrid French king a lesson for stealing the Angevin Empire. Everyone knew that. Boredom? Stuff and nonsense!

Indignantly, as if she saw the opinion as a personal insult to her husband's integrity, Lady Camoys felt bound to ask, "But surely you cannot believe the *cause* ignoble?''

"England's cause is noble enough, my lady, though somewhat contrived!"

If Ermgarde had come right out with treason, the lady couldn't have been more shocked.

As agreed, the gentlemen spent the rest of the daylight hours at the lists in the meadow beside the Avon, humorously tearing each other's fighting prowess to shreds; the ladies—those who had excused themselves from such tedium—were left to occupy their time as best they might under the somber hostesship of dull Lady Beauchamp.

Lady Camoys put aside Ermgarde's unfortunate outburst in the quest for lively company—though even her ideas of how best to fill the time left the Lady of Synford sighing—and together they made for the town, or more precisely to the church of St. Mary's which, Lady Camoys had been told, was as fine a parish church as could be found. Years of accompanying Maud to church stood Ermgarde in good stead for an hour of kneeling beside her devout companion, though in truth she said no prayers and occupied her time taking in her dignified surroundings.

Richard Beauchamp's grandparents lay before her, their alabaster effigies in quiet repose, their place before the high altar honoring their standing while alive. Thomas had fought valiantly in all the French wars of Edward III, had commanded at the battle of Crecy, had been guardian to the minor Black Prince, and had fought at Poitiers and at the siege of Calais. It had taken a dose of plague to finally finish him off!

'Twas strange to think of her grandfather fighting under such a man's command, stranger still to think of herself now accepted into the bosom of Beauchamp's all-encompassing family. Ermgarde: the shepherdess who dines with earls!

CHAPTER
1 5

IT WAS EVIDENT that sometime during list practice Gloucester had imparted to his elder brothers the wish that England make ready for war. In the great hall that night it was the leading topic of conversation.

Humphrey was speaking loud enough so that the hushed assembly could hear. "Harry doth propose bonuses for any who bring more than thirty men to the muster. Our scales of pay are yet undecided, but I can tell you that for myself, and any other duke who takes the road to France, there will be at least thirteen shillings a day; for earls, six shillings and eight pence, or thereabouts; four shillings for barons, two for knights, one for men-at-arms and six pence for the archers. Me thinks we should go to war more often!"

There were satisfied "Um's" from the higher tables, though below the salt the knights mumbled indignantly at their expertise in battle only being deemed worthy of two shillings a day.

"Let us not forget the extras," Gloucester reminded them. "The yield from a sacked town is high, and there is the ransom for any prisoners taken."

To a man, the males nodded. Aye, never mind the rates of pay. It was the potential for plunder on the chevauchee that filled a man's purse.

The feasting continued, a lull coming only when the king's minstrels started another song or ditty and the diners paused to listen. And when the feasting was done and the tables cleared by efficient serving wenches, the dancing began.

Ermgarde tapped her foot in time with the lutes and recorders, hoping that Wauter would condescend to partner her, yet sensing that his dislike of so unmanly a pastime would stall him. He much preferred discussing the approaching muster with Sir Gilbert Umfraville.

What a waste of good tuition! Lady Margaret had spent

hours taking her through the steps of the court dances until
she had reached proficiency in each, her body's graceful ways
lending themselves readily to the slow, precise footwork and
intricacies that the dances demanded.

Then, saving her from boredom, came Humphrey of Gloucester, bending over her shoulder and breathing of her perfume with a veritable sigh of pleasure. "My lady, I could not
see you languish for want of a partner."

"My lord?" She looked her husband askance.

Having warned her already, Wauter saw no harm in her
dancing with the duke. 'Twould save him the infuriating duty,
after all! "Feel free."

Oh, he could be so riling at times! Even as she rose when a
page removed her chair, Ermgarde saw that he had already
gone back to his favorite topic, war, and seemed to forget her
existence.

She danced well, smiling each time her graceful path
reunited her with the duke, curtsying to his studied bows,
knowing that in her black and silver garb she had captured
everyone's attention—even her husband's—as she moved the
area between the tables. She'd take his mind off war!

"I'm bewitched," breathed Gloucester, taking and leading
Ermgarde to the summit of the line of dancers, where he had
to relinquish his grip and reluctantly take his solitary steps to
Thomas Erpingham, listening for what seemed an eternity before the mellow strains of music brought them back together.

"Would that this hall was deserted, save for you and I and
the musicians. I would blindfold them and take sole pleasure
from the movements of that lissome body."

"My husband has given me warning of your ways, my lord
duke. But I admit to liking your flattery. Pray continue, so
long as you mean nought by it."

The duke gave an exaggeratedly affronted look. "That
which passes my lips is the solemn truth, my lady. If I said you
are the moon and stars, 'twould be no exaggeration. Alas, the
flowery compliments I am used to issuing at such times as
these now seem quite inadequate. Will it suffice to say that
never have I met your like before?"

Wauter spotted the way Humphrey was fawning over his
wife, yet could discern nothing that would warrant the slap he
had instructed her to use should the duke's advances get out

of hand. He looked about the tables where conversation had lulled. All eyes were on the handsome dance partners. Whether Ermgarde encouraged it or not, it was evident that Gloucester was bewitched, the admiration in his eyes transgressing the borders of decency.

Angered, yet at pains to hide it, Wauter resumed his conversation, though the attention of even that old warhorse, Umfraville was now divided and his answers became laconic and mechanical, eyes straying time and again to the couple.

Damn Gloucester! These university types were all the same! Spouting knowledge in that aloof manner all their own, wooing women with well-learned phrases that spilled from their tongues with ease! And look at her, his wife, lapping it up! Why had she consented to another dance with him? Wasn't she aware of the spectacle she made?

The Lord of Synford doubted that the onlookers could have been more struck by the sexual undercurrent that charged the hall than if his wife had disrobed and danced naked before them!

An eternity later the dance finished and Ermgarde was escorted back to her lord's side. He had purposefully centered his attention on the knight facing him and gave only a curt nod when Gloucester enthused over her grace and beauty, before tactfully withdrawing on seeing the fire in the lord's eyes.

It appeared to Ermgarde that her husband hadn't missed her company and she felt hurt by it. She forced herself to smile brightly. " 'Twas pleasant to be able to put into practice the steps Lady Margaret taught me. Of course the gay atmosphere did lessen some of my fears, and my lord duke of Gloucester was courteous enough not to comment if I misstepped."

Wauter held out his goblet so a page could refill it. He answered caustically, "If you'd danced like a yoked ox I doubt your partner would have noticed! His eyes were seldom on your feet."

Hurt was replaced with indignation. "If you'd thought to dance with me, husband, I would not have had to accept another partner! Could you not forsake your discussions of war long enough to go through the steps with me?"

"I think you've danced enough this night," he told her, slamming his goblet down on the table.

Umfraville watched in amusement. Could it be that the

lovebirds were heading for a bout of irate feather-flying?

Then one minstrel began to sing, sauntering between the tables as he strummed his lute:

> "A maiden fair, with raven hair,
> Hath stole away my heart;
> One smile, or kiss from such
> Strawberry lips, and my spirit
> Would soar with the lark. . ."

Ermgarde blushed as she felt the lute player's eyes on her, and giggled in pleasure at the flowery, somewhat thrown-together words in her honor.

The rest of the diners were watching too, though their eyes were on Wauter. His face burned a crimson red, his mouth formed a tight line of barely suppressed fury. First Gloucester, now some pipsqueak musician! Eyes watched his fingers grasp the goblet, half expecting him to crush the silver.

Instead, he rose, then caught his wife about the arm and brought her to her feet beside him. Her giggles stopped, her smile vanished. Paling, she watched as he executed a stiff bow for the Earl of Warwick, and began to speak. "If my lords and ladies will excuse us, but my wife professes herself fatigued after the day's travel and must seek her bed forthwith."

Warwick looked skeptical, but kept his peace. No doubt if he'd possessed such a wife his reaction to this evening would have been similar. "Of course, we all understand. Goodnight to you. A servant will conduct you to the chambers that have been prepared."

Feeling humiliated, color returned to her cheeks as she was nigh on dragged from the hall, the presence of a guiding servant keeping unspoken the words she wanted to hurl.

A far-from-gentle hand propelled her into the bedchamber. "Get you to bed."

She turned at the command, spitting defiance, but the door closed before her eyes, leaving Ermgarde alone with her rage.

CHAPTER

16

"HAVE YOU SEEN Lord Wauter?" Ermgarde asked Lady Camoys, sitting down beside the woman in the hall and taking the platter of bread and honey extended by a servant.

"Briefly. He took a hurried breakfast, then made off to the lists with my husband and half a dozen others. They'll be preparing for this afternoon's tourney. We ladies are instructed to make our way there after the midday meal, so that we might *enjoy* the sight of them trying to knock each other senseless."

Ermgarde smiled in mild amusement, glad to find that her ladyship had something of a sense of humor after all.

"But for this morning we may forget about that ordeal. The Duke of Gloucester has promised to escort us ladies about the town. 'Tis market day and 'twill make a pleasant diversion."

Dubious of the idea, Ermgarde shook her head. "I don't know whether I ought, considering Wauter's attitude toward the duke."

"But, my dear, you'll be with at least a dozen other women. Surely he couldn't object to that? Besides, being occupied as he is, I doubt he'll even know."

She felt satisfied with the rationale. And if he could disappear without even a thought for her lingering discomfort among these strangers, then she felt entitled to amuse herself and come to know them without his help or blessing.

Veiled and wimpled—sometimes both, if the ladies were truly diligent about protecting their countenance from the gaze of commoners—they strolled near the north gate of the town. An escort of Warwick's guards kept the overly curious townsfolk at bay with halberds and threatening snarls, while the Duke of Gloucester divided his charm and wit equally between his willing charges.

Oh, that Lady Ermgarde! Surely there had never been one

so superbly created as she? Her body promised unimaginable delights; her smile turned him into a callow youth with two left feet and no worthwhile conversation. She catapulted the word "sex" to sublime heights, so that it was something to revere, or to seek in a painful quest as Galahad had sought his Holy Grail. And, most amazing of all, she had no real idea of the effect she created even as she turned men into willing slaves.

Gloucester worked his way through the ladies, smiling here, making a witty remark there, until he had gained her side, mentally cursing Lady Camoys for never leaving the girl alone. "I trust you ladies are enjoying the morning? More fun, is it not, than lingering within the castle waiting for this afternoon's entertainment?"

"Indeed, my lord duke," agreed Lady Camoys, stepping gingerly aside as a stray pig upturned a cart, whose contents of marrows and green gourds skittered in their general direction.

Gloucester saw his chance for closer contact with the fair lady and took it, encircling her waist with an enthusiastic hug and pulling her away from the vicinity of the avalanche of vegetables.

Ermgarde, though, didn't see the hazard coming and made indignant objections to the duke's overly familiar manner. She squirmed from his grasp and haughtily straightened her houppelande, slapping out blindly, until she stumbled on a marrow and realized what he had been about. She broke into a winning smile. "Pray forgive me, my lord duke. I did misread your intentions."

"I'll forgive you only if I'm allowed to escort you ladies around the remainder of the stalls and keep you from further harm with more knightly deeds—circumstances warranting," he said laughing, ignoring his cheek where her palm print showed angry red.

"Agreed," said Ermgarde, relieved that he'd gallantly overlooked her violence against his royal person.

He crooked his arms, offering them to the ladies and then escorted them around the marrows, leaving chaos in their wake.

The market stalls displayed the usual produce brought in from the outlying crofts, but the market also was jammed with caravans brought in by merchants who hoped to draw the wealthy to their more expensive wares. And this day they were in luck. The ladies of the court were known to be frivolous.

"Have you ever seen the like?" Ermgarde asked no one in particular, captivated by the glitter of gold and silver before her eyes. She reached out tentatively to examine the objects held before her by a hopeful merchant. Rings, heavy chains with heraldic devices, gems in precious settings; jewels for every occasion.

Of course Gloucester had seen the like before. He had coffers bursting with trinkets that he'd never even bothered to look at, let alone wear. But he would never have told Ermgarde that. 'Twould have sounded monstrously pompous to one as naive as she.

"Oh, Lady Camoys, will you take a look at this! 'Tis so clever," gasped Ermgarde.

Lady Camoys was genuinely impressed by the golden horse which reared on its hind legs, then bowed on an alabaster plinthe and nodded its head to imitate a snorting neigh. "Indeed, 'tis splendid. But how does it work?"

The merchant directed his banter at her then, seeing Lady Camoys as a prospective client. "The mechanics of the piece are a mystery even to me, great lady. I acquired it from a Bristol merchant, and he from a goldsmith in Germany. 'Twas made at Nürnberg, to be precise, at one of these workshops that also create the timepieces so greatly in demand. One has to insert a key, thus, and the horse is instantly set into motion."

Ermgarde was ecstatic and, searching in the purse hanging from her girdle, she asked, "And how much do you ask for the piece?"

"Well, my lady, 'tis one of the finest items I have to offer. The gold and alabaster alone are precious . . . and then there are the unique movements of the horse. Seventeen pounds is not an extravagant sum, me thinks."

"Seventeen?" Ermgarde's hand fell away from the purse. She had but five pounds on her in gold and silver, and thought that a princely sum! Mightn't she go beg the money of Wauter? He could be so indulgent at times. But at the moment he was angry and she doubted he'd be receptive to her whim. "Your price is too high," she told the merchant, leaving Lady Camoys to stare as she calculated whether Lord Thomas would take kindly to her buying it.

" 'Tis nought but a pricey, useless toy," Ermgarde told herself, unaware of Gloucester at her side witnessing her disappointment. "My lord would have a fit should I squander his money on a horse that does nought save rear and prance."

She stopped at a stall which sold religious paraphernalia. There were garnet rosaries, gold and silver crucifixes. Better to spend her money on something useful for Maud, she decided, and picked a cross at random, handing over the desired amount of coin.

Then she wandered on. Gloucester had disappeared. So had Lady Camoys. Ermgarde looked about, hoping to spot the guards, but the many stalls blocked her view on all sides. So it seemed sensible to head for the castle walls, for surely she'd meet some other lady on the way.

She had barely cleared the town gate when Gloucester's voice reached her ears, calling with breathless insistence from behind.

"My lady, wait. My lady. . . ."

She paused in her unhurried walk, turning to make some desultory comment, when her eye was caught by the gleaming object in his grasp. She had no doubt that it was the golden horse.

Humphrey had reached her, the other ladies and the guards trailing far behind. He was panting, and a wide grin transformed his youthful looks to sheer boyishness.

"You have bought the horse? Oh, how splendid! Perhaps you would let me turn his key? Just once."

He thrust out his hands. " 'Tis for you I did buy it."

"My lord duke!"

"Take it, take it. 'Twould give me more pleasure than you can imagine. I can well afford it."

"But my husband—"

"Take it. You'll think of some story to tell him. Say the merchant fell in love with the color of your eyes and gave you it for the total sum of your purse. Say anything, but take it."

Ermgarde held out her hands and received the object with careful joy, her eyes clouding ridiculously. "My lord, I don't know. . . ." She laughed, but it sounded strangled in her throat. " 'Tis *too* fine."

"Nay, not for you."

She kissed him. It seemed the most natural way of showing her thanks. She grazed his smooth fair cheek with a kiss that went unnoticed by none of the pursuing ladies and guards. And she didn't care. As Hotspur and Warwick had been and were champions of England, so Humphrey of Gloucester, scholar and laze-about was now her champion.

Ermgarde turned the key in the appropriate slot and together they watched the antics of the horse, the beast's audience growing as the ladies converged upon them.

CHAPTER

17

SEATED BELOW the gaily striped canopy bearing the Warwick arms, Ermgarde tried to spy Rogue, or Brodrick—serving as her husband's squire in Robert de la Vallée's absence. She studied one of the crest-topped pavilions that had been erected in the meadow beneath the castle walls, and before long she spotted the argent device on top of Wauter's tent. She was able to pick out Rogue tethered nearby.

She could well imagine the chaos behind those silken walls, having witnessed Wauter being fitted with his harness of steel plate on a couple of occasions and finding it the most tedious of businesses.

Leg harnesses would be secured first, over his hose of mail; greaves, fan-plated poleyn and cuishes. Over a linen under-tunic would be fitted the breast-and-back plates, which followed the bodily contours faithfully and finished on the hips in a dagged fringe of mail. For the arms there would be vambraces, and, about the throat, a gorget of plate or mail. The gauntlets and helm—which had a hinged visor that left only a slit to see through for the tourney field—were not donned until before the fray.

Trumpets sounded and the seated dames tittered among themselves, smiling gaily as husbands and lovers rode to the tourney field in magnificent procession. There were only two men absent from the field: York, because he didn't possess the inclination; and poor Lord de la Pole, who had slipped on the wet turf that morning during list practice and suffered a bruised posterior. It was impossible for him to sit a horse in comfort.

The knights made a colorful sight, from the steel-grey and silver of their harnesses to the jeweled sword belts and scabbards at their hips. And their mounts were no less impressive, emblazoned with multi-colored caparisons, stell chafrons to protect their faces, and gaudy bridles and Hessian saddles.

Flourishing painted lances, the lords rode before their ladies and saluted them. They then lowered their blunted lance ends so their ladies could tie some token there, to be caught up by the favored knight and reverently tucked beneath his armor—the lady's champion for the day.

Ermgarde looked for Wauter as she unknotted a lengthy piece of ribbon from her hair. But he didn't come forward, and instead hung back within the crush of mounted knights, his eyes under scowling brows telling her that she was still out of favor. Blast him! 'Twas so humiliating.

About to enfold the crimson ribbon in her skirt to prevent some not-so-preoccupied courtier from taking note of her husband's chilly behavior, and providing food for court gossip, Ermgarde's heart lurched guiltily as a voice enquired, "Could that token be for me, sweet lady?"

Relieved, she smiled warmly at Gloucester, thinking him quite the most becoming knight in his harness of white steel. Her eyes slipped past him to Wauter as she wondered if the sight of his rival might soften his stand about accepting her token. It hadn't. He hid his emotions behind a sardonic mask, then fitted his helm on his head and clapped down the visor, wheeled Rogue about and made his way back toward the pavilions.

Somehow Ermgarde kept the glare from her eyes and broadened her smile for the duke. "Of course 'tis for you, my lord. I pray you'll guard it well?"

"With my life."

"I trust 'twill not come to that!" she laughed, then tied the crimson velvet ribbon about the tip of his lance.

Once in his hands, Gloucester kissed the token and, oblivious to the watchful eyes about him, wrapped the ribbon about his arm like a personal pennant, causing Ermgarde to blush and the ladies to titter once more. Lady Camoys' lips pursed in faint disapproval.

Positively beaming, Gloucester secured his helm, saluted Ermgarde once more and headed back toward the knightly ranks, positioning himself—whether by design or by coincidence—beside the Lord of Synford, so that the latter could not help but notice Ermgarde's token.

The tourney ran its course, the lesser knights quickly making their exits from the field under the skillful attacks of

Beauchamp, FitzSimmons, Gloucester, Holland and Corn-wall. To win or lose at this stage held no disgrace, for those who remained knew they were the elite of England's warriors. But the fighting was no less earnest for that knowledge. Most had a dream, an ambition to bring either FitzSimmons or Beauchamp to his knees, so they could say they had fought and bested the finest in the land. And they tried, *desperately*. But it wasn't to be. Wauter, because of sheer strength and well-learnt techniques, and Richard, as the acknowledged Champion of England, beat all comers and, as expected, finished up fighting it out between themselves for the day's honors.

Ermgarde cared not who won, though grudgingly she acknowledged to herself that her husband must surely triumph. He was in fine form. And, sensing that Warwick couldn't afford her the pleasure of seeing her arrogant husband sent sprawling into the dust, she stood up without an ex-cuse and left her companions, ignoring Lady Beauchamp's questioning glance.

Nay, she was not going to stay and watch the inevitable out-come. She didn't want to see her husband's haughty mien reach its limits as he was proclaimed victor of the day!

She followed the banks of the Avon, not once looking back to where the combatants blurred colorfully against their watching ladies and squires and the bold hues of the pavilions.

FitzSimmons the Bastard, he was called affectionately. A fitting epithet in every way, she decided.

"Could you not have stayed to witness the outcome?" Wauter demanded, swinging from Rogue and leaving the horse to feed on the tall meadow grass.

Ermgarde ignored him, her chin stubbornly set as she walked, and with her dainty slippers kicked at the dandelions lining the field. He caught up with her, moving with surprising swiftness for one in full harness, and grasped her upper arm to whirl her around.

She flinched at the steely grip of the gauntlet, trying in vain to pull away. Her eyes narrowed so that Wauter could see little save the thick black lashes. "I'm surprised to see you here, my lord. Should you not be back at the castle basking in your win-ner's glory?"

"Warwick won!" he snarled.

"Oh!" She was genuinely surprised.

Won, thought Wauter furiously, because I was too interested in what had brought about your departure before the end of the tourney! Though nothing would have dragged such information from him.

"It was ill-mannered of you to leave."

Her indifferent shrug brought a blaze to Wauter's already stormy eyes. Shaking her like a dog with its quarry, he railed, "I am your husband, madam. You are supposed to show a semblance of interest before others, even if you do not feel it!"

"Why should I, pray? My husband you may be, but this day you were not my champion by your own design! Don't you dare to expect a show of allegiance from me when I suffer nought but your pridefulness in return!"

She struggled to free herself, but it was futile. He was as sound as any castle and, with a painful expulsion of air, Ermgarde found herself backed none too gently up against a horse chestnut trunk with Wauter looming over her, his anger vanishing with astonishing speed.

She knew that light in his eyes instantly, but was still too angry and possessed of a feeling that she was ill used, to be obliging. Steeling herself as he found a nipple and toyed, she tried to push him away, to move her face when his head descended and he sought her mouth. Useless. She bit his lip, feeling a moment's triumph before he bit her back, bringing forth a moan that was stifled by his pillaging tongue.

She couldn't defeat him, she realized, but mayhap his harness would. How could one perform the act of coupling in steel plate? She almost giggled aloud at the thought and allowed his fierce kisses and probing hands to continue. When he reached the point of discovery and found that he could not have her, oh how she would laugh! 'Twould be a suitable punishment.

In the meantime, however, it was becoming difficult to remember that she was supposed to feel outraged and humiliated. He could kiss so thoroughly, so expertly, that her pulse quickened and soon she was kissing him back, her tongue toying with his, her breathing growing labored.

Arms locked about his neck, unmindful of the joined steel that caused discomfort against her tender flesh, her knees began to tremble weakly as her desire mounted and his hand sought and caressed with greater insistence, sending shudders through her.

Eventually she forgot that the armor was supposed to shield her from him, and began wondering instead how she might broach it to get at the man underneath!

While Wauter kissed her—his low moans filling her ears as he pressed her more ardently against the tree, hot breath searing—she tugged vainly at the mail hose that protected his manhood, making little headway. The finely knit links stubbornly resisted, scratching her fingers until she cried out in exasperation.

"Where there's a will . . ." he said determinedly, releasing her and throwing down his gauntlets, his calloused hands finding the unwieldy garment easier to deal with than his wife had.

'Twould have been more agreeable, perhaps, to have tumbled with him in the soft grass at her feet, but she didn't doubt Wauter would have crushed her in all that steel plate. Up against a tree would do just as well. And the quicker the better!

Her legs separated willingly as Wauter caught the hem of her silken gown and pooled it around her waist, his eyes sparkling fiercely at sight of the midnight triangle. Then his mouth found hers again and Ermgarde moaned as his fingers sought between her legs and she was galvanized by the shock of pleasure that spread upward through her belly.

When his manhood found the same soft, welcoming haven moments later and made a hungrily swift entry, Ermgarde was left gasping, her feet gradually leaving the soft earth as Wauter rose proudly to his full height and gave support by cradling her buttocks in his hands.

The striving upward motion of his body swept her along with him, his nearness and knowledge that there was no route of escape, save at his choosing, heightening the intensity of the steadily building waves of desire. Her mouth, locked with his even as their bodies were, made gurgles of abandonment that spurred him on, her arms slackening about his neck as all there was to give was given and hungrily received.

The end when it came was violent and simultaneous, shaking them both greatly and, without the tree to lend much-needed support, the pair would no doubt have landed in an unromantic heap in the grass.

As it was, Ermgarde didn't come through completely

unscathed, and after the heat had given way to tranquil contentment she felt the first twinge of discomfort where Wauter's breastplate had bruised her, and could guess at the ruination of her fine silk gown against the rough bark of the tree.

On entering the chamber, the first thing that caught Wauter's eye was the golden horse crowning the sideboard. He strode toward it curiously and picked it up, then smiled when the steed pranced when he turned the key. He looked inquiringly at his wife.

"How did you come by this?" he asked, reasonably enough.

Ermgarde cursed herself for having left the automaton on show, thinking that this wasn't perhaps the best time to speak of it. She was as evasive as possible. "I did see it at the market this morn and took a liking to it. A merchant from Bristol brought it."

"Cost a pretty penny, no doubt. Did you borrow from one of the other ladies? If so I'll give you coin enough to make good the debt."

"Nay, I . . . I didn't buy it. 'Twas a gift."

"A gift?" One of Wauter's dark brows rose suspiciously. "You should not have accepted; 'tis too fine. A gift from whom?"

Her throat felt suddenly restricted and Ermgarde coughed nervously. " 'Twas from my lord Duke of Gloucester. He saw how I had taken to the thing and, knowing I had not the coin, he did purchase it for me."

"Gloucester! You took so valuable a gift from him!" Wauter was upon Ermgarde in an instance, his face darkening with fury that no artful session of lovemaking would dispel, his mighty hands clamping about her shoulders like a vise. "How could you? Did it not occur to you that he'll undoubtedly expect something in return?"

"No, you're wrong. Gloucester seeks nothing of me but perhaps to be my champion. There is nothing impure in this, Wauter; you must believe that, or else I should not have accepted the horse," she tried to explain.

But Wauter would have none of it. He jeered at her, hardly deigning to listen, "No impure thoughts? Madam, either you are a fool or you take me for one!"

"Not so!"

"I can see this thing will have to be nipped in the bud. I think it best that you return home, therefore relieving obvious temptation all round."

"You are sending me away because of this?" She looked stricken, as if he'd struck her.

"It seems the most obvious course," he said, more ruled by anger than common sense. He wanted to put as great a distance as possible between her and that opportunist, Humphrey. Buy her expensive gifts, would he? No more!

CHAPTER

18

WAUTER WASN'T HAPPY about Ermgarde going to Bristol, considering that Humphrey was in their party, but there was no way he could decline the invitation. When the king—who was in Bristol on a pilgrimmage to rally adventure-seeking Englishmen to his proposed cause—requested something, there was no denying him. Royal requests were orders, no matter how cordially they were put. And Henry, no doubt piqued after listening to Humphrey's flowery spurtings on the subject, wished to see Ermgarde in the flesh.

Wauter quietly seethed. Apart from demanding satisfaction from the duke with no real cause, there was no way to still his tongue. One couldn't fight a royal duke simply because he'd complimented and flirted with one's wife.

And now she was on her way, after months when he'd received only one appallingly misspelled missive that spoke not of love but of castle affairs. Then she'd dutifully made mention of her wish that he would soon be home! Prideful witch!

If not for the king's curiosity she would still be at home, and he'd have delayed going back until every conceivable excuse for staying abroad had been used. He would make her realize that he was the only master in the household, that such irritations wouldn't be tolerated in the future.

The lack of her presence and, most annoyingly, his enforced abstinence from the delights of her body, were things that discipline and willpower made bearable. Want her, he did, but reconcile their differences so that he might have her, he wouldn't!

But if she was at Bristol, mightn't he be cutting off his nose to spite his own face to ignore her? He needn't be completely cold, need he? And, oh, it would be good to lose himself in the pleasures of that temptress's body, to assuage the need that had grown out of all proportion since their parting.

He need not have stayed celibate, of course, for there were those women who followed in York's and Warwick's train who would gladly have raised their hemlines and fluttered their eyelashes if he'd but clicked his fingers. Yet they'd lost whatever appeal they'd once possessed. Having had the Goddess of Love herself, how could he be content with a mere handmaiden?

Wauter snarled at his eulogizing. Christ, he was beginning to think like that flowery-tongued Gloucester.

On the knightly progress from Warwick, there had been work aplenty to keep his mind from women and their devious way of getting under one's skin. At Gloucester city they made indentures, hundreds of longbowmen arriving at their camp from the surrounding villages, Herefordshire, and the Welsh hills beyond the marches.

Stoke Gifford lay just beyond the city-county boundary northwest of Bristol, and boasted scattered farms and clustered cottages beneath the crumbling ruin of a Norman keep. The lands had been owned by the Giffords since the year of the Norman Conquest, but when one of the descendants, John Gifford, made the mistake of robbing Edward II's baggage train—and was captured, then hung, drawn and quartered at Gloucester in 1332—the manor was given to the Berkeleys.

It was here that Wauter again met up with his old friend.

Thomas FitzHarding, portly though he was, could be impressive when bedecked in his finest harness of plate and surrounded by a sea of servants and banners upon the village green. There were few yeomen who didn't feel the urge to take the sixpence he offered and follow him into battle.

Seated upon an equally portly horse, he watched over the proceedings, believing that there was nothing quite like the personal touch.

Wheeler, wheelright; Jones, archer; Wintle, infantryman; Bowyer, Fletcher, and so on, whose names described their skills at war and whose presence was due to tales of plunder and glory. The monkly scribe, who had been brought along to set names to parchment, suffered acutely numbed fingers—as well as feet, because of his open-toed sandals—by the time the January light began to fail.

When all willing yeomen had sworn themselves to Thomas, they promised availability whenever he returned and bid them follow. Then the dukes, lords and knights took to the road once more, heading for the south and Bristol City proper.

Bristol Castle and its walled city had the added protection of two encircling rivers, the Avon and Frome. To the south was the manor of Bedminster, Redcliffe and Temple Meads; to the east the King's Orchard and Earl's Mead; to the north was Broad Mead, Lewins Mead and, more westerly, St. Augustine's Back. It was in these latter districts that Bristol's religious houses were most prolific, and the city boasted some half a dozen orders. While within the sprawling city walls, which could be entered by any of a dozen gates, there were some nine parish churches.

But Bristol was known primarily for its castles. The premiere castle of the west lay on an area of eleven acres, its curtain walls and manmade banks following the natural bends of the two rivers, bridged by three gates leading into the compound. Some thirty-six yards by thirty in length and breadth, the keep rose imposingly, overshadowing the heavily fortified Newgate, its northeast tower rising higher than the rest, topped by the royal pennant.

The future King John had become Earl of Gloucester in 1183 after a marriage to William's daughter, Isabel, and had spent considerable sums of money on the castle's upkeep, perhaps seeing the need for a stout fortress during the crisis that ultimately paved the way for the Magna Carta. Having control of the castle meant control of the town, the barton and Kingswood forest.

Ermgarde, parting the damask curtains of the litter so that she and Alice might catch their first glimpse of the city, faltered with words to describe the beauty that loomed before her. Spires, towers, ship's rigging, and a conglomeration of half-timbered shops and houses vied for attention. If Warwick and its castle had been impressive, then surely Bristol was without equal.

Ralph LeRoy, sergeant-at-arms, slowed his mount to keep abreast of the litter and smiled at Ermgarde's astonished look. "Impressive, is it not, my lady? Only London has the edge over this fair city in terms of wealth. As for the castle—this keep is the equal of London's White Tower."

Once inside, the inner ward's bustle was overwhelming, with soldiers and grooms, lords and pages all mingling together in a seemingly purposeless welter of activity.

"Make way! Make way!" Officiously, LeRoy herded the curious townsfolk who blocked the castle street that ran through the green.

Wauter stood watching as Ermgarde and Alice alighted from the litter set in front of the arched portal of the hall, yet he would not come forward and, when his wife stood before him, he gave her nothing but a formal bow and a kiss of her hand.

His head nodded to each. "Ermgarde. Alice. I trust your journey was not too discomforting?" Without waiting for a response, he turned and headed back inside, leaving them to follow. He circled the main hall that ran to the right and led them directly to their chambers.

"You'll no doubt want to rest, so I'll leave you now. Please dress with special care this evening, my wife, as you are to be presented."

He was about to leave when Ermgarde stopped him, placing a tentative hand upon his arm. "Presented? To whom?"

"Didn't I make mention of it in my missive? No? Oh well, must have slipped my mind. The king is a visiting with us for a week or so. He's come to spectate at the mustering and see how work goes on the siege guns being cast for him. My lord Duke of Gloucester—being unable to keep himself from singing your praises—has led to Henry insisting he meet the woman who's besotted his brother!"

Ermgarde's spirits sagged. So he hadn't asked her to Bristol to be reconciled! 'Twas the king's curiosity that had brought her. The king! She was to be presented to him? Oh lord! Her continuing battle with Wauter would have to wait in the light of this newly sprung, no-less-worrying development.

The panic-stricken look on her face brought a smile to Wauter's mouth for the first time that day, but it wasn't a pleasant expression. "I'll be back at the supper hour to escort you," he told her, and with a curt nod, he was gone.

Ermgarde's glower changed to a look of despair as she moaned to her sister, "How could he be so cruel, Alice, as to spring such news on me out of the blue? And then for the devil to take himself off so that I can't even ask his guidance on which gown to wear...!"

Alice was out of sorts as well, but for an entirely different reason. She began to lift the lids of the coffers that had just arrived at the chambers and commenced unpacking their belongings. He'd had not one look to spare for her save at the moment of greeting, and then his gaze barely touched her!

'Twas obvious the fool still felt tenderly disposed toward his flirt of a wife. But what if she could manipulate Gloucester —who by the sound of it didn't need much persuasion—into greater contact with her sister? Was Ermgarde above temptation? The duke was handsome—by all accounts rich and powerful. But did he possess what it would take to steal Ermgarde from Wauter? Ermgarde seemed immune to the charm of any save her husband, blast her and her sense of morality!

Alice decided to see which way the wind blew, to observe events and, where possible, influence them to suit her own ends.

If Ermgarde succumbed to the charming duke, she, Alice could console Wauter. But if the high-principled bitch remained true to her husband and Alice couldn't find a way to steal him, why then she'd console the duke! He was rich and powerful enough to make it a pleasant task.

CHAPTER

19

ERMGARDE LOOKED UNEASY, though undeniably stunning in her scarlet-and-black velvet houppelande and sable-trimmed, reticulated headdress, from which cascaded a shimmer of black gossamer. Wauter, lithe and vibrant with energy, glowered nearby at no one in particular.

Henry came gallantly around to the front of the supper table and gave a practiced smile of welcome, calculated to put others at their ease. The Lady dropped into her curtsy, too awed even to look him in the eye.

Enchanting. Now he could see that the reports he'd received about FitzSimmon's jealousy were true, could even understand his own brother's mooning over her even though retribution from an irate husband hung over him.

Ermgarde thanked the king for his rather automatic speech of greeting, thinking him the most sexless creature she had ever met, then dutifully fell silent as her husband aired news of the muster in the city.

News given, the FitzSimmonses took their place at one of the lower tables.

Then the king gave the command: "Let the feasting begin."

The evening was a long and tense one, through which the lord and lady exchanged curt words only when necessary.

Lady Camoys pressed for the reason behind Ermgarde's sudden departure from Warwick, undeterred by her evasive answers. Jacqueline Holland, a rather waspish descendent of Joan of Kent, and the girl—it was rumored—who would be affianced to the Duke of Gloucester, cast Ermgarde venomous looks down her long nose and engaged in subtle innuendo to the detriment of her supposed rival.

Ermgarde sensed her husband stiffening by degrees as the woman's tongue ran on without restraint, knowing too that his doubts about his wife kept him from silencing Lady Jacqueline. So it seemed as though it was up to her to act, or bear the barbs in stoic silence. She did a while longer, but then. . . .

"Rumor has it there is one here this night who is better used to and more suited to the company of sheep," the earl's daughter whispered to her matronly neighbor, though loudly enough for those in the immediate vicinity. The receiver of the news, Umfraville's wife—who knew Ermgarde from Warwick and found her a pleasing addition to the court circle—cast her eyes to her platter in embarrassment and voiced a silent prayer that her neighbor be struck dumb.

Ermgarde felt the color rising to her cheeks, some from discomfort, most from her growing temper. She set a hand on Wauter's forearm, fearing that he was about to rise to the bait and deliver a spanking, which would have been quite unpardonable.

She smiled falsely at her antagonist, bringing surprise to the girl's widening eyes; then, with cold deliberateness, she knocked over her goblet of wine and watched as the well-aimed flow of ruby ran across the table into the lap of the unprepared girl.

There was an indignant squeal as Jacqueline found herself suddenly wet and jumped to her feet, brushing ineffectually at her sopping silk skirt. "Why you. . . !"

"Oh dear, how clumsy of me. I shall, of course, pay for any damage," Ermgarde told her, looking suitably aghast at her supposed accident.

Everyone was watching. The king raised a quizzical brow, while Humphrey snickered behind his hand, having sensed that Jacqueline was dishing out ill will in overabundance. And the girl, now finding herself the focal point of mild amusement, fled the hall in mortification.

Ermgarde bowed her head and allowed herself a secret smile of triumph. She could sense Wauter relaxing once more and, when the smile waned and she raised her head, it was to intercept a comradely wink from Lady Umfraville.

Merely one day had passed in Bristol and Alice hadn't been slow to reap the rewards of new conquests. How wonderful was this place after the unbearable months at Synford without Lord Wauter's presence—and with a consignment of soldiery that offered no new challenges.

She snorted down her nostrils at the thought of her would-

be lover, even as her loins throbbed from the usage they'd
received at the hands of Sir John Marshfield, a secretary in the
king's household. And the stupid, oversexed John had been *so*
generous, presenting her with a circlet of gold with which to
adorn her hair, so enraptured had he been.

Which was more than one could say for Wauter of Synford!

Alice seethed, watching him now from the gallery that overlooked the hall, he and that regal bitch, Ermgarde, partaking
of supper in the royal presence, to which *she* had not been invited! Nothing more than a gruff greeting had Simon of Waverley's bastard given her since her arrival, as if he—dubious
though the circumstances of his birth might be—would always
be her superior. Alice sighed and sat down heavily, drawing
the momentary attention of the minstrels as they played for
the honored assembly through supper. She had had one goblet
too many of Somerset cider with Sir John and was now feeling
positively woozy, her hands searching her crown to ascertain
whether her circlet was still in place.

Oh, how that man angered her! Nothing seemed to break
the bond between him and that *oh-so-sweet* wife! Nauseating.
And such a waste. Wauter was man enough for several
women. She felt despondent, though was loath to admit failure as she watched him covetously. There had never been, nor
would be again, a man who so enflamed her. A pity then, was
it not, that the one man she craved was so singular in his adoration?

Alice then turned her bleary eyes to Gloucester, knowing
him instantly from the descriptions which Ermgarde had
volunteered on her return from Warwick to Synford. A slight,
impish, sun-bronzed man, still boyish in his ways, and possessing none of his brother's pious airs. Now there was a lively,
vibrant looking man. . . .

What power might not be hers if she could captivate a royal
duke? Brother of the king? Alice giggled uproariously at the
thought, intoxicated in every sense of the word.

She could destroy Ermgarde, the favored one, the beloved,
and bring the proud Wauter to his knees. Mistress of the duke.
The duke's mistress. Hmm, she liked the sound of it either
way. Her hazel eyes narrowed under her thoughtfully lowered
brows and a feral smile set itself upon her face.

"Could you not go one day without causing a stir?" Wauter

asked in obvious exasperation, clothes flying about the room as he undressed.

Ermgarde ceased the unlacing of her houppelande and planted her hands on hips. "Would you rather I'd allowed that silly chit to continue? She had a libelous tongue, as you'd have realized if you'd not already been blinded to the truth by your doubts about me. It's been a long winter, Wauter. Let us forget about the duke, please."

"My acquaintance with the man is longer than your own. I should have thought myself a better judge of his character!"

"All right! Have it your own way!" She continued undressing, ignoring him.

The houppelande came off, discarded thoughtlessly over the nearest available chair, then her undertunic of fine wool. Finally she sat on the edge of the bed to remove her slippers, garters and stockings.

Each furthered their state of nudity obliviously, facing the other to issue more heated words. Their eyes met, then hers traveled unwillingly down the body she knew and loved so well. Wauter appraised her in the same manner.

Was it any wonder others sought to gain a smile and more from that full, red mouth, any wonder they harbored lustful thoughts about such a body? A man would have to be blind or in his dying hours not to want her. Could he blame Gloucester? Wasn't his sense of outrage just a little ridiculous? She was a good wife, a true wife, he felt sure, and had given him few qualms—save when she had accepted that golden horse from the duke. Instead of harboring doubts, mayhap he should give thanks for being the one to win her. Yes, *he* had all of her while Gloucester and the rest went begging for a smile or crafty inhalation of her perfume. Poor Humphrey, he thought with as much sincerity as a cat who's got the cream while a stray looks hopefully on. Looking at things from this new angle, 'twas the duke who needed sympathy and understanding, not himself!

In one stride he was upon her and Ermgarde was in his arms, being carried to the bed, her lips searching and finding his as they sank onto the bed and the leather slats beneath the mattress groaned in protest.

She was ready for him without preamble, her hips straining against him, legs parting to grant him entry, but Wauter was of a mind to worship her body before possessing it completely

and began a sensuous trail of kisses over her flesh. His teeth
nipped, then his tongue probed a calculated path across her
breasts and down over belly to her inner thighs, setting
Ermgarde to moaning.

He sought to pull her legs wider but she murmured a languid
"No" and forced herself to close temporarily against him. She
remembered how efficiently he could work upon her with his
lips and tongue, and feared that should she not protest
'twould all be over for her before she had savored him and the
enslaving force that emanated from that powerful shaft. It
had been a *long* winter.

She grasped the stiffness between her fingers to emphasize
the point. "I want *you!*"

Alice's first encounter with the Duke of Gloucester had not
been overly promising. They met—seemingly by chance, but
very much by female design—on the castle street one warm,
cloudless morning. Alice had taken special care over her appearance, had even chanced stealing a gown of emerald velvet
from her sister's coffer, yet even so he did little more than
bestow a passing glance.

She followed him persistently, though at a safe distance,
certain that he could not be going far since he was on foot. He
passed through the gatehouse, moving out with an athletically
light step, then stopping on the gently humped bridge over the
river that acted as a natural moat about the sprawling castle
precinct.

Alice slowed and paused in the deep shadow of the
gatehouse. What was he about, leaning over precariously and
shouting down at the waters? She started forward, deciding
that she would ask him—as good a conversation opener as
any.

"Careful. *Careful!*" he was barking below to the harassed
bargee who had dropped a cask with nervously clumsy fingers
and now had to retrieve it from the bottom of the shallow
vessel. "If any damage be done to that wine, I'll have your
neck stretched!"

"Yes, my lord duke," mumbled the man, as he got the first
of the casks safely into the rope net suspended from the crane,
then signaled for the laborer on the bridge to hoist it up.

"Good day, my lord duke," said Alice, standing beside him
now.

He straightened up and drew his eyebrows together. "Good day, young woman. Do I know you?" Humphrey was stand-offish. Her gown was immaculate, but her vulgar amount of jewelry and veilless face made him suspect she was some prosperous whore from the docks.

" 'Tis doubtful, my lord duke. Though I believe you be acquainted with my elder sister, the Lady Ermgarde of Synford?"

"Oh yes, *indeed*." There was instant enthusiasm, Alice noted. "So you are *her* sister! Pray tell, how is she? I hardly dare to inquire personally because of a difference of opinion between her husband and I."

Alice was not unaware of the "difference of opinion." It was the subject of much gossip. All knew that FitzSimmons and Gloucester snarled and snapped like leashed dogs after the same tasty bone. "She is well, my lord duke, and happy to be here in Bristol."

"Good, good. Steady there, man! Load the cart more gently. This fine old wine must be treated with reverence. 'Tis a gift from the Duke of Burgundy himself."

Alice looked suitably impressed, though wondered aloud, wryly, "Is it altogether politic to accept his wine when we are supposed to be neutral concerning the turmoil across the Channel?"

Gloucester laughed at her quickness of mind. "Young woman, you may have something there. If you promise not to tell, thereby avoiding a diplomatic incident, mayhap I'll let you taste some of it tonight."

She trilled prettily in mock outrage, "My lord duke, are you inviting me to your chambers?"

His eyes fairly popped and he looked scandalized, to Alice's utter surprise. "God forbid! A lady's reputation is precious indeed. I meant that you might partake of a cup or two at the evening's supper in the hall."

Inwardly Alice sighed with irritation, while outwardly appearing quite woebegone. These overly chivalrous types could be tiresome, holding to their virtuous ways like a lot of silly virgins!

"Heavens," mused Humphrey, "what cloud has drifted across your inner sun?"

"I have no title and am not invited to sup in the hall this night. What a shame."

He frowned. "Indeed. But were I to personally invite you, no one would dare to say nay."

"You would do that for me?"

"For Ermgarde's sister nothing is too much."

Besotted fool! He mooned after the unattainable, while she—just as fetching in her own way—was willing and available to help him forget his devotion to another.

The casks were now safely aboard the cart and the laborer presented Humphrey with parchment and quill, while some scruffy urchin hovered nearby with a pot of ink.

"All seems in order," decided the duke, and signed at the bottom of the scroll while Alice looked on avidly.

"Thank you, my lord duke," said the laborer humbly, bowing himself out of the royal presence.

As far as Humphrey was concerned, the man no longer existed. His attention was now on the man driving the cart. "See those casks safely to the hall, carter, or you will never work for this household again."

"Yes, my lord duke," said the man, trembling.

"Was that your mark you made, my lord duke?" asked Alice, curious.

"What? Oh, yes. My *G*. Much less fuss than having to sign everything Humphrey, Duke of Gloucester. My initial is enough. Everyone knows it. I may have gone to Oxford but that doesn't automatically mean that I like putting my writing arm to constant use. I have a scribe who writes my letters when need be, and I sign them with the *G*."

"Very sensible for a man required to keep in touch with his many important interests."

"Quite so. My work is done; I'm returning to the castle. Might I escort you?"

"I would find it a great pleasure."

It was remiss of him, Humphrey realized awkwardly, but he hadn't thought to ask her to cite her name.

CHAPTER
20

ON HIS RETURN to London, Henry summoned his uncle, Bishop Beaufort, Chancellor of England, and informed him that he had decided to take a sea voyage.

When a French delegation arrived in England in July headed by Guillaume Boisratier, Archbishop of Bourges, negotiations seemed but a formality.

Seemingly attentive, Henry listened—an elbow on the arm of his chair and chin in hand, his severely cropped hair giving him the look of a studious monk.

Their new concessions were unacceptable to him, though they included the ceding to England of many important territories, the hand of Charles's daughter Katherine in marriage and the unprecedented dowry of eight-hundred-thousand gold crowns.

They made a better offer. No. Henry would have none of it. He continued to insist that all his claims were just and that Charles VI would be responsible for the unavoidable deluge of Christian blood if they were not met.

Such hypocrisy was too much for the Archbishop. He stood tall before the king and told him, "Sir, the King of France, our Sovereign Lord, is the true King of France. And, with respect to those things to which you say you have a right, you have no lordship, not even in the kingdom of England, which belongs to the true heirs of the late King Richard. Nor with you can our sovereign lord safely treat."

Such outspokenness was too much for Henry. He rose haughtily from his chair, signaling that discussion had ended. Fling Bolingbroke's usurpation in his face, would they! "Depart for France and be not long about it, for I'll not be far behind you!" he spat.

The household was instructed to make ready to move to

Southampton, for inside three weeks the king's fleet would be ready to sail.

Humphrey lay heavy-limbed in his damask-canopied bed, the result of newly arrived Burgundy wine causing his sleep to be deep, his snores resounding.

Alice approached in the dark, setting down her taper and disrobing in its poor light, a sneer on her face. If she was to share his bed often—and that was now her aim—then some cure would have to be found for that infernal noise. He was about as regal as a hog in a wallow! She lifted the covers and slipped in beside him, setting to work immediately with her artful hands upon his sleeping body.

Humphrey stirred and sighed, dreaming of violet eyes and raven hair, then opened his eyes.

"God in heaven! Young woman, *what* are you about?" he demanded, voice high like some outraged maid about to be raped. He sat bolt upright, snatching her hands away from his loins and pulling the covers protectively about him.

" 'Tis only I, dear duke, come to please you," coaxed Alice, arms coiling again. "You needn't fear me."

"Stop it," he ordered, shocked, catching her wrists and pushing her away, then retreating himself. "For shame! Your behavior is most unseemly. Two cups of wine and one dance do not give you the right to come here like this, uninvited. How did you get past the guard?"

"I told him you were expecting me," volunteered Alice, crawling across the bed toward him, then kneeling seductively. "Don't be shy. Let me show you what *real* love is all about. For too long I fear you've been indulging in that courtly variety, which is without real substance. Adoration for someone who can never be yours is without point, while I, her sister, would fill the role you choose for her in your dreams."

Humphrey gaped at her in stupefaction and heightening vexation. "You think yourself a suitable substitute? Sisters you may be, but I've seen nothing in *you* that I admire in your sister. You are as vinegar compared with wine—your taste is unpalatable."

"You are angered because I came here without your bidding. Come to bed and I'll make amends," persisted Alice, ignoring the personal slight and moistening her red lips with her tongue as invitingly as possible.

Humphrey's mouth frowned, and he wrapped himself in the coverlet from the bed and padded across to the door. "I will not use violence to eject you, for that is against all the teachings of my childhood, but if you do not go *now* I shall call the guard; then this unsavory episode will be the knowledge of all. Is that what you want?"

"You are not a man to reject me so," she snarled, retrieving her bedgown. "Where are your male instincts, some show of natural desire? You're not a *real* man. Nay. You're pathetic. A royal weakling, as sexless as your brother!"

His voice was low and threatening. "Take care. It would be dangerous to indulge in any more such outbursts. Now *get out*, you disgusting creature, and never again address yourself to me either publicly or in private."

Humphrey opened the door and Alice passed by him, her eyes blazing with such hatred that a shiver ran down the length of his backbone. He crossed himself when the door was once more a safe barrier between them, but he felt no relief.

If Wauter was still surly in his attitude, Ermgarde overlooked it, for at least he was once again on speaking terms with the Duke of Gloucester.

Since their reunion there had developed between them a tentative truce. Through the months of May and June they were made welcome at Nunney Castle in Somersetshire, as the guests of Sir Elias de la Mare, savoring its idyllic beauty and peace after weeks of Bristol, rife with rumors of war. Once assigned to Mary, one of the Bohun heiresses—before her marriage to Bolingbroke—Nunney nestled amidst a sleepy village; a round-towered keep was surrounded by a wide, water-filled moat, over which spanned the obligatory drawbridge.

They were happy there and, without Gloucester's presence, Ermgarde sensed their relationship returning to the blissful state it had enjoyed soon after their marriage. But it couldn't last for long, and even that far into the country rumors had begun to penetrate and yeomen arrived at the castle daily, offering their war skills to the knight, de la Mare.

So they returned to Bristol, the castle teeming with dukes and lords and knights, all waiting for the word to take up arms. And Ermgarde began her nightly sessions of weeping after their lovemaking was done and Wauter was asleep, knowing that soon he would be gone.

She watched the ladies of seasoned warriors through the month of July, as tension mounted and each day threatened to send their men scurrying toward the south coast. She could only marvel at the control they exerted over their emotions. There was no weeping in public, no outward show of fear that their husbands might never return. They talked of duty, the upholding of England's good name, the need to right a wrong. Not one of them doubted the wisdom in invading France.

The messenger—one of dozens sent out about the country by Henry—came while Ermgarde was paying Maud a dutiful visit at the Magdalen nunnery. It had been a somewhat pointless exercise, she had found. Maud was glad to see her, but in a detached fashion, as if they had never been sisters. But at least Ermgarde felt at peace with herself as she reentered the city by the Frome gate, for she didn't doubt that her sister was happy, that the order gave her what she needed.

If the castle had been bustling with activity the first time she had entered its gates, this evening, with darkness falling, it was as if everyone within the walls had succumbed to madness. She knew the cause and realized that her time with Wauter had run out. Drawing back the curtains, she lowered herself from the litter, not caring to wait until LeRoy appeared. Each moment that passed without him was another lost chance at one last memory to cling to.

Picking up her skirts, she ran, dodging aside when more knights and their retainers came charging through the confusion in the inner ward. Ermgarde made it through the crush with nothing more severe than an accidental elbow in the ribs, and then commenced to battle her way along the narrow, human-filled passage off her chamber.

Her arm was taken and Ermgarde propelled through the crush, an imperious male voice ringing out, "Make way there! Make way!"

She looked up, surprised. "Gloucester! Where did you come from?"

"I was in the ward when you returned in the litter, and followed you because I must talk."

"Your choice of time and place are rather unfortunate," she laughed, drily.

"I would have spoken weeks ago, only I was summoned to the muster and did not return until this morn. I'm here now only to cart up my accoutrements, then make haste to Southampton. But I had to speak before I left.''

"Let us try to reach my chamber, then. At least there I may hear you clearly. What a din! Everyone seems to have forgotten their manners and sense of decorum.''

"No, not your chamber. Think how that might look if your husband walked in. He's not the most understanding of fellows. Further along the passage there is an alcove with a window overlooking the river. Mayhap it will be quiet there.''

Very well. Lead on,'' said Ermgarde, rather puzzled. What did he want? The man was without guile and had no unchaste designs, she knew. She couldn't for the life of her guess at why he sought her out with such urgency. She would have much rather been in her chamber with Wauter, sharing what little time was left before the great upheaval.

They reached the alcove where the crowd was thinner and they could observe a steady stream of courtiers, serfs and servants bustling by with coffers and plate from harnesses, armfuls of weaponry and fragile ladies' headdresses.

"Speak. Time is precious.''

Humphrey looked awkward. '' 'Tis about your sister, Alice.''

Ermgarde was instantly alert with suspicion. "Yes?''

"There were a few nights shortly before my departure, when I arranged that she be invited to sup in the hall—''

"I recall. Go on.''

"Well, on one of those nights. . . . Heavens, it sits ill with me to recount this. After all, reputations, once lost, are hard to rebuild. I break a code of honor by not taking this secret to the grave with me.''

"Be plain, my lord duke,'' urged Ermgarde, growing more restless as the moments passed and he continued to battle with his conscience.

"She stole into my chamber uninvited and I awoke to find her in my bed.''

"*What!*''

"Nothing happened, believe me,'' Humphrey reassured her hastily. "I was shocked and ordered her away in no uncertain terms.''

"I apologize in her name. Alice has always been uncontrollable. Once she sets her mind upon something. . . . I'll speak sternly to her.''

"I think you should. And watch her, too. Her hatred when I

ordered her away was frightening to behold. It's absurd, but
she believes that it is my regard for you which has led to her
being rejected. Be wary, sweet lady."

"I will. And I thank you for having taken the time to tell
me. 'Tis just as well, perhaps, that we leave for Synford
shortly. Goodbye then, Humphrey, and return unscathed
from your brother's excursion of folly across the Channel."

He chuckled and took Ermgarde's hand, kissing it with
knightly reverence, her palm to his mouth as another male
voice, beloved and dreaded alike, rose angrily above the hub-
bub, "Good wife, should you not be about your packing?"

Humphrey dropped Ermgarde's hand as if it was a hot iron,
and she, all conversation done, could only stand there looking
awkward—guilty—with nothing to say.

She blurted, "Why, Wauter, the duke craved a word and
this was the only quiet place we could find."

"You neglect your duties," he muttered, barging through
the procession of deserting guests and reaching her side, face
stony and arms filled with saddle, bridle, plate and caparisons
retrieved from the castle mews.

Humphrey smiled, shrugged and sidestepped into the fast
moving crowd, eager to be away. "Farewell. I neglect *my* duties also."

Wauter scowled after him, then turned to Ermgarde, narrowing his amber eyes coldly beneath dark brows. "What
brought the two of you to this quiet little niche?"

"A domestic problem, Wauter, with which I shall not burden you at this chaotic moment in time. Let us go to our chamber and prepare to leave."

"But for these final items, my preparations are done. Any
delays which ensue, wife, will be down to you." He forced his
way into the crowd and brought Ermgarde before him, his
bulk protecting her from any jostling as they headed for their
chambers.

"Don't be petty, I beg you. Gloucester had but a moment or
two of my time, and none begrudged it more than I. You are
leaving and our time is precious. Let us fill it with smiles and
fondness."

He digested her words and snorted, his steely fingers, which
guided her forward unerringly, squeezing her upper arms
gently in response. "Synford is not so many miles away. I

shall escort you safely there, then take my leave in the *proper* manner.''

"I hope so, my lord," she told him lovingly, shoulders swaying back momentarily to caress his chest, "for your farewell will have to sustain me until your return."

"There you are," said Alice, curtly, a scowl on her pretty face. "I was beginning to fret, wondering where you were. This place grows quieter by the moment, as if the life drains from it."

Wauter dropped Rogue's paraphernalia in the middle of the floor. "Your time would have been better spent in packing our belongings than indulging in idle worry."

"Oh, I've seen to my own things, few that they are, but I hesitated over yours and Ermgarde's. I did not think it my place to delve into the personal effects of others. All are entitled to privacy."

Ermgarde had doffed her gown and was now struggling into simpler traveling attire. "Having lived with Wauter and me for such a long time, Alice, I doubt there is little about us you do not know, and vice-versa," she said, remembering Gloucester's words and thinking that there would be much plain speaking between them when they reached Synford.

"Then I shall commence collecting your things together forthwith," Alice chirped.

Wauter sighed and sank onto the bed to exchange one pair of boots for another. Alice's making much of nought agitated him, as did her painstakingly careful and *slow* placing of Ermgarde's effects into her coffer.

His wife girdled her gown and, noting his deepening frown and impatiently drumming fingers upon the furniture, was quick to lend a hand. "Come, Alice, I'll pack. You fetch."

"The night draws in," said Wauter, hovering at the window now and watching his men waiting in the ward.

"I know, husband," snapped Ermgarde, "but I'm working just as fast as I can."

Two servants arrived and hefted out a coffer between them, faces turning red with the strain.

"Where do you want these?" asked Alice, scooping the contents of a cupboard, casket and rolled parchment filling her arms.

Ermgarde barely spared her a glance. "There should be just enough room on top. Then we are done."

Alice appeared to trip, the scrolls scattering, then steadied herself against Wauter, saving herself and casket from crashing to the floor. "Phew! That was lucky. Must have caught my toe on a board."

He righted her and stooped for the ribbon tied missives, curiosity piqued.

"Are you all right, Alice?" inquired Ermgarde. The last thing she needed was for her sister to sprain an ankle. Wauter would be furious.

"Yes, nothing broken."

Thus assured, her gaze passed to Wauter, puzzlement on her face. "What have you there?"

"You ask *me*?" he snarled. He had unrolled a parchment and was reading it between outstretched hands, each word quickening the beat of his heart until it felt like a hammer pounding his insides.

"Wauter?" Ermgarde rose from her knees before the coffer, concerned.

"Explain this, if you can," he challenged, striding forward, until he loomed above her, his giant's body trembling with rage.

Petrified, Ermgarde could only stare uncomprehendingly at the letter before her eyes, her head shaking feebly and knees turning weak with fear. "I . . . I cannot. I've never seen it before."

"Ha!" he roared in derision, making Ermgarde jump then stifle a scream of terror, while Alice shrank into a corner, looking suitably mystified and worried.

He forced her to watch while he read those terrible words which were unknown to her, but which pained him to speak aloud and caused his voice to break.

She listened but didn't hear all, only disjointed words lavish with filth and destruction. ". . . savor of your mouth . . . caress the smoothness of the flesh and kiss trembling thighs . . . when will you be mine again?"

"*Again!*" shouted Wauter, dropping the missive in disgust. "There is my proof!"

"*Ermgarde*, how could you do this to Wauter?" bewailed Alice in shocked outrage.

Wauter turned, snatched up a shoe from the coffer and

hurled it at her. "Get out! Haven't you wits enough to know when you're intruding?"

Alice shrieked and bolted for the door, crying, "Turn not your ire on me. *I* am not disloyal."

Wauter didn't hear the slamming of the door. He had grabbed a fistful of Ermgarde's hair, bringing pain to the eyes already spilling with tears.

She choked on a sob. "I do not understand. You must believe me when I say that I've never seen these missives before this evening. I am innocent of the crime with which you charge me. Wauter, for God's sake."

"Do not draw the Almighty into something so base! You hope to soften me, no doubt, with those beautiful, deceitful eyes. But I am no fool. How many times did you lie with Gloucester? There have been ample opportunities, and this castle is vast, could easily conceal lovers for an hour of ecstasy."

"No, that's *not* true!"

"Don't bother lying to me. His mark is on the page as bold as brass. When you produced his bastard was I supposed to accept it meekly, perhaps even take pride in the fact that we'd have royal blood in the family? Well? You have little to say, madam. Haven't you spirit enough to defend yourself?"

"Knowing the bounds of your jealousy, is there any point? The moment you saw that *G* at the bottom of the page you doubtless recalled my meeting earlier with the man and condemned me on the spot. My love is yours, always, but telling you so is not enough to convince you. I have no defense. I swear my innocence, but that is not enough for you either."

"Quite so. You have no defense because you are guilty. I must believe the evidence of my own eyes and not be swayed by one as artful as you," he spat, releasing his hold at long last and shoving Ermgarde from him.

She fell onto the bed, and remained there, fearing he would murder her if she moved, so mighty was his rage. While inside her, fear warred with anger, pain, pride and wretchedness, though they were as nought compared to her utter bewilderment. It had to be a dream—a terrible, stupid dream.

He had pulled his voluminous, fur-trimmed black mantle about his shoulders, all his movements quick and violent with fury.

Ermgarde clutched at the bed and pulled herself up, crying

out desperately, "You cannot go, walk away and leave me.
'Tis ridiculous. I love you."

"And I loved you too, madam; once. Though it seems that
was not enough for you. You wanted a tame duke for your
plaything also. Well, you have *him* but you cannot have us
both!"

"No, don't say that. There is treachery here. Can you not
feel it? Someone wants to force us apart."

"The only treachery is yours, and I have found you out.
Not before some time had passed either, it would seem. You
have made a fool of me. What pleasure that must have given
you; a living, breathing jest for you and your lover to laugh
over. No, don't bother. Your protests are pointless. And do
not rise, royal whore, unless you want to be laid out per-
manently, ready for your funeral."

He went. All had been so simply done. All destroyed.

She wanted to go after him but dared not, so Ermgarde
cried herself into a state of exhaustion atop her bed, lying
there numb and empty.

Who hated her enough to write those missives? The Duke of
Gloucester certainly hadn't done the penning. He probably
wasn't even aware of the fact that she could read after a
fashion. And who hated him enough to implicate him in
something so dire?

Alice.

"No!" she cried aloud, horrified by her own thoughts. She
must not believe that, not of her sister. She was distraught,
and thus suspicious. But even as she reviled herself for thinking so wickedly, the kisses, flirting and derogatory remarks at
her own expense came forth in an unwanted rush of memory.

She always felt queasy where Alice had been concerned.
Lady Margaret had warned her and so had Gloucester. Was it
just coincidence that she, the supposed erring wife, was cast
off, while Alice had departed with her husband?

Ermgarde closed her eyes, her thoughts muddled. Nothing
was clear. Just suspicions, and she couldn't act on those, no
matter how they might appear to develop into certainties. She
had no real proof. Should she think ill of someone who had
never given her any real reason to doubt?

Or had she?

Alice had been clever and careful, even as a young

child—when she stole the possessions of her brothers and sisters, she never left evidence of the crime. Ermgarde hadn't suspected her, only discovering the truth one day when she came across Alice burning one of her missing dolls on a fire in the woods near Dillbury. Then she had realized that Alice hadn't wanted the doll for herself, had just wanted to deprive Ermgarde of it. And after Edward had soundly whipped her, voicing his shame at her destructive jealousy, it was Ermgarde who had borne the brunt of the sister's subtle animosity. That was the thing about Alice—nothing ever came out into the open. There were no fights, no outbursts of rage. Whatever she felt and thought she mostly kept hidden.

Had Alice—with her liking for the possessions of others— seen Wauter as such? And then, finding him unresponsive, had she decided that Gloucester would do just as well? After all, he had some regard for the Lady of Synford, so Alice would be stealing him *and* his affection away from another. It was preposterous, yet it all came together and made sense in Ermgarde's head. But Gloucester had rejected her too, fueling her hatred. Alice wasn't the type to forget, to let bygones be bygones.

She never had been. Ermgarde rose from the bed and filled a goblet from the chalice atop the light oak cupboard, drank deep in an attempt to banish the thoughts. She was reading too much into this, seeing evil where there was none, none that concerned Alice anyway. Or had she merely deluded herself in the past out of loyalty to her own flesh and blood?

Rowen—dear scamp of a younger brother—had had a litter of puppies once, engaging black and white curs. Alice had wanted one of them in particular, but Rowen had already ear- marked that intelligent pup as a future sheepdog and would not part with him. He gave Alice the pick of the rest, but she had apparently lost interest in the idea, disinclined to settle for second best.

The poor, favored puppy hadn't lived long. Rowen had found him one morning dead and savaged, killed—Edward had told them knowledgably—by some wild creature of the night. Ermgarde and Rowen had clung to each other weeping, but Alice, as ever, had stood aside, detached and quiet, without a tear in her eye.

Ermgarde had always wondered about the true cause of the animal's death. But it was such a horrible accusation that she had curbed her tongue and thoughts, obliterating it from her mind. Until now.

Ermgarde stood at the window looking down into the empty ward, another goblet in hand. Those times flooded back all too vividly.

Mother, as quiet and unremarkable in her way as Maud, had detested the Baron de Witt and counseled her husband to keep the children out of sight whenever he might be abroad. But Alice had received a wink from the baron and, eager to learn, had stolen off into the woods one August when the moon was high, drawn by the tales from the other girls in the village.

Ermgarde had heard the tales too, but the repulsive baron had never piqued her curiosity. He was free with his coin and easy to please, but she would have been none the wiser save that when she awoke one hot and restless night, she saw Alice's empty bed and instinctively knew where her sister had gone.

Should she go to her parents? Or perhaps wake Maud? She did neither, worried for the wayward Alice, and instead stole off, thinking to bring the girl home and have done with such foolishness with no one the wiser.

That night had brought revelations concerning Alice's true character.

De Witt and his friends—his squire, whose mind was as preoccupied with filth as his own, and half a dozen high-born guests, who no doubt lamented the passing of Richard II's perverted style of court—cavorted beneath the trees in the light of the moon, naked save for their short undertunics, which barely covered their private parts. All of them were over 50 years old, and their licentious lifestyles had left their marks upon the various bodies. None were handsome, some were vaguely unpleasant, and one or two frankly repugnant.

But the girls hadn't seemed to mind, imperfections cast aside for the sake of money. They'd taken their pennies and performed as required, their laughs and giggles, shrills and shrieks unsettling the birds in the trees.

Ermgarde remained at a distance, safely out of sight, concluding that Alice was past saving—in both the physical and spiritual senses of the word.

Ermgarde had seen enough and fled for home. And that should have been the end of it, but. . . .

The next morning, when their father mentioned noises in the night and looked about the breakfast table for the culprit, it was Alice who piped up as bold as you please.

"Mayhap it was Ermgarde off to a tryst with her lover?" she giggled, spooning her porridge ravenously.

Her mother had frowned at the possibility and Edward, stony of expression, was far from amused. "I want no daughter of mine bringing shame upon this house."

"I have no lover and I never left my bed," Ermgarde had declared, hotly.

Maud had shaken her head. "That is not entirely true, sister. I awoke once, and your bed was empty."

Blast Maud. Why couldn't she have just remained quiet? But she saw everything in black and white, right and wrong. As one of God's chosen she had always possessed an infuriating compulsion for telling the truth, no matter what damage it might do.

All eyes had fallen on Ermgarde. It would have been easy to tell the truth, to extricate herself from the increasingly unpleasant situation. But Alice would have suffered horribly. Edward would probably have dragged her to the river and held her under until she drowned. So Ermgarde had kept her peace, lamely manufacturing a call of nature to account for the empty bed, and thereafter had experienced her parents' doubt.

Yes, Alice was clever. Clever enough and most capable of employing a scribe to pen those love letters and sign them at the bottom with that incriminating *G* for Gloucester!

She threw her silver goblet against the wall, a ruby stain flowing to the wooden floor.

If only she had acted upon her feelings when that female first joined Wauter and herself at the castle. . . . *If only!*

Certainty grew.

Alice, who for pennies had been the willing plaything of that foul old toad de Witt, had turned into a young woman who expected a little more for her favors. She had aimed high, wanting her conquest to be powerful, wealthy *and* handsome enough to complement her fetching good looks. And, although FitzSimmons and Gloucester might have initially rejected her advances, this night Alice controlled them all. She it was who traveled with Wauter while his spurned wife tarried, abandoned, in Bristol. And she it was who had the clever brain to concoct the situation!

Ermgarde slammed down the lid on her coffer and donned her mantle in righteous anger. Not another moment would she stay there crying over her loss. She would find a carter or the like and pay him well to get her to Synford before the dawn. Once there—always presuming that the gates were not barred against her—she would make them pay: One for her evil treachery, the other for his lack of faith.

BOOK

Two

Owre Kynge went forth to Normandy,
With grace and myght of chivalry;
The God for hym wrought marvelously,
Wherefore Englonde may call, and cry
                              Deo gratias:
Deo gratias Anglia redde pro victoria.

He sette a sege, the soothe for to say,
To Harfleur toune with royal array,
That toun he wan, and made a fray,
That Fraunce shall rywe tyl domes day.
                              Deo gratias:
Deo gratias Anglia redde pro victoria.

—Verses 1&2 Agincourt battle hymn.

CHAPTER

21

"WAUTER! Son, whatever has happened?" Lady Margaret demanded worriedly, negotiating the spiral stairs from the solar, Alice's presence at his heels doing nothing to dispel her fast-growing fears. "Where's Ermgarde?"

In the grip of blackest rage, he kicked open the stout door to the bedchamber and disappeared inside, his growl barely reaching the lady as she stared at Alice who blocked her path.

"The whore is at Bristol with her lover."

"What's that you say? Get out of my way, girl!"

Alice merely smiled, shaking her head arrogantly, her arms barring the doorway.

"I will *not* speak of it, Mother. Go away!" And to make the point clear, he shoved Alice aside and closed then barred the door against the astounded woman.

"Well!" She glared at the blank door, dumbfounded by his uncharacteristically brutal dismissal. I should have thrashed him more often when he was a child! she thought angrily. And what was this about Ermgarde having a lover? No, surely not? Knowing the girl as she did, Margaret thought it utter piffle.

But there didn't seem much point in standing before his door looking foolish. It was evident she would get no answers from her son this night. He had closeted himself with that sniggering strumpet who should long ago have been sent packing. She cried out severely, "I shall expect some explanation in the morning, my lad!" Then she strode haughtily down the passage to her own chamber in the farthest wing.

Wauter looked out on the black early hours through the embrasure, his mind unable to rid itself of the tableau the pair of them had made when he came upon them. He could not be more wounded if he'd found them naked in bed together. She had saved her last moments for Gloucester, forgetting her hus-

band so that she might secretively bid her lover farewell in
some dimly lit passage.

Faithless, deceitful female. And when he had just begun to
trust her again, too! What a fool. His fingers laced together,
trembling with rage that could not be vented right away.

He turned, surprised to find Alice standing there. "What're
you doing here?"

She looked suitably serious for the occasion, remembering
to play the part of a sister shocked by Ermgarde's actions. "I
thought you might be in need of company, lord. If there is
some way in which I might lessen the pain my sister has caused
you, you have only to ask."

"No one can lessen the pain," he cried, a hand warding her
off as he headed for the jug of wine on the sideboard. He
drank deeply, not even bothering with the niceties of a goblet.
He wanted to become obliviously drunk. Then, uttering an
oath, he caught sight of the golden horse beside his timepiece
and, snatching it up, hurled it toward the embrasure. His aim
was off, however, and instead the mechanical device smashed
against the tapestried wall and fell with a mournful clatter to
the floor.

Alice, aware of the fury within him, and strangely charged
by it, made a tentative attempt to caress him, her fingers running down his arm. "Perhaps the company of one who cher-
ishes you will bring some comfort?"

His face grew harder. "You are no different from she, are
you, wanton Alice? You'll spread your thighs for anyone, so
I've been told by those who've enjoyed you!"

A scowl creased her face, wiping clean all semblance of prettiness. "But I differ from my sister in so far as I *do* love you!
Let me show you how much. I can make amends for the wrong
she has done. I can make you forget."

"Could you now?" It was a coldly issued challenge, done
out of nothing but spite. Alice meant nothing to him, but as
Ermgarde's sister and with physical attributes that were not
dissimilar, she might make a suitable substitute on whom to
vent some of his pent up rage.

"Let me show you." With betraying swiftness, Alice
unlaced her houppelande and pulled it over her head, stripping
off stockings and undertunic in so unalluring a fashion that
Wauter sneered. The sight of her naked body stirred him only
slightly, his manhood rising to stiff prominence beneath his

hose through purely animal instinct. Any well-proportioned
and naked female would have brought a like response.

Alice's eyes fastened immediately on that part of his
anatomy, triumph welling within her. But when she made to
spread herself atop the gold coverlet of his bed, he stopped
her.

It was *their* bed and, although to take Alice atop it might
have been fitting exorcism of that other panting bitch,
somehow he couldn't bring himself to such an act.

"No, not here, slut. There's a chamber much more suited to
our purpose just along the passage." So saying, he unbarred
the door and, taking a torch from a wall sconce, led the intrigued, unabashedly naked girl in that direction.

Alice's reaction to de Witt's chamber and its tasteless furnishings was one of surprise that quickly grew into avid
curiosity and, as Wauter unbuckled his jerkin and pulled off
linen undertunic, she studied the various positions on view
until her pulse raced.

Wauter scowled as he witnessed her ever-increasing lust, the
way her eyes strayed from the copulations on the woven silk to
his body, which was bit by bit coming into view: first broad
chest, then flanks and tight-muscled legs as he pulled off his
hose. Her pupils dilated and breath caught at the sight of his
erect manhood and she came forward, kneeling before him
and taking him between her hands, rubbing her cheek against
him, kissing him.

Detached, almost disinterested, he let her indulge her likes
for a moment or so, the couples about him on the walls arous-
ing nothing sexual in him. He could only fixate on those
adulterers—Ermgarde and Humphrey. Shallow creatures! The
mistrust of them that he had always felt was proved correct.
They were all the same. Even this one, obliging Alice, her lips
working away on him, hoping to arouse him further. She was
the same as her sister, willing to have her heat cooled by the
first available man. Deceitful, scheming. . . .

He grew bored with her ministerings and pushed her backward onto the crimson coverlet, bringing up her knees and
forcing her thighs wide apart. A finger found her wet and
more than ready. Ignoring her expectant features, not attempting to kiss her, Wauter thrust home, like a knife to the
hilt.

Alice cried out under the attack in both pain and pleasure,

cringing as he seemed to push further than she could rightly bear, yet reluctant to fight against him. She'd never seen such power in a man. He worked upon her like someone in a trance, his furious drive precise and unchanging, and the relentless stabbing would have inched her to the head of the bed had he not kept two steely hands upon her shoulders, forcing her to endure. She thought she might die, but instead she reached an orgasm that mimicked death, so fierce did it come upon her.

His need to hurt and humiliate a woman—any woman—and the mechanical way in which he carried it out meant that Wauter soon found joyless relief and sank beside a sated and happy Alice. Her smile was more than he could bear, for it gave evidence to the fact that she had enjoyed what had taken place, whereas he had not intended her to.

"Out!" he ordered her, pulling the coverlet over himself and looking into space as if she no longer existed.

Alice's smile faded. What had she done? Or perhaps it was something she *hadn't* done. Might he have found it displeasing that she had not participated with greater adventurousness in the act? Had her sister proved a more eager mate? But under such an onslaught it had been impossible to contemplate a more active role. Surely he had understood that? He'd nigh on killed her as 'twas!

She couldn't believe that he really wanted her to go. After all, there was no reason to *now*. Ermgarde was disowned and her place could be filled quite adequately, given practice. "Wouldn't you rather I stayed, Wauter? You may feel the need for *company* again later."

He laughed scornfully, no mirth in his amber eyes. "I've sampled all of your company that I care to. Now *out!*" With a foot to her buttocks, he speeded her passage from the bed.

She began to cry, seeing her dreams shattered before her. She pushed back the heavy tresses from her face to implore him with her eyes. "But I love you, Wauter. You know that. I'll learn how to please you, so help me I will. Just tell me what you want and I'll do it."

"You can get out and that will please me greatly," he told her, finding a way of hurting her more effectively than his brutal fornication had been able to achieve.

Alice couldn't believe her ears, couldn't believe that he still rejected her. You have no grounds! she wanted to scream at him, but common sense prevailed. A tongue out of control in anger might say more than was safe or wise.

Taking on a woebegone expression and forcing another tear solely for his benefit, she crept dejectedly to the door and let herself out. He'd had his fill of defiant females after coexisting with that termagant, Ermgarde, for two years, so perhaps a show of meek subservience would hold more sway. Some sleep would not go amiss and with the dawn she could attack these unforseen problems with new vigor.

If Alice slept, Wauter could not, and, after she had gone, he quit de Witt's room with a shiver of disgust for what had taken place and went back to *theirs*. Thank God the bedsheets were fresh and clean and bore no trace of Ermgarde's scent. The tables and sideboards were clear of her feminine accoutrements as well. He doubted he could withstand too many reminders of his lost love.

Even so, the ghosts did walk as he lay propped against the bolsters, staring ahead. He could see her clearly at her bath that first night at Synford, recall with painful clarity her skin and the pleasure that had been his as he sponged her to a peachy glow.

It had all been right then. Whatever had gone wrong? His throat felt dry, constricted, as if, heaven forbid, he was going to succumb to womanish tears! Nay, not him. He needed a drink, that was all. Everything would be fine on the morrow. He'd be on his way to Southampton—France. Away from these memories 'twould be simple to forget her powers. Surely her image would wane with so great a distance between them? And there would be fighting in France—men dying. What better way than that to end pain once and for all?

"Gloucester? Nay, I cannot believe it! What could Ermgarde have seen in him?" scoffed Lady Margaret incredulously, not quite able to swallow all that Wauter disclosed. 'Twas preposterous, no matter what he said about his wife's unfaithfulness.

"What did all the others before her see in him? Wealth, power, not to mention a measure of charm," Wauter muttered acidly. He rose from the breakfast table, having found it impossible to stomach more than a crust of bread. "Now, please, you have the facts. I don't wish further words wasted on it."

"But—"

Impatiently, he dismissed her. 'Twas a pain of greater intensity than any battle wound could have wreaked upon his body.
"Word came last night when I was at Bristol," he said instead.
"The king waits at Southampton and the army is to assemble
there with speed. I sent out my sergeant-at-arms on arrival
here, to round up all those men from the villages who had
enlisted under me. They should be here by now. And I must
make haste. Brodrick!" The lad, ever conscious of the honored position he held as squire, appeared as if conjured from
thin air at the lower end of the hall. "Away with me to the
quadroom, lad, and help me into harness."

Lady Margaret's plump features creased into a heavy
frown. She liked not the unsatisfactory way in which he had
dismissed discussion of his wife. Liked even less the smug
smile that Alice wore as she took Ermgarde's chair at the high
table and demanded a speedy breakfast of the servants. The
disrespectful chit did not even deign to say good morning! She
was pleased by the Lady of Synford's downfall, that much was
obvious, and Margaret felt a twinge of suspicion that she had
to let die because there was no time to investigate.

Brodrick appeared again not long afterward, feeling splendid in breast-and-back plates of black steel, a courteous bow
executed for Margaret. "My lady, your son is in the ward and
wishes to take his leave."

Margaret and Alice rose simultaneously, consternation on
the former's face as she caught sight of the girl's bundle for
the first time.

"What have you there, girl?"

"Never you mind!" Alice tried to pass her, but Margaret
grasped her arm determinedly.

"Surely you don't think to go with him?"

"That's *exactly* what I mean to do. Ermgarde is no longer in
favor and I've a mind to make that favor my own!"

"You're mad! He goes on a chevauchee, not some uneventful progress! A woman has no place there."

"Don't try to rule me. Last night I shared his bed and he
demonstrated his feelings for me quite clearly. He'll want my
company. And I *shall* go!"

"We shall see," challenged Margaret, deciding that Wauter
should settle this mess of his own making. Lifting her skirts,
she fair flew down the stairs to the ward with Alice on her
heels.

Wauter sat atop Rogue, helm under his arm and shield secured to his saddle. He wanted only to be away, rid of the memories. So the sight of Alice scurrying after his mother, a traveling bundle under her arm and that determined look on her face as she elbowed Margaret aside and ran to him, destroyed what little patience he had left.

He glared down at the girl as she flicked a sausage-like plait angrily over her shoulder, before fastening upon him her coyest smile. The contrived gesture made him glare all the fiercer. "For what reason do you handle my mother so roughly? Has no one ever taught you respect to your elders?"

Alice argued, "But my lord, she would try to sway you in regard to taking me along. She seeks to keep us apart. After what happened last night—"

"*Nothing* of import happened last night! I go to war, you foolish girl. And, even if I might, I would not seek your company. Didn't I make myself clear when I said I didn't want you? You are nothing to me, Alice; you never could be. Last night only happened because you reminded me vaguely of her and gave me a chance to vent some spite!"

"No!" She clung to his stirrups, shrieking, still not inclined to believe him despite his savage words. "No, it cannot be so! You cannot mean it, not after all I've done so that we might be together!"

Wauter wheeled Rogue about in a dazzle of white caparison until Alice was forced to let go of his stirrups or be trampled. Lady Margaret caught her by the elbow as she made to grab for Wauter's leg, hissing and shrieking her incoherent hate of them all.

With relief, he said, "I give her into your charge, Mother, to do with as you will."

With a tight grasp on the writhing form, Margaret managed a dry reply, "Well, don't expect any thanks! I'd rather you gave me the care of a basket of vipers."

"I have confidence in your being able to cope," he told her fondly, the undignified prisoner in her arms making it impossible to do more than smile at each other before Wauter headed out through the gate. Brodrick rode at his side—trying to overcome his shame at his sister's unsavory behavior—and the mounted men-at-arms and marching archers were to the rear.

They made an impressive sight: shining steel, colorful ban-

ners, and homespun tunics gaping from beneath leather jerkins. They overflowed with optimism and the excitement of
adventure yet to come. Only Wauter remained sober-faced
and made no attempt to join in on the chorus of an old battle
hymn. And Margaret prayed that this campaign might bring
him forgetfulness and renewed spirit.

She watched until the last man had quit the ward, then
shoved Alice back toward the keep. "I would have words with
you, my girl. There are a few questions in my mind that demand answers."

Rowen stood at the massive oak doors with his now-faithful
following of greyhounds, a grimace of distaste on his face as
he watched the malevolent features of his sister. "If you've a
mind to thrash her, Lady Margaret, then do so without a
qualm. If my father had witnessed her actions this dawn, I
don't doubt that's exactly what he'd have done."

Margaret smiled grimly. "I hope it doesn't come to that,
and that Alice tells me what I want to know without recourse
to such action. But I thank you for your permission, young
man, and bear it in mind."

CHAPTER

22

LADY MARGARET, for all her visible signs of strength, couched in an aristocratic manner, couldn't intimidate Alice from her stubborn silence. The girl had no fear of the older woman, and she was about to go ask Rowen if she might borrow his dog whip to lend weight to her demands when Martin Carter knocked at the chamber door, informing her that Lady Ermgarde approached with a paid escort.

From that moment on Alice was a different creature. She began to tremble; her eyes, in a suddenly pale face, darted about the room as if searching for an escape route. Ermgarde would have worked out the duplicity by now and could be expected to be angry. Mightily so. Alice began to see that her plan had not borne fruit. She hadn't reckoned on Wauter leaving her behind.

Lady Margaret allowed a secret smile as she sensed the girl's growing disquiet and, positioning herself before the chamber door lest Alice think of bolting, she waited, her own frustrations fading as she said softly, "Very well, my girl, we'll leave the questioning to your sister. I'm sure she'll discover the truth more easily than I."

Alice didn't doubt it and her voice was tense as she pleaded, "Please, let me go before she arrives. I only did it because I loved your son and thought I could make him love me in return. 'Twas for him."

"Save your explanations for her. And whatever you did, I doubt not it was but for yourself."

When Ermgarde entered the chamber shortly thereafter, the gaze she fastened upon her seated sister, with intense violet eyes, was enough to shrivel the girl. Margaret laid a hand upon her arm, fearing murder, or maiming at the least. "Child, I know she deserves it in all probability, but think of the consequences."

"I have, my lady, I have," Ermgarde muttered between clenched teeth. "I should like to kill her, but that would be too merciful. I've thought of a suitable punishment."

Alice dropped off the footstool and onto her knees, bringing into play every gesture of penitence she could think of. "Ermgarde, don't hurt me, I pray. I'm sorry, truly I am!"

"You are sorry only that you've been caught out, Alice. And frankly, knowing the deviousness of your mind, I am surprised you could think of no better way to take Wauter from me. Forging letters from Gloucester, indeed!"

"But it worked!" Alice reminded her sneeringly, a hand flying to her mouth a moment later as Ermgarde came and stood over her, spitting in fury.

"It worked because my lord was already in the grips of jealousy and was quick to believe the evidence of his eyes. And I must say you picked a peculiar time to try to win him. Surely the eve of his departure for France was bad planning on your part. Or did you have the notion that he would take you with him? How little you know him!" jeered Ermgarde, resisting the urge to slap her sister. She had promised herself she wouldn't touch the girl.

Lady Margaret had been absorbing the scene staged before her, and could fit together the bits and pieces that her daughter-by-marriage had disclosed to get a clear picture of prior events. She shook her head at Alice. "Have you no conscience? God forbid, but does it not occur to you that my son may lose his life in France and go to his death believing his wife unfaithful? How could you knowingly bring this pain upon us, and upon Wauter, whom you profess to love?"

Alice created the perfect picture of wretchedness, casting down her eyes and shaking her head in woe. In truth, she would have destroyed them all if it meant having Wauter for herself.

Ermgarde moved to the corridor, making it plain she was closing the door on any more discussion, her voice emotionless as she aired her opinion. "I have decided that you are in need of solitude in which to meditate over your lack of Christian fellowship, and in solitude you will remain—until such time as I see fit to have you released. Lady Margaret—if I can presume upon her to undertake so distasteful a task—will accompany you, along with an escort of six men-at-arms who are impervious to your obvious charms and therefore unlikely to aid you in an attempt to escape.''

Along with Alice's relief at coming through this episode relatively unscathed, there was also a steadily growing unease. Ermgarde talked as if of a prison. ''Where are you sending me?''

''To the Magdalen nunnery at Bristol, dear sister. You will be able to keep Maud company, and there are others who, for reasons not dissimilar from yours, have been left there: recalcitrant wives, wayward daughters, ladies suffering from unrequited love. . . . You'll feel at home.''

''You jest?'' Alice looked appalled. To be locked away in a *nunnery*!

''Nay, I'm *deadly* serious. You will leave on the morrow, if Lady Margaret is agreeable to traveling at such short notice?''

Margaret nodded. ''The sooner this viper is snatched from the bosom of the family the better, I think.''

''Good. Until then, Alice, you will keep to this chamber. I shall have a guard posted outside should you require anything.''

''You can't be serious? You'll not get away with it!''

''I am. I will. You did make an error of judgement when you sought to steal my husband. What is mine I do not give up easily; neither do I care to have it tampered with. 'Tis for that one night you spent with him that you are being punished, rather than for your scheming. For having coaxed him to your bed I can never forgive you.''

The loser in a position that couldn't possibly get worse, Alice gave in to malice, feeling more at home with such an emotion. As Ermgarde opened the chamber door, the younger sister's voice took on its more familiar acid tone. ''You can't forgive me because he had me and enjoyed it! He told me so. 'Alice,' he said, 'compared to you my wife is like a stone cold corpse in my bed'!''

Standing beside Margaret in the passage, Ermgarde winced at the words, slamming the door before more came forth to freeze the heart within her.

''Don't you believe her, child. 'Twas said solely to spite you. When Wauter left this morning he was far from appearing the satisfied lover. Truth to tell, he said nothing of importance happened last night.''

But it had! Whether satisfactory or not, Wauter had bedded Alice, and that knowledge left Ermgarde feeling sick to the pit of her stomach. A controlled rage had possession of her body, along with a sense of betrayal, first by Alice, then by her husband.

He was gone, out of range of that rage, and there seemed no way that she could get retribution from him for the wrong he had done to her; no way to make him pay as Alice would. But she couldn't leave it at that, waiting patiently for his return from France . . . a return that might never come. One couldn't revile a ghost for his lack of faith!

CHAPTER
23

WHEN LADY MARGARET DEPARTED the next morning with Alice beside her in the litter—bound at ankles and wrists because she had proved uncooperative—she sensed that her daughter-by-marriage would not be residing at Synford on her return. Flooded with warmth, she grasped her hand long and tight before the litter trundled away, saying only, "Take care."

Ermgarde nodded, full of spirit now that she had made up her mind and cast a clear course of action. "I will."

The litter passed through the barbican with Alice issuing one last piece of ill will: "I hope you rot in hell! And I hope he's killed on foreign soil never knowing the truth!" For which she received a smart cuff about the head from her angry wardress.

Ermgarde made for the kennels in search of Rowen, Alice's words not troubling her much. He *wouldn't* die—not before she'd had a chance to confront him with her justified ire, her scathing reproaches! She felt certain the fates would keep him safe until then.

Her brother still slept. He lay atop a bed of straw, with a blanket and several greyhounds to keep him warm. He seemed oblivious to the piquant smells of the kennels.

"Rowen!" She kicked him in the ribs impatiently, her soft slipper bringing forth nothing but a mumble and grunt. "Rowen!"

The heavy lids opened slowly. "What?" he yawned.

"Where do you keep your clothes?"

"Huh?" He gave her a bemused look, shifted reluctantly, and laughed as one of the greyhounds licked his face. "Cut that out!"

She repeated, louder, "Where do you keep your clothes?"

"In a chest in Master Knolly's room. But what do you want with them?"

"To borrow some items."

Sitting up, he scrutinized her face worriedly. "What have you got in mind?"

" 'Tis no business of yours. And now that I know where I can find what I seek, you may return to your slumber."

She was up to something, he could tell. He knew that set, purposeful expression of old, and there was no way that he could go back to sleep. More than likely he'd awake and find that she'd already done what she intended, and he would have missed it altogether! Nay, he wasn't daft!

Struggling into his hose, Rowen ran after her.

In Knolly's cramped quarters next to the kennel, Rowen found his sister already busily sifting through his meager belongings—hose and jerkins, shoes and hoods flying about the floor to untidy it further.

"What are you about?"

She didn't bother looking up. "I told you, I want to borrow some things."

He slammed the lid, barely missing her fingers, and was struck with an angry glare from violet eyes. Nay, he wasn't about to be intimidated by a female, albeit his sister whom he knew was quite capable of delivering as sound a blow as any lad his age. "You'll get nothing until I know what's in your head." He thought he sounded suitably firm.

"Oh, don't be so tiresome!" She tried to hit his planted foot from the lid it kept firmly shut, but couldn't budge him. He must have grown some since those days when they used to fight and wrestle and Ermgarde had been in the habit of winning. "Very well, if you must know, I've decided to go after Wauter. There are certain things I would have out with him that just won't wait."

Rowen was aware of the goings-on about him more acutely than any would have guessed, so Ermgarde's decision came as no real surprise. Couldn't really expect less from someone as willful as her. And he wasn't even arguing with her about it. "Well, why didn't you just say that in the first place? But why the need for my clothes?"

"I think I'll be less likely to attract attention if I go as a boy. 'Tis not so bad in England, but if going to France becomes necessary, I don't want to have to protect my honor on top of everything else. There are brigands infesting the land, so I've been told."

"I can see your need to go and I'll not try to stop you, Ermgarde."

"Thank you, Rowen."

"But I'll have to go with you. You couldn't defend yourself against anything, and well you know it."

Was there any point in arguing? Rowen was as stubborn as herself and he was right about her lack of knowledge concerning self-defense. There was no point in getting killed before she could reach Wauter. Even so, she didn't like the thought of Rowen being put in danger because of her. This was *her* grudge, her quest to mete out retribution. Still, if she refused his protection he'd likely see to it that she didn't go either.

"Very well, you'll come with me."

On the deck of the *Trinité Royale*, the king, surrounded by a crowd of lords, sailors and servants, cast eyes over the great fleet that choked the Hampshire coast opposite the Isle of Wight. He glowed with pleasure at the new look of this navy—a royal navy.

Anchored around the king's ship were the *Katherine de la Toure*, the *Petite Trinité de la Toure* and the *Rude Coq de la Toure*, their decks crammed with lords and men-at-arms, archers and infantry.

As far up and down the Solent as the eye could see, ships of differing tonnage floated, their multi-colored sails clashing, their red waists decked with strange serpents, bulwarks gaily painted with checks and hung with the shields of knights. The creatures of heraldry abounded, worked upon sails, pennons and woodwork.

At three o'clock that afternoon the armada lifted anchors. The shore crowd cheered and waved their goodbyes. Priests prayed and sailors shouted.

Wauter stood at the rail with his fellow soldiers as wind caught sails, but he didn't wave to any of the receding figures. There was no elation within him at what might await across the Channel and no sorrow at leaving England either. He didn't care if he never returned. Synford, once promising so much, meant nothing now—not without her.

Just three days after slipping from the Solent, the English

army, in hundreds of small boats, landed on the beaches to the
west of Harfleur. The shingle beneath their feet was heavy
going as they unloaded livestock and horses, provisions and
baggage, guns and armor, with the unmanned ditches and
banks of boulders—hurriedly erected by the townsfolk on
sight of their approach—an added nuisance. Still, that was the
only resistance toward them thus far.

The hill north of Harfleur was soon resplendent with pavilions, tents and marquees, their emblazoned charges gay in
the August sunshine. And everywhere thronged knights and
dukes, heralds, minstrels, surgeons, chaplains, pages, grooms
and clerks. What the citizens of Harfleur thought, as they
watched from their wary vantage points atop town walls, was
difficult to imagine, but the English appeared to be enjoying a
picnic or its like, rather than planning military action.

The town was surrounded, though not before the Sire de
Gaucourt, on the French king's orders, had entered the town
with some three hundred men-at-arms to add to the garrison
commanded by the Sire d'Estouteville. And when Henry made
the expected demand that the garrison surrender, d'Estouteville indignantly refused. With four hundred men and the
stout walls at his back, plus earthworks and the barbicans of
Harfleur to beset the English, the French commander was confident that more help would arrive to give them deliverance
before the siege began to effect the town.

After a frustrating week when the town was reconnoitered
and no weakness found in its defenses, Henry was forced to
admit that to take the town by conventional methods or starve
them into surrender would take a very long time. And time
was something that the English couldn't spare. He tried to
tunnel under the walls, but with poor results, and eventually
brought into play his guns from Bristol—reluctantly, for such
impersonal mechanisms were held to be unchivalrous.

The positioning of the guns gave Wauter and his fellow
knights their first real taste of action, for the infantry—struggling with levers and ropes in the intense August heat—were
prime targets for sallying bands of French knights who rode
down on them from momentarily opened town gates, to ha-
rass and take prisoners before just as swiftly reentering the
town.

But it was intriguing how, even when detached from the action in spirit, Wauter still functioned effectively, knowing when to slice a mounted assailant with his sword, or when to instinctively aim a blow with the barbarous mace so that a foe's helm caved in along with his skull. While those about him fell, or were taken prisoner, or hobbled back to the English camp with debilitating wounds, he remained whole, unscathed—the perfect killing machine.

Henry began to use him to protect the gunners with greater frequency, knowing not what had turned the man into such an automaton of hate, but seeing the advantage of putting it to good use.

The French began to recognize him, the bravest of them singling him out on their sallies—and always regretting being drawn to the figure in silver-gray steel atop a ferocious horse. They nicknamed him the "Sire de Morte" because of the chilling roar he gave before dispatching one of their number to the hereafter.

But Wauter was not the only one to be given a nickname at Harfleur. There were the guns and, although such clumsy oddities had been infrequently used in battle over the last hundred years, they still had great curiosity value. The soldiers watched in proud awe as "London," "The Messenger" and "The King's Daughter" were trained upon Harfleur and their powder was ignited. The deafening roars and choking smoke that engulfed the gunners was an incredible sight; the millstones and boulders weighing five hundred pounds soon weakened the masonry of Harfleur's walls and towers.

When September arrived, Harfleur still held, but only just, and the king was confident of her fall within the week. For, besides the guns, he had also ordered the ancient siege machines to be brought to bear, such strangely named mechanisms as mangonels, arblasts and springalds still proving effective despite the antiquity of their design.

CHAPTER

24

"I THINK MY LORD is pushing himself too hard," Brodrick boldly volunteered, his close acquaintance with Wauter over the last month affording him the privilege of outspokenness. "That mistake today nearly cost you dearly. Could you not forego guarding the guns tomorrow, my lord?"

"What, and sit here and like as not go down with the bloody flux like others of my noble lords? Nay, 'tis bad enough listening to the suffering at night when I try to rest, without enduring it needlessly in the day," Wauter said brusquely, wincing as the salve he applied stung the raw edges of his cut cheek. A little more to the left with that Frog's slice of blade and he'd be minus his nose! Careless. He'd *forgotten* to lower his visor! As Brodrick rightly pointed out, that uncharacteristic carelessness almost cost him.

But, truth to tell, he didn't care. Nothing mattered, had the power to move him any longer. Whether Harfleur fell or not was of little import to him. There was no satisfaction to be had from this way of life any longer, no feeling of exhilaration. When he fought it was by instinct, well-learned skills displaying themselves automatically, unbidden, as he felled his adversaries, one by one, wondering when his own finale would come. But he neither feared it nor consciously guarded against it.

Dusk was falling, the thundering guns obliterating the moans from surrounding pavilions at monotonously regular intervals. The king would no doubt start his nightly rounds, visiting the gun emplacements and dishing out encouraging words to the men on guard. And they certainly needed it, thought Wauter wryly, lying down on his couch and cursing the breeze that blew warm and stale from the salt marshes.

There was no escaping the heat. By day it exhausted him just to stand in full harness, while to actually move was something of an endurance test, his body feeling as if it were baking alive. At night, in nothing but a loincloth, he sweated and rolled restlessly, irritated by the cries of the unfortunates about him and the virulent air that stifled all thought.

The bloody flux—dysentery—had been the scourge of armies throughout the ages, and here at Harfleur it was taking a disturbing hold. The heat, the air, the forced inactivity of the army as a whole, the indigestible cockles and mussels the men ate to supplement their rations, as well as unripe grapes and raw wine, undermined the spirit and heightened ill health. The Earls of Suffolk and March were laid low with the disease and young Bishop Richard Courtenay of Norwich hovered on the brink of death, the king in frequent attendance at his bedside.

Brodrick frowned at his master. The man who was now nothing but an unfeeling shell, didn't even trouble to see to his own cleanliness, except after considerable cajoling and assistance from his squire. And he allowed Brodrick to crop his hair and shave him only on occasion. Loving his sister, Ermgarde, as he did, still the lad could decry with shame the destruction her actions had wrought.

"I'll go see if I can find us something for supper," decided Brodrick, who was himself suffering the pangs of hunger. He watched Wauter—who appeared to be asleep, but wasn't—in the hope of some favorable response. There was none, save a grunt of acknowledgment. Eat and sleep the lord did in small measure, and with the same lackadaisical attitude with which he did everything else. Disappointed, the squire left.

"My lord, do you sleep?"

Wauter opened one eye. The voice was not Brodrick's, yet was equally familiar. "Robert?"

"Aye, 'tis me, my lord." Robert de la Vallée replaced the flap over the entrance and came to sit at Wauter's feet, a smile of friendship mingling with self-importance upon his face.

Wauter sat up, dishing out an affectionate slap on the back. "Well, I never! 'Tis good to see you again. Did you sail with the king? Then why have I not seen you before?"

"The king put me under the command of Michael de la Pole. I've had scant opportunity to seek you out until now."

"And how fares my lord Earl of Suffolk?"

"No better."

"And how fare you? Was your time with the king instructive and profitable?"

"Indeed, my lord. He gave me my spurs when we landed at Harfleur. I am now Sir Robert."

Wauter nodded proudly. "Rightly so. You'll drink with me? And soon Brodrick will return with whatever food he can find. Then we'll eat."

"I shall be glad to sup with you, on one condition."

"Oh, and what's that, pray?"

"That you'll not press upon me seafood." Wauter laughed at the look of abhorrence on Robert's face. "My lord Earl of Suffolk's rations grow low and we've all bridged the gaps in our bellies with cockles and the like. The sooner we head inland and are able to hunt decent fare, the happier I shall be."

"Poor Robert. I promise: no seafood."

Humor abating, Wauter studied the other, wondering what lay beneath the mask of knightly arrogance, the commendable show of lightheartedness. Did he still want for Alice? Or could the spell away from Synford have worked the healing upon his heart that Wauter had hoped for? Either way, Robert must never learn of *his* dealings with the strumpet on his last night before leaving for war.

The quietness within the pavilion evaporated the ease that had engulfed them only moments before, their heartiness becoming more forced as Wauter poured wine and they drank. Then Robert, it seemed, could control his tongue no longer and blurted out the question that had brought him to Wauter after weeks of self-restraint.

"How is she, lord. Does she ever speak of me?"

Wauter muttered into his goblet, Alice being the subject he most wanted to avoid after Ermgarde. He managed an abstract, "She was her usual self when I left."

Robert was instantly downhearted. "But she had no word for me?"

"Nay," Wauter said regretfully, cursing the wench in his mind. "I'd hoped you would have forgotten her, Robert. 'Twould have been best."

"I tried to forget her, lord. At court there were many women who offered solace, many marriageable maids put into my path by hopeful parents. But I only want her."

Wauter was thinking of Ermgarde, his thoughts akin to the lad's. Love was a murder of the soul, he decided, and clapped the knight's shoulder to offer a measure of comfort that he knew to be useless against such pain. "I understand."

"How can you?" Robert gulped at his wine, fearing that under such sympathy he'd make an ass of himself and start crying. "How can you understand? You've found love with the lady Ermgarde. She is a true and lasting love."

Wauter's voice turned hate-filled and vehement. "Nay, Robert, in matters of love I'm as much a fool as you. My true love," he jeered, "has proven herself as false as her sister, Alice."

The knight shook his head, disbelieving. "How can that be? Nay, I cannot credit it."

" 'Tis hard to swallow, I'll agree, for her act of faithfulness was convincing right up until the end—until I came upon her with her lover, discovered his love letters to her!"

"Good God!"

"And he is here, that high-born lover, and one day soon upon some field I shall call payment for his black deed and spit him through like the deserving swine he is!"

"Who is it, lord? Who stole your lady away?"

"Gloucester, with his Oxford ways and courtly graces. But being the king's brother won't save him!"

"My lord!" Robert was aghast, his eyes anxiously casting about for any eavesdroppers. "Calm yourself, please, before the guards descend and drag you away in chains!"

"What do I care?" growled Wauter morosely, drinking deeply of the bad wine and grimacing. "They can only kill me for treason, and frankly, that eventuality seems palatable. I've nothing to live for, Robert. *Nothing.* That bitch, my wife, has seen to it that I'm so bewitched by memories of her that no other could ever take her place. What's left for me? In truth, I might as well be dead."

Heavens above! Robert watched in sad amazement as his once proud, arrogant master slumped to his couch, eyes a thousand miles away, and sipped unconsciously at his wine. If love had tortured *him*, then it was slowly killing this man.

The knight refilled both their goblets and decided, "Let's get drunk, lord, gloriously drunk. Women? Bah! Who needs them?" His mind came forth with the unbidden, unwelcomed answer: we do.

CHAPTER

2 5

ON THE SEVENTEENTH DAY of September, the garrison made its final sally, as obstinate as ever in this last gesture of defiance. In the thick of the melee, Wauter was conscious of Robert guarding his back as in days gone by, but this time that presence, instead of being reassuring, was somehow annoying. It was as if the knight were watching him, guarding him—a job Wauter could adequately do himself.

The Lord of Synford cut through the air with his sword, making contact with the mace-wielding arm of the French knight who seemed to have singled him out for special treatment. There was a moan of pain from behind his black steel visor as the man found his arm suddenly useless—broken, or worse, since the armor plate had cut into his flesh. He reined his horse away with his good left hand, seeing the wisdom in falling back before more harm could be done.

Then Wauter turned his attention back to Robert in exasperation, resenting this guardian angel who seemed to be constantly hovering nearby. The growl from beneath his basinet reached the squire: "Get off my back!" it threatened.

Nay, not likely, thought Robert with determination. He'd seen that look on his master's face the night of their reunion, knew a death wish when he saw it and how desolation turned anyone's mind to self-destructive paths. No woman was worth it. Even longing for Alice as he did, nothing would have prompted Robert to make so futile a gesture to prove that love.

Around them the temptations played. Rogue snorted and nipped at anything that came within reach of his sizable jaws; men cried out personal mottos or gave the oft-used battle cry, "Saint George!" Horses whinnied in terror and men-at-arms locked with opponents in single combat. The melee was a writhing mass of color, steel and death.

Wauter saw the flail swing out toward him from an unknown foe, mused in the split second that followed on the barbarity of the object—a spiked iron ball linked to a length of chain—yet he didn't think of death, nor anything else. Worse still, he didn't *do* anything.

Robert screamed a warning, his own sword striking out at the same time and catching the Frenchman at the neck, where there was nothing to protect him save a gorget of mail. It was a lucky stroke, aimed wildly in panic, and the man fell dead from his horse. The flail blow bounced harmlessly off Wauter's basinet and caused little more than a ringing sound in his ears.

The lord looked at the knight in consternation, wondering what had set the young hothead to rant at him, and not seeing the half-decapitated form being trampled by Rogue.

"Die, you may want to. But I'll make it bloody difficult, so help me I will!"

Die? What was the fool talking about? I'm dead already! 'Tis only my body which refuses to acknowledge the fact. It keeps working of its own accord, without any prompting from me to keep this reluctant carcass on the move. And when I grow careless and peace seems about to descend, some watchdog with an infuriating sense of loyalty has to come to the rescue!

"Forget about me. Guard yourself," he commanded the lad, making to wheel Rogue about in search of new prey.

'Twas then that he caught sight of the charging knight out of the corner of his eye, cursing the Frogs for not knowing when they were beat.

"Look to your left, Robert!" he warned, certain that his former squire could beat off such an adversary without too much bother. But Robert was angry, his eyes and mind still fixed on his master.

"Look to your left, I say!"

Too late. Wauter closed his eyes momentarily, fearing to look as he heard the clash of steel against steel. Then, a second later he was engaging with the French knight, a blow from his furiously wielded mace catching the man in the chest with a reverberating *bong*. Knocked askew in the saddle, the man tipped sideways, his foot still in his stirrup, as his body fell groundward to be dragged unceremoniously by his mount.

Wauter looked about him. The melee seemed almost at an

end, the French retreating toward the gate of the town, with John Holland at the head of a counterattack.

He brought Rogue up close beside Robert's mount, spying the dent in the knight's basinet and the way he reeled drunkenly in the saddle. "Are you all right?"

Robert couldn't answer. Suddenly the heat was too great, his basinet seeming to suffocate. He blinked, trying to clear his vision, wondering dazedly at the red mist before his eyes, then realizing with a chill that it was blood. *His!*

"Robert!" Wauter snatched the reins of the knight's horse as the young man slumped against its neck, terror growing in his chest. If the lad should die because of him. . . !"

He led him hastily back to the English camp, calling frantically for a surgeon as he released the boy's limp legs and feet from the stirrups and lifted the knight gently to the ground. "He should have been looking after himself instead of playing nurse to me," Wauter chided morosely, helping the surgeon remove the basinet, then shaking his head fearfully at the congealing mess of red in the lad's sun-bleached hair. 'Twas his foolishness that had caused this. He had committed the gravest sin any knight could be guilty of, by placing another in unnecessary danger. Well, no more. Courting death was done with, for it seemed obvious that God had no mind to let him die just yet.

The surgeon probed the wound methodically, mumbling to himself as his patient moaned unconsciously.

Wauter bit his lip. "Well? What do you think?"

"He'll be all right. It does look far worse than it is. I can detect no damage to the skull."

Thank God! The knot of fear in Wauter's chest began to unwind.

"We'll just stop the bleeding, and maybe put in a few stitches. I wager he'll have nothing worse than an excruciating headache when he awakens."

He cauterized the wound with a hot iron, then knitted together the raw flesh to stop the bleeding and lessen the risk of infection. Wauter carried the steel-clad knight back to his pavilion, where Brodrick set to work on the laces and leather straps of the harness, and his master took up a wineskin to drink thirstily.

Henry's terms of surrender were harsh and, not surprisingly, the Sire de Gaucourt felt obliged to reject them. Very well. The king made no attempt to change his mind by modifying those demands, but instead trained every gun and instrument of siege warfare upon the walls of Harfleur.

The already battered walls were bombarded, the houses beyond were reduced to rubble, while millstones took great chunks of masonry out of the steeple of the church of Saint Martin.

The French came with the dawn to the Duke of Clarence's camp to reopen negotiations. The offer was accepted and the Earl of Dorset, Lord FitzHugh and Sir Thomas Erpingham were chosen to lead the English delegation. After much haggling, the French were forced into agreeing to surrender on the following Sunday, September the twenty-second, at one o'clock in the afternoon.

Henry was confident that Harfleur would soon be in his hands. It was unlikely that either the dauphin or his father, Charles VI—carrying his sacred red-silk banner of St. Denis as an object to boost patriotism—could bring a unified force of Frenchmen against the enemy. Armagnacs hated Burgundians much as the Welsh, Irish and Scots hated the English. But whereas the people of the British Isles would most times stand together against a foreign foe, the many factions of France would not.

Both Charles d'Albret, Constable of France, who tried at Rouen to assemble an army, and Jean Boucicaut, Marshal of France, who was stationed at Honfleur on the southern shore of the Seine estuary opposite Harfleur, were finding indifference among the commoners. What peasants in their right minds would donate military service to a king who refused to pay them, whose armies suffered from non-cooperation and petty bickering among the officers' ranks, and whose officers refused to fight side by side with mere peasants?

The Duke of Burgundy, mindful of his secret promises to Henry, promised Charles VI help but found convenient ways of excusing himself from rallying it. And when his son, Philippe, the Count of Charolais, asked to join the army, John had him locked away in the castle of Aire near St. Omer, where he could do no more than vent tears of frustration.

When an Orleanist was appointed Captain of Picardy, the Duke of Burgundy refused to recognize his authority and most of his lords followed suit, refusing the dauphin their support without their overlord's permission.

Even the Orleanists and Armagnacs were proving less than cooperative. The Duke of Orleans sent the king five hundred men, lamely promising that he would be following them later, while the Dukes of Bourbon and Berry withdrew their support altogether in protest against the dauphin's unspecified scandalous intrigues.

So it was that when a weary Sire de Hacqueville returned from Vernon to Harfleur, he messengered no promise of help from the dauphin. And, accordingly, the conditions of the truce were fulfilled. Harfleur surrendered.

It was humiliating to the French commanders to cede their town to Henry, yet on Sunday, September the twenty-second, Raoul de Gaucourt and Lionel de Bracquemont were obliged to don the hairshirts of penitents, along with twenty-four French hostages, and have themselves brought before Henry.

The king sat enthroned in his silk pavilion on the hill opposite Harfleur, Sir Gilbert Umfraville standing to his right and bearing a pike-staff that held Henry's tilting helm adorned with crown. All around him stood his lords, wearing their finest apparel this afternoon instead of yesterday's armor.

Wauter watched, as fascinated as ever, as Henry savored the moment. Any word he might speak would go down to posterity, and the young monarch was acutely aware of the fact. He wanted to make this as historically memorable as possible.

He refused even to glance in the general direction of the French, forcing them to kneel a long time before he instructed the Earl of Dorset to relieve them of the keys to the town.

They had done him a grievous wrong, he told them in an elaborate peroration. They had denied him access to *his* town, but as God had made them see the error of their ways and they had given themselves up to his mercy, so he, Henry, would be merciful to them.

The king entered Harfleur on Monday morning, determined that this become an English town as Calais was. His instructions about the future of the inhabitants were quite clear. The rich would be held for ransom; the not-so-rich would be allowed to continue life as before, so long as they took an oath of allegiance to the English king; the poor and infirm—seemingly of use to no one—were escorted from the town with nothing but the clothes on their backs and five sous.

With Harfleur in their hands, the English set about burying their dead and sending home the sick. Beside the usual casualties of war, more than two thousand men were dead or struck seriously ill by dysentery. The Duke of Clarence had contracted it and Michael de la Pole, Earl of Suffolk, William Butler, Lord of the Manor of Warrington and John Philip of Kidderminster, besides many others, had perished. Henry's ten thousand men had fast been whittled down in numbers.

Having envisioned a triumphant march along the Seine to Rouen and Paris, eventually to end in Bordeaux, Henry now had to accept the fact that such valiant plans were fantastic. But out of pride he insisted on a chevauchee—some show of strength in the French king's own back yard. First, though, he dispatched Guienne Herald and the Sire de Gaucourt to the dauphin with a personal challenge. He deferred his decision to march for eight days until he got a reply. Single combat to decide who inherited the French crown after the death of Charles VI was what Henry proposed. The fact that Henry was twenty eight and no mean fighter was not considered preposterous or distasteful, even when the challenged dauphin was a sickly, fat youth of nineteen!

And while they waited, they counted the number of deserters, assigned men to the defense of Harfleur, and then distributed the extra weapons and armor that the dead would no longer be needing. The remainder numbered no more than six thousand; five thousand of them were archers, the rest men-at-arms.

To try to march to Paris would be lunacy, even taking into account the dithering confusion of the enemy. Autumn would soon be upon them and no army relished forced marches and food shortages in the face of worsening weather, let alone the possibility of meeting the enemy on the way. Such arguments did Henry's lieutenants put to him at a war council at the beginning of October. But supported by his younger, more adventurous officers, the king argued for the less tasteful alternative—namely to evacuate Harfleur, save for the garrison. But might not they march boldy to Calais, there to take ship for home having proved their fearlessness?

Wauter understood the king's reluctance to back down. The Lancastrian sense of honor wouldn't stand for it, and there was also the matter of England's pride. Having boasted to Charles VI of taking the French crown and becoming master of them all, how could Henry possibly go home with but one sea town under his belt?

Perhaps, without his own clinging disinterest in life, the Lord of Synford might have thought more carefully about standing behind the king, might have argued the unlikelihood of their carrying out the king's plans without annihilation. As it was, he backed Henry recklessly in his intention to march to Calais, and the king, in turn, with piety and sense of purpose, spoke eloquently.

"I am possessed with a burning desire to see my territories and the places which ought to be my inheritance."

Who could deny such a call from the heart?

Two days later, there having been no answer to Henry's challenge from the dauphin, the army marched out of Harfleur with enough provisions for eight days, but little else. Their march would be fast, to try to keep them one step ahead of the French, but flamboyant enough to give a good report of Henry on his return to England. On no account must it seem to his people that he had turned tail and run.

CHAPTER

26

ARRIVING AT SOUTHAMPTON and finding the army had already departed was disappointment enough, yet Ermgarde was to experience worse. There were no ships to be had. It was a preposterous state of affairs. And Ermgarde—who had decided against pocketing large sums of money, knowing that brigands were inclined to kill for a heavy purse—had not enough coin to persuade even a fisherman to transport her across the Channel.

After several days of waiting for a sail to appear on the horizon, she was in favor of following the coast to another port, for surely the king couldn't have commandeered *every* ship around Britain? But Rowen argued that more days would be lost on the road to Dover than if they remained patiently planted where they were.

It was nigh onto a month before the longed-for ships slipped into port, and then there were several but they carried the less-than-glorious dead and many sick men who had found little reward for their brief sojourn across the Channel.

Ermgarde half wished that Wauter be among them. Not seriously wounded, of course, but incapacitated to the extent that he couldn't evade her and would have to lie docile while she tended him and admonished him soundly. But it wasn't to be. He was still in France presumably in good health.

When the ships had cleared their human cargo, Ermgarde sent her brother to inquire of the captains if any were returning to Harfleur, and if so, whether two lads might be given passage. Rowen was to tell the curious that he and his lord's page—Ermgarde in disguise—were endeavoring to bring news there of the birth of their lord's first born son. The Lord of Synford had charged them to bring the joyous news immediately, no matter where they might have to travel. The captain of the *Rude Coq de la Toure* was convinced without any

trouble, knowing how much store these high-born fellows set
by the arrival of their sons and heirs. He would book the
messenger and page on his next provisioned crossing, but he
wouldn't be departing for several more days. Having ferried
the putrid bodies of the dead and dying from the siege, he explained, he needed to scrub the vessel down to make passenger
voyages palatable.

Their crossing of the Channel was uneventful. The weather
was blustery but never approached anything as unpleasant as a
storm. Life on deck continued to be tense. Archers manned
the castles of the ship in the unlikely event that a French ship
intercepted them.

Stepping along the shingle beach with Rowen—and some
dozen merchants who planned to take advantage of this new
English stronghold—Ermgarde tried to calm the wild rhythm
of her heart, which beat faster with expectancy and dread.

She was almost there. In a while they would stand face to
face, she told herself, fighting off the premonition that it
couldn't possibly be *that* easy. And how was she going to approach him? All fire and retribution? Nay. She had thought to
vent her anger when she saw him, but now she just wanted to
take him in her arms. There would be no recriminations. No
mention even of Alice! Just so long as everything could be as it
was before.

Around the walls of the town lingered evidence of the siege.
Masons and carpenters busied themselves as they rebuilt the
mangled walls and barbican. Great trenches scarred the slopes
where the English had made their camps, filled now to overflowing with the crow-pecked, rotting carcasses of horses that
had been killed during numerous attacks and melees. The
stench was unbearable and Ermgarde prayed unconsciously
that Rogue had evaded so ignominious an end.

Inside the walls, her premonition began to seem unwar-
ranted. There were literally hundreds of soldiers milling about,
watching over the Normans who went about their daily business as if they'd never been enemies. Wauter *had* to be somewhere.

"Where do we start looking?" asked Rowen drily, knowing
they could wander the town for days and probably never stum-
ble across their lord.

Ermgarde paused and thought, dropping her pack of provi-

sions at her feet with a sigh of relief. She would be glad to find
Wauter, if only to do away with this disguise of being a lad.
'Twould be heaven to unbind her breasts, take a bath and put
on a gown. "There's no point in just wandering about. We
don't even know where the army has billoted. Best bet is to ask
someone where the king is. Wauter will doubtless be nearby."

"All right. You stay here with the belongings. I'll see to it."

Rowen was not gone many moments. He stopped the first
soldier who happened by, and the leather-clad, basinet-helmed
figure leaning on a halberd told the lad all he wanted to know.

"Well?" asked Ermgarde impatiently, picking up her backpack once more and hoisting it over her shoulder. "Which
way do we go?"

"The king is no longer here."

"What?"

Rowen saw her frame sag in disappointment and was quick
to bolster her spirits. "Now don't get all despondent again.
The king isn't here, true, and neither is your Wauter. But
they're only a day away from us. The soldier said they left yesterday morning on a forced march. Their destination is Calais.
He also said that the Earl of Dorset has been appointed Governor of Harfleur. We could find out the king's plans from him,
if you like."

"Nay; there's no point." Ermgarde looked suddenly more
determined again. "Just one day ahead of us, you say? Then
let us take time only to buy more provisions and be after
them."

"But . . . Ermgarde, wouldn't it be better to speak to the
governor, find out what sort of problems we'll be faced with?
Where the dangers might lie?"

She shook her head resolutely. "The earl will argue against
our going. I'll not justify my actions to others." Besides
which, she decided as she crossed the thoroughfare to a vit-
tler's shop, the dangers that lurked ahead of them were better
left unwarned against. *If I hear too much talk about hostile
French and roving brigands, this trembling frame might get its
way and stay safely here!*

Rowen hurried to keep up with her, jostling among the
morning shoppers. "All right . . . well, if we don't find out the
lie of the land from the governor, at least let us be armed so
that we can put up a fight should the need arise. While you

purchase foodstuff, I'll go find a bowyer and a fletcher. This dagger is next to useless and I'll feel more at home with a bow."

"Yes, you do that. But be quick."

He frowned, though she was too busy selecting pies to notice. Where was her stubbornness going to lead them this time, he wondered, hardly daring to think. If she wasn't his sister and her happiness not at stake, Rowen would have trussed her up like a chicken and put her aboard the first ship back to England.

CHAPTER

27

ARQUES, FOUR MILES SOUTH of Dieppe, guarded the River Bethune; its chateau, rising high above the river, overlooked the bridge.

It was with some surprise and annoyance that Henry Plantagenet found the castellan there disinclined to let the army bridge the river unmolested. After the French had had the audacity to open fire upon them with cannon from their lofty heights, the king sent one of his customary messages expressing his displeasure at such behavior and demanding his army be allowed to pass over the bridge, *or else*!

Threatened with the razing of Arques to the ground, the castellan immediately adopted a more convivial frame of mind and even went so far as to cart down to them a load of bread and wine to speed them on their way.

By nightfall of the following day they had reached the River Bresle, half a mile or so to the east of Eu. And again there was resistance to their advance—first with cannon fire, then with a charge of cavalry that left casualties on both sides before the French were driven back into Eu.

Almost word for word, Henry issued the same strict message that had been so effective at Arques the day before. Success. The English crossed the bridge, then settled down to enjoy fresh bread and more wine with Eu behind them.

Things were going well. The army was well fed and in a pleasant, wine-drugged mood. They'd crossed two rivers and trekked eighty miles with little loss. One more major river lay ahead and that was the Somme, but thirteen miles away. There they expected to cross by means of the Blanche-Taque ford, which was supposedly being kept open by a force of men-at-arms from Calais.

The next day, with seven miles covered after their dawn start, the army moved down into the valley of the Somme, marveling at the absence of any French people in sight.

Riding in the vanguard beside his confederates, Umfraville and Cornwall, Wauter was as taken aback by the peculiar sight of a solitary Frenchman as the rest.

Umfraville shouted for the man to stop, momentarily at a loss as to what else to say. It wasn't every day that one of the enemy, unarmed, popped up before them in the middle of nowhere.

The Frenchman didn't seem inclined to take his chances at running away and waited for the knights to reach him and dismount. Wauter eyed him suspiciously, noting the total lack of arms, the homespun tunic and darned hose. A wandering peasant, mayhap?

"Who are you?" he asked, praying his French was good enough for the man to understand.

"A Gascon . . . lord, in service to Charles d'Albret, Constable of France," muttered the man worriedly.

"What's he say, Waut?" queried Cornwall, whose French was so poor he could not follow the prattle.

"He says he's d'Albret's servant," Wauter told him skeptically.

"What's he doing here, then?"

"That's what I'm wondering."

"Lord, I am Gascon, with no love for Armagnaque or Orleanist. I come to give you warning," gushed the prisoner with eagerness born of fear. "You cannot cross the Somme at Blanche-Taque. Marshal Boucicaut guards it with a force of some six thousand men, and they have driven sharpened stakes into it to hold you at bay."

"What's he saying now," Cornwall asked, this time with impatience.

Wauter repeated the man's words, wondering at the truth in them. Or could it be that the man was a plant to try to alter their planned route?

"Good God!" thundered Sir Gilbert Umfraville. "Surely, he lies? Boucicaut was at Honfleur, last I heard of him."

Under further questioning from the Lord of Synford, the Gascon said that both d'Albret and Boucicaut had been at Rouen by the time the challenge of single combat was received by the dauphin, and that both marshal and constable had been dispatched with their men to the Somme, their orders to pursue and fight the enemy.

phin—found the English enjoying a Sunday rest from their march toward Calais.

The king, whether surprised or not, kept a bland face before the heralds as they delivered a challenge from the dukes. He had hoped, upon managing the difficult task of crossing the Somme, that God might stay with him and see the English host safely home. But it seemed that the Almighty ordained there be a confrontation.

The heralds spoke of the English king and his army's intent to conquer towns, castles and cities in the realm of France. And then of their own king being compelled to raise an army to defend his people, an army that would meet in combat with their foes before they reached Calais, there to take revenge for England's conduct.

Henry's face didn't change. It remained devoid of expression, and when he spoke neither anger nor compromise laced his voice. If he had to meet the French, so be it. He'd do so with the same spirit he'd shown them even before this campaign began.

He told them, when asked what road he meant to take: "Straight to Calais, and if our enemies try to disturb us in our journey, it will not be without the utmost peril. We do not intend to seek them out, but neither shall we in fear of them move more slowly or more quickly than we wish. We advise them again not to interrupt our journey, nor seek what would be its consequence—a great shedding of Christian blood."

Each given a hundred gold French crowns, the heralds departed and the English broke camp.

Where the road to Albert crosses the road to Bapaume, the English were left in no doubt to where the French were headed. The previous day's rain had turned the road crossing to mire, and the English could see thousands of bootprints left by a vast army on the move. Before, there had been only rumors; now, they knew what they were up against.

Wauter brought Rogue to a halt and cast an eye over the wide band of countryside pocked by the French, whose path led only slightly more northerly than the route their own king had plotted to Calais. He removed his basinet and felt the rain matting his dark locks, felt the chill of it down his neck. Somewhere, before they could reach Calais, there was going to be one almighty battle. Somewhere, not too many miles away,

lay an easy death, the likes of which had eluded him since setting foot in this cursed land.

    He watched the chaplains leading the soldiers in fearful
prayers for deliverance, and felt some pity for them. But he
was calm and welcomed the road ahead. Not many days, he
guessed, and he'd be free of *her* for ever.

CHAPTER
28

To say that Ermgarde and Rowen were bewildered would be to understate the situation. Having crossed the bridge at Arques under cover of darkness, and carefully bypassed Eu in the same manner, they eventually found themselves in the valley of the Somme. Ahead lay the Blanche-Taque ford, yet the army's tracks veered eastward. What was going on?

"They've changed plans." Rowen stated the obvious.

"Anyone can see that. But why? Everyone we spoke to said the king intended to march to Calais. Well, the port is that way." She pointed north in consternation. "Oh dear, I never counted on them changing plans. What do we do now?"

"I suggest we go to the ford. Perhaps there's something there that can clue us in to the king's reasoning. One thing's certain—I don't relish the thought of traveling further inland."

At the quiet ford across the bottleneck of the river, they found evidence of the French blockade. The fact that the English had had to change direction to avoid an unfavorable confrontation filled Ermgarde with foreboding. Who could say that a battle had not already raged inland where the king must have gone to probe for another crossing place?

"Oh God, Rowen! What if he's dead?" she cried, looking along the path down which Wauter had traveled on Rogue, Brodrick at his side. "We must make haste."

"Where? Nay, sister, I've just said I don't relish going further inland. Now, be sensible and stop wailing like a raped nun!"

Momentarily, Ermgarde looked shocked at his unholy comparison, then the fearful tears gave way to reluctant giggles. "Rowen, for shame! If father could hear you he'd clip your ear!"

" 'Twas *from* father that I learned the saying! Now listen to

me. 'Twould be folly to go inland. We'd get lost sure enough
and like as not run into trouble with the peasants. In Normandy they were bad enough, even with their supposed allegiance to the King of England. But beyond Normandy—we'd
get ourselves run through with pitchforks or suchlike. I'm too
much of a coward to want to pursue the army, Ermgarde. I
say we continue to Calais. If the king said he was going there,
then he'll get there sometime. The army's probably already
found a crossing place and is turning back to its original
course."

"You make your way sound so sensible. But what if something should happen to Wauter in the meantime?"

"You've trusted God to keep him safe for you so far. I
think he'll hearken to your prayers a while longer."

So they had chosen Rowen's way and, after resting the night
on the south bank of the river, he set about dislodging a
couple of the sharp stakes that the French had wedged into
position, thereby giving them passage across the ford.

That day they traveled ten miles, for Ermgarde's left boot
had worn through and her foot was blistered. The next day
they traveled even less, since her ill-clad foot, even swathed in
lumpy bandages cut from the generous hem of Rowen's cotehardie, was now lacerated too, causing her to wince whenever
she stepped forward.

When dusk came and brought with it the rain, brother and
sister were decidedly miserable. They didn't dare to light a
fire, but found an out-of-the-way copse where they sheltered
beneath the heavy blanket of fern and elms. Her stomach
rumbled hungrily, but she wouldn't give in to it. If she could
just get to sleep then hunger wouldn't play upon her senses. As
for her foot! Of all the damned, blasted . . . !

"We should have bought extra boots at Harfleur," she
mumbled to the green fronds behind which her brother shifted
about uncomfortably.

"We should have *stayed* there, that's what we should have
done," he retorted.

The next day they crossed a river, though they had no idea
as to its name, and sat down beneath the overshadowing trees
to eat a little of the dried meat and fruit left in their backpacks. Ermgarde's teeth chattered and she shivered noisily, to
her brother's great annoyance.

"Lord above! Can't you stop that infernal noise?"

"Nay, I can't. 'Tis these clothes. They're still wet from yesterday's soaking. I'm sure 'twould cease if only I had something more substantial in my belly."

"Aye. Well, we're not really in a position to pop into the nearest village and ask to buy something, now are we?"

"Indeed we're not! And who was it warned me against pitchfork-wielding peasants? You made it sound as if coming this way would be safer, but it isn't, is it? The peasants of Picardy are a menace to travelers, chasing us and setting their dogs after us. We might just as well have followed behind the army—at least then we'd know where we were, which is more than we can say for ourselves now!"

"Typical female! The first sign of hardship and she begins to mutter and fling recriminations!"

"You may say that, Rowen, but don't forget who's wearing the pair of whole boots! Any gentleman would have offered me the use of his by now!"

"You'll not get these boots even if you have to walk barefoot! They're the first pair I ever had made especially for me, and if it comes to trouble and one of those peasants skewers me on his pitchfork, I intend dying in them!"

"Well, you do just that!" Ermgarde hurled at him, jumping to her feet and cursing the pain, making as if to start off without him.

She didn't go very far. Coming up from the trees and heading back toward the bridge where they had crossed earlier, Ermgarde heard voices—foreign voices—and the soft jingle of horse bridles. She ran back to Rowen, the pain in her foot quite forgotten.

"I knew you wouldn't be stupid enough to go off on your own; you've got no sense of direction," he jeered.

"Ssh!" she caught him by the arm and dragged him with her beneath the trees.

"What's happening. What's—"

"Frenchmen. Crossing the bridge, I think. We'd best be quiet."

Rowen needed no prompting. He'd gone deathly white, shrinking among the foliage in the manner he'd learned during his poaching days.

The approach of the Frenchmen grew noisier, covering the

fearful whispers not too far away.

"Travelling north by the sound of them," Rowen calculated.

"Yes."

"I suppose we've done well to get this far without coming across any. Have to take care from now on, though. Could be more where they came from."

"Perhaps we'd better move only at night from now on?"

"Good idea. That way, if those Frenchies are camped anywhere on our route, their camp fires should warn us to detour."

The small band of soldiers had vanished, but it wasn't until dusk that the two mustered enough courage to leave the cover of the trees and start again on their way.

That night they came upon a smoldering cottage on their slow northward trek, the smell of what they presumed to be roasting pork drawing them warily to the gutted building. They should have known better, really, for what would a pig be doing roasting in the ruin of a house? But stomachs ruled heads in this instance.

Rowen went first with dagger drawn, sneaking about the side of the blackened hovel where a shutter banged unrhythmically in the night breeze. Ermgarde crept apprehensively behind him, ears alert to the sudden, inexplicable night noises.

Her brother stopped short, stifling a shriek as he trod on something soft, then a strangled gurgle of revulsion catching in his throat as his eyes made out the bloody, brutally raped form of a young girl. An axe in her chest had killed her after God knew who had had their pleasure.

"Oh, dear God!" Ermgarde, inquisitive as always, had come up behind him. Her stomach lurched and, retracing her steps blindly, she found a bush behind which she could empty the slight contents of her stomach.

"Stay there," Rowen ordered, stepping about the body and coming to the door of the cottage. He didn't go in, for what caught his eye from the threshold was enough. A man—it was difficult to tell and the lad wouldn't go closer—lay atop the charred remains of his kitchen table, his blistered, twisted body testament to an agonizing death; his feet—which someone had set over the now gently smoldering logs of a fire—burned to blackened stumps.

Poor tormented soul. Tortured, no doubt, while he was made to hear others taking turns with the girl outside, then left tied to that table while they set the building on fire!

Rowen was no stranger to violence. It was a violent time, after all, but the atrocity here was more than his stomach could stand and he fled, finding Ermgarde still doubled-over behind the bush and joining her.

She wiped a sleeve across her mouth and inquired wretchedly, "What did you find inside?"

He retched again, and kept doing so even though his stomach was quite empty. "Nothing." Not for anything would he have spoken of that sight. He wished to God they had never come. 'Twas enough to give a man nightmares for the rest of his days.

Ermgarde wasn't convinced. Something had set him to shivering and crying. But she sensed, that it was best to remain ignorant.

At last he straightened up and seemed to take hold of himself, wiping his eyes and setting his jaw in a jutting angle of determination.

"Mayhap if we look we can find a spade with which to bury her," suggested Ermgarde, half-heartedly. It was their Christian duty, and yet the thought of it made her tremble violently again.

"Nay." Rowen shook his head adamantly. "We can't take the risk of others coming to investigate and finding us here." In truth, nothing could have induced him to linger at that place and, taking his sister by the arm, he hurried her off into the thankful blackness of the night, away from the roasting smell.

When the last of the dried meat was gone, they went two miserable days on nothing but nuts and berries gathered along the way, tempers shortening further and desperation growing. They *had* to find something to eat. Wildlife was nonexistent, and they'd been able to catch nought save one paltry lark some days before, hardly enough to fill their need.

With trepidation, Rowen robbed an isolated family of serfs, the deed lying heavily on his conscience since they were hardly better off themselves, their large eyes dim in haggard faces. So he took nothing save a round, flat loaf of unappetizing black

bread and paid generously with English coin, withdrawing
from their hovel with bow and arrow trained warily upon
them.

The bread, unpalatable though it was compared to the
yeasty, brown-crusted loaves of England, was savored that
night as if the tastiest morsel at any banquet; the remainder
was carefully put in Ermgarde's backpack.

With something in their bellies to cheer them on, they
pressed through that night, slowly, careful of Ermgarde's
worsening foot. But for the infected appendage, she would
have been in high spirits, and cursed eloquently with each
painful tread. At this pace it would be Christmas-tide before
they reached Calais!

When they crossed another nameless river and the sky began
to lighten with the first hint of dull grey daylight, Ermgarde
lingered in the chilly water, forgetting that her sopping hose
would mean hours of shivering and discomfort ahead. She
only knew that the water felt like balm to her lacerated sole,
cleansing the dusty wounds and freeing bandages that had ad-
hered to her flesh because of seeping blood.

"Heaven," she breathed.

Rowen was on the far bank already, frowning at her. "Oh,
do come on! There's another village ahead and I want to be
around it before we take a rest. There appears to be woods to
the north of it from what I can see. We'll stop there."

Reluctantly, Ermgarde extended her hand and was hoisted
to the bank, scrutinizing the tower of a church and rooftops
visible above the trees in the distance. "Looks more like a
town to me. 'Tis too large for a village."

"All the more reason to get past it before the light comes
proper."

They made their way from tree to tree between the south
and southeast roads that ran out of the town, thankful when
the scattering of trees grew more dense and became a wooded
area that afforded them cover. When the town was lost to
sight behind this autumn-hued screen, they stopped, set down
their provisions and supped on black bread and hazel nuts.
Dawn found them sleeping the sleep of the exhausted.

It was Rowen who woke first, alerted to danger by the growing noise to the south. He sat bolt upright and trained an ear in
that direction. More French? God forbid! He urgently shook

his sister awake. "Ermgarde, rouse yourself! We've got to get moving."

"Why?" She blinked sluggishly, certain she'd slept no more than a moment or so.

"More French, I think, entering the town from the south. We've got to go while we still can. North."

"French!" She jumped to her feet, almost screaming out loud when pain pulsed up her leg. Her face drained of color. "I shan't be able to go very fast."

"Then I'll have to carry you, piggy-back fashion like we used to do years ago, remember?" he told her with cheerful resolve after witnessing the sudden fear in her eyes. "I want no arguments. No doubt you don't care for the indignity of such transport, but there is no alternative. Up you go."

With her arms clinging about Rowen's neck and her knees clamped about his waist, where he pinned them down, they made slow passage through the trees, their backpacks—empty and expendable—were left behind.

Pushing aside the branch of the last tree as they emerged from the wood, Ermgarde's eyes turned saucerlike and her mouth fell open.

"Christ!" It was evident that Rowen had seen them, too. For a moment he froze, couldn't think, and it was only after Ermgarde pinched him and whispered urgently that he backed into the trees.

"My God, have you ever seen anything like it? We must be surrounded by the devils!"

Through the trees they watched the seething mass of color on the distant slope to the north, a vast area widening out fanlike for as far as they could see between the two woods; it was filled to overflowing with a French army, their camp a sea of banners and fleur-de-lys pennants, pavilions and cooking fires.

"Lord, Rowen. Of all the woods in France, you have to choose this one! How will we ever get around them?"

He coughed as if that would dispel his terror, but had no answer. "We'd best go back a way."

"But there are French behind us as well. You said so."

"I know I did! Just be quiet for a moment, if that's possible. I need to think."

Ermgarde pursed her lips, flesh crawling fearfully at the

nearness of so many enemies. There were thousands of them, tens of thousands. A veritable army. And she couldn't even run!

"But I didn't see the army coming from the south. I only heard them," Rowen was saying, to himself rather than his sister, trying to get things clear in his mind. Did *that* army also have to be French? Wasn't it just conceivable. . . .

"We're turning back," he told her, retracing his path through the woods. Ermgarde cried out as branches caught across her face and scratched her.

"You are mad! Let us lie low until they've gone."

"I don't think they're going anywhere, not just yet. And I want a closer look at the army behind us."

"You are mad! You'll get us killed!"

Rowen paid her no heed, his pace possessed of more vitality than had been evident in days past, her added weight not slowing him at all. He knew, as surely as he knew the sky was blue, what awaited them beyond the woods near the town.

Ermgarde was still pleading with him to stop as they broke through the trees that surrounded the north of the town. She thought the lack of food over a continued period had unhinged his mind. Whatever drove him was purely suicidal. She didn't want to end up like that poor girl at the cottage they'd come across.

"Rowen, I beg you to stop!"

"Don't you see them? Lord above, sister, stop thinking I carry you to your death and look down the road. What do you see?"

"I . . . well, soldiers, of course. That's what I've been trying to warn you against these past moments!"

"But look at the surcoats of some of them. Since when have Frogs worn the cross of St. George?"

"They're . . . English?" she gasped, tears pricking her eyes as she spotted a tattered white surcoat emblazoned with a red cross. "They're English!"

"Quite," Rowen beamed as she cried for joy, attracting the attention of the soldiers entering the town further down the road.

Through listless groups of sleeping or talking soldiery, they made their way. Most of them looked ill. They all looked hungry. And, even as Rowen set her down so that she might appear before her lord on her own two feet, priests wandered among them hearing confessions.

"Excuse me, sir. Can you direct us to the billot of Wauter of Synford?" asked Rowen of a knightly figure passing by in white steel.

"Direct you? I certainly could, though I must say I haven't a mind to. My brother has seen fit to lodge us in the same dwelling and . . . well . . . for reasons that honor demands my silence, we do hate each other passionately," growled the voice behind the steel, with tantalizing familiarity.

"Hell's bells, Gloucester, is that you?" cried Ermgarde, laughter and tears in her voice.

The visor flew up and indeed it was he. He glared down at her, puzzled by the forwardness exhibited by this scrawny boy. "You presume greatly, lad, to address me so. Who is your master? 'Tis evident he did lack in his schooling of your manners."

She laughed in his face, to his heightened consternation. "Don't you recognize me?"

"Nay, I consort not with riff-raff and lackeys!" he told her disdainfully.

"Not even now?" She pulled back the hood so that his eyes could feast upon the coal-like tresses pinned atop her head.

"Heaven preserve us! Ermgarde! Madam, you are mad!" He flung his arms about her, only lessening his hold when she squealed in pain because of the bruising metal encasing him. "However do you come to be here, and so filthy!" He wrinkled his nose in mock disgust.

"We walked from Harfleur, and I've the holes in my boots to prove it."

"And all for him? For that man up there who won't listen to me although I've tried to explain our innocence a hundred times? I pray you have not come all this way for nought, sweet lady, though in my heart I fear it to be so. My brother, knowing of the animosity between us, did room us together in the hope that we might settle our differences. But it won't work. I intend staying well away from the place in the interest of self-preservation."

"Will you point out the house, then, my lord, so that I might go to him? I fear by the looks of things that our time together will be brief."

Gloucester nodded reluctantly in affirmation. "The battle will like as not take place tomorrow. You will find your lord in the house yonder, the one that has a baker's sign over its door."

"Thank you, my lord duke. And if I should not see you again, good luck tomorrow."

He kissed her hand, unmindful of its filthy state. "We shall need it."

At the door of the baker's shop, Rowen seemed reluctant to go further. "Considering that you and he will be seeing each other for the first time in many weeks, I don't think my presence will be needed. I think I'll go see if I can find Brodrick. Mayhap he'll have something for me to eat."

She gave him a loving hug. "You are the best of brothers. Give me an hour or so."

She watched him move off among the soldiers, her hand lingering on the door to the bare shop. Now that the moment was upon her, Ermgarde was nervous about seeing him, apprehension growing into terror as the moments passed. Unconsciously, she let her down her hair, fluffing it freely about her, so that there would be something feminine in her appearance —a hint of her former self.

Like a thief, she mounted the stairs.

On the first landing were two doors. She knocked on the left one and waited, then inquired of a passing page as to who might occupy the other.

"My Lord Camoys and the Duke of York," he told her, looking her over oddly.

"And the room opposite?"

"The Duke of Gloucester and the Lord Synford."

"Thank you, you've been most helpful. Don't let me detain you longer."

Her voice was so authoritative that he found himself following orders without question. If it hadn't been for the preposterous garb, he'd have sworn her a high-born lady.

When the door was closed and Ermgarde turned her attention to the portal on the right, she gave it a hesitant knock. How would she greet him? Perhaps it was best not to think about it until it happened. There was no answer from within. Lord, don't let him be abroad! She couldn't stand the suspense. She breathed deeply, once, twice, and entered.

He lay atop a bed that had been stripped of its sheets and coverings, his giant's body sprawled so that his booted feet projected from the foot of the bed. His hair had been cropped short like an unruly cap upon his head, and his face shaven. There was darkness circling the eyes and hollows beneath his cheek bones; like the rest of the army, he looked tired.

He slept restlessly, muttering incoherencies as his arms made reflexive movements. Ermgarde closed the door behind her and came to his side.

"Wauter." She spoke softly, lacing fingers in his, squeezing his hand in a surge of love. "Wauter."

She bent over him, lowering her lips to his and kissed his mouth into response. He moaned, an arm coming around to capture her across the shoulders and drag her nearer.

The passion she blazed to life within him also had the power to wake him, and as his sleep ended, so too did the dream.

Amber eyes stared incredulously up into violet ones as reality came flooding in. He bolted up and sent her sprawling with the back of his hand, then wiped his mouth as if her kiss were poisonous.

"You!" Instant rage made it impossible to think of anything else to say. *"You . . . !"*

CHAPTER

29

"AYE, ME!" Ermgarde straightened up, touching her chin indignantly where it had scraped the floorboards, then sat back on her heels. "I had hoped for a warmer welcome after traveling so far."

"You'll get no welcome here, harlot!"

"Obviously. But you will at least listen to me, Wauter, for I will have the truth heard and my innocence proven as fact."

"Nay, I want none of your artful lies!" He made as if to eject her from the room by force, but Ermgarde was not about to be so easily put aside.

In an instant, Rowen's knife was drawn from her belt, its wicked blade pointing at his stomach. "You *will* listen. At least then I shall be at peace with myself, knowing I did all in my power to make you see the truth."

He laughed, an unnerving, vibrating bellow that filled the room and made Ermgarde shrink. Then a hand shot out and caught her wrist with force and pressed until she cried out and dropped the dagger.

"Madam, you are ridiculous. Do you forget I've been schooled for years in the ways of disarming an enemy?"

"I forget nothing, pig-headed mule!"

He leaned over her, resting on one knee, his fingers still about her wrist, forcing her arm backward in a new attempt to inflict pain. She struck out with her free hand, catching him about the ear and cheek where the flesh instantly colored.

She buckled under the force he exerted on her arm, back hitting the floor and legs caught painfully beneath her.

"And I damn you," she choked, "for closing your mind against me!"

"A pointless exercise, my sweet," he spat. "I was cursed the day I laid eyes upon you. You've inflicted more pain than any battle!"

"Nay, I'll not take the blame for that which was self-inflicted! 'Twas nought but your jealous mind that brought about the floundering of our love, that and some wicked planning by Alice."

His face loomed closer, eyes bright with viciousness. "Ah yes, Alice. Would you like for me to tell you about her performance that night we returned to Synford?"

Ermgarde struggled against the hands that grasped her by the shoulders, her head shaking, voice pleading. "Nay, don't speak of it! I know what you did well enough, for she did fling it in my face when I sent her to stay with Maud. I don't want to hear—"

"But surely you don't take exception to my having the consoling talents of another? You had Gloucester, after all. And she was so accommodating, my dear. I think you should take family pride in that. She gave herself with the abandon of a true whore; much like yourself in fact."

"No more, I beg you! You will not be content until you've destroyed everything there was between us, will you?" Ermgarde cried, turning her face from him so that she'd not have to watch him gloating over her hurt.

" 'Tis already destroyed. And tomorrow nothing will matter anyway. We are to fight the French and there are few among us who believe we'll still exist when the battle is done. You are as dead to me now as I shall likely be on the morrow." It took all his will power to say those words, to sever the slender thread that held them together and, contrary to his expectations, he felt no peace or satisfaction in his rejection.

"You lie." Her face turned to him again, the violet pools awash with tears at those words. She would never believe him.

He shook his head stubbornly, avoiding that gaze that sliced to his very soul.

"You want to hit at me and wound me with your tongue, but still you want me, Wauter. You hate yourself for that weakness, yet you cannot be rid of it."

"No!" His voice was gruff in denial as he drew away, he the one now feeling threatened.

"Yes, I say. I'll never be dead to you. And this proves it." The palm of her hand glanced down over the front of his hose where he was rigid with longing.

"Don't touch me." He slapped her hand away, chest expanding powerfully as if to burst the leather thongs that held the jerkin together about his waist. "What I feel for you I would feel for any well-proportioned whore who lay thus before me! I've no love in me, only a basic need to satisfy."

Ermgarde raised herself higher on an elbow, her body coming closer to him, seductively, yet not quite touching him. "More lies, my lord. No doubt you've told yourself them so often that you're half convinced of the truth. But what you feel for me you could never have with another or with whores, because there is love between us, a bond too strong—"

His arm went about her like a band of steel, forcing her breasts against his muscled chest, crushing her with calculated brutality. His mouth found hers and his tongue plundered her, sending the breath from Ermgarde's body.

He broke away, a hand still tangled in her hair where he had held her firm but a moment ago. "Was there love in that? Nay, I'd hardly call it so. Nor in this. . . ." His hands caught the neck of her cotehardie and broke it down the front, buckles rending from cloth. Then he eyed the bindings about her bosom with a frown, disinclined to spend time unwinding them. He took up the dagger Ermgarde had been forced to drop and cut through the fabric ignoring her squeal of fright.

"Do you call this love?" he demanded, certain in his own mind at least that it was not.

He tore the remnants of jerkin from her, then her boots, Ermgarde howling because of the excruciating pain from her roughly handled foot. He gave the bleeding sole a cursory glance, frowned, then took her hose in his hands and forced them down over her flat belly and writhing thighs, throwing them away with a triumphant cry.

"Neither can you call this love." He tossed aside his jerkin, pulled down hose and kicked free of them, knees forcing her modestly closed legs apart.

Ermgarde didn't fight him, knowing that he expected her to, but when he brought her up against him, hands raising her hips so that his first thrust would strike home assuredly, she did admit to a certain amount of trepidation. She cried out, pushed against his chest as if to relieve the pressure that filled her.

He jeered, "Was that a cry of ecstasy I heard from your lips, my sweet? Do I please you?"

She wanted to scream at him that he was a brute, to lash out at him and deny him his pleasure. But that was what he expected. Wanted. For her to say that this wasn't love, that what had been between them was finished. Nay, he wasn't going to win! She had taken him so far; she would bear whatever else came.

"You do please me mightily, lord," she cooed, running arms about his back and bringing his chest down to make sweet contact with her breasts.

Wauter's face hardened, even as his flesh shivered at the nearness of her, at the prominence of her nipples pressed against him, which sent more heat through his veins. Try to play him at his own game, would she?

"What say you to this, then?" His hands ran over her inner thighs so that she parted them still wider, limbs trembling and moving of their own volition. Then he moved at last, not withdrawing a little as she might have hoped, but moving in a circular, grinding motion, his loins molded against her thighs, seeming to burn her flesh.

If his plan was humiliation, to turn her body into a writhing mass begging for mercy, then he had made the wrong move. It was uncomfortable, certainly, to be used so, and she turned her face so that he might not see her teeth sink into her bottom lip to keep her from crying out involuntarily, but it was also . . . .

"I . . . I . . . oh, heavens!"

He stared at her in disbelief, not comprehending for a moment the violent contractions he felt in her depths. She wouldn't dare! But it seemed she *did*. She was actually enjoying it! And as he watched, hypnotized by the misting of her eyes and ecstatic lolling of her head, she caught her fingers in his hair and pulled him down relentlessly until her lips could touch his.

He wouldn't respond, damn it, no! But she was so warm, so soft, her breath searing, her arms clinging about him as if she clutched at life itself. He pushed his tongue between her lips and at that same moment her whole body convulsed and writhed against him.

And the kiss became endless and he lost himself in her, drowning in oceans of sensation, aware only of her desire as he worked upon her, and of his own desire growing, consuming him. When she cried out a second time, legs wrapped about him and fingers kneading his back, her sobs muffled against the harshness of his mouth, he went along with her, took flight and hoped never to return to earth.

The grip of her legs loosened and Wauter eased himself away, coming drunkenly to his feet and looking around for his hose. He'd never bargained on such an outcome. Defeat! She was more lethal than any French knight! He pulled on his hose, found his jerkin, looked anywhere but at her. He could imagine the smug expression on that face, and it was more than his pride could handle.

Ermgarde drew her knees beneath her and sat back on her heels, wondering absently what she would do for clothing now that her cotehardie had been rendered useless. Then she looked up and watched him triumphantly as he hurried about his dressing.

She asked innocently, voice still husky, "What *would* you call that then, dear husband, if not love?"

His jaw clenched in defiance as he went to the door, needing air. "I've no time for classifications now. There are things to do, things to ready for the morrow." Reluctantly, his eyes traveled over her, seeing her creamy flesh as the weapon that had brought him to his knees. "I also have to find something for you to wear."

She smiled, but his frown remained. And then he was through the door banging it resoundingly.

To say that he was stunned by her appearance out of the blue was an understatement. To say that he'd envisaged a meeting between them after what had transpired, ending in his making love to her on the floor of his room, was incredible.

Wasn't he supposed to hate her? Why hadn't he wrung her neck instead? She'd come all this way to protest her innocence. Had walked, like the men in his infantry, her boots wearing out and her feet bloody. Could there be a grain of truth in her story? Would someone of guilty conscience have risked so much to reach him? If only there were time to think about it clearly, to demand her story and scrutinize it. But it was too late this day. There were his men to see to, his harness to be readied, encouragement to be given to the lower ranks. God, he wished he might offer them more than that. Most of them thought they were going to die on the morrow. What comfort or note of optimism could he dish out that sounded remotely true? All he could ask was that they fight their damnedest and die with honor.

At Wauter's pavilion to the north of Maisoncelles, Brodrick was grooming Rogue whilst listening to Rowen's account of his journey. Wauter eyed the younger brother wryly and shook his head. So she had had some protection on her trek, albeit of so useless a kind!

"Rowen, if you and your sister are here, just who is left behind to protect Synford?" he inquired drily.

The lad, faced with a Lord Wauter who was neither thunderous nor out to do murder, was amicable in return. "Why, Lady Margaret, of course, my lord."

"And what am I going to do with you? There will be a battle tomorrow in all likelihood and I don't wish you two involved. You and your sister picked the most inconvenient time to come visiting."

Rowen smiled. "If it pleases your lordship, I thought I might be assigned to look after Rogue and the other horses? That way I'll be away from the battle and you'll have your peace of mind, while I'll be able to watch the spectacle."

"Fair enough. But promise me that should the French break through our ranks and reach this point, that you will go stay with Ermgarde at the town. If you are taken prisoner, do not fight, but state your relationship to me and yield yourself to their protection. The same routine applies to your sister, should the need arise. You will be ransomed."

"Do you think she will agree to staying in the town if you are in danger?" asked Brodrick skeptically, patting Rogue's silky rump, to which the destrier replied with a friendly snort.

"Whether she agrees or not is neither here nor there. She stays at Maisoncelles if I have to manacle her to the leg of my bed! And that reminds me—somehow I must find her some clothes. Who of her size do we know?"

Dusk was falling. There would be no battle this day, since it was unfitting for high-born men to fight in the dark.

Straddling the north road out of Maisoncelles to block the English advance, the French camp was noisy and high-spirited. To the right of the English lines, hidden by one wood, was Tramecourt, many of its houses sacked and set ablaze by the French that day as they marched to their northerly position. To the left, nestled behind the other wood halfway between the armies of France and England, was a nondescript village and its modest castle. It was known as Agincourt.

It was the eve of the feasts of Saints Crispin and Crispinian,

and in the English camp the chaplains prayed to those hal-
lowed two as well as to God to deliver them from their expected doom, to protect them, or at least grant them an
honorable death. A steady rain continued to fall.

When darkness arrived Ermgarde stood with Rowen at the
second-storey window of the baker's shop, feeling better since
donning Gloucester's clothes. The hose were of a dashing
crimson; the cotehardie of black velvet was tucked with a hundred pleats to draw it in snugly at the waist before it flared
again at the hips. Her hair, plaited once more, was fastened in
thick coils about her ears.

"They haven't got a chance, have they?" she stated rather
than asked.

Rowen shook his head in glum agreement.

Around dotted camp fires, the many archers and men-at-
arms who could find no sleep that night made moody conversation or sat in bleak silence, trying not to think of the hunger
gnawing at their bellies, their wet clothes and what their lot
would be on the morrow.

The French, on the other hand, kept up a merry din that did
nothing for English morale. They had traveled as far as their
enemies, true, but they had been well fed on the way, either accepting what was offered by the peasants or taking what was
not. And they felt fresh enough to sit through the night and
throw dice for the prisoners they would take on the morrow,
and to paint a cart in which they intended to carry the captured King of England through Paris.

When, in the dark hours before dawn, her husband and
eldest brother entered, she and Rowen still stood at the window. She turned, heart taking up a speedy tatoo at the sight of
Wauter, his leathers dulled and hair matted by the steady
downpour outside. Then she smiled in a winsome manner that
belied sorrow and kissed her brother, he hugging her with the
gentility of a bear.

He chided jovially, "Of all our father's children you are,
without doubt, the idiot of the brood. You should have stayed
at home."

"Nay, Brodrick, even with tomorrow looming over me. I'm
glad to be here. I would have it no other way."

"We cannot stay long," Wauter told her, feeling, she felt,
uncertain; his thumbs were lodged in the thick belt that drew

his tunic in about the waist, his fingers fidgeted. "We've just come to make our farewells before seeing to the positioning of our men. Dawn will soon be here and the king expects them to attack soon after."

"Of course." She wouldn't make any fuss, for she had never counted upon them having *any* time. She had barely expected him to come and say goodbye. That in itself was a bonus.

"Rowen desires to look after my horses and that I have allowed. But you will stay here. 'Twill be the safest place, Ermgarde. And if . . . if the French should come, don't do anything foolish, *please*! The coffers back at Synford hold enough for your ransom. You understand?"

If she protested at being left there alone, Wauter was capable of locking her in, she knew. So she gave a resigned sigh. "Aye, I understand."

Thank God she appeared to be showing some common sense at last, he thought. He glanced out the window, watching the blackness of sky giving way to the gray light of dawn. He should be gone. Still, he lingered. His eyes settled on her composed features, committing the beautiful face to memory.

"Take care, my lord," she begged him.

"Aye, the greatest of care, never fear. I now have reasons aplenty to stay alive."

Brodrick was at the door, signaling urgently for Rowen to make a hasty exit with him. The younger brother looked back in bemusement. What was he about, gesturing like that? Huh? Ah, yes—the lovers needed a moment to themselves. That must be it. Nodding in understanding, he slipped out of the door unobtrusively to wait below with Brodrick.

Wauter took his wife's hand and raised the palm to his lips, before gathering her possessively into his arms and feeling the silk of her hair against his cheek. "Would that I'd lingered in Bristol long enough that night to listen to your explanations —or this morn for that matter, when you tried to set things straight. God grant that there may come a time when I know the treachery of which you spoke. But if it should not be . . . know, Ermgarde, that in my heart I feel you to be true, am sure of your love."

"Aye—you have it always."

"Then I'm content."

His lips traced her brows and eyelids, cheek, then mouth,

lingering there with a passion that was desperate, as if both wondered whether this last embrace would have to sustain them through eternity.

She wanted to beg him, "Don't go! Don't leave me!" But 'twould have been preposterous. Instead, as he pulled away reluctantly she smiled—a little forced and sad perhaps, but a smile even so—just as Lady Camoys and the rest would have done on seeing their husbands off to war. And it did seem to lift his spirits a fraction, for he smiled back and blew her a kiss before stepping through the door.

CHAPTER
30

AS MORNING BROKE, the two armies—separated by the corn-field where later that day they would fight—prepared themselves for the battle, taking up their positions and making final checks upon harnesses and weapons, longbows and arrows.

The English formation consisted of three main bodies: Lord Camoys commanded the left, the Duke of York commanded the right, and the king—as expected—led from the center. Archers filled the areas between formations and at the flanks, so that they could subject the enemy to a hail of arrows from all sides. Everyone, including the king, would be on foot.

The French formation was less easy to discern, for every duke and count thought it his God-given right to be in the front line, jostling aside the archers and crossbowmen who had the audacity to presume they might fight side by side with their lords! Thus squeezed out onto the flanks, the archers where now blocking the view of the gunners, who found it impossible to keep open a field of fire.

Eventually, the front line consisted of not only the frustrated figures of Constable d'Albret and Marshal Boucicaut, but also the young Duke of Orleans, the Duke of Bourbon, the Counts of Eu and Richemont and hundreds of their knightly companions. They were all on foot, their armor weighty and allowing for little freedom of movement, unlike the English plate which had been developed over the past decades to give something approaching agility to the wearer. So it was with clumsy and deliberate movement that they waited in the front line, shoulder to shoulder, unable to move any way save forward, the ground beneath their feet a wallow of mud.

Behind them was the second, far-less-congested line commanded by the Duke of Alencon and the Duke of Bar. These, too, were on foot, while to the rear and on the flanks were the horse-mounted men-at-arms, commanded by a half-dozen more dukes.

From the English lines, the French were hardly discernible behind their sea of banners, yet their confidence seemed to permeate the cold air of morning, causing the English chaplains to go to work again giving what comfort they could to down-hearted soldiers.

The king appeared after hearing his third Mass of the morning. He was splendidly attired in armor, over which he wore an embroidered surcoat quartered with the arms of England and France—the leopard and fleur-de-lys. His helmet was plated with gold and encircled by a sapphire-and-ruby-studded crown, which also had the added luster of one hundred and thirty pearls.

With sword in hand he addressed his men, reminding them of the just cause for which they fought; of their families back home, for whom they should strive to be victorious; of the victories they had already scored against the odds, in this land; and finally, of the rumor that had reached his ears of the French boast that they would cut the fingers off the right hand of every archer captured. If that wasn't an incentive for them to remain able-bodied and not become prisoners, what was?

Three hours after dawn, with no sign of an attack by the French, the king—though he would rather have been struck by a thunderbolt than admit it—began to worry. It had to be today! Already his men were on the brink of starvation, weary and ill. By the morrow he sensed they'd by *unable* to fight. Could it be that the French were waiting for exactly that to happen, thereby avoiding a battle altogether?

If he started this battle he'd be at a disadvantage, yet neither was he prepared to wait. So he called Sir Thomas Erpingham, who always reminded him affectionately of an old gray goat, and instructed the knight to see that the archers were in readiness. They were, of course. Reluctant but ready, their arrows poised against bowstrings; many of them were naked of armor or mail and, in a few cases, even of their clothing and boots.

Marshaled into an arrowhead formation, Erpingham gave the obligatory cry "Nestrocque!"—now strike—and dismounted to take his place beside the king, a page appearing to retrieve his horse.

Moments later Henry gave the command, "Banners advance! In the name of Jesus, Mary and St. George!" The army fell to its knees and kissed the soil, then standing and drawing weapons, it advanced neither too quickly nor too slowly, since one might be construed as too anxious, the other as too reluctant. A hundred voices called, "St. George," as horns echoed their war cry.

She should have stayed in her room as promised, sat patiently praying and hoping, but neither was Ermgarde's way. Wauter would be furious if he knew. But why should he ever know? His world centered now on meting out death and skirting it himself. He wouldn't ever know.

It was the trumpets that had stirred her, making it impossible to sit still a moment longer, so that in minutes she had scampered into the deserted square of the town and run toward the English camp.

She reached it in time to see Henry and his men crossing the track that ran through the cornfield connecting Tramecourt and Agincourt. And she stood rooted as the advancing body stopped and the longbowmen, using the stakes they had complained about ever since the Duke of York made his suggestion back at Corbie, thrust the sharpened boughs into the ground to form a lethal fence. Behind this fence they took arrows from their belts, nocked them and pulled until goose feathers rested against their cheeks.

Aim. Release. The noise defied description—like a loud whisper or hiss, fast running water, or an ill wind whipped up from nowhere. And in the sky there was a gray cloud that mesmerized the young Frenchmen who knew nothing of Crecy or Poitiers, while those of maturity said their prayers and hoped their armor would deflect the deadly downpour.

All hell broke loose.

Goaded, the army of France went ponderously into action, men-at-arms breaking through the front line of their own men to charge at the enemy, their horses impaled upon the deadly spikes, while many of them sprawled helplessly at the feet of the English archers, who slit their throats or clubbed them to death in double-quick time, the sooner to get back to their own brand of fighting.

Other horses, infuriated by the arrowheads embedded in their hides, ran amok and made a shambles of Charles d'Albret's advance, knocking down knights who were finding it difficult enough to progress. With extreme difficulty, pages pulled their angry masters from the mire and set them lumbering forward once more, heads down to protect their faces from the pelting arrows.

Hoping to present the English archers with less of a target, the French main line split into columns, but the flank archers were able to pick off as many as before. And as the French advanced it became easier still, because the woods drew in toward each other like the narrowing neck of a bottle, forcing the columns closer, until they were a solid mass once more. Their crossbowmen could offer little support at all, fiddling as they were with the ungainly contraptions, while their Welsh and English counterparts were quicker and more accurate with their longbows.

Piles of bodies amassed, with the English archers scrambling over the top, killing the wounded and those who had stumbled and were unable to rise again because of the weight of their armor, Henry's words still fresh in the archers' minds: no one was going to cut their fingers off!

The Duke of Alencon managed to rally some knights about himself and strike against that section of the English army led by the Duke of Gloucester. Gloucester fell wounded, a dagger thrust beneath his breastplate. A cluster of English knights—FitzSimmons and de la Vallée among them—fought off further harm while the king was informed about his brother. They dragged Humphrey—he protesting at the indignity—from the thick of the fight, and in the melee the Duke of Alencon was knocked to the ground.

He couldn't rise, but holding aloft a hand, he called to the receding back of the king, "I am the Duke of Alencon, and I yield myself to you."

Henry turned and held out his hand, but some overzealous Englishman was already dealing death to the duke with an axe.

Carried from the field with much fussing and palaver, Humphrey spotted the lone figure of Ermgarde beside her husband's pavilion almost immediately, instructing his stretcher-bearers to carry him hither.

With his helm removed and in that sparkling white steel, Ermgarde knew who lay atop the stretcher and ran anxiously to him. "My lord duke, are you wounded? Is it serious?"

"Not serious enough to keep me from talking to you. Have you not one ounce of brains in your head?"

"Indeed I have, my lord duke," she stated indignantly. "But I couldn't stay at Maisoncelles and not know what was happening. I've been unable to spot Wauter, but being close to the field gives me a strange kind of comfort."

"I saw your husband but a moment ago. In fact he did fight off those who would have slain me as I lay wounded, much to my great surprise." The duke coughed and grimaced, the surgeon who hovered near looking worried. "I presume 'tis pointless to order you back to Maisoncelles?"

She nodded, bestowing upon him a stubborn smile.

"Then take my helm, at least. 'Twill offer some protection should the need arise, and hide from good men, who need no such diversion at this time, the fact that you are a woman."

"Thank you. By and by, how goes the fighting? From here 'tis little more than a confusing mass of color."

"Better than I had hoped. As yet we are holding our own." He turned his eyes to the surgeon. "Get me to thy tent. My guts are mightily sore."

Better than he had hoped? Could she trust Gloucester's word, or had he consoled her, keeping false hope alive? Nay, her friend would not be so cruel. If it was hopeless, he would have told her.

Ermgarde put on the helm, instantly claustrophobic inside the steel shell, and lowered the visor. Vision was limited to straight ahead, but she could see well enough. Thus protected, mightn't she go forward just a little more?

After all, Rowen was disobeying orders, too, standing at the rear of the English men-at-arms instead of staying at the pavilion as he had promised Wauter. And from here she really couldn't tell what was going on, couldn't make out her husband . . . .

The Duke of Brabant, younger brother of the Duke of Burgundy, arrived late and missed the beginning of the battle. It was a wonder he was there at all, being ordered to stay away by John the Fearless, who used a christening party as his own excuse for his absence.

And, as the French spirits sagged a little, knights falling in their hundreds while striving ineffectually to better the paltry number of English, the Burgundian appeared on the scene in a suit of armor borrowed from his chamberlain, for his own harness had not yet arrived at camp with his servants.

He charged down the field, attempting to rally the French—
some of whom were even then sneaking away. He stopped and
grasped a fallen banner from a trumpet, slashed a hole in it
with a dagger and put his head through the hole to wear it as a
surcoat. Then off he charged again, a few loyal followers behind him now as he brandished his spear at the English and
shouted, "Brabant! Brabant!"

He was knocked to the ground and captured forthwith, but
Henry was made decidedly uneasy by the display of defiance.

The French captives were so numerous now that should the
reluctant rearline under Lammartin, Marle and Fauquem-
berghes decide to charge the enemy, Henry guessed those prisoners might well take up what arms they could and attack their
captors from the rear.

It was a dangerous state of affairs.

Only the removal of strong leaders kept the French inde-
cisive upon their next move, he knew. With Charles d'Albret
dead, Boucicaut and the Duke of Orleans and Duke of Bourbon captured, the French had begun to indulge once again in
their favorite pastime—interfactional bickering. Burgundians
wouldn't serve under Armagnacs and vice-versa; Brentons,
Gascons and Poitevins refused to serve under any of them!

All the prisoners would have to be killed. It was Henry's
only way to hang onto the advantage he had and avoid dis-
aster. His men took the order badly. It wasn't that their feelings were any more compassionate than Henry's, but rather
that they did not wish to give up expected ransom money.

The slaughter ceased only when it became clear that the
French attack would be a half-hearted affair; Brabant had
died amongst them, his borrowed armor and improvised surcoat leading his captors to believe he was of little value as a
prize of war.

"Oh, the blood! If there were ought in my stomach, 'twould
be up by now," groaned Ermgarde, as gray-faced and ill-
looking as the brother beside her.

"Let's go back to town and wait. I've had enough of this
place," urged Rowen, looking very childlike at that moment.
It would be several years before he could approach battle and
its subsequent carnage with the same coldness and dedication
as Brodrick; perhaps not even then.

Ermgarde was willing to go. She had spied Wauter and her

brother not long since and neither looked the worse for wear. But Brodrick was calling to her brother now, urging him to bring their horses quickly, for they were at a disadvantage against the mounted French.

The lad ran back to the pavilion and untethered Rogue and Brodrick's mount, Boris, both fully equipped in case of just such an eventuality.

She could see Wauter among the hay-stack-high piles of dead and wounded. Robert de la Vallée—who had already gained his horse—gave the lord what protection he could against the final French assault. Yet Wauter seemed hardly aware of the danger, contemptuous even, and pressed forward against one mounted figure after another, cutting the mounts from beneath them, then finding the vulnerable area in the floundering knight's harness and attacking it with sword or dagger.

The "Sire de Morte." The French had named him well. At this moment he looked immortal. Even so, Ermgarde's fear was acute, causing her heart to thump in her breast as she called out impatiently, "Don't dally, Rowen!"

In truth, he was hurrying as fast as he could, Boris needing a great deal of coaxing to cross the battlefield that stank of death and made his ears prick back warily. Brodrick ran to meet him, jumping into the saddle and spurring the reluctant Boris forward. Rogue's reins were firmly in his hand, though the veteran destrier needed no coaxing to taste battle.

When Wauter was atop the steed, Ermgarde's fears lessened and she allowed herself a sigh. He *wasn't* immortal, and it only took one slip, one lapse in concentration . . . . Even the king, guarded jealously though he was by the knights of his household, had had one of the fleuron struck from his crown by an unknown assailant, and his helm had been dented by a battle-axe.

The French, humiliated and angry, seeing this last attempt to save the day coming to nought, began to disperse from the field in all directions. Ermgarde took cover behind the nearest cart as one of them came charging by taking vengeful swipes with his sword at anything that moved, hacking his way through servants and pavilions, then disappearing into the wood of Maisoncelles.

She lifted her visor to determine better what had become of Rowen, and saw him running toward her—with two mounted

French knights bearing down upon him. She could tell by the
lack of concern on his face that he was merely running to be
quit of the battlefield, had no inkling of what was fast coming
from behind. She shrieked with terror, the horror in her voice
seeming to reverberate inside her steel helm, distorted and
deafening.

"Rowen! *Rowen!*

What she could have done to save him was negligible, but
she ran forward, ran and ran, yet seemed to get no nearer; she
howled as the first knight sliced Rowen's cheek with his sword
blade, and willed her brother keep moving, to reach her outstretched arms.

But he'd stopped, shock running through him, though
strangely he felt no pain. It was as if his body had been
drained of bones; he collapsed and sank to the ground.

"Oh, Rowen!" With an anguished wail she ran still, went
through the motions of moving her legs even when the first
knight had caught her beneath the arms and scooped her up to
lie across his saddle.

The battlefield receded through the slits of her visor, her
older brother and Wauter still fighting, oblivious to her plight,
not yet aware of Rowen's death. She tried to call out and
couldn't, choking on her sobs, her view growing blurred and
uncertain with tears. Wauter was but a shadow growing dim-
mer.

BOOK
Three

Then for sothe that knyghte comely,
In Agincourt feld he faught manly;
Thorow grace of God most myghty,
He had both the felde, and the victory.
                    Deo gratias:
Deo gratias Anglia redde pro victoria.

Ther dukys, and erlys, lorde and barone,
Were take, and slayne, and that wel done,
And some were ledde into Lundone,
With joye, and merthe and grete renone.
                    Deo gratias:
Deo gratias Anglia redde pro victoria.

—Verses 4&5 Agincourt battle hymn.

CHAPTER

31

By LATE AFTERNOON, the light fading fast as rain again set in, Ermgarde was in deepest despair. Each mile they covered took her further from Wauter, safety and the haven of Calais that had been so tantalizingly within reach.

Riding behind her abductor on a swift horse, her arms linked about his waist and cuffed to impede escape, she looked over the straggly column of mounted soldiers with whom she rode and damned them all vehemently. One in particular, though, dressed in rusty colored leathers, was doubly damned; every brutish facet of him burned in her mind, to be remembered. He had killed her brother.

Her throat constricted once more and the sobbing began, lessening only when the man seated before her jabbed an elbow into her ribs, sick and tired of her intermittent wailings, his hissed words of annoyance so much nonsense to her ears. She gulped, sniffed, forced grief into silence once more.

When, in mounting darkness, they approached a poor-looking hamlet and many of the peasants stole off seeking safety in the night, Ermgarde could understand their fears only too well. These soldiers were disappointed with the day's work. They relieved their frustrations on whoever and whatever was still in the hamlet. Ermgarde was left hobbled amongst the horses as a prize of war, able to do nothing save close her eyes behind the visor.

The humble dwellings were sacked; anything of value was pocketed by the soldiers or, if unappealing, thrown into the mud of the street. The unfortunates who hadn't managed to flee in time were put to the sword, or, if they were female and not yet turned haggard with age, raped and then killed.

Ermgarde moaned, her empty stomach rolling in nauseous waves, her eyes opening as she heard the agonized breathing of someone running in her direction and saw an old man, who

screamed when the point of a pole-axe was thrust between his
shoulder blades. He twitched awhile near her feet, then was
still, the horses backing off skittishly from his form.

Oh God, help me!

Her abductor, his hose hanging down about his knees, was
finding relief between the legs of a screaming woman, her
limbs spread-eagled by helpful soldiers who urged him on and
laughed uproariously at the spectacle.

Would that be her lot when her helm was eventually taken
and they discovered her a woman instead of a male member of
the Duke of Gloucester's household? Nay, they wouldn't
dare, would they? She was a lady, and not to be so used! And
mayhap, she prayed, after taking their pleasure of and frustrations out on these poor wretches, they would not be inclined to
want a woman for some time. She would be able to reason
with them, warn them that any abuse to herself would bring
savage retribution from her husband. She would dangle her
ransom like a tasty morsel before them, but only on condition
that she remained unharmed, untouched.

But what if these brutes knew no other but their own
uncivilized tongue, what if she couldn't make herself understood, or they were unchivalrous enough to violate her and
then demand ransom? There was little to give her hope of
being treated according to her station.

The man behind whom she had been forced to ride had now
finished his cold and methodical rape and stood rearranging
his hose, face as grim as ever through his raised visor.

A cottage further down the road was set on fire, black
billows of smoke belching from its unshuttered windows.
Somewhere a woman, having satisfied these men's appetites,
screamed and begged for mercy, her shrill cries ending in a
gurgle as she was stabbed in the heart.

Nay, I'll *not* let it happen to me!

Crouching behind the horses and lurching toward the dead
man before her, Ermgarde resolutely put aside her horror at
the ghastly sight of his pierced back, and took his hood. Then,
behind cover of their mounts, she exchanged helm for hood,
certain that they'd have little interest in the latter and therefore be unlikely to relieve her of it. The longer her identity
was kept secret, the better. It would give her time to think,
something that her brain was reluctant to do at that moment,
dazed and numbed as it was with grief. Give her time.

*   *   *

The Chevalier Saint-Luc was only slightly mollified by taking a hostage, the one and only compensation in this whole disastrous business.

Who could have said with conviction that before noon of the same day the might of France would lay trodden in the mire of Agincourt by so piffling a foe? It was a monstrous humiliation, even for him, and as a Burgundian he had no love for Charles VI and his Armagnacs and Orleanists.

Ah, but why so glum? Didn't he have a hostage? That was more than most of the French could boast of achieving that day. And weren't his deadly enemies, Bourbon and Orleans taken temporarily out of action? With luck it would be years before Charles VI's treasury could shoulder the burden of paying their ransom!

One had only to look at the helm he had taken from the lad as a trophy of war to know he'd pulled in a handsome catch. And crested with the arms of Gloucester, the cotehardie was spun with sumptuous fabric. A member of the duke's household, obviously, and of rich background. Aye, someone would want him back, crybaby though he was. It was just a matter of ascertaining his rank and from whom a ransom was to be demanded; that, Etienne Saint-Luc would do once he reached his home in Burgundy. Up until then, however, he must concentrate on crossing Charles VI's lands with the minimum of incident.

At Reims they stole fresh horses and, twenty-odd miles further south, after crossing the River Marne, stole more food from frightened peasants living in a hamlet on the outskirts of Epernay. It was a staunchly pro-Armagnac region, so the Burgundians wisely refrained from further sacking and murder, keeping as low a profile as possible and only surfacing when more food was needed, much to Ermgarde's relief.

What struck her most about the countryside was the lack of human habitation away from the great cathedral cities like Reims, and the widespread desolation. The peasants seemed to have given up in favor of a safer haven behind the fortified walls of the towns.

On most roads were shells and decaying ruins of what had once been cottages and farms, deserted by people sick and tired of raising crops or livestock only to have them razed to the ground or slaughtered for someone's army. The war in France had gone on for many years and the end was nowhere in sight.

Moving westerly down through Champagne, Troyes not many miles ahead, they were set upon by soldiers from the duchy of Bar, located not too far to the east. The marauders swarmed down upon the road from their hiding places in the trees. Both sides looking to be equal enough in numbers, her abductor encouraged his men to fight rather than flee, his own mount already wheeling to face the first of the attackers head-on.

Ermgarde, loath as she was to make closer contact, clung tighter about her abductor's waist, head low against the rough leather of his jerkined back. She closed her eyes and prayed for herself *and* for the men with whom she rode. Better to be in the hands of Burgundians whose duke was allied to Henry V, than be taken by supporters of Charles VI.

Having beaten off the attack successfully and with only minor injuries, they left the retreating soldiers cursing behind them and sped on, the Chevalier Saint-Luc possessed suddenly of the strangest sensation.

The lad clinging fearfully to him was extraordinarily soft against his back, the contact even pleasant. Saints preserve him! He shivered in self-disgust, pulling instantly away from his alluring passenger, a cold sweat breaking out on his forehead. God strike him down for having even remotely entertained such forbidden thoughts! What he needed, most definitely, was a good woman, and no, he wouldn't think about the thighs contoured around his own, the clinging arms. . . .

After their next stop for rest, Ermgarde found herself hoisted behind another rider and wondered briefly at the change. The vile fact was that her new companion was the monster who had slain her brother and, when her hands were tied in front at his waist and his closeness was inescapable, she couldn't control her enraged trembling.

They moved on, Burgundy before them, the Chevalier Saint-Luc feeling easier now that he rode alone, certain that his friend, Guillaume Lansier—who was not averse to taking his pleasure with others of his own sex—would relish the disturbing presence of the lad as he could not.

CHAPTER

32

THE MIRACLE had happened. God had listened to their prayers and had blessed them, Henry was apt to believe.

When the battle was ended and the few French who had not already done so, either fled or surrendered, the English saw before them a clear road to Calais. Though the road was heaped with bodies, there was jubilation.

The clearing of the field began, the king knighting Dafydd ap Llewelyn ap Hywel as he lay dying in the mire, then listening sadly as more names were recited to him as being among the dead: The young Earl of Suffolk, following quickly in the wake of his father who had died of dysentery at Harfleur; Sir Richard Kyghley; Walter Lord and, perhaps the most distinguished of the English dead, the Duke of York, who had stumbled and fallen during the battle, unwounded, to die of suffocation beneath a pile of other bodies. But the losses were low, barely over a hundred, while the French dead numbered around eight-and-a-half thousand!

It appeared that half the nobility of France had been wiped out in one morn, as surcoats and banners were identified and bodies were relieved of their valuables. Charles d'Albret, Constable of France; the Dukes of Brabant, Bar, Alencon; the Counts of Nevers, Marle, Vaudemont, Blamont, Graupre; and so on. There were also prisoners, some one thousand six hundred of them in all. Marshal Boucicaut, the Dukes of Orleans and Bourbon and the Counts of Richemont, Eu and Vendome were among them—what ransoms there would be!

Wauter laughed in amazement, hugging and being hugged by his fellow lords as they came dazedly from the field, spirits as high as if they were drunk. He reined the sturdy Rogue behind them.

" 'Tis hard to believe, hey, Waut?" choked Thomas Erpingham, his emotions about to boil into tears of relief and wonderment.

"Scarcely . . . scarcely. And the archers—were they not magnificent?"

"Filled me with pride. I think it was the talk that the king gave them. Put the fear of the French, if not God, into them."

"My lord!" Brodrick called to him, voice atremble with emotion.

Wauter's joy disappeared instantly and he left a startled Sir Thomas as sudden fear flooded over him. Oh God, it was Ermgarde! Nay, nay, she was safe at Maisoncelles. She had *promised*. . . .

He drew near to Brodrick, could see the awkwardly prone figure half shielded by the kneeling squire, and knew it to be Rowen by the color of his hose. "Oh, dear God!"

He sank to his knees on the other side of the dead boy, half his mind bathed in relief that it wasn't his wife, the other half aflame with remorse. If he'd never allowed the lad to attend to Rogue and Boris at the pavilion. . . . Too late!

Rowen, poor thing, looked startled even in death, his eyes wide and blank. Wauter wanted to shake him, cuff him about the ear as he had on past occasions when the boy indulged in some prank or mischief, wanted to say brusquely, "Enough, stop your silly-assing and get up!" But this time it wouldn't work. Rowen wasn't suddenly going to jump to his feet and laugh at them, jeering, "Ha, fooled you again!"

"Who could have done it, lord?" questioned Brodrick, gently wrapping his own surcoat embellished with a St. George cross about the torso of the lad, wishing to cover the unsightly wound so his brother was whole again.

"A man devoid of honor, Brodrick. I know no more. But Rowen wore no helm, nor harness and he was unarmed."

"Would that I knew his name and could track him down."

"I know. But there can be no way of telling, no chance for revenge. Were there any, I would seek it above all else, for 'twas my doing that Rowen was near the field . . . my fault. . . ."

"Nay, lord, nay!" Brodrick clasped the other's hand, denying it vehemently in the hope of stalling the lord's distraught tears. " 'Twas as he wanted it—to be near the battle. There's no fault or blame to be shouldered. Please, lord, go break this news gently to my sister, for I could not undertake such a deed. She always loved him dear because he was the baby amongst us. You'll know better than I how to console her."

"Aye, I'll do that." Wauter nodded, reluctantly rising to his feet. "But shall I not give you a hand with him first?"

"I'll manage. He weighs but little. The king has instructed that a pyre be built in one of the barns near the town. I'll find a priest to say a few words over him, then take him there."

Wauter nodded, drying his face on his sleeve. Better that finale than the one for the Duke of York and Earl of Suffolk, whose bodies would be boiled so their bones could be more easily ferried back to England.

Wauter searched until the light began to fade—through the camp and pavilions, the town and approaches, then the battlefield itself, sifting through the bodies amassed there and stripped of clothing and armor. He never expected to find her among the dead but was compelled to probe every possibility. Surely if a woman had been found among the dead someone would have commented on the fact.

His fears multiplied as he made his way to the barn on the outskirts of Maisoncelles. It was already beginning to burn, the torch-brandishing soldiers falling back as a red glow glared through open doors and loft moments before flames engulfed the structure. She wasn't in there! She couldn't be.

"Brodrick!" He swung the startled youth about to face him, face frantic. "Have you seen your sister?"

The squire shook his head in bewilderment, ceasing the prayers he'd been mumbling beside the chaplains. "No, of course not. Why should I have? She's at Maisoncelles."

"She's not. Gloucester says she came to watch the battle. I've looked everywhere, but there's no sign of her. Nothing. They wouldn't have put her in there, would they? *Would they*! My God, don't let her be dead! Don't let that be my punishment for having mistrusted her!"

Brodrick looked at his master agape. The older man seemed to teeter on the edge of insanity, the human bonfire igniting a crimson brilliance in his eyes that made the lad want to cross himself.

"She's not in there, lord, believe me. More than likely she's helping tend the wounded back in the town and you've overlooked her. Come, let us search some more."

"Yes, yes, let's do that. Of course she's not dead. I'm not

thinking logically, that's all. She's some place I didn't think to search, in no danger at all," Wauter told himself reassuringly, a nervous laugh escaping him.

Brodrick prayed it was so, and cursed Ermgarde for causing the man such anxiety by her disobedience. He didn't doubt she'd receive a thrashing for this day's piece of idiocy, and well she'd deserve it.

"Look out for a white steel helm. Gloucester told me he lent her his," Wauter informed the squire as they moved away from the barn.

"A white steel helm?" Instantly a scene from that morning flashed into Brodrick's mind: Rowen leading the horses onto the field so they could be ready for the final attack from the French. Beside an empty cart that had been used to carry armor plate, stood a youth in crimson hose and black cotehardie, wearing a white steel helm. He remembered the lad solely because of the stunning helm. The image had fled from his mind as the onslaught had peaked. Now he realized, without a doubt, that the lad had been his sister in disguise.

"I saw her, lord," he said quietly, voice a little tremulous, for he couldn't know what Wauter's reaction would be. "She was standing near where I found Rowen. I remember the helm."

Wauter took the news better than the lad had expected. "Then there is some hope of her being alive, don't you see? If she had been killed, wouldn't we have found her body near Rowen's? She's been taken, that's the only answer if a further search of the town yields nothing. Someone saw the helm she was wearing and thought her a fair prize."

He was clutching at straws and they both knew it, but nothing would have induced them to say so, to have broken that thread of hope.

"Sounds plausible, lord. But who would have taken her? How can we seek them out if we know not who we're after?"

Wauter frowned at this far from slight problem. Who indeed: Orleanists, Burgundians, Armagnacs or Gascons?

"If she had been taken, lord—and there seems no other explanation—there will be a ransom, surely? Wouldn't it be better then to go back to Synford and await the demand? We'll only be looking for a needle in a haystack otherwise."

"Nay, I couldn't sail for home knowing she's still here. Think. . . Think. The final attack made by the French came

just after that piece of pointless bravado by the Duke of Brabant. Half the men in the attack were his followers, Burgundians. There's a fifty-fifty chance therefore that she was taken
by one of them."

"You'll go to Brabant in search of her?"

Wauter was thoughtful. "Nay, I doubt I'd find her there.
Most of the duke's followers are from Burgundy itself. I'll go
to John the Fearless, offer myself in exchange for my wife
until ransom is paid. He'll know if any of his own hold her."

When Humphrey of Gloucester, stiff with bandages and
stony faced, entered the king's quarters that evening for a
select celebration supper, no one noticed. They were all too
busy being surprised by Wauter of Synford at his side. The
two men actually appeared to be together—even talking, by
God!

As they stepped up to the king's table, Henry's eyes glinted
at the sight of the reconciled knights. He held aloft his goblet
and some swift-footed prisoner refilled it, no doubt seething at
having to serve at the table. Henry ignored him. He was
watching his brother and Wauter, his lids curtained over eyes
like a wise and watchful owl. "Well, why do you not take your
seats?" They wanted something, he could tell.

"My king, brother. . .I would have your ear first, for Lord
Wauter wishes a favor."

"Then speak, my lord. This night you find me in an ame-
nable mood."

"Sire. . ." Wauter paused, every avenue of approach
sounding doubtful to his mind. "Sire, yesterday, and with
considerable surprise, I found that my wife had followed me
here."

"She *what*!" Henry gave an unregal splutter with a mouth-
ful of chicken.

"We had some bad feelings between us when I left England
and she came to set things aright."

The king had recovered himself. "And I take it, seeing you
once again on companionable terms with my brother, that
things *were* set aright?"

"Indeed, sire."

"Then where is the lady Ermengarde now? I'll admit the notion of women in army camps does not greatly please me, but I
can forgive her that, she being young, impetuous and *very*

beautiful. Is it that you thought to ask my permission to have her attend this supper, mayhap? If so, of course there is a place for her. We would enjoy her company greatly, my lords, would we not?''

There was a rumbled "Aye" of approval.

"Nay, sire, 'twas not for such a favor I pleaded your ear. You see, she is gone. Abducted, I believe, by some Burgundians during the final attack. Her impetuosity, as you called it, drew her to the battlefield when I had forbidden her to leave my quarters."

"Gone, you say? What, as a hostage? Well, confound it! No conception of chivalry, these French, that's the trouble with them. Making war on women—where's the honor in that, I ask you?''

An air of indignity permeated the room.

"She was dressed as a lad, sire, in your brother's clothes and helm, to be precise. And 'twas for a lad, I believe, they took her."

Henry lifted a brow. "What is your part in all this?" he asked of this brother.

"Nothing of import, my king. I but lent her badly needed clothing, as my Lord of Synford has already said, and later, my helm. I've come here with my lord because I feel a duty to help him. 'Twas because of misunderstandings betwixt us— the nature of which you are aware—that this lady undertook so perilous a journey on foot to reach him. I wish to help him find her by putting myself and my men at his disposal."

Henry shook his head steadfastly. "I cannot permit that, brother, and well you know it. When I return to London your place must be beside me in the victory procession. You understand this, don't you, Wauter? Not for anything would I hamper your quest, but . . . ."

"I understand, sire, and have already put such arguments to the duke. I've men enough under my command already and, if you would return to my service the Knight de la Vallée, I will ask no more, save your leave to part on the morrow."

"You have it."

"But I *want* to go!" protested Humphrey, expecting arguments from his brother ever since this notion of rescue had surfaced in his mind. "I swore myself her champion and I have the right—"

"My Lord of Synford is his lady's champion, brother, before all others. I think we can safely leave him to cope with all that such a position entails. Now come, let us eat. I'll call for the Count of Vendome to serve you your wine. That will cheer you."

Humphrey remained petulant.

CHAPTER
33

GUILLAUME LANSIER WAS indeed enjoying the company afforded by the unwilling passenger who sat stiffly behind him; stiffly, but no less exciting for that. He'd enjoyed the women at the village they'd sacked, his appetite sated only after two violent rapes that ended in death. But this boy was stirring him anew, the slim firmness of thighs pressed into the back of his legs. His loins were roused to a hungry throbbing. He prayed that Etienne would leave him alone with the lad on their arrival at the chevalier's fortress of Chemille-sur-Seine, which he held for his liege-lord, John the Fearless; he grinned and licked his lips at the prospect.

Ermgarde could never recall with clarity her arrival at the chateau of Chemille. She saw neither the ancient gray stone walls jutting from a natural ridge, nor the towers scraping the low clouds, nor the dry ditch straddled by drawbridge. Seated behind her brother's murderer, she held nothing in her mind but a loathing so strong that she plotted one scheme after another for his speedy demise.

They entered the ward as green-tunicked servants scurried to take the reins of horses and tried to anticipate their masters' wishes.

The Chevalier Saint-Luc seemed weary and slid stone-like from his mount, acknowledging no one as he strode toward the outside wooden staircase that led up to the first storey of the keep.

"Wine and food are being readied, monsieur," informed an obsequious servant, shuffling behind him with a servile stoop to his shoulders.

"I want nought but my bed. I trust the sheets have been changed since the last time I slept in it?" He still didn't bother to glance at the eager-to-please retainer.

"Of course, monsieur. And a sprig of lavender or two to lend a sweet scent."

The chevalier mocked him. "You did not need to go *that* far! I will have an afternoon of rest, then you may bring me food and wine, and a comely wench—if such can be found in this pest-hole."

"Yes, monsieur, it will be seen to. There is a new girl in the kitchens; Daphne. A virgin still and fresh as a daisy."

"Then go tell her to prepare for the honor of being bedded by her master with the coming of evening," said Etienne in a bored tone.

Guillaume was calling to him from below, his gauntlet-encased hands about the shoulders of the English captive. "What are your orders concerning the hostage?"

Guillaume champed at the bit, it seemed, and Etienne saw no reason to deny his pleasure. It might put the English brat in a more cooperative frame of mind when he came to deal with him later. "You see to him for now. I've neither the stamina nor inclination."

The Chevalier Lansier's grin turned lascivious. "With the greatest of pleasure."

Ermgarde was worried. She had expected to have her identity unveiled by now, and her captors parceling out some degree of hospitality as befitted the wife of a lord. She didn't expect to be dragged off somewhere by the brute who had slain Rowen without a qualm, and from whom she could expect little courtesy.

At best she had expected to be escorted to a chamber, at worst, an oubliette beneath ground level, but the stables, where she found herself with the paunchy brute who seemed in charge, made a disquietingly odd prison.

"What are we doing here?"

His grin didn't falter and it was obvious he knew no English, had no interest in what she said anyhow. He closed and barred the door, snatching her to him instantly and caressing the roundness of her buttocks. "Ah, mon petite guerrier!"

"Get your hands off me, you vile pig!" she shrieked at him in disgust and horror, suddenly knowing what he was about. He believed her a boy and, heaven forbid, he wanted to enjoy her as one!

Her body recoiled so violently that she was free of him momentarily and ran to reach the bar across the door. But he was too close behind and tore at her clothes and, though she struggled and shrieked, he tossed her into a pile of hay in the stable corner, his corpulent weight atop of her, hands ripping, tearing.

The cotehardie of good-quality velvet resisted his savage fingers for a while as she fought him off, but the fabric tore and she felt the chill air about her back. She shrieked again, a louder, more frantic cry this time.

Her hose came down, baring soft buttocks and slim thighs and as the knight would have fallen upon her with his own hose about his knees, and taken his pleasure, Ermgarde rolled away from him as best she could.

He caught her angrily, wrenched the cotehardie away from her arms, and was about to snatch her hood with the same impatience, when his eyes caught sight of her breasts. Ermgarde didn't know for sure but guessed that he was swearing, a string of heated, incredulous words spilling from his lips.

He ripped the hood away, eyes opening wider in a way that heralded greater danger, and Ermgarde writhed to be free of him, choking disgustedly as words of appeal seemed to fail her.

Guillaume couldn't believe his eyes. He'd hoped for a slim, handsome boy, but had captured a goddess instead, her rosy nipples causing him to lick lips, her opulent form as she struggled beneath him, resembling the body of Venus. So creamy soft, like silk or velvet; the tiny curls between her legs a midnight sky lit by stars! Ah, oh, that face and hair!

He caught the braids, wrenching them savagely from her crown, unwinding them with frantic fingers as his weighty torso kept her trapped. Magnifique! Such a crowning glory.

If only she had a red-hot poker! Ermgarde screamed, her harrowing cry seeming to make the walls of the stable shudder.

Etienne found the shrieks annoying. They kept him from sleeping and, climbing from his bed in nought but a loincloth, he descended the external staircase of the keep and demanded of his sargeant-at-arms, "Why such an infernal din?"

"The English boy has no liking for Monsieur Lansier's approach, I think."

"He sounds more like a girl."

"I was thinking the same, monsieur. But what else would you expect from the English?"

There was another piercing scream, this one causing every soldier and servant in the ward to pause in their occupations.

Etienne scrambled quickly down the stairs, drawn to the barn and the crowd who had gathered about it, peeping through the gaps of planking where the caulking had broken away.

"Monsieur, 'tis a woman!"

"I was watching," volunteered another, "when he took away her hood. A vision of beauty. How come no one knew?"

"A woman?" Etienne pushed through them, ignoring the urge to peep as they had done, feeling that he should appear above such behavior. He pounded on the barred door of the barn, calling icily for Lansier to open up.

Inside, the knight barely heard, so busy was he trying to keep his vision still long enough to gain entry to her harbor of earthly delights.

"Open up, I say!"

Ermgarde was sobbing by this time, her flesh bruised about thighs and hips where he had pinched and probed at her, trying to unlock her legs.

Then the door caved inward and there was the far greater shame of everyone beholding her nakedness, as Lansier sprang away from her, his face florid with rewardless exertion and anger at the interruption.

"Guillaume, explain!" Saint-Luc demanded.

Ermgarde tried to cover herself as the soldiers moved forward, their leader before them.

"I cannot." Guillaume pulled up his hose self-consciously, trying to hide the throbbing in his unsatisfied loins as the soldiers sniggered behind their master. "I thought him . . . her . . . . Hell, I cannot explain. 'Twould seem our hostage was a well-disguised woman!"

The Chevalier Saint-Luc scrutinized her from hooded blonde brows, startled but relieved by the revelation. The desire he had felt with her behind him on that horse had not been so unnatural afterall, then! He wasn't becoming jaded or perverted as he had feared, but had responded healthily, albeit unknowingly, to female flesh. He felt better.

But how come he had never suspected? She was undeniably a woman! Kneeling in the straw, her delicate oval face crimson with shame, her limbs and body barely covered by her mantle of blue-black hair, she was having a devastating effect upon his men. Etienne could sense the rising anticipation and de-

sires, his own along with theirs, barely contained by the linen
of his loincloth.

Who she was or what she had been doing on a battlefield
dressed as a boy, he couldn't begin to imagine. At the moment
he wasn't really interested. He could think of nothing but
creamy limbs, a luxurious black mane, and two pools of bottomless, fear-glazed violet. Let Guillaume find his pleasure
someplace else, he decided. She was Etienne Saint-Luc's prize
of war!

He turned to one of his men and demanded a cloak of him,
throwing it to Ermgarde. "Cover yourself, demoiselle."

She needed no coaxing, fearing that the men's patience
might waver at any moment and they would fall upon her like
a pack of wolves. The flimsy cloak of threadbare wool was not
much protection, but she felt safer, her terror receding. It appeared that her captor had something of the gentleman about
him after all; he might show her some measure of compassion.

Etienne turned and his men instinctively made a path for
him to the open door, then he barked another order over his
shoulder, which Ermgarde guessed was directed at her. "Follow me. There is a chamber beyond the stairs where we will be
more comfortable."

Perhaps he wasn't so awful, Ermgarde decided, putting
from her mind the sacked village where the knight's lusts had
shown themselves in their basest and cruelest form. Armies
always did such things and there was no point denying it, even
to one's self. Pious Henry's force had committed violations
against church and mankind at Fecamp.

The French knight was, she guessed, in his mid-twenties,
with a youthful frame and lean physique not troubled by the
maladies of his seniors. Decency forbade close scrutiny of a
man in such a state of undress unless he be one's husband, she
reminded heself. No, she wouldn't think of Wauter now. It
was difficult enough to stay level-headed as it was without her
loss filling her with forlornness.

Aye, the knight had a handsome physique and the noble
features to complement it. He was blond, his close-cropped
locks fine and pale like sun-ripened corn, his face evenly fea-
tured and perhaps unremarkable—save for a determined chin
and almond-shaped eyes the color of cornflowers. And when
he smiled, as Ermgarde had noted just now, his pleasant face
was faintly disarming.

They moved through a gloomy hall that was devoid of banners and the like, past trestle tables and laboring servants who were frantically seeing to the preparations of some sort of meal. Up winding stairs that were lit by small embrasures and arrow slits, to the chamber of which he had spoken.

Ermgarde felt unease. She expected a solar or a visitor's chamber, but it was easy to guess whose room he had brought her to. His personal effects were everywhere; arms, clothing and dusty old volumes were thrown carelessly into a corner, the odd cloak or hood pin scattered atop dusty tables. He made no comment on the mess and seemed quite at home.

Ermgarde steeled herself as the door was bolted behind her and the knight kicked aside a well-worn shoe to stand before her. Nay, there was no need to be afraid. She had but to explain and chivalry would win the day.

"Sir, I think I should explain, the quicker for you to send to England for my ransom. I am Ermgarde of Synford, wife to—"

He snatched away the cloak, leaving her nothing but her mantle of raven hair, the calm decisive look upon his face making her take a few steps backward to the door, a gasp of fear escaping her lips.

Instinctively her hands covered her woman's self, then beat against his chest as he leaped upon her and pulled aside the heavy tresses.

"You can talk to me later. For now, demoiselle, I've but one pressing desire." He hooked his fingers in the hair of her crown and forced her to remain still for a kiss as he caught her in a firm embrace.

Feeling his manhood already hard against her belly, she fought the harder and managed to free her mouth and cry in outrage, "Lay a hand upon me and my husband will slice you like bacon!"

"Where is this husband of yours? I do not see him," the chevalier reminded her, acidly. "I'll solve such problems when and if the time comes. For the moment I'm interested only in discovering the secrets of your body, of enjoyment. Forget about your husband. He need never know. I certainly wouldn't be unchivalrous enough to tell him. Come now . . . ."

"You're no better than that fiend below who would have taken me in the barn! I spit on you, French dog!" And she did.

He wiped the moisture away from his face with his arm, then caught her wrist and hoisted her arm up behind her back.

He pushed further and further, until tears pricked her eyes and she thought her arm would snap.

"I am better suited to bed you in one respect and you had better remember it. I'll only make use of you in ways to which you've doubtless become accustomed, but Guillaume, well. . . . I don't think you need me to tell you of his inclinations. If not me, then him. The choice is yours, demoiselle. Only choose wisely. Guillaume is the generous sort; he might pass you around the men afterwards."

In answer, Ermgarde tried to bring up her knee and maim him. Nobody was going to rape her. Nobody! She had been treated roughly at times by Wauter when he was in one of his angry spells, but it had been him then, not some stranger. And he could be tamed to kittenish sweetness. She was completely unprepared for this situation. She knew only that she couldn't give in, mustn't allow it to happen. She was Wauter's. Only his!

He had turned aside momentarily so that her knee made contact only with this thigh, then, as she staggered under the impetus, he caught her by the hair and dragged her, screaming, to the freshly made bed.

Flung on her back, she instantly rose again to her knees and hit out at him with fists and nails. He slapped her and by the time her vision had cleared, he was free of his loincloth and kneeling before her, his thighs glancing against her own, his penis dominating the space between them.

She gave an outraged moan and tried to scramble free, but his arms entrapped her, drawing her back against him like a vise, his thighs forcing their way between her own trembling limbs. A hand clenched her buttocks and, as Ermgarde moved instinctively forward away from his offensive touch, so his manhood found her and gained brutal entry.

Her constitution was such that she could bear the initial pain with but a moan and reflexive spate of fighting against it, her body twisting to and fro, her arms chafing against his torso, seeking to be free. She was afforded not even the mercy of a swoon. And all she could think of as she writhed, sobbing, as he rammed her, was that she had failed—and what was Wauter going to think?

CHAPTER

34

"EAT!" He thrust a platter of cold meat and fresh brown bread at Ermgarde as she sat quite still, yet visibly trembling in the chamber's only chair, her nakedness covered by the linen sheet she had snatched from the bed when he had departed in search of food.

She shook her head, her eyes downcast, loathing him and his smugness. The thought of food was intolerable to a body already threatened with sickness. Idiot to have thought him a cut above that other loathsome creature, Guillaume! He was far worse to her mind because he had used trickery, had fooled her with his hospitable smile and manners.

She wanted to spit in his face again or shriek her contempt, but she was frightened of his brutality, of having to submit her most coveted possession once more.

It was the shame of it that hurt most, that and her fear of Wauter's reaction when he found out someone else had possessed her. He would understand, of course, that she had not given in willingly, but could things ever be the same? She had only just found him again and their love was a tenuous thing that needed no such catastrophe to test its strength. When they were reunited, would he look upon her with the same shame she felt for herself?

Etienne Saint-Luc shrugged his shoulders indifferently and stretched himself atop the bed, smacking his lips over his meal and smiling in a well-pleased manner. A rare delight indeed, this English lady, and such a fighter! He doubted he'd be tired of her—not mentally at any rate—in a day or two, so Guillaume would have to wait with greater patience for scraps.

But why did she show such an anguished face? It wasn't as if she were a virgin, and if England's court was anything like Burgundy's, she doubtless had more than one lover, even making allowances for her tender years. So why all the fuss?

Wasn't he handsome enough for her? Nay, even if he was

not handsome to the same degree that she was beautiful, still he was not lacking in appeal to the opposite sex. Was it then, perhaps, that she was the type of woman who felt honor bound to show false modesty before finally giving in without restraint? That rang more true to his mind. Yes, give her a couple of days and she would plead for more.

But why was he bothering to analyze her mind at all? She was only a prisoner, albeit a beautiful one, of importance only because of the ransom she would bring. He'd enjoy her while he might, but there would be an end to the matter.

His jovial voice was enervating and made Ermgarde's mind fester with impotent rage.

"Come now, demoiselle—or I suppose I should call you dame, seeing as how you declare yourself to be married—you had best eat. We don't want you looking all peaked and mistreated when your husband comes to pay the ransom and collect you. For myself, I've worked up quite an appetite."

Ermgarde would have ignored him as before, except that he talked of ransom for the first time and hope kindled within her. She forced herself to look at him, her violet eyes transmitting her feelings toward him.

"I pray you'll see to the matter of ransom without delay, Burgundian, for I've no mind to partake of your questionable hospitality longer than need be. I can give you the information as to where you can send your demands right now. 'Twill not be a moment too soon to set the wheels in motion, me thinks. A fair ransom will be paid, just as *you* will pay for my violation!"

The chevalier exaggerated a yawn. "But for the moment I've not the inclination to set about such a tiresome task. I must think on it, dame, and set a figure that seems appropriate to your worth. How much do you think your husband will pay? Five thousand gold crowns? Ten thousand, maybe? One cannot rush into such a thing. And in the meantime . . . ."

He had cast aside his platter and rose to pour wine, two brimming goblets from local vineyards, tut-tutting when Ermgarde made no move to take the silver cup he extended.

In the meantime, what? Did she even have to guess?

Well, she would fight him again, keep on fighting no matter what the consequences might be. But was that wise? Honorable it might be, but why risk angering him to such an extent that he handed her over to Guillaume? You don't want that, do you? Oh nay! But not to fight, not to resist the abhorrer would be like a betrayal of her love for Wauter. She *couldn't* just give in.

He had finished his wine and was now downing the draft she had rejected, his half-naked body and the arousal she sensed in him once again turning her into a tense mass of silent outrage. Nay, she'd never accept this as her lot, for, besides feeling it a betrayal of Wauter, she possessed an inbred force that would not allow her to meekly bow down to anyone. She would not be bested by any man simply because he was physically her superior; not this man at any rate.

So when the chevalier set down his goblet and focused his full attention on Ermgarde, she stared back at him with defiance, hands already curved into bird-like talons that could wreak havoc.

For a moment he watched her speculatively, smiling, then moved so swiftly that she lunged at him in blind panic. He drew in a sharp breath as she raked a cheek, but dragged her from the chair nevertheless, across the boards to the bed, she twisting and fighting all the way.

He dragged the linen sheet from her and his loincloth from his body to form a pool on the floor. He lay beside her, manipulating her body by pure brute strength, catching a wrist as her claws made to strike, and ordering, "Touch me, pleasure me, beautiful dame. See what you have caused to grow into such a torturous stalk of desire."

She tried to draw her hand away, made a gurgle of disgust in her throat as his grip forced her reluctant palm to encircle the throbbing girth of his manhood, forced her fingers to close about him and work the desirous flesh to further prominence.

"I would feel your lips."

Her recoil was answered by his other hand clamping about her neck and forcing her head down, putting her lips in contact with him. Ermgarde shuddered, straining to pull away and, knowing she couldn't endure it a moment longer, she bit him. It seemed the only thing to do.

He howled, pushing her away and jumping to his knees to examine his abused member, afraid to look too closely at first, lest she'd destroyed him as a man. Relief swamped him when it appeared she hadn't even drawn blood.

Of all the. . . ! He'd never thought that she might. . . . Smarting, but otherwise unhurt, he delivered Ermgarde a punishing cuff to the jaw and mounted her before she recovered and knew what he was about.

*   *   *

"Well, why am I still waiting?" demanded Guillaume, in a hiss of impatience.

"Because as yet I still find her intriguing, my friend, and would keep her to myself a while longer," Etienne told him stonily, hating even to admit the fact.

It was a week since she had been brought to Chemille, seven days and nights of fighting and fierce passion, and still she cursed him and showed no sign of becoming docile.

It was time, he perceived, for a slight change in tactics. Perhaps to be treated more like the lady she professed to be would produce better results than his inflicted humiliation. And so he had given her a dress and the services of a tiring woman to restore the dignity that prior treatment had denied her. This night, in the hall of the castle she sat beside him, though it must be admitted she looked as if she did not enjoy the privilege of their company. Infuriating wench.

It was turning into a matter of pride and self-esteem with the chevalier now. He *would* have her willingly!

Ermgarde ate in a quiet manner, deigning to look at none, her haughty expression hiding, she hoped, her fear of these men. Still, a week had brought changes. Even if there was no respite from the carnal demands of Etienne Saint-Luc, at least she had noted less brutality. She guessed that her refusal to submit was the very thing that kept his interest. Detesting him as she did, she still saw the wisdom in keeping his yearning for her; it kept her out of the clutches of Lansier and the others.

So this evening was a victory of sorts. She had clothes again and a place beside the castellan of Chemille at supper—a step up from despair even if his company and that of his men would gladly have been forfeited for the pleasure of supping alone.

The week past had required her to tap every resource she possessed to fend off attack, even knowing those efforts might be futile.

Her feelings for the chevalier were purely hateful and could never, she vowed to herself, be any different no matter what persuasion he used.

She loved Wauter FitzSimmons and brought him to mind during the attacks she suffered; his image, and memories of the love they had shared, fueled her loathing of the man who sweated and panted atop her, leading her to more frantic attempts to repulse him.

But how much longer could she continue to fight? Already she sensed herself weakening by degrees—not mentally, but physically. And she perceived that it was guile rather than might that would prevail against Saint-Luc. But how did one go about trying to outwit so wily a fox? Let her rescue be executed soon, pray God!

With thoughts of ransom and deliverance fresh in mind, Ermgarde turned her attention to the chevalier and spoke to him for the first time since coming to the table, the meal almost done by this time. "Sir, might I inquire when you intend sending to England for my ransom? Time marches on and my family will be frantic for news, just as I am to be back amongst them. I believe you have had all the necessary information from me to make the claim for your money all the easier; therefore, I hope you'll not be unchivalrous enough as to cause unnecessary delays."

Saint-Luc was amiable, though Ermgarde had learned the hard way to distrust such a friendly facade. He undid the topmost buttons of his wine-velvet cotehardie, the better to be comfortable, and sank into the heavily carved chair, smiling, delaying comment.

"Well, sir, when are these things to be seen to? You have a duty to inform my family and name your price; those are the dictates in regard to prisoners of war," Ermgarde told him, sharply.

"Dame, you need not remind me of the finer points of chivalry. And all, I can assure you, has been seen to."

She took in his handsome smile suspiciously, her black brows drawing together above watchful eyes. "Explain."

"All has been seen to. Could I possibly put it more simply? I dispatched a messenger yesterday, having arrived at a satisfactory sum of ransom with Guillaume. We thought you a prize worthy of redemption at fifteen thousand gold crowns."

"Fifteen thousand!" Good God, could Wauter raise such a sum? It would beggar them.

"Not exorbitant, dame, considering your station *and* beauty. Were I your husband, I'd pay twice the sum to have you back."

Ermgarde didn't deign to reply. Fifteen thousand was a princely sum, but Wauter would pay it, would raise it if it was not readily available. Yes, yes, of course he would. And soon she would be home. Home. Thank heavens! Hope and tranquility settled over her. Satisfied, she turned her attention once more to her fare, the cherry tart suddenly very appetizing. For the first time in a week she actually felt hungry. But the chevalier was disinclined to leave her in peace, for this was the closest yet they'd ever come to a conversation.

His face quizzical, he pressed on. "Now that I've set about the business of your exchange, will you return the favor and tell me what took you to Picardy?"

Ermgarde remained evasive and terse, telling him, " 'Tis no business of yours, chevalier. A mere domestic problem could not possibly interest you."

"But it does. 'Twould have had to be a problem of some magnitude to necessitate your traveling with the army."

"I traveled with my brother and only met up with the army at Maisoncelles."

"Your brother?"

"Aye, he accompanied me to offer protection."

"Then he did a poor job, no? Snatching you from the field was simplicity itself," the knight pointed out, a mocking note in his voice.

Ermgarde's face turned tense with rage, her eyes boring into his, making the smug smile falter. "Monsieur, the reason I was open to your mercenary attack was simply that my unarmed brother was slain by that corrupt heap of flesh who sits beside you! I ask your permission to retire. I've sampled enough of your company this evening!"

She was on her feet, trembling from head to toe in her hastily procured gown of dull brown that suited her not at all. Etienne was of two minds—whether to make her stay, to retire when *he* allowed it, or let her vent her anger alone. Perhaps it would be best if he did the latter. Oh, damn and blast it all! And things had begun to look so promising this day. He couldn't even clearly recall Guillaume slaying the lad, so many other deaths had he witnessed that day. Oh, damn the knight, too, for putting yet another barrier between them! Was it any wonder she hated and shunned him, loathed them all, when her own kin had died at his friend's hand?

He nodded. "You may retire."

The castellan of Chemille-sur-Seine retired soon afterward amidst vulgar jesting from his men, who had unveiled envy in their eyes. But this night he was going to give the lady the pleasure of going without him. Not that he didn't want her —no one had ever cast the spell upon him that she did—but because there were other things that pressed urgently, especially now that he'd told her a messenger was on his way to England. He gauged her relief, and felt she would eventually honor his conditions without too much reluctance. And his conditions would be that the lady tell him about herself, her husband, family, all. Yes, he had to know *all* for his plans to work.

He wasn't going to touch her? Ermgarde was suspicious even after he swore to it on his oath to St. Andrew, sitting stiffly in her chair, garbed in the brown dress that felt akin to armor after days of nakedness. No, he told her, this night he wanted only to hear about her, to try to understand her better.

His interest was genuine, not, she felt certain, manufactured solely to put her off guard; yet her unease prevailed and was lessened only slightly when she took a goblet of wine the third time he insisted. One's mouth did get so dry with so much talking, and his questions were endless. He wanted to know about Synford, her husband, her life at court, unimportant things that Ermgarde answered readily enough, seeing each moment that passed as a moment to escape his sexual advances. And when the second goblet of wine turned reluctance to eloquence, she saw no reason not to go into details of her quarrels with Wauter, and when pressed, to speak of dear Gloucester and her scheming sister, her journey to France. . . .

"Oh, poor, cheri, how testing for you. But everything will work out right, no? This Alice is locked away in a nunnery, is she not, and unlikely to tempt your husband on his return to England? That is supposing she has not . . . no, of course she cannot escape, can she? Those places are not unlike prisons, yes? And you said she meant nothing to him, that he made love to her only out of spite. Within a month your ransom will be paid and you can go home."

Why did he sound so uncertain? Ermgarde wondered, the unburdening of her stormy marriage hardly satisfying. He frowned at the mention of Alice, as if the girl was still a threat. No, Alice was locked away, and besides, Wauter hadn't really cared for her despite the words he'd spoken at Maisoncelles. There was nothing to worry about save her present position, and in a month or so not even that. She would be home.

CHAPTER

3 5

THE NOVEMBER CHILL penetrated the soldiers' clothes and slowed their progress. The sight of Dijon before them was welcomed, though they knew not what kind of reception they might expect.

Wauter, Robert de la Vallée and Thomas Berkeley had parted company with their king on the morning of October the twenty-sixth, leaving the hungry yet triumphant army to march toward Calais. Gloucester flared and blazed, yet didn't quite dare to go against his brother's wishes. And Henry gave the inland-bound party letters of reference and intent, knowing they'd fare well enough. A sizeable band of soldiers would escort the threesome since Lord Berkeley had elected to go with them, his taste for adventure not yet satisfied, and his invitation to those still not homesick accepted by many. And France was, to a comforting degree for any foreign travelers —especially English soldiers—without an army now. Aye, Wauter and the rest would be able to cope alone. The king took his leave cheerfully.

They entered the ducal city as unobtrusively as possible; no pennons, cotes d'armes or identification were on display for the citizens. Yet it was impossible not to be just a trifle conspicuous. No body of fighting men could go unnoticed, yet their progress along busy thoroughfares went unchallenged, and they were stopped only at the gates of the palace itself.

"Your business?" The guards—only two of them—looked uncomfortable faced with so rough and ready a bunch.

Wauter mustered up the stilted French that Bolingbroke had taught him at such pains. "Be at ease, men. We come from Agincourt in Picardy where our King Henry did take victory over his enemies. We do seek an audience with your most illustrious duke."

"A victory?" One of the guards looked gleeful at the news

of defeat for Burgundy's foes. The other had gone scurrying off beyond the gates to summon a higher authority. He returned, panting, red in the face, with a somberly dressed servant on his heels.

"Noble sirs, if you would come this way, stabling will be found for your horses and the soldiers will be shown to the kitchens where they may eat."

These things seen to, the lords and knight were preceded up a narrow stairway mostly used by servants, and into the interior of the gothic splendor that was Dijon's palace.

The servant apologized by way of explanation for such clandestine treatment. "I'm certain you understand, good lords, that the duke has not openly declared himself either for your king or his own cousin, Charles VI. Therefore he thinks it prudent that this meeting be conducted privately, that your presence in Dijon, welcome though it is, does not become widely known."

"We understand," said Wauter, a hint of cynicism lacing his voice. John the Fearless wanted a finger in everyone's pie.

The tapestry-hung chamber where they awaited the duke looked out upon a secluded courtyard. The double arches of an elaborately carved embrasure allowed the last light of dusk to enter the room. The furniture was of light oak; box chairs and tables were decorated with the solemnity and grace of a cathedral choir; the floor was a geometric wonder of triangles and squares in multi-colored Italian marble.

Impressive, if somewhat garish, Wauter decided; the tapestries of crimson, black and gold assaulted his senses. The entrance of the duke and his son was no less dazzling.

Jean-sans-Peur, Duke of Burgundy, entered the room garbed in a deep-green brocaded houppelande that trailed on the tiles behind him. Its collar and sleeves were trimmed with silver fox, his shoulders were draped with a dag-edged cape of russet wool, and his short-cropped hair was hidden beneath a wide and fussy hat of black wool that was also dagged and trailed over the shoulder with a lengthy liripipe. A ruby was embedded in the hat, a ruby-and-pearl brooch was pinned to the cape, rubies and gold were at his belt and, of course, on his fingers.

He was regal, but by no stretch of the imagination, handsome—his features thin and sharp, the nose prominently bridged. But he had nice hands—delicate and graceful for a man—and he gesticulated with them continually to draw attention to the fact.

He looked over the three men with interest, his gaze coming back to Wauter, whose sheer size and bearing identified him as their leader. "Seigneur, my servant informs me that there has been a battle in Picardy and a victory for the English. Is this so?"

" 'Tis true, my lord duke. At a place called Agincourt. The King of France's forces were soundly beaten and many of them were taken prisoner."

The duke nodded, his face giving nothing away. "No doubt Orleans and the rest used the antiquated tactics that led to such folly at Crecy and Poitiers. Some cannot learn by their mistakes. Were any of my noble cousins taken prisoner or wounded in the fray? And Brabant—did you see aught of him? It displeased me greatly when he ignored my advice and went to fight for Charles. I have hot heads for brother and son."

Wauter answered with as much diplomacy as he was able, airing the good news first and saving the worst till last. He grew increasingly aware of an angrily glowering duke's son. "The Dukes of Orleans and Bourbon, and the Counts of Eu, Richemont and Vendome, head a list of hundreds captured, my lord duke."

John the Fearless couldn't quite control his emotions this time and a smile of satisfaction flitted over his face. Soon there would be only Count Bernard of Armagnac himself to champion the king!

"Your brother was captured also, but there was some confusion as to his identity. He did not declare himself your brother, my lord duke. At one point it became necessary to put some of the prisoners to the sword and, regrettably, he was amongst them."

The duke's brow creased, but there was no spontaneous grief—no anger unleashed at these men who had been on the side that had meted out his brother's death. He expelled heavily and shrugged his shoulders. "Trust him not to declare himself! Knowing him, he wanted not that I should have to pay his ransom for him, prideful ass! And he was right, of course; 'twould have angered me greatly. But better that than him dead. Take note, Philippe, 'twas for this reason that I forbade you to go join the king's forces."

Philippe of Charolais, distressed by the news of his uncle's death, cried passionately, "Your reasons were never so noble, Father! You locked me away so I could not fight because you had sold yourself to the English, not because you feared for my life! You wanted not the embarrassment of me fighting against your allies."

"You will be quiet," ground out Jean-sans-Peur between clenched teeth, angered and discomfited at the lack of control displayed by his son before strangers.

"I will not! Charles VI is my liege-lord, and as such he has my support. I am married to his daughter and hate my allegiance being called into question because of your dealings with the enemy!"

Soft gray eyes—in a finely boned face devoid of the father's coarseness—shot a look of hatred at Wauter and his companions.

"You had best leave us," ordered the father.

"With great pleasure!" retorted the son.

After the door slammed noisily behind the impetuous nineteen-year-old, John shook his head in exasperation. "My pardon for such unseemly behavior, my lords. Philippe has much to learn. Alas, he is wildly in love with his little Michelle de France and sees it as his duty to champion her father whenever opportunity arises."

"I understand, my lord duke. For one still so tender to believe passionately in something cannot be so uncommendable an emotion," assured Wauter, diplomatically.

"Um, yes. . . . Now where were we? Ah, yes, the battle. 'Twas good of your King Henry to send you with the news, and please be certain that you convey my pleasure of it to him in exchange. I'm certain you understand that I cannot commit such to paper for reasons politic, but my shared jubilation with your king is no less for that."

"My lord duke, 'twas not for such reason that we traveled here, though I am glad to be the bearer of good tidings. 'Tis a personal matter to do with my wife."

"Oh?" The duke's brows lowered.

Wauter explained his theory that Ermgarde had been snatched away by one of Brabant's knights and was somewhere in Burgundy.

"And on mere supposition you have traveled here? Your feelings for her must be more intense than those displayed by my son for his beloved! Wouldn't it have been more sensible to return home and await a ransom demand?''

"I cannot leave the country believing her still here, my lord duke. I thought, and in this I must beg your assistance, that you might be able to find out who holds her, and that I might then take her place as hostage until the sum demanded is paid.''

Such substitutions for hostages were not uncommon. When King John of France was taken prisoner at Poitiers, his son, Louis of Anjou, went to London as hostage in his stead. But Louis had escaped to France, dishonorably breaking his word in the eyes of a world besotted by the notion of chivalry, and John, mortified by such actions, had handed himself back over immediately.

John the Fearless gave a ponderous nod of agreement. "I can see no objections to you taking the lady's place. But finding her will present something of a problem. Burgundy is vast and, too, there are my brother's lands in Artois and Flanders. She might be anywhere, *if* indeed she was taken by Burgundians at all.''

" 'Tis a sizable task, I know, my lord duke, but I ask only that you keep an ear open for news. Courts are renowned for knowing all.''

"Aye, 'tis so,'' laughed the duke. "And gladly I shall listen and urge others to do likewise. Also, I shall send word to the northern territories, ordering the Lady Ermengarde of Synford's whereabouts reported to me should it become known. Will that suffice?''

"I'm indebted to your grace.''

"But what will you do in the meantime?'' asked the duke, waving aside Wauter's thanks with a dismissive flutter of those elegant hands. "Will you be my guests?''

" 'Twould be difficult for me to sit idly about, my lord duke, though I thank you for your offer of hospitality. If I could but travel your lands . . . perhaps pick up some information myself? We will, of course, act at all times as befitting guests in a foreign land and bear arms only if the need for protection arises.''

"Yes, yes, I think that is acceptable. Before you leave Dijon I shall see that you have papers with my seal to authorize your search. That will smooth the path a little, no?''

"My lord duke is indeed generous.''

Jean-sans-Peur indicated that the audience was at an end. Thomas and Robert, who had remained silent spectators throughout, bowed along with Wauter and backed from the room.

"Whew!" said Lord Berkeley, "that young Philippe gave me a few uneasy moments, I can tell you. If he'd been armed, I don't doubt he'd have tried to take on the three of us. Such passion!"

"Blow him! Let's go join the others in the kitchens. I could do justice to a decent meal," said Robert.

Thomas patted his protruding belly. "And I."

Wauter laughed and shook his head. The greatest concern of their lives was keeping well fed.

They set out the next morning, well rested and well fed, carrying the duke's authorization for their search as promised, and a generous amount of provisions from the palace kitchens were packed aboard the cart that also stored their harnesses and knightly trappings.

Three weeks later they had visited every chateau and fortified dwelling within a hundred mile radius south of Dijon, never staying to enjoy the hospitality of the castellan or chatelaine for more than a day. Though they were oft pressed by isolated nobility starved of interesting company to stay several days, they always left with the pledge of news should the mysterious Ermengarde show herself in their vicinity.

When December arrived and the weather became increasingly uncharitable, they turned once more to Dijon. Mayhap the duke had heard something by this time, or perhaps Lady Margaret had news of the ransom—Wauter having sent word of his wife's disappearance to England and instructed his mother that he might be contacted through Jean-sans-Peur.

On both accounts he was disappointed. There was not so much as a whisper, the duke told him solicitously, but then 'twas only just past a month since her disappearance. Give it time and, in the meantime, his noble English guests could spend Christmas-tide with him, yes?

Wauter was reluctant, but the eager faces of his fellow knights and soldiers swayed him. They had been either marching or riding since landing at Harfleur. They were tired and in need of a few weeks recreation. Let them have it, he decided, then when Christmas was done they'd be eager for the hunt once more. For himself, the thought of sitting idle for so long made him as irritable as a chained hound.

From Lady Margaret there was no joy. And no comfort, either. No, she had received no word from Ermgarde, no ransom demand. And if he'd not been so eaten by his own groundless jealousy, none of this would have ever happened. Wauter read her scathing missive with a deepening frown, resenting her loading him with the blame, yet acknowledging it. Yes, he was all the things she said: arrogant, overbearing, sanctimonious . . . and no, if he didn't find Ermgarde he wouldn't blame his mother if she never talked to him again. Lord, such hostility from one's own flesh and blood!

He hated, too, this inactivity, lolling around a court that concerned itself only with fashion and honor, chivalry and intrigue, because it presented him with ample time to worry.

Why had there been no ransom demand received back in England? A messenger shouldn't take so long to travel. Who had her? Was she being treated with due courtesy?

Dangerous ground, that. Whenever he envisaged her a prisoner, her beauty caused him disquiet and fear. Few men were immune to it—none that he knew of, save perhaps King Henry, who now saw himself above something as earthly as carnal lust. Would her gaolers keep to their chivalrous vows and not touch so fetching a morsel who was unwillingly in their charge? At this point Wauter would unfailingly find himself atremble with frustrated rage. If any dared. . . . One hair on her head harmed, one honorless deed perpetrated against her, and the offender would regret it tenfold . . . nay, a hundredfold! Wauter would tear him limb from limb, hack him to pieces, have his balls. . . !

CHAPTER
36

A MONTH AND MORE had passed since the day Etienne Saint-Luc had told Ermgarde of his sending a messenger to England, and in that time she had fought against him as hard as ever, holding strictly to her principles. There were nights when she longed to lie back and let him get on with the deed, knowing that she could have saved herself a great deal of violence by doing so. But she was another man's wife, she loved that man and it was her duty to fight. She was weary but not bested.

But then a messenger came.

She remembered vividly huddling before the fire in the chevalier's chambers, struggling over the book he had given her by one Chretien de Troyes, the few words of French she had picked up useless in trying to decipher the Arthurian legends that sprawled across the velum. And she had slammed the book shut in disgust, cursing the French for their unfathomable language that denied her avenue into books.

Etienne had entered, smiling that not-quite-true smile of his, and had handed her a packet wrapped in linen. For some moments she turned it disinterestedly in her fingers. He had taken to bringing her gifts from time to time and she refused them all with the same lack of courtesy.

"What is it this time? I've told you before, monsieur, that I care for nothing from you."

"But this time I think you will not say nay. 'Tis from England, cheri, concerning your ransom, I don't doubt," he told her, seeming as interested as herself with the contents. Ermgarde ripped the covering with a wail of joy and began to straighten out the folded sheet of parchment. Here it was, here it was! A little late, but never mind that. Oh, dear God, she thought she would choke on the lump in her throat.

She read to herself, Etienne peering over her shoulder, elation ebbing away with each line that she labored over. No, no, he *couldn't* do that to her. No!

She squeezed the parchment between her fingers as if it were some living thing from which she wanted to choke the breath, her breathing shallowed alarmingly as she erupted into sobs of shocked misery.

Etienne grabbed the crumpled missive from her hands, his face frowning. "Let me have a look at that."

He read out loud, each syllable confirming that Ermgarde's eyes hadn't deceived her, that the thing sounded no less devastating no matter who read it.

"To the custodian of Ermgarde of Synford, penned this, the twenty-second day of November in the year of our lord 1415, by Margaret Parfrey, at the bidding of one Wauter Fitz-Simmons, Baron of Synford. Concerning ransom of the aforementioned female: It is with regret that I must inform you that fifteen thousand crowns is a sum beyond the immediate capabilities of the Lord of Synford, even desirous as he is for the return of his wife. Therefore, we do direct you to keep her safe and to inform her, for her own peace of mind, that her husband is in good health and being cared for in her unfortunate absence by the lady's sister, one Alice Shepherd, lately returned from Bristol. A term of two years grace is asked for, in which time it is hoped that the ransom sum can be raised."

"Oh, my *poor* sweeting. I never imagined that it would come to this," said Etienne, his arm enveloping Ermgarde's shoulder even as she flinched from the touch.

"Couldn't you lower the price for ransom," she begged him suddenly. The thought of two years at Chemille while Alice ruled at home filled her with desperation.

"I should like to, cheri, to make you happy. But fifteen thousand is no great sum, not if he really wanted you back. Oh, pardon me that slip of the tongue . . . it was without tact . . . I never meant. . . ."

She shook her head, not really listening. All Ermgarde could contemplate was the fact that he had brought Alice back from Bristol. Wauter, her beloved, whom she had fought to honor in the arms of this lascivious knight, whose love had sustained her this far, had brought Alice back to keep him company while he went about the tiresome business of raising the ransom!

He hadn't even taken the trouble to pen the letter to her himself, but had delegated the task to his mother. She, it would appear, dictating the content to some scribe whose calligraphy had a monk's anonymous uniformity of character. Hadn't even signed his name to the bottom of the document! Otherwise occupied! her mind screamed, with Alice in his bed! And he expected her to languish here for two years? Mayhap longer—if Alice proved entertaining and kept his mind from duties.

When Etienne took her that night, using all the tactics he had acquired with former loves, Ermgarde lay numb beneath him, no longer fighting, true, but totally unresponsive. He was not pleased. The fighting he had disliked, but making love to a corpse was worse still. He could have done anything, she wouldn't have cared, and knowing that, he wasn't fulfilled.

"Come now, dame, 'tis no good to mope. Your husband will surely pay the ransom when he is able." Etienne was growing exasperated by her total disinterest in life, in him more especially. With the obstacle of her husband done away with and himself appearing sympathetic to her distress, he had expected change to come more quickly in their relationship, had expected her to respond, if only out of spite toward the man who had supposedly cast her aside for another.

She seemed not to have heard him, his harshness of voice bringing no response. Ermgarde sat up in the bed, staring at the monotonous expanse of gray winter light through the embrasure, the chill turning her flesh to goose bumps, though she was loath to have the shutters closed and lose what small glimpse of freedom she had during these inclement days.

Etienne's lips tightened. What was one to do with her? She wanted none of him or his gifts, ignoring whatever he might bring, her face cloaked in sorrow. 'Twas obvious she still pined for that husband of hers, must truly have loved him. Well, Lord Wauter was something that Etienne wasn't prepared to give, not now, perhaps never. *He* wanted her, wanted her ecstatic response when they made love, just as that other man had. Why was it so hard for her? He was a man, ardent, capable. There was nothing he wouldn't do for her, were she to give him the opportunity.

He schooled himself to keep his temper, to cast aside the biting edge from his voice. "Won't you rise? The day is not so hostile that you must seek protection from it in bed. Not that I have any objections to feasting my eyes on those handsome shoulders or those delicious. . . .''

Distractedly, Ermgarde lifted the sheet higher to assure herself that any further feasting of his eyes would go unrewarded, and he laughed. ''Ah, so you *can* hear me, Silent One! Leave that bed and come put on this gown I've brought you. 'Tis fine, and I chose the violet because of your eyes. The match will be devastating. No? But I had one of my men travel to Dijon to purchase it for you. Wear it for his sake, if not mine, so that he won't think he undertook the journey for nought.''

Ermgarde gave the gown a cursory glance, if only to prove that she still had some manners. It wasn't his fault, after all. He had sent to England for the ransom in good faith, was solicitous, even kind now when it appeared her stay would be longer than anyone had anticipated, when her distress was obvious. Aye, the gown was fine.

The faint spark of interest didn't go unnoticed by the chevalier and he was quick to press for advantage. ''If you dress quickly there will be time to go riding before I deal with the day's business. The land along the banks of the Seine is quite beautiful even in winter. I presume you ride?''

He was going to let her outside the confines of these thick walls? After weeks of staring about one chamber and hall, the news brightened her countenance. Then again, if she was to endure two years of this place, some concessions of the sort would have to be made if her gaoler had any heart at all. She was no hardened soldier to be chained in some oubliette year after year. Etienne realized this, it seemed, and would make her stay not too uncomfortable.

''Yes, I ride,'' she told him, the thought of fresh biting air sending a shiver of enthusiasm through her.

CHAPTER

3 7

"HE DOESN'T LOVE you. He has another," Etienne had reminded her cruelly that winter past, and little by little Ermgarde had come to accept it, rarely thinking to escape in search of revenge. She wouldn't have survived a journey through enemy territory on her own. Starvation, rape, murder or robbery were possibilities too fearful to contend with.

Once she'd taken her revenge, what would she have done then, anyway? She was no Robin of Loxley to play fugitive in some greenwood. She was no high-born lady to throw herself on the king's mercy. They would have seen her only as Ermgarde Shepherd, the crofter's daughter who was raised by the good Lord Wauter to a desirous position of lady wife. 'Twould not be an eye for an eye to their minds, but plain old murder, and they would have hung her for it, hung the peasant who presumed to go too high.

So Ermgarde resigned herself to life at Chemille, where the castellan at least seemed to want her, though heaven only knew why, for she still would not deign to offer him any encouragement.

She asked to be quartered in her own room, telling the knight that she could not abide someone as untidy as himself, and he had acquiesced. The ready agreement on his part caused her some surprise. She had expected refusal, anticipated him raising hell over a change that would mean the end to his having her at his leisure. But Etienne didn't see it that way, found her making of terms wholly satisfactory. The demanding of her own chamber, and the furnishings and accoutrements that went with it, was the first step, as he saw it, in her accepting her lot. She had begun to approach Chemille with thoughts of permanency—thus, his indulgence. Anything was possible, so long as it made the lady feel at home.

The purple gown was joined by others, all chosen by

Etienne to compliment her coloring, match her eyes or hair, or contrast vividly so that every man who glimpsed her was struck with awe. And, to go with the gowns, girdles of precious metal and surcoats trimmed with ermine and fox; reticulated headdresses that swept like gossamer wings from her head, veils framing her beautiful face; cylindrical cauls worked in gold filigree held the lady's hair in place; chain necklaces—which Etienne insisted were the latest in good taste —and fillets, signet rings, brooches and so on for every occasion.

Ermgarde accepted it all with mild gratitude, not really seeing the point in so much finery when she was never permitted to venture further than the lands of Chemille-sur-Seine. But it was as Etienne wanted—for her to always look like a queen just for him, even going so far as to have made a collection of coronets and crowns of silver to be worn with her veils. The Duke of Burgundy was generous toward his castellan and Etienne had precious little else to spend his money on, so why not on Dame Ermgarde?

Not for him the nuisance of having to guard a treasury that contained miserly full coffers. They only awaited the perfumer from Dijon, who had cosmetics and the like that ladies seemed to set such store by, and then he could feel content that every chance to please and ingratiate himself toward her had been taken.

Only in one matter did it seem he could not please her, and that was over Guillaume. That she detested the man was obvious, and Etienne had noted how her flesh crawled and lips tightened whenever she was forced into the man's vicinity. To please her, Etienne would have cast aside the friend of long standing, but he had other considerations. Guillaume resided at Chemille to help the Chevalier Saint-Luc in his duties by order of Jean-sans-Peur, and no one went against the dictates of the most powerful duke of the Western world; certainly not without a good reason. What kind of excuse did he have? That the sight of the man displeased his paramour? Jean de Bourgogne wouldn't wear that!

She'd just have to get used to the idea of having him around, put aside the fact that her brother had gotten himself slain by the man. Such things happened in times of war. 'Twas regrettable, but one had to go on, had to forget.

Ermgarde knew her keeper's mind concerning Guillaume

Lansier and it played a key role in her continued coldness. He would not do the one thing she asked of him, and seemed to think he could compensate for the fact by buying still more gowns and trinkets. It wouldn't work.

'Twas just past noon and the garrison took its customary break from duties by crowding into the hall to eat. Guillaume caught hold of a luckless lad who was carrying logs to the hearth and began kissing and fondling his trapped prey. The others looked on; Etienne and the soldiers laughing raucously; servants going sheepishly about their business with one eye on the proceedings; the poor lad trembling with terror in the man's hands.

Ermgarde set knife to plate with a clatter and rose to her feet, hissing at him in a language he couldn't comprehend, any more than she understood the lascivious suggestions he was making to the lad, though she could guess. "Sir, you are contemptible, a disgusting, corrupt lump of lard! Can you not, in this pest-hole, find someone willing to accept your advances, instead of forcing yourself upon a mere boy who finds you just about as charming as a snake?"

Lansier laughed at her outrage, that being what he had set out to incite in the first place, and toasted her mockingly as she ascended the stairs with disdain.

Etienne made no comment and his friend had been counting on that, sensing that Saint-Luc was reluctant to have his deep feelings for the lady turn him into something of a laughing-stock amongst his men. How they would roar and jeer to hear tell how Etienne Saint-Luc had come to the sorry predicament of falling in love! But Guillaume wouldn't tell. One didn't do that sort of thing to friends. And soon Etienne would be out of love again, Guillaume didn't doubt, knowing how his friend's love affairs blew hot and cold. Chemille would then cease to be a fortress that functioned, it seemed, solely for the convenience and comfort of the English dame. And the sooner the better, for he had liked things the way they were before. Just him and Etienne, comrades-in-arms.

"Monsieur!"

Etienne looked questioningly as a watchman entered. "Well?" His voice was gruff, his thoughts still half occupied with the lady who had just retired. How he wished Guillaume would cease his deliberate baiting. 'Twas childish, and left him with the not-so-easy task of placating her later on.

"There be riders approaching from the northeast. 'Tis difficult with the mist so thick and light poor, but they look English. Some wear the red cross on their tunics."

"English?" Etienne mused aloud, a frown drawing his blond eyebrows down. "Now what could they want here?"

"Could it be the lady's husband has come searching?" offered Guillaume, smiling at the thought of maybe being rid of her sooner than he'd expected, greed visible in his eyes as he recalled the matter of ransom and his percentage.

"Quiet, you fool! She might hear!" Etienne was on his feet, ignoring Guillaume's fierce stare, and ordering the watchman, "Get back to the walls and let me know what develops. Are the gates shut?"

"Yes, monsieur."

"Good. Keep them that way. I shall be back directly." So saying, he headed for his chamber.

The mist did the strangest things, Ermgarde thought as she leaned from her window and observing the countryside. Sounds hung eerily in the air and objects—trees and suchlike —disappeared altogether except for an occasional branch that poked through the whiteness. It was early afternoon, yet it felt timeless.

At first she thought she heard muffled echoes of singing from the guardroom which stood near the main gate of the chateau to the north, far away from her southerly window. But the tune was strange, its distant whisper leaving her puzzled, disquieted. Come to think of it, she'd never heard the soldiers of this castle sing.

It was growing louder, as if the choristers drew near from the north. Not the guards of Chemille at all then, she was certain. How interesting. Perhaps they would have guests.

Curious, she slipped through the door and took to the passage and stairs that led to Etienne's chamber. His window faced north and she might be able to see who came. The door opened as she reached it, Etienne hesitating at the sight of her, wine sloshing over the rim of the goblet he held.

"Cheri, what are you doing here?" He smiled, his free hand catching her elbow to lead Ermgarde back the way she had come.

"I thought I heard someone approaching the castle. I wanted to see who had arrived."

"Visitors? No, you are mistaken." He tugged a little more persistently at her arm. "Come, let's go back to your chamber. I was on my way there, to bring you this wine and apologize for Guillaume's behavior."

"But there it is again, Etienne. Don't you hear it?"

"Peasants singing in the fields, I expect."

Why hadn't she thought of that? She allowed herself to be led back along the passage, nodding in agreement with his explanation, and yet. . . .

He closed the door behind them and led Ermgarde to the bed, handing her the goblet and placing a bolster behind her head like a fussing hen. "Drink. You had no wine with your meal, I recall."

She sipped, allowing him to remove her shoes and ruby-studded garters, puzzling still over those odd singing voices. 'Twas loud enough now for her to catch the words, but even hearing them, they made no sense.

"*Deo gratias. Deo gratias, Anglia redde pro victoria.*"

"What nonsense." she decided.

"'Tis Latin," Etienne corrected her.

"Oh." She grimaced at the edge on the wine and he said, jokingly, "Ninety-five was not a very good year."

"Quite." She made to put down the goblet but he shook his head.

"Drink it all. 'Twill help you to sleep."

It was nearly all gone anyhow, so she obliged, relaxing and sighing. She usually took rest in the afternoon, there being precious little else to do at Chemille, but today for some reason the need for sleep lowered over her alarmingly fast.

"Rest, precious one."

His voice had such a soothing, compelling quality, she thought detachedly. And then she heard the voices again, seeping into her brain as her lids closed and her black lashes brushed her cheeks. Their song had ended minutes before, but now it seemed they were going to chorus through it again, just for her, she felt sure.

> "Our king went forth to Normandy,
>   With grace and might of chivalry,
>   The God for him wrought marvelously,
>   Wherefore England may call and cry,
>   *Deo gratias. Deo gratias, Anglia redde pro victoria.*"

Deo gratias, indeed! Who'd ever heard of a peasant
schooled to the extent that he could chant Latin, lest it be in
parrot fashion at his prayers? And what was that about the
king . . . England . . . Normandy?

She wanted to open her eyes, to ask something, but the
question flew from her mind and the voices grew fainter, died.

Etienne surveyed the soldiers from his position on the watch
tower, about to ask who they might be, then changed the question to, "What business brings you to Chemille?" What was
the point in asking who they were? He already knew, didn't
he? There was no doubt in his mind that the imposing figure
astride the fearsome beast at their head was Wauter of Synford, and, accordingly, something within him withered.

The man was magnificent—a ruthless looking giant, even in
the black leather jerkin and woollen hose that accented his
figure. The dark face, framed by hair and untidy beard, contemplated Etienne from beneath his raised visor with a thor-
oughness that matched the other.

Wauter's voice boomed up at him, sending Boris jumping
about skittishly, to Brodrick's chagrin. The beast would never
make a good warhorse.

"We come with safe conducts from your duke, in search of
a missing wife."

"You've lost your wife? Indeed that was careless of you,
sir," said Etienne, hoping his voice had just the right mocking
note in it.

Wauter glowered momentarily, finding no amusement in
the matter. Eight months they'd been searching now without
reward, not so much as a false rumor of her whereabouts.
There'd been no ransom demand received at Synford, either.
His hopes were beginning to wane.

"Tell me her name, sir. Perhaps 'twill recall something to
mind," suggested Etienne, helpfully.

"Ermengarde of Synford."

Etienne mused, shaking his head. "Nay. Sorry. I should
have recalled so fine a French name had I heard it. But let us
not continue to conduct this conversation on so distant a level.
Will you not enter and partake of our hospitality?"

"Do you forget about the ransom money?" reminded Guillaume in a hiss at his shoulder.

'Twas a little reckless perhaps, Etienne conceded to himself, totally ignoring the furious knight beside him, but Ermgarde was safely asleep, and would be that way until dawn because of the powders he'd added to her wine. He'd used them before to ease the battle-wounded, and their soporific powers had never failed. He wanted to speak to this lord, *had* to, feeling compelled to learn, if he might, what it was that the Lady Ermgarde found so memorable. Perhaps when he knew *that* he could make her love him with the same passion she had felt for Wauter.

But Wauter shook his head, declining. "Thank you, but no. We wish to reach Chatillon before dark and that will be no easy task as 'tis with this mist, monsieur. I'm sorry, I don't recall you giving your name."

"Saint-Luc. Etienne." His voice was laced with disappointment.

"Good day to you, then." Wauter back-stepped Rogue from the dry ditch and knocked his visor back into place. The others followed behind, their mounts wheeling and snorting as they turned about with none of the old destriers' poetic motion.

Etienne watched until the mist swallowed them, that multi-versed battle anthem reaching him again, grating on his nerves. He bristled with the indignity of one who had fought at Agincourt and lost, seething that an enemy could sing self-praising rubbish on his lands, whilst carrying safe-conduct papers from Jean-sans-Peur.

Guillaume was swearing, eyes murderous as they beheld the other knight. "I knew 'twas too good to be true, your talk of ransom. You never meant to hand her over at all, did you —*did you*!"

"No."

When Ermgarde awoke at dawn, the mist had gone; but it was the first thing she remembered—the mist and the singing.

Etienne must have woken her as he left her bed, and she sat up to confront him as he pulled on his hose, her mind in a turmoil of queries and uncertainties. No, she was certain she hadn't imagined those English words, hadn't dreamt them, either. And why had she slept so long? That wasn't natural.

"Etienne." Her voice was cold, demanding.

He turned, smiling that untrustworthy smile. "Ah, sweeting, so you are awake at last. You must have been very tired to have slept so long."

"They were singing in English; I heard them before . . . before I fell asleep," she told him, defying him to argue.

He nodded instead. "Quite so. They were English visitors and not peasants as I had thought. After all, what peasant would know Latin? It never occurred to me at the time."

"They *were* English? Who . . . who?"

"Sir Harold of somewhere-or-other. Can't remember. He was on his way to Dijon on king's business but got lost in the mist. I merely redirected him."

She gave a heavy sigh of disappointment. She hadn't really expected Wauter to have a bout of conscience and come release her. But there had been the hope that someone might stop at Chemille and bring news—if not of Wauter, then of the movements of King Henry. Was he still in London being feted for his great victory, or had he returned to secure Normandy, as he must surely do? The taking of one town and a battle victory could not be termed total conquest, after all.

Why couldn't it have been Gloucester or Warwick who'd stumbled across Chemille instead of some bumbling knight? Nay, the duke and earl would never succumb to anything so humiliating as getting themselves lost!

"I'm sorry I did not wake you to meet him, my sweet. I know how you must yearn for news of home. But he seemed so insignificant. I didn't think you could possibly find him of any interest."

" 'Tis of no consequence."

"But it is. I've deprived you of a diversion. How can I make amends? How would my darling like to go to Dijon to hear all the news her ears can cope with?"

"Dijon?" Her eyes widened at him. For eight months she'd been nowhere, save on tours of his vineyards. Now he would take her to the premiere city of the duchy!

"I go once or twice a year to report to the duke and receive fresh orders, should there be any; he seldom comes here."

"I should love to go."

"Good. 'Tis about time you ceased a cloistered existence and made a fresh start. And perhaps you should have a new name to go with it."

"Whatever for?"

"Ermengarde is of the past. There must be only the future for us. But you needn't lose it altogether, if you like it that much. 'Tis a pretty name, after all. Mightn't we just shorten it a little more, say to Ermen? Ermine, hmm, I like the sound."

To be called after the regal fur that trimmed the clothes of the nobles struck Ermgarde as ridiculous. But she would indulge him. The changing of a name changed nothing at all. She was still the same and the past would always be with her. "Call me what you will."

"Ermine, then." There, everything was solved, he thought, smugly. Lord Wauter was heading north, away from Chemille and Dijon; soon, no doubt, he would return to his native land, having given up the futile search for a wife who had vanished. And if he took his love to Dijon as Lady Ermine instead of Ermengarde, 'twould take a very shrewd mind to connect the two. He doubted that any would be so intrigued as to probe into her origins, as long as there was a plausible enough story.

The perfumer arrived before their departure for Dijon, accompanied by servants who shouldered their coffers of wares to the lady's chamber for Ermgarde's inspection, he covering every available surface with pots, jars and phials that mystified her.

Wizened and wizardly looking with snowy hair and beard, his bony frame lost in the folds of a scarlet houppelande, he explained the properties and benefits of each preparation for enhancing a woman's beauty.

"Not that you are without unquestionable beauty, dame, but to enhance is no bad thing. Take for instance this rouge. Your color is marvelous and so healthy, but there are times, no, when one is wan? In such times just a little applied to the cheekbones will make you look radiant with health."

"I never feel wan or in ill health," Ermgarde told him, truthfully. Frustration flooded over him and colored his cheeks.

"But there may come a time, dame. Women who bear children, for instance, can suffer months of fatiguing sickness."

"God forbid!" she breathed out loud. Since coming to Chemille and having the chevalier in her bed, she had employed a conglomeration of all the remedies she'd ever heard of to avoid such a happening—unbeknownst to her bedfellow, of course. She had not Wauter's child and she wanted no one else's.

"What's this?" She picked up a pot that looked to contain charcoal, and stuck a finger in it curiously.

" 'Tis for the eyelids, to emphasize the whites and irises of the eyes. You simply smudge the color onto your lids."

Ermgarde went to the mirror and tried it. The effect was pleasing. "I'll have some of that," she decided.

"It becomes you, dame," he agreed, thankful to have captured her interest at last. "And perhaps a vial of belladonna for the eyes themselves? In Spain, 'tis the women's habit to put a few drops in each eye to add luster and enlarge the pupil. What man could resist your violet eyes sparkling with added brilliance?"

"Well. . . ."

"Is it because the substance is extracted from the nightshade plant that you hesitate? If so, let me put your mind at rest. One has to swallow the stuff in considerable quantity for it to be harmful." He didn't add that repeated drops in the eyes would produce blindness in years to come. That would have been bad salesmanship!

The word nightshade meant poison to Ermgarde's mind, making her recoil inwardly from the harmless looking liquid in the corked vial he held up for inspection. Yet even as she shied from it, a terrible, unbanishable thought kept running through her mind.

"You can leave me two vials."

"Two?"

"I have large eyes, therefore I'll need more, won't I?" she said, with studied naivety and conceit.

'Twas hard for the old man not to chuckle at the absurdity of her logic. "Of course, of course. Now shall we look at the perfumes? I've jasmine from the east, lavender, essence of roses. . . ."

Ermgarde put the vials on the table before her mirror with trembling fingers, not daring to catch her own reflection, lest what was in her mind showed on her face.

"Yes, let's look at the perfumes," she agreed, forcing lightness into her voice.

CHAPTER
38

THE QUEEN OF FRANCE had been a fourteen-year-old Bavarian princess when Philippe the Bold, Duke of Burgundy had engineered her marriage to Charles Valois back in the 1380's. Supposedly she was to be a political puppet, but Isabeau of Bavaria was ruled in all things by whim, love or hate, rather than by outside forces pulling strings. Therefore, Philippe soon gave up on her.

The young king had found her captivating at first, but then, as his bouts of madness became more frequent, the enchantment gave way to aversion. And she, a voluptuous woman who embodied sensuality, took his younger, licentious brother, Louis d'Orleans, for her lover.

The murder of her lover at the instigation of Burgundy's next duke, John the Fearless, meant that politically she swung toward the Orleanist cause, and for a while she enjoyed a powerful position—the loss of Louis bringing her a rare flood of sympathy from the commoners. Then the Count d'Armagnac had risen as leader and Isabeau found herself thrust into the background.

At forty-five, and with a string of lovers and twelve children behind her, she was to be found at her own court of Vincennes on the outskirts of Paris, having left her husband Charles in the compassionate care of his young mistress, Odette de Champdivers.

She'd done her duty, bore his children, put up with the madman, and now she wanted to retire, her contract fulfilled. At Vincennes she would have no talk of politics, no mention of that irritant, Armagnac; only the continuous exploration of courtly love, as specified by Christine de Pisan in her literary works. Courtly or otherwise, rumors as to the goings-on at Vincennes had become a public scandal.

It was toward Paris and Isabeau's court that Wauter now

traveled, knowing it dangerous to go to the heart of enemy territory, yet daring to be reckless since he was desperate. Burgundy had yielded nothing and this was the last chance, his last inquiry before conceding defeat and going home to try and live with the knowledge that she had gone forever . . . was probably dead.

At Montereau he had dismissed Thomas Berkeley and Robert de la Vallée, sending them on their way with a commendable show of heartiness. Thomas clapped Wauter about the shoulders solicitously, telling the man to have faith, though his own had run out months before. 'Twas only his deep friendship that had kept him loyal to Wauter's cause, even when in his heart he had felt the mission futile and had to mask his feelings behind a cheery facade. Well, he could no longer show false cheer in a lost cause, and so he was going home. Things in Gloucestershire had been neglected long enough, and, if in truth that didn't bother him at all, it did give him a good excuse for leaving.

That Robert had wished to go with the lord had surprised Wauter. It wasn't that he questioned the young man's loyalty, but had never thought that Robert would give up, leave him. They'd been together for so long. He tried not to look hurt, to smile amiably as the knight took his hand and clasped it long in friendship.

"Lord, I pray you'll understand my need to go with Lord Thomas, for 'twould grieve me to think I'd fallen in your esteem. But as you seek your whole reason for being, so must I do likewise. My plans I keep to myself, for I fear you would upbraid me as to their soundness, but just as you take a chance going to Vincennes, so too must I stick out my neck for what I want."

He's going after Alice again! Was there ever such a pig-headed fool? But perhaps his determination would count for something this time—that, and a great deal of growing up. The knight had gained more than his spurs since setting feet to French soil. Naivety, shyness and uncertainty had given way to manly traits, many of them picked up from Wauter and the others he'd served under at Harfleur. And many lessons had he enthusiastically enrolled upon with the ladies of Jean-sans-Peur's court. If France had taught him anything, it was how to deal with women. Only time would tell if he could deal with Alice.

Wauter had hugged the young man briefly and tousled his hair, then watched as Robert mounted his horse and crossed the bridge over the Seine, calling out a farewell to Thomas, then counseling the knight, "There is a Magdalen nunnery on the outskirts of Bristol. There I think you'll find more than God."

The knight had looked over his shoulder, then nodded thoughtfully, a smile of understanding gone as he tapped down his visor into place.

Now it was only him and Brodrick—the oldest and most adventure-loving of the Shepherds sticking to him like feathers to tar. They had no soldiers to worry about and only themselves to please, and that was something of a relief.

At the town of Vincennes they lodged in a ramshackle inn, where no one took too much notice of them in their dusty traveling clothes and lack of heraldic display. For any who showed interest in the harnesses of plate and destriers, there was the not-so-improbable tale of mercenaries from Gascony looking for a lord under whom they might serve. Wauter did the talking while Brodrick limited himself to surly grunts; this having the tendency to make people steer clear of him.

Headquarters established, the next objective was to get into the queen's presence. This was not so easy. One could not simply go up to the gates of the royal residence and state one's business as with Jean-sans-Peur. Here they were on enemy ground, likely to be taken captive and held for ransom themselves if they were not careful. The queen's mood would somehow have to be gauged, her feelings upon consorting with an enemy of France ascertained before any steps were taken. One thing was for certain: her growing dislike of Bernard d'Armagnac meant that she would have some sympathy for anyone in an opposite camp.

The first step upon the ladder to the court was taken without too much delay. Barely two weeks after slipping into Vincennes, Wauter accidentally-on-purpose stepped on the trailing hem of a likely looking lady as she strode from church after hearing vespers. He'd given her face but a cursory glance, his calculating mind centered upon her clothes. Clothes told a lot about people, and this one was dressed in infinite splendor, like a lady-in-waiting or mistress of the robes. When she turned upon him angrily, trying to pull free her train, Wauter was mildly pleased to find her not only poten-

tially well suited for his plans, but also quite beautiful. The
task would be all the more pleasant.

Anne de Bois opened her generous mouth to rail at him,
then closed it again nonplussed, blinking at Wauter while
he removed his sole from the ermine trim of her robes and
flooded apologies. Well, well, well . . . for once it looked as if
going to church was going to prove fun, she thought, smiling
her forgiveness and ordering a maid to dust her kingfisher-
blue hem.

"A thousand apologies, demoiselle. But these trains do
have a way of hampering the wearer and those who would seek
to get closer to such loveliness, too."

"You were trying to . . ." She broke off and tittered prettily, the veil of her horned headdress framing honey-colored
hair and lending some color to her small, gray eyes.

Twenty-five, perhaps older, he gauged, leastways old
enough not to be too naive to suit, and definitely *too old* for
the show of modesty she was now indulging in for his benefit,
blushes and all!

"Monsieur, you are too bold!" she cooed.

"Seigneur," he corrected, feeling that a lord would impress
more than a knight. "With apologies once more for having
been so outspoken, I take my leave. 'Tis obvious I offend—"

"Oh no, I mean. . . ." Her hand was on his arm, thrilling at
the play of muscle under his garb, her words giving way to a
flustered silence as his amber eyes set her afire.

"Still, I must go. I would not jeopardize your reputation."

"You offend and jeopardize nothing, seigneur," she assured him, ignoring the women and waiting attendants at her
litter as if they didn't exist. "I am a widow of some years now
and my reputation has long since been lost."

Well spoken! At last some honesty. He liked that, liked her
the more for it. "Dame, I should like it if we could meet again.
Is that possible?"

"Yes . . . yes, I think so. The queen is exacting, but I do
have some time to myself, as now when I come to church, or
maybe in the evenings when others entertain her for an hour or
two."

"Is tomorrow too soon? We can meet here, if you like, at
the same time."

"No. I've a better idea. You could come to the palace. We

can walk and talk there and mayhap there will be some courtly entertainment to amuse us."

She was heaven-sent to aid him, it seemed. "And your name, sweet dame, so that I may speak it caressingly in anticipation of our next meeting?"

"Anne de Bois, lady-in-waiting to Queen Isabeau."

She extended her hand and he kissed it before handing her into the litter. Then, as the conveyance drew slowly away and she peeped excitedly at him from behind a brocade curtain, he blew her a kiss and stood erect and tall, determined that she would remember her first glimpse of him with relish and seek more.

For a week they met in the same manner, using the gardens at Vincennes as a screen for their lovemaking, which had commenced with lack of preamble on both sides on the morning of their first rendezvous.

Anne was openly eager. She fumbled with Wauter's hose to get at him the quicker, and Wauter gave a memorable performance. He'd had years in which to learn how to please women to the full, and those poignantly vivid memories of days with Ermgarde added polish to his style. But he tried not to think of her when he was with Anne, fearing that to do so might dampen his feelings for the woman. And it was vitally important that he please her, win her over so that he could get to her mistress. This was for necessity's sake, nothing more, yet even so he prayed that Ermgarde never found out. She'd never understand, no matter how noble his motives!

Well, it appeared he had pleased Anne de Bois, for she agreed to meet him again, then again, and the third day was all but begging for his assurances of love and by the promise of more delights on the morrow.

"Of course I love you, my delight," he had told her casually, pleased with the easy way it slipped from his tongue—as if he told every woman he bedded exactly the same, the words meaning nothing. He could almost see the determination in her eyes to make him mean those words the next time he spoke them. He'd won. And from now on he needn't try so hard to please unless it suited him.

When he told her he was English, thinking it time she was prepared for her role as mediator between him and Isabeau of

Bavaria, she showed no surprise at all.

"Ah, now the funny accent is explained. I never did entirely believe that yarn about Gascony. So what is an Englishman doing in Vincennes? Could you be a spy? You are my enemy, you know, but never fear, in regard to politics I am not unlike the queen. She hates the Armagnacs more than the English at times, I think, and she dislikes all her own family, save her youngest daughter, Katherine. You will be safe here so long as you do not shout your nationality from the rooftops."

" 'Twas to see the queen that I came here. I have a wife who has gone missing, you see, Anne—"

"A wife?" The lady looked instantly stricken. "You never said anything about a wife."

"I did not want her to come between us, delight, please believe me. She means nothing to me and our marriage was purely political. But I've a duty, you understand, feel honor-bound to try to find the foolish girl. This won't change anything between us, Anne."

"Won't it? I had thought, hoped . . ." She broke off with a petulant puckering of her lips. No point talking of marriage now and making a fool of herself. She asked coldly, unable to quell her curiosity, "How did your wife go missing in France?"

"She was with me at Agincourt. Even then we were quarrel-ing, you see, and she had followed me to try to patch things up. And come the end of the battle she was gone, someone had snatched her away." It was reassuring to keep repeating that story, for 'twas the only thing that could have happened.

"So how can Isabeau help you?"

"I doubt that she can, but I feel honorbound to make in-quiries as far afield as I'm able. I've already been to John the Fearless, but Burgundy has heard nothing of the lady. If I can possibly gain an audience with the queen, I shall beg her to make inquiries at her court to see if any of them, or any of their neighbors have made mention of Ermengarde of Syn-ford. 'Tis my last hope. If there are no leads this time. . . ." He couldn't say it, wouldn't acknowledge her death.

But Anne read his mind and it kindled a spark of hope within her. If she could bring about the audience and the queen's inquiries proved fruitless, he would give up his wife for dead. There was some hope, after all. Anne of Synford. Um . . . she liked the sound of that.

She lay back in the grass and laid provocative fingers to the shoulders of her deeply V-necked gown, inching down the fabric until her breasts peeked above the ermine necking and Wauter could take her nipples between his lips at leisure.

He would please her this day because it suited him. She was going to get him that audience, he felt sure, and this was payment in advance in the form she liked best.

The very private meeting between the queen and the enemy of France took place in the consort's bedchamber, such intimate surroundings owing more to the fact that the queen suffered from agoraphobia than a need for secrecy.

Anne escorted him to the chamber, then left immediately when Isabeau flashed her a dismissive wave. She then waited anxiously for him beyond the door.

He advanced, dropped to one knee before the queen and took the fat hand extended to him to kiss it, mindful not to knock her limbs, which he knew were afflicted with gout. Anne had warned him of this condition that often induced the queen to bad temper.

Perhaps once she had been beautiful, but the features were bloated now, the plucked brows and swollen forehead making it difficult to distinguish her features. She seemed to rely on bold colors to hold the attention of others, and this day she was dressed in a high-girdled houppelande of crimson brocade that matched the color of the divan on which she sat and the royal bed that stood at the far side of the chamber. The walls, in startling contrast, were hung with royal-blue tapestries smothered in golden fleur-de-lys.

"Rise. The Dame de Bois has begged of me this meeting, my lord, but I must straightaway voice my resistence. If 'twas not a matter of love and honor, as she informed me, I should not be receiving you. Though love for whom, I'm not certain. Anne says you seek this missing wife out of honor, but would honor alone bring you to the heart of an enemy land? I would know your feelings for Anne, and your wife, before pledging help."

On his feet once more and wearing his most elegant traveling clothes in honor of the occasion, Wauter seemed to loom over the queen, dominating. She liked not feeling the disadvantage.

"Sit yourself down."

He did so. Having decided that honesty was best, he began, "Gracious lady, I have been searching for my wife for nigh on nine months and have just come from Burgundy, where there was no hint of her presence, though I would have staked my life on her being taken by Burgundians after the battle."

"What battle?"

"Agincourt, lady."

She rolled her eyes in exaggerated horror. "Breathe not that name about here again, my lord. I'm loyal enough to France not to care to be reminded of that fiasco. Continue."

"You are my last hope, lady. I pray you can have inquiries made. Perhaps someone at your court has heard mention of the lady. I offer myself in her place until ransom is paid."

Isabeau cast upon him a cynic's eye. "*Honor* means everything to you, my lord. Or is it that you do love this wife dearly and the tales of duty and honor were for Anne's benefit?"

"I am found out," he conceded.

"You are transparent in your love, my lord. And your distress over her loss is obvious, that is all. I wonder that Anne has not yet noticed it. But then, they say love is blind."

"I did not intentionally set out to hurt her, gracious lady, but I had to get to you."

"No need to explain. 'Tis easy enough to understand. Though I pray you'll let my lady down gently. She truly believes herself in love with you."

"I shall endeavor to soften any hurt. I owe her that much at least, though I've hopes of our relationship dying a natural death."

Isabeau shook her head skeptically. He was the handsomest looking rogue. Her heart had gone all aflutter at his entrance. No woman was going to give him up easily once she had him. "I shall make the necessary inquiries for you, my lord, but 'twill naturally take some time. Until then the hospitality of Vincennes is at your disposal, though I pray you'll continue to masquerade as a Gascon, even with that appalling French. My husband's spies would like nothing better than to find an Englishman at my court."

"Thank you, lady, and I shall bear your warning in mind."

"What if we cannot find this wife for you, my lord? Would you consider Anne then?"

"I would rather not think of that eventuality at all, gracious lady."

CHAPTER

39

THE MOVE TO DIJON had to be delayed due to the sudden illness and death of Guillaume Lansier.

One moment he was arguing vehemently with Etienne, using his native tongue to exclude Ermgarde, though she felt certain she entered into the conversation. The next he gasped, holding hands to his stomach, and hardly quitting his chair before beginning to vomit.

"Someone help me. I feel . . . pain."

"Guillaume? Do as he says," Etienne commanded his servants. "Get him to his bed."

"Perhaps the hare he ate had been hung too long. It happens some times," Ermgarde offered disinterestedly, her tongue tripping over such a sentence.

"Maybe so. Has anyone else eaten of the hare?"

"I did, monsieur."

"And I."

The two soldiers looked ominously at each other, expecting any moment to be struck violently ill like their leader, the food and wine before them palling as having any gastronomic appeal.

"Then go to the guardroom and stay there. We'll keep an eye on you both."

The two men remained free of food poisoning, as Ermgarde knew they would, but it did no harm to send out a false scent. While the kitchens were being blamed, no one thought to examine the knight's own supply of wine in his chamber—supposing a sot like Lansier had left any wine not drunk to be examined. And when Etienne came to inform her that the man had died—his face sadly surprised, his head shaking—she maintained the same stony expression, exhibiting neither grief nor satisfaction at hearing the news.

"I do not understand it," he muttered, sitting down in quiet bewilderment.

I do, she thought. 'Tis called vengeance. "An act of God perhaps?"

His look was hard and questioning, but she met it without a waver of her gaze, before going calmly back to her needlework.

He might suspect, knowing how she had hated the man, but he would never allude to it because he didn't want to know the truth.

She should respond to him, she knew, for he was as patient and skillful a lover as any woman could wish for, but there remained that infuriating mental block, an inability to feel pleasure. Poor Etienne.

She'd begun to think of pretending, of simulating a passion that wasn't there. Wasn't that the way with harlots: to tell their momentary mate that he was the best, that no one would ever be able to do it better? But she wasn't even capable of that to save his depleted prowess. Somehow she couldn't act the lie, felt he'd see through it.

So this time when he finished, his body coming to a pulsating halt atop her, she held him close, caressing his lean muscled back, as she hoped that comforting him might take away the sting of another less-than-perfect coupling.

Panting still with exertion, his body atremble with pleasure, his voice, filled with hurt, came to her ear. "In the name of the Almighty, how much longer must I endure this? What are you, a block of ice?"

"I cannot help it!" Her small voice was apologetic and anguished. "Believe me, I try, every time, but something just won't let me lose control. I want to, Etienne, for I am fond—"

"Fond!" He withdrew abruptly and rolled away. "*Fond*! I burn with love for you and you hurl *that* at me! One feels fondness for a friend or favorite hound, not a lover! Why do you still persist in your love for him?"

"I don't! I hate him."

"Do you? Really? I bet he never made love to so cold a lump of womanhood! You're keeping your love for him; even though he's gone, deserted you, still you love him!"

"I don't, I tell you!" Ermgarde made to quit the bed but his hand shot out and grabbed her about the waist, holding her in place.

"The year is almost up when your ransom was supposed to be paid. How many years are you prepared to give him? Three, five, ten maybe? Must I wait till I'm in my dotage before you accept me as your lover? I'm patient, but good lord!"

"I don't expect him to come. I gave up on him when the missive arrived and I read that he had brought Alice back. And there is hate inside me aplenty. Still I have no control over the impulses of this body. If I did, Etienne, my love would be yours. Please give me more time."

"Always more time," he said in a mocking voice, releasing her and rising from the bed. He splashed water over himself before pulling on his houppelande, his frowning silence gnawing on Ermgarde's nerves. This night she was to be presented to the duke as the Chevalier Saint-Luc's wife, and she could well have done without this episode to put her on edge.

Washed and gowned in olive-green velvet tailored with a low V neckline and trailing hem of midnight sable, she sat before the beaten steel that served as mirror. There, her tiring woman braided her hair and set in place the reticulated headdress from which floated a leaf-green veil. Emeralds set into a heavy golden chain blazed at her bosom; more shone on her fingers and her headdress. When the illusion was complete, she rose and allowed Etienne to give her an appraisal.

"Quite beautiful. Now, have you remembered what I said?"

"About your having met and wed me at Harfleur, do you mean?"

"Aye. You understand the reasons, don't you, cheri? If I said I'd captured you at Agincourt and your husband won't pay the ransom, 'twould only look bad for you. No one will question my meeting and wedding you at Harfleur. The place is teeming with English women since King Henry gave the English merchants an incentive to cross the Channel."

"I understand and I'm grateful."

"And don't forget either that this night and henceforth you are Ermine, Lady of Chemille."

The curfew bell of St. Jean sounded as Etienne draped a

black mantle about her shoulders. "Let us away; one does not keep the duke waiting."

She followed, her hand linked through his arm, but even so something rebelled against the change. She was Ermgarde of Synford. Always.

From the vast kitchens below to the great hall above, the ducal palace of Dijon was given over to fanatical ritual.

The chief cook sat on high, holding his wooden ladle like a staff of office, while scullions ran and prepared food to be tested by his discerning palate. If it did not suit, the ladle in his hand turned into a weapon and he rapped their crowns. The cup bearer and keeper of the bread were ranked below him, but still above cook and carver because bread and wine figured in the Mass.

Above, Jean-sans-Peur watched in approval as his goblet was borne on high so that no lowly breath might pollute it. And, before he ate, six physicians tested the fare for poison with a piece of unicorn horn.

Dining done, he would then either join his court in their amusements, as the key figure whom they strove to please, or three times a week he would sit on his high throne draped in tapestry, and hand out judgment.

At such audiences, which could drag on for hours, petitioners, clerks and the *audiencier* stayed dutifully on their knees, while the court—from the lowliest of squires to the princes—were made to attend and hide their boredom.

Forty *valets de chambre* looked after John personally, while sixteen squires of good family found it their lot to keep him amused, to read him the latest chivalrous works, to play lute and lyre, to sing away his worries. For his protection, he was encircled by one-hundred-twenty-odd men, and a special body of archers.

The court was a place of extremes, especially in fashion. Any trend unfortunate enough to travel from another land via ambassadors and their entourages was immediately seized upon by the Burgundians and adapted, usually without sense of style, and almost always with disastrous results.

Here, the fashion to pluck out eyelashes, eyebrows and hairline reached its most dramatic heights; the fashion to wear pointed-toe shoes grew to such lengths that the shoes had to be

fastened about the wearer's knees with dainty chains to keep
the wearer from tripping; and certain points of the anatomy,
both male and female, were displayed without qualm. It was
fashion, and Burgundy would be second to none. Cotehardies
became indecently short and the necklines of the ladies
plunged until there was little material above the high waists.
Nipples nestled against ermine and sable necklines for everyone to see and became a commonplace sight that drew no great
attention.

The niceties of etiquette meant everything to this court and
their duke occupied an exalted position among them. Nothing
base must ever come near him; nothing common must offend
his greatness. Dijon was Camelot, and Jean-sans-Peur was
their King Arthur. Even his toothpick and the collars of his
hounds were forged from precious metals and studded with
gems.

'Twas into this atmosphere that Ermgarde now came, her
fingers tightening nervously on Etienne's sleeve as he led her
through a parting sea of startling color and jewelry, to the
throne of the duke. Beside the duke sat his wife, Marguerite,
and at her feet, on tassel-edged footstools, were the princesses;
at his right hand stood Philippe de Charolais, his Michelle absent from the audience due to some unspecified malady.

Jean-sans-Peur was fixing thoughtful attention on Etienne,
thankfully seeming unaware of herself. She sensed that he was
having difficulty putting a name to the face before him.

Etienne dropped to one knee, bringing Ermgarde down with
him into a deep curtsy that made the green velvet of her skirts
shimmer like the weeds at the bottom of a lake. She looked up
once and found Philippe musing over the peaks of breasts
above the sable of her neckline, and let her eyes wander speedily on until the inquisitive stares of his sisters, the princesses,
sent her gaze to the fleur-de-lys and other heraldic devices
upon the steps of the dias. Her gaze locked there to keep from
breaking some rule of etiquette.

"My lord duke, I have the honor this day of being able to
present to you my wife, Ermine, the new Lady of Chemille."

Ah, Chemille. Inwardly John the Fearless sighed, thinking
of his northern fortress, then remembering its name. " 'Tis a
pleasure to see you again, Saint-Luc, and with a wife? Let us
hope she presents you with a good many sons to fill the role of

castellan in the future then, no?"

"Indeed, my lord duke."

"Dame, you have found yourself a worthy husband. The chevalier serves me well at . . . um . . . Chemille."

Ermgarde felt Etienne nudge her arm and looked up in bemused guilt, her face coloring. The words had obviously been addressed to her.

"My lord duke," Etienne explained, "Ermine is English and did meet and accept my marriage proposal at Harfleur. Her grasp on our language is as yet poor."

"I see." Then to Ermgarde, in English, "Dame, welcome to Burgundy," before reverting to French and telling Etienne, " 'Tis a pity you come so late in the year. But a short while ago we had guests from England among us. Their leader was looking for a missing wife. But he gave up in the end and departed."

The duke suspected nothing, Etienne felt sure, yet even so he quaked inwardly, able to manage only a lame, "How unfortunate for him," in reply.

"Indeed 'twas. Never have I encountered a man so unabashedly in love. He seemed to diminish before my eyes during the months he spent in Dijon, to lose all interest in life. But enough of that. Enjoy your stay at Dijon, chevalier, and I'll have your annual reports in the morning."

"Of course, my lord duke."

"The duke's family could use a few pointers from Henry of England in putting his guests at ease. I didn't dare to do anything, lest it be against the dictates of their ridiculous protocol," said Ermgarde in a whisper as they melted into the crowd.

"Our duke sets great store by manners. There was a time, at the coronation feast of Charles VI back in 1380, when his father had to literally fight for his rightful place at the table. John will not tolerate such appalling goings-on here, and I do not blame him."

Philippe of Charolais loved his Michelle, but even so could never resist a new and pretty face. If there came a new flower to court that appealed, he set about with relish the business of plucking it. And the Dame Saint-Luc appealed greatly.

Why the duke's son should seek her out to dance with was not altogether hard to decipher. Ermgarde supposed it was connected with his earlier ogling. She was, accordingly, on her guard. Too, she could have done without the attention it drew to her, and dreamed of a quieter period of settling in to the court at Dijon. There had been enough tongue-wagging in England, back in the far-off days when Gloucester lost his head just a little, and she had no mind to repeat such experiences, this time with Etienne playing the jealous husband.

She felt the young man's gray eyes upon her, along with those of many others about the hall, and wished the dance soon ended, a stop put to his subtle caresses each time the music brought them together.

"No doubt Chemille has been deadly dull for you, lovely dame, but perhaps we can make your stay in Dijon more eventful, no? Your husband will be occupied with my father on the morrow. Mightn't we then find some way to amuse ourselves?"

Ermgarde stiffened and put on her most haughty expression. "Seigneur, I have slapped the face of an English royal duke for less than that!"

Then the music parted them and when it next brought them together Philippe was more intrigued than ever. "A royal duke?"

"Gloucester. But he had the good grace to know when to give up."

"And how might you know Gloucester? I thought your husband said he'd met you at Harfleur?"

Stupid, tripping tongue! She could almost hear his mind working overtime, cursed herself for lack of caution. "And so he did. But I came originally from Gloucestershire. 'Twas there that I did come to know the duke."

"And your family, Lady *Ermine*, who might they be?"

She liked not the way he laid stress upon her name, and she could have kicked herself for the fumbling delay that ensued before she could think of an answer. "They were shep . . . that is, they own lands upon which the peasants farm sheep."

"I see."

She knew that he did, only too well. She'd lied and the speed with which he'd caught on puzzled her.

Etienne was going to be cross if this Philippe de Charolais bandied it about court that she hadn't been wed to him at Harfleur at all, that she was indeed a prize of war from Agincourt. But how could she have known that so charming a male could possess so devious a mind? If the truth was unveiled, at least this silly pretence would end. So what if everyone knew her husband had not thought her worthy of ransoming? The shame might be humiliating for a while, but courts were in the habit of forgetting one scandal in favor of another, more recent one. It wasn't as if she was new to being a choice morsel for gossip.

"Will you reconsider our meeting on the morrow?" asked Philippe, as the music ceased, a threatening undercurrent lacing his voice.

"I think not, seigneur," she told him, steadfast in her rejection of his advances even if it meant returning to Chemille-sur-Seine in near-disgrace.

"Then I thank you for the dance, Lady Ermengarde," said he, bending a knee, his eyes intent upon her face.

"Thank you, seigneur." She was thinking solely of how she could break the news of her blunder to Etienne as she left the duke's son and made her way to her pseudo-husband, thinking perhaps it might be best to refrain from the news. Philippe might not do anything, after all; his threat could be hollow. It did not register in her mind that she had been called Ermengarde and had challenged it nought.

CHAPTER

40

THE FALL OF CAEN in Normandy to Henry and his forces in the autumn of 1416 signaled that the duchy had at last been tamed. Thereafter, as he traveled south the fortresses and castles in his path surrendered with no more than token gestures of resistence. Not to surrender, in the vain hope of French reinforcements from Paris, would ultimately mean a bloody siege and a sacked town. Caen had tried to hold out, and had suffered terribly at the hands of the English in retaliation. No one wanted another Caen. Too, there was the promise of reduced taxation from their conquerors. So they gave in, and by winter Charles VI's France had shrunk dramatically. Anjou, Maine and Brittany renewed their truces with King Henry and he—on his way back from personally visiting these provinces—besieged and took Falaise before February of 1417 was out.

In Paris the Burgundian mob fought the Armagnacs, whose leader, Constable Bernard, seemed more than ever to be ruling the country in his mad master's stead. Jean-sans-Peur was no longer content to sit back and let Henry of England grab whatever came into his path, and was beginning to set his sights on the control of France for himself. Charles was more mad than sane these days, the dauphin—to whom Henry had sent his challenge of single combat during the Agincourt Campaign—had died during the winter of that same year and now there was a new one—no stronger or less degenerate than the last.

Methodically and stealthily, Jean-sans-Peur began to incite the towns and garrisons along the Seine to throw out their Armagnac soldiery and let him protect them. In a time of need—and few were unaware of the English menace breathing down their necks—he, John of Burgundy would not leave them to fend for themselves as Charles had left the people of Harfleur and Caen. Rouen and many other towns along the route of the

English advance took his offer.

At Vincennes it was difficult to imagine the fighting on the streets of Paris not too many miles away. The queen was forty-six now, but her appetite for young lovers had not waned since the time of Louis of Orleans. She was keeping happy her latest lover, Louis de Boisbourdon, and showed no interest in the worsening state of her husband's faction, save to gloat if new misfortunes beset the Count d'Armagnac.

For Wauter it was a winter of deepening hopelessness. The queen, waspish as always and with a tendency—when they were not overheard—to refer to him as "English Dog," had done everything in her power to gain the information he so desperately sought, and had become increasingly infuriated and apologetic at the lack of reward for her efforts.

Bit by bit he had schooled himself to the truth. Ermgarde was dead and he had to give up the search. But even then he would shake his head stubbornly. No, no. And his mind would say, you delude yourself, Wauter. Better you join the army in Normandy as Brodrick keeps pressing you to do. That would be better than Synford without her, better than mother's reproaches. Nothing to be gained save unease from staying longer at Vincennes.

Not quite. He was overlooking Anne as usual, seeing her as little more than the instrument to engineer his meeting with the queen, and using her conveniently over the past months because she was always there, ever willing.

She wept a whole day and night before his departure, her eyelids puffing and her face stained with tears, as she beseeched him to reconsider and stay.

"You know I love you, fool that I am. What is there away from this place that I cannot give you? Don't go!"

Composed, he filled his saddlebags with the few personal items he kept at her rooms in the chateau. "I must. My army is to the west. You cannot ask me to sit here in the middle of England's enemies while my countrymen fight not too far away. If you love me, Anne, let me go without so sad a reminder of our parting. It may be that this is not the end for us. I've grown fond of you, and. . . . Well, I must have time alone to adjust to things without. . . . Give me time. Maybe I'll come back."

Her sobs diminished to nothing. 'Twas the nearest thing to a promise she'd managed to wring from him in their time together. Perhaps, if he could be away from her to reflect upon his situation, he might see her worth. She wouldn't make him a bad wife and she'd be faithful, just as she'd been since lying with him that first time. If only he would forget Ermgarde. Nay, she was not simple, though at times she thought he took her for such. 'Twas love, not duty, that had compelled him to search for that phantom-like Ermgarde whom she had come to detest, as it was love that had made him whisper her name forlornly in his dreams at night when Anne lay unhappily beside him. But ghosts must be laid to rest, memories allowed to fade. And when he was able to handle his wife's death, Anne de Bois would be waiting.

She dabbed her eyes with a handkerchief and sniffed bravely, a tremulous smile on her face as she handed him his razor and silver comb. "Go then, and find your peace of mind. You know where I am if ever you want."

She was in his arms, standing on tiptoe to offer her lips as her fingers locked in his hair, words quite forgotten.

So sweet and understanding a woman. Perhaps there might come a time when he could turn his thoughts seriously in her direction. A delicate hint of rosewater drifted to his nostrils, a fragrant reminder to take with him, along with the kiss that was thorough and passionate.

Two gentle-yet-firm eyes stared at the young man through the grill of the door; the woman had a thin, sallow face framed by a white starched wimple and drab veil. The head shook.

"Again, sir, I can only say that as a man you may not enter here. Go sleep off the brew someplace else and leave the souls within to their prayers."

Robert was beginning to get irritated. The night was cold and the rain steady, and even under the porch of the nunnery, the wet seeped through mantle, hose and boots, chilling him uncomfortably. "Mistress . . . sister, or whatever you may be called, let me tell you here and now that no drink has passed my lips this night! I've traveled far to reach here; from Burgundy, in fact, and I shall not quit this place until I have spoken to Alice Shepherd. Surely 'tis not so much to ask? She is not a nun, after all, and my need to see her is most urgent."

"Wait there." A panel slid across the grill, excluding him like a leper, blocking out the light from within so that he stood once more on a darkened street.

The Knight de la Vallée shuffled his feet restlessly, hating this further delay. What if he were to batter his shoulder against the door? Nay, they built these nunneries like fortresses! He eyed the oaken door with malevolence. 'Twas a good six inches thick in all likelihood.

Then those daunting inches swung inward and the porch step on which he stood was bathed in comforting light. The last nun was replaced by another, this one more forboding than the first. She looked him over thoroughly before waving a hand impatiently to enter.

Her height and girth exceeded his, and in her austere habit adorned with ornate, bejeweled crucifix, he guessed she'd prove quite an adversary if it came to using force to reach his goal.

"I am the abbess. Could you not have found a better hour for your business, young man? 'Tis well past curfew. Sister Celia mentioned Burgundy. Could you have connections with Synford? Do you have news of the missing sister? Pray God you bring good news and then you shall be truly welcome."

"I'm sorry, I carry no such joyous tidings, though connected with Synford I am. I have just come from Burgundy, where I was searching with Lord Wauter, but when I left we'd found no clue to the lady's whereabouts at all."

There was a long sigh from the woman. "Oh dear, and I was *so* hoping to give Alice some comfort. Maud took the news in her stride and set about methodically praying that her sister be returned to the bosom of her family unharmed. But Alice . . . such remorse."

"Could I see her, do you think? The sister said men are not permitted, but I have traveled far for this purpose. We are old friends."

"Could you be Robert?"

"Yes; why?"

"Oh, nothing. She speaks of you sometimes. That is all. I'll have Sister Celia take you to the cloisters. You may speak with Alice there."

The two figures who approached him along the arched gallery, which swept upward into a fan-vaulted ceiling, were so alike in build and dress that momentarily he couldn't decide which was his love. For an awful moment the thought flashed through his mind that Alice had become a nun, but then the two passed a wall sconce and Alice's veil turned out to be her mantle of unbraided hair. There was a tremulous sigh of relief within him that turned to dread as they neared.

Was this his Alice, the substance of a thousand torturous fantasies over the last years since he'd left Synford? Where was the cat-like gleam in those blue-green eyes, the wickedly fleeting smile or indifferent stare?

Instead of the spiteful fifteen-year-old he'd carried in his memory to France, there was a quietly beautiful woman whose eyes were now brimming with tears, whose once cruel mouth trembled with uncertain emotion.

He hardly acknowledged Maud's presence beside the other, but thought fleetingly that at last she'd learned to tolerate the weaknesses of others and made silent thanks for it.

"I'm supposed to act as chaperone, but I feel the need of a walk. You two stay here and meet me at the fountain in the garden when you've a mind."

Alice didn't know really why she had begun to cry. Partly she supposed it was the abbess's news that Ermgarde still hadn't been found, and partly the inexplicable pain and joy she felt at seeing Robert.

He had changed so she scarcely recognized the youth she'd treated so shoddily and carelessly before. But he was a youth no longer. The soft adolescent features she had come to appreciate because of the pure memories they evoked, were gone now, hardened and scarred, the pageboy locks shorn severely like every other soldier. Yet hard and imposing as he seemed, his eyes beamed warmth as he beheld her, a tenderness that she neither expected nor felt she deserved.

"Oh, Robert!" The silent weeping gave way to heart-rending sobs that brought him to her side in a quick stride, taking her in his arms and smoothing her hair, both dazed.

Could it really be happening? Alice seeking comfort from him, pressing so close against him that he rocked on his heels?

"'Tis all right," he soothed lamely, voice cracking.

"Nay, nothing is right. How can you even bear the touch of me, to be near me?" she sobbed against his chest. "I've killed her, Robert, with my childish spite. What right had I to play so awful a trick, to think I could ever win him? I can see it all so clearly now, but why couldn't I have been wiser sooner? He loved her, only her. And I tore them apart! I wanted him because of a silly infatuation. Because I couldn't have him I wanted him all the more resolutely; I didn't care about the consequences of my actions. Oh, I thought I loved him at the time, but now I know it was rather because of my jealousy of Ermgarde, and him being the first real man I had ever encountered. 'Twas the same when we were children; I coveted her possessions even then; I was *bad*!"

Robert folded her more tightly in his arms.

"Don't give up hope, Alice. We don't know for certain that she is dead. Lord Wauter certainly doesn't think so, and is searching still."

"Let it be so! I pray continuously for him to find her, for her to be safe. But . . . if. . . . Robert, when last I laid eyes upon Ermgarde I told her I hoped she'd rot in hell! No one can forgive me that, most especially myself. But I never really wanted her dead, 'twas just words . . . terrible words. . . ."

He led her to a seat that had been carved of stone, into the old Norman structure of piers and arches, looking out onto the contemplative gardens of the nunnery where the merry tune of a fountain was all but lost in the barrage of raindrops. And while he spoke, trying to encourage hope to blaze within her, she kept noting how he had changed.

He was like a kindly stranger, his deep voice ringing no bells of remembrance, the unconscious clasping of her hands between his, making her tremble as she had never done in her worldly-wise younger years. In truth, she was acting like some scared-yet-excited virgin! But that was ridiculous. She wasn't, and this was the very man who had relieved her of it. Alice gave silent thanks for the darkness that hid her crimsoning face, but couldn't hide the shiver that passed through her.

"You are cold?"

"A little," she lied, feeling surprisingly warm inside despite the appalling night and the rain that fell in torrents beyond the arches of the cloister. How could she speak her mind? Her remembrance of that night with him on the hill at Synford filled her with grief and shame, another callous act for which she had done penance while at the convent. He'd been but a lad and she had treated him cruelly, her heartless response to his inexperience enough to destroy him as a man forever.

'Twas fanciful and pointless to wish one's past back, to be able to try again. Yet with this Robert, the stranger who seemed as vivid as Lord Wauter was in her memory, she felt that there might have been a chance. Here was a mature male grown up from uncertain youth, a man who could and would have loved her if she had but let him. She'd lost him because of a compulsive dream, a need that *would* be satisfied. But it could never have been like that; Wauter was more than she could ever have handled.

"How could I have been such a fool?" She looked out at the rain, putting the question to the elements.

"Children do thoughtless things. 'Tis part of growing up."

"But I was thoughtless with everyone! My sisters, Lady Margaret, you. . . . I know not why you took the trouble to come with your report of the search, Robert, unless 'twas to inform Maud, for I deserve no such thoughtfulness from others."

"Yet it was to see *you* that I came, Alice. I have things to say that have been inside me for too long. I left my lord in France because my mind was on nothing but you and I found I could not serve him wholeheartedly."

"Oh." The inane little noise escaped from her lips and she waited, her heart accelerating and her breath catching in her throat.

"I want us to be wed, Alice," he said in a rush, glad to get it over with.

"Oh!"

"I know I'm nothing special, but I've been knighted now and am able to provide adequately for us both. We'll go away somewhere; they're always crying out for knights to do service on the marches or the Scottish border. We'll make a fresh start." There, he'd managed that, too, without a pregnant pause or blush. But his tension mounted as her face, concealed somewhat by the dark, remained expressionless. Was this the old Alice resurfacing? He waited for the bite of her acid tongue, feeling better able to cope with it now. After all, he had been expecting precisely that when he rode into Bristol.

But then there was a sound in the dark and, setting a hand on her trembling arm he realized that she was crying again.

"Alice?"

She didn't deserve it; she mustn't accept it. Everyone had suffered so much because of her, what right had she to be happy, to just walk away from the misery and chaos she had caused?

"If only 'twere possible. But I cannot, Robert. I shall stay in this place and continue to pray for Ermgarde. My penitence cannot be ended."

"You can pray elsewhere for your sister. And what about me? Must my suffering continue? Mayhap you find it impossible to love me still, but my feelings are as they always were. Say me nay and I shall be desolate." Vehemence gave way as he realized another rejection would be his destruction.

She took his hands in the dark, lacing her fingers through his and squeezing. "I do love thee, Robert, with certainty. Even knowing me corrupt, still you would have me. Yet even if there were not my guilt to hamper me in doing your bidding, still there is the fact that I am a prisoner here. I cannot be released, save on my sister's word. 'Tis fitting I remain until such time as . . . if she returns and finds it in her heart to set me free."

"Nay! Ermgarde wouldn't be so cruel. To know that you are reformed will be enough for her. And reformed you are, Alice, and are coming with me this night even if I have to clear a path to freedom for us!"

"Robert, nay; I want no violence! No more sinning to answer for."

They came to their feet together, clinging, lips fused while the rain dropped noisily beyond the cloisters, hearts pounding in hectic unison.

Alice drew away, feeling her knees suddenly weak. "I cannot go."

"You will."

He lifted her aloft in his arms so that argument was useless. Momentarily she squirmed against him and tried to free herself, but his grip was like steel, his lengthy strides taking them back along the cloisters to that part of the holy house where earlier he had spoken with the reverend mother. No one was there, and the door, when he turned the wrought-iron ring, opened with a groaning of oak on hinges, the street beyond beckoning them.

Alice found herself hoisted onto his horse, and Robert's body pressed close behind her. He took the reins, spurring the beast's flanks to bolt them into motion.

She could have screamed out for help, she supposed, but there was no telling what he might do in so determined a state. She didn't want any violence. And, then again, neither did she really care to be rescued from the clutches of this impetuous man.

As the horse carried them away from the convent, she allowed herself to relax against Sir Robert, luxuriating in the feel of his chest and arms about her, letting her head loll upon his shoulder. Later she couldn't even recall that it had been raining and that her hair and clothes were sopping.

Maud picked herself up and plodded across the grass path to the refectory, shaking the wet layer from her habit as best she could.

The reverend mother was inside waiting for her, an inviting goblet of wine extended. "Well?"

" Twas as you foresaw it. They talked, they did kiss and such, and then he took her up like a babe and carried her off."

A smile of satisfaction spread across the elder woman's face. "Then all will be well, I think. Alice was never one to find comfort for her sins in God alone. Sir Robert, from what I have learned from you, sister, will help her in ways we cannot. Drink your wine now, then go change your clothes."

Maud gave a derisive chortle, though in truth she was well pleased by the night's work. "I'll like as not take a chill. And they didn't even take the time to say goodbye to me."

"Isn't that the way with lovers—to forget about the world around them?"

Maud turned pensive a moment as she sipped her wine. "I really wouldn't know, and neither do I have any wish to find out."

Gloucester and the Earl of March had gone west, their aim for 1417 to bring into line the petty nobility of the Cotentin peninsula; Clarence had turned east with Salisbury, determined to make up now for the lack of glory that dysentery had dealt him at Harfleur. They conquered in their own names, the spoils theirs, yet still at their eldest brother's bidding. Henry's energies, meanwhile, centered on the conquest of upper Normandy.

Striking out for Normandy in full harness atop their destriers—it seeming prudent to be well protected and ready for any eventuality in the heart of enemy territory—Wauter and Brodrick found themselves encountering English soldiers instead of the expected French ones; bands of them laden with loot called out to them cheerily on the road, their captains beaming with the smugness of victory as they catalogued their exploits for Lord Wauter.

They had reached Evreux, and half the distance to Caen was covered when they met up with and joined Richard Beauchamp. He and his men were methodically bringing to heel the people who fringed the County of Blois. They were friends of old, the kind of company Wauter needed, having reached the depths of despair. Dick would keep him—once he'd told all about his loss—from doing anything foolish, and from the rotting of the soul the likes of which had set in that other time when he'd thought her lost to him.

He wasn't alone, after all. There was still Anne, though guiltily he realized that away from her he thought of her hardly at all, Ermgarde still reigning supreme even in death. He lusted after a ghost! And he cursed her, too. Christ, get out of my mind, woman! Give me peace, for pity's sake. I searched for you, so did Burgundy, so, too, did Isabeau of Bavaria. You are dead, lost to me forever. Now let me be.

For several months his work with Warwick set her ghost to the back of his mind. They took villages and towns, and sometimes helped other captains short of manpower with the taking of cities. There were contents of coffers to be divided, women to be taken—whether by rape, or by cajolery. He'd reverted to a brutish way of life reminiscent of those far-off days when he participated in the Welsh Campaigns. And with such dogs of war upon the prowl, the inhabitants in their path gave in with sullen meekness or fled before them.

The news of 1417—apart from Harry of England doing very much as he pleased in the west—was of the queen's exile to Tours.

The Constable d'Armagnac, who passionately returned the dislike she showed toward him, had informed the king—in one of his now rare moments of sanity—of her latest adulterous affair. Poor Louis de Boisbourdon was tortured then sewn into a sack that read "*Laissez passer la justice du roi*" and thrown in the Seine.

The queen was taken and kept under strict guard, her treasures seized by the dauphin and d'Armagnac. She had borne twelve children, but the dauphin was her only surviving son. Even so, his collaboration with her enemy was enough to turn her against him forever. When Isabeau hated, she was thorough.

Wauter wondered briefly how Anne had weathered the storm, feeling neither a sense of justice nor pity toward the queen and her comeuppance. But there were more towns to be taken, an agenda for to follow. She was resilient; he needn't bother himself.

Then, when he thought the incident done with and Isabeau of Bavaria tamed once and for all, she took everyone by surprise by writing to Jean-sans-Peur for help. Time healed, it would seem, and she was willing to forget about his having had her dear Louis d'Orleans murdered ten years before, if only he would deliver her from the detestably drab life imposed on her at Tours.

John had eight hundred horsemen ride to her rescue and bring her to him at Chartres, seeing only good in a queen who could support his faction as wholeheartedly and blindly as she had supported her lover, Orleans. Isabeau might be a cantankerous old witch, but she was still Consort of France and commanding of authority; a useful pawn if handled with delicacy.

Wauter pulled up hose over his now flaccid manhood and threw a handful of coins at the girl who lay sprawled across the filthy straw pallet. Some relief, but not much satisfaction there, he mused cynically, feeling cheated by the business-like tone of the act. But what could one expect when one was obliged to pay? Rape meant a struggle, prostitutes meant a limp, mechanical affair.

Combing his hair into place with his fingers Wauter rejoined his companions in the main room of the drinking house. They'd virtually rode into town uncontested, and now the innkeeper was ingratiating himself with a servility that Wauter found contemptuous. No man should have to grovel like that to be assured of his own safety, and he, Wauter, contributed to that condition.

Warwick called him over, shouting for more ale in the same breath. Wauter looked about the hovel that boasted nothing but a few crude tables and chairs, a rickety trestle on which the casks of beer and wine were set. He realized that Brodrick had disappeared—no doubt to some other flea-infested hole to find a moment's pleasure between the legs of another money-grabbing harlot. Well, might the lad find more fun than had Wauter. What he needed was a good, willing woman.

He perched himself on the table before Richard, one leg bent so that his boot rested on a stool. "Why don't we head for Chartres? Surely a close look at the courtly goings-on of John and Isabeau will be of interest to Henry? We may be able to find out something to his advantage, gauge better Burgundy's disinclination toward further alliance with us."

"Um." Warwick was more interested in the flouncing redhead with freckles who was making bodily overtures toward the speaker, thrusting breasts against his jerkined arm and inclining her head toward the door at the back of the taproom. "She's hot for you, Wauter."

"Hot for my money, more like." Wauter shrugged away the insistent touch, ignoring the girl as his amber eyes quizzed Warwick for a reply.

"Aye, the king will be interested in any information we can obtain. But I'm not so sure about just dropping in on Burgundy. Can't be certain of a welcome nowadays."

"We'll get a welcome, don't you worry. I'll just say I wanted assurance that the queen was safe. I'm not unknown to either of them, so 'twill not appear strange. And there's a certain lady-in-waiting. . . ."

"Ah, now I see the real reason for wanting to go to Chartres," laughed Warwick, glad that Wauter's mind of late dwelled less frequently on the woman now gone. He'd liked Ermgarde too, but one had to start over again even if no lady matched the other's caliber. "Very well, we'll go to Chartres."

Anne gave herself as never before, her former abandon as nothing when she found that Wauter had come back. She knew she possessed him fully and that his Ermgarde was nought but a painful memory.

Her body felt like fire to his touch, and when they rolled in pleasure upon the rug, she raised her knees and beckoned him in, sighing at the fullness that spread waves through her belly, scratching at his back when he took her to the heights of blissful timelessness and kept her there. "Oh, Wauter, I've kept myself for you, for this evening, and I've not been disappointed."

He rolled her over and stroked the honey hair, hands straying over her curves and globular buttocks; he caressed in languid silence, pleased at having an enthusiastic partner once again instead of nameless, faceless bodies who felt as numb as he did.

She quivered and her legs inched apart as a finger stroked with well-learned sensitivity between her legs, then raised herself as he sought entry again, her buttocks rotating against his loins, a soft moan escaping her as his hands cupped her breasts and kneaded gently.

"Oh, I almost forgot. . . ." Anne rose from the bed where they had lain, sleepily recounting the events that had transpired since their last meeting. From a jewel-inlaid casket that held her more precious items of jewelry, she took a rolled sheet of parchment and handed it to Wauter, nestling down close beside him once more. "It did come the day after you left to rejoin your army. Bad timing, don't you agree? 'Twas given to the queen, but she gave it to me to hand over to you if you should ever return. Who's it from? Not that I expect it matters now. The missive is months out of date."

" 'Tis from Philippe of Charolais." Wauter spoke in a ponderous voice, the brief lines of the message confusing:

"At my father's court there is a lady endowed of midnight hair and purple eyes. To us she is Ermine of Chemille. To you I think she is more."

Chemille . . . Chemille? The name was vaguely familiar, yet he couldn't think. Midnight hair, purple eyes—! Oh, lord in heaven!

Wauter turned to Anne, in his eyes a brilliance she had never seen before and which she found disquieting. "Where resides the Burgundian court?"

"Why, here of course, for the time being—until the queen and duke decide upon a more permanent residence for her. Wauter, what is wrong? You are acting very peculiar."

"Take no notice. Get some sleep, my sweet. I shall go see that my squire is comfortable for the night. My eagerness to be with you did cause me to forget about him."

"But it's the middle of the night! Surely he can fend for himself? Come back to bed, Wauter."

But the Lord of Synford was already dressed and didn't even hear his lady as he opened the door and left, didn't hear her indignant little call for him or her pleading, "Wauter? Wauter?"

He knew not what he did, save that he couldn't sleep after such news and wandered in the general direction of the stables where he knew Brodrick would be sleeping with the horses. Hating the English as he did, might not Charolais be playing some spiteful trick? But then how could he know of the black hair and violet eyes? Somewhere in the city, maybe even in the royal residence of Chartres, his wife might be sleeping this night! His Ermgarde; his life. How could he sleep on such a possibility?

CHAPTER

41

CHARTRES, OVERLOOKING THE RIVER Eure and the plains of Beauce, was teeming with Burgundians; the twin spires of the cathedral stretched heavenward in a vain attempt to escape the chaos below on the streets. Every lodging house, inn and religious house mindful of the needs of travelers was filled to overflowing, and the quick-thinking shopkeepers had also begun the lucrative business of renting out rooms for the duration of the royal stay.

Because Etienne had been among the eight hundred who had rescued the queen, he was better able to secure rooms before the onrush of the court. So their room at the Pilgrim's Rest was better furnished than most, and Ermgarde was spared the harassment that many of the late arrivals had to endure.

Since that worrying episode with Philippe of Charolais, nothing more had happened. She could only deduce that he had mulled over the possibility of exposing her as Saint-Luc's paramour and found the idea weak. 'Twould not be out of character for him to find such scandal too smutty even for *his* involvement! Whatever, something had stalled his hand and her short stay at Dijon had progressed smoothly enough.

They'd not long returned to Chemille when Etienne was called to duty by his duke to bolster the queen's rescue party. To Ermgarde, the time—until his request for her company arrived—was like a tranquil rest. No one dared displease her, no man dared anything improper. She had peace, a reprieve from the unharmonious relationship with her lover. His impatience at her lack of reciprocation in the matter of love was turning into bitterness, and that bitterness caused him to be angry with her. It was difficult at times to even feel fondness toward him, being continually regaled as a heartless creature, a cold bitch.

And then came his request. After months of absence it

wasn't difficult to look forward to his company again, to pray
that when next they bedded there would be something, an
elevation of minds and bodies that would turn it into something more than a mere coupling. If it didn't happen naturally,
then she would manufacture it, act the part of ecstatic bedfellow. Didn't she, after all, have a store of memories to draw
from? All those nights with that libertine husband of hers!
The sighs, gurgles of pleasure, murmurs in candlelit chambers.
Something in that repertoire could be reenacted convincingly
enough to satisfy Etienne's ego. She owed him that much.
And 'twas fitting that her performances for Wauter should
now go into the pleasing of his successor.

She unfolded the parchment missive. It announced that the
duke would trumpet Burgundian affluence in a colorful display staged for the queen. Etienne added that Ermgarde was
to come without delay and bring the best of her finery in her
train. He missed her, he said, and his enforced separation had
made him see how dear she was to him.

The missive had been penned, as always, by a monkly scribe
in Etienne's stead, known only through the spidery, hurried
"Saint-Luc" at the foot of the page, scratched with awkward
quill—his own—though the dictated content was fond and devoid of anger. And so Ermgarde arranged an escort and saw to
her packing, then set out quite cheerfully to join him. Perhaps
Chartres would be the turning point in their uneasy relationship—the very place for resolving differences.

There had been no time at their reunion to put her con-
nubial plans into practice, a session of kissing and caressing
through garments having to suffice for the chevalier.

"We cannot tarry," he had told her. "The duke holds a
feast and will have every available courtier there to impress the
queen. Wear your gold-and-crimson brocade for me, sweeting. The color does suit you so well."

Bathed, perfumed and dressed, Ermgarde had looked a true
Burgundian. The paisley-brocade houppelande—plunging
neckline at the back and front, sleeves dagged and lined with
black silk, a train trailing a good yard behind—together with
matching steeple headdress from which floated a lengthy wisp
of black gossamer, guaranteed that she would be the most
beautiful creature on show.

From Etienne's contemporaries and John the Fearless there

was praise for his wife's faultless beauty; from the queen's household—which seemed to Ermgarde to consist mainly of young men and ladies-in-waiting—openly appraising glances.

As the supposed wife of a petty noble Ermgarde was given no formal introduction to the consort, Isabeau making it plain that she would entertain strict formality only for the likes of counts and higher-ranked nobles. Mere knights and their spouses were only there to add to the spectacle, in her opinion, to be seen and not heard, and certainly not spoken to at any length, lest they be of the handsome variety that appealed to her jaded tastes.

She had turned once and looked toward the throne, surreptitiously, feeling no small amount of disquiet to find the royal eyes fixed on her. One of Isabeau's eyebrows was raised in query, her lips tight with thoughtfulness. Ermgarde's mind raced, trying to recall if she had committed some blunder of etiquette, but she could think of none that could cause the queen to stare so.

The royal gaze shifted momentarily to glance at the honey-haired beauty who sat on a cushion at her feet. And the Lady of Chemille looked there too, intercepting a narrowed stare from small gray eyes.

Perturbed, she had plucked at Etienne's sleeve. "Why do the queen and her lady-in-waiting stare so? Have I done something I oughtn't?"

Etienne gave a low, reassuring chuckle. "How would you feel if you were fat and forty and Venus walked into the room? The queen is probably just mortified by your beauty and her own faded looks. As for the lady—as a beauty herself, I should say she is assessing your points of merit and weighing them against her own."

Etienne was right, at least about Anne de Bois's scrutiny, but what went through the queen's mind as she examined the Lady of Chemille was not clear, even to herself. There was something about that face, the ethereal beauty, that niggled in her brain, and she had turned to Anne hoping that the lady might know what it was. But Anne saw the lady only as one she-cat sees another—with inbred suspicion. It played on Isabeau's mind long after the feast was done and she'd escaped into the sanctuary of her bedchamber.

The strange behavior of the queen faded from Ermgarde's mind. She held out her arms like some stiff-jointed doll as

Etienne unfastened her golden girdle and then slid the voluminous houppelande down over her shoulders. Sheer weight and
the force of gravity sent it collapsing to the floor in a shimmer
of red and gold, and then she stood before him naked save for
her jewelery and silk stockings, her dancing slippers already
kicked into a corner.

If she could not feel, then she would act.

His fingers toyed with the clasp of her heavy golden necklace, then that too fell, cushioned by the gown heaped on the
floor. His touch lowered, caressing her breasts, rubbing dark
nipples between thumb and finger, tugging like an infant a
moment before his lips took up the sensuous teasing.

Very well, if the body still refused, then she would pretend.

Ermgarde encircled her arms about his neck and arched
her body against his, an invitation that had never failed to
work with Wauter, not that her lover needed encouraging. Her
thighs rubbed his, and his manhood swelled further against
her belly as his lips traveled upward, seeking hers.

Is his body not handsome, his face not fair with the pale
gold locks and eyes like the sky? Then love him, give him a
little.

For the first time ever her lips worked against his in a concentrated effort that brought a moan of delight from Etienne.
His arms tightened around her until Ermgarde thought the
breath would flee her body, and she smiled, curving her body
into an inviting repose as he rushed her to the bed then set
about scrambling from his courtly garb. Ermgarde found it
rewarding to see him so happy. You will not tense, she told
herself, neither will you lie like a lump of clay when he joins
you.

He lay beside her, murmured French words of love as his
hands ran over her parted thighs. Where the fingers went the
lips followed, covering her body with kisses. She moaned, ran
her fingers through his hair, spurred him on with a softly
groaned "Yes, oh, yes" until Etienne mounted her frantically,
determined to ignite the passion within her.

She arched to meet his patient thrusts, clung about him with
a possessive gesture she felt sure would spur him on, and returned his kisses when they came.

She had begun to feel, tuning her nerve ends to torturous
sensitivity that sent waves of pleasure through her.

It only took a little initiative, Wauter. Now I'm rid of you!

Perhaps it wasn't wise to bring him to mind at such a time, but she had felt such exhilaration at her victory, a need to deal a death blow to his memory. . . .

Her passion ebbed. But it didn't really matter, not this time, for Etienne, enflamed by her, was already crying out his pleasure, thrashing away as though no longer a part of this world.

She'd made him happy, even if she'd cheated herself of pleasure with one ill-timed reminder of the past. Next time she wouldn't think of Wauter at all, she'd best him. This night she'd broken down the barrier, and when Etienne learned some control, could keep himself in check until she'd found fulfilment. . . .

"My darling, my precious!" Etienne cradled her in his arms, ecstatic, it seemed, at the longed-for breakthrough. "That was wonderful!"

"It will be even better next time," she told him, wondering why the sated body atop of hers touched no cord of tenderness within her, was irritating even.

Isabeau was growing restless, not so much because she tired of the company of Burgundians, but rather because Chartres meant being too close still to her husband and son for her liking. Paris lay not many miles to the northeast and there was always the possibility that that accursed devil, Armagnac, might try to recapture her. She needed a well-fortified city, preferably one endowed with a grand residence where she might keep court in style. Chartres was a temporary ploy, so she found it difficult to relax, and although these Burgundians had proved themselves entertaining and courteous, they were not her own kind.

She had spoken to John on the matter and he appeared to be in favor of Troyes, which lay still further to the south beyond Orleans. And so she had been weighing the suggestion—now that All Hallows was past—that she should settle in to her new residence in time to celebrate Christ's Mass with her own intimate circle.

But in the meantime the courtly atmosphere prevailed, everyone celebrating their recent triumph in colorful trappings designed to please the queen. There was the endless feasting, journeying to the cathedral to give thanks for her safe deliverance from her enemies, plays performed by mummers, and so on. She smiled through it all, though the to-ing and fro-ing for prayers taxed her patience to the limit, especially when the winter weather worsened her gout and she longed to be back indoors where the open sky and endless plains didn't seem so threatening.

This night for her delectation there was another endless meal, certain to be dragged out torturously slow by Jean-sans-Peur's predilection for ritual and sumptuous elegance. And, to keep her amused, a minstrel had been enlisted to sing in praise of her beauty! She'd almost laughed out loud when her Burgundian host had informed her of such, wondering how he could keep a straight face when mouthing such nonsense. Could it be, she wondered, that he was so used to monstrous flattery from sycophantic courtiers that he truly believed *she'd* savor such drivel? Isabeau knew what she was, and a beauty she was no longer. Still, if it pleased them to fete her, let them do it. There might yet be amusement for her in it.

Isabeau moved her bad leg tentatively beneath the table and leaned toward her host, whispering, "Who might that girl be? The one in black, down below the salt. She doth intrigue me, exasperatingly so."

"You mean Dame Ermine Saint-Luc, me thinks. A rare beauty, is she not? Though I'm afraid I can tell you little about her. Her husband met her at Harfleur, so he says, after the English had taken the town."

"So she is English, then?"

"Aye."

"Strange that she has such a name. Ermine." Isabeau said it to herself, musingly.

"Not so strange or uncommon as it might seem. I had at my court, back in the winter of fifteen, a man who's English wife was called Ermgarde. One can only assume that the English are learning a little taste at last in the naming of their offspring."

"Surely you don't mean Wauter of Synford?"

"Indeed I do!"

They looked at each other, startled.

Isabeau told him, "He did come to me at Vincennes, asking for help in finding her. I tried, but nothing came of it."

"Well, I'm blessed! The lord certainly was one for putting his all into the task! I wonder what became of him?"

"He's here at Chartres, my lord duke," she informed him with a superior smile born of knowing such news would come as a surprise. "He arrived yesterday with the English earl, Warwick, supposedly to ascertain that I was well after my ordeal. But between you and I, I think it was more to do with taking up where he'd left off with one of my ladies-in-waiting from Vincennes."

"So he's over the loss of his Ermgarde, then?"

"It appears so. It's funny, duke, but when you mentioned the name I couldn't help thinking that Ermine does sound strangely similar to Ermgarde. Coincidence? Yes, of course it must be. . . ."

Two royal pairs of eyes scrutinized the black-clad figure far down the rows of tables, their minds humming. Synford's wife had disappeared after Agincourt, Saint-Luc's wife had appeared soon after. Yet how could she be *the* Ermgarde they'd all been seeking so painstakingly those two years past; what would she be doing masquerading as the wife of another?

Jean-sans-Peur nodded, though his mind was still uncertain. "As you say, my queen, coincidence." He decided to corner Saint-Luc the following morning and ascertain just where and when his marriage to Dame Ermine had taken place.

When the eating was done and the tables moved aside, the court took to the dance floor, their flurry of colors softened by weak light cast from the few giant tapers set in wrought-iron holders around the room. Drinking cups were filled and the night grew noisy with chatter and song, laughter and intrigue, while the queen and duke watched the gaiety from the calm island that was their twin throned dias.

Ermgarde was enjoying the dancing, pleased to find Etienne as nimble on his feet as she.

They made a striking couple—he in beige-velvet cotehardie and matching hose, she in a black gown that exposed back and bosom in two deep *V*'s. Lying heavily between her breasts was a necklace to match her ruby-encrusted girdle; and her hair, drawn into cylindrical cauls of silver filigree, was topped by a coronet of matching metal.

That the men drooled while their women fumed silently had crossed her mind but bothered her not. She'd grown used to such attention, to attracting female hostility despite her attempts to blend in. They were no different from the court back in England, save perhaps that their suspicion of her was doubled because she was foreign as well as beautiful.

The dance ended and, rising from her curtsy with a helping hand from an attentive Etienne, she moved beside him in a gliding motion to be escorted off the floor in search of refreshment and a seat. Her grace only heightened the envy of every woman in the room.

"Shall we leave soon?" pressed Etienne, more ardent than ever since the night he'd had a taste of the heady pleasure that could be found when she was wholly willing.

"Yes, all right. I've danced my fill. But perhaps a little wine first?"

"Certainly." He signalled to the nearest cup-bearer.

Ermgarde drank, standing beside Etienne as no seats were available. She noted, as she glimpsed above the rim of her goblet, that Queen Isabeau was watching her yet again. It had become so common an occurrence since that first time that Ermgarde no longer worried, and felt bold enough to stare back unwaveringly. But then two figures, their backs to Ermgarde, blotted the queen from view and she gave her attention to Etienne who was sliding a hand about her waist, caressing lightly.

"I burn for you, precious. Hurry up and finish your wine," he breathed against her hair.

"A little waiting can only serve to sharpen your desire, my dear. Surely that can be no bad thing?" she teased.

" 'Twould be a bad thing indeed if my sharpened desire was to go out of control at such a gathering." Accompanying the joking threat came a kiss that was barely decent in so public a setting, and the roving hand came to rest on her left breast.

She pulled away from him with barely concealed annoyance, disliking the way he tried to stamp her as his property before others, her eyes darting about self-consciously in the hope that there had not been too many observers. Then almost as swiftly, she fell back against him, her eyes blinking in startled disbelief, a shocked gasp rising from her lips.

From the royal dias strode her husband, his eyes locked on hers, the shards of amber galvanizing her thoughts to life. Beside him hurried the blond lady known to her as Anne de Bois. Behind him came the Duke of Burgundy and Queen of France, their faces showing relish of the moment.

Her legs felt suddenly boneless and it was only Etienne, a hand about her waist once more, who kept her from falling.

The whole court was held in a state of suspension. Chatter died, the minstrels ground to a halt—leaving dancers stranded in confusion amid the floor—and all eyes turned to the commanding figure of Wauter FitzSimmons, who had a place in the memories of most. They could tangibly feel the menace about him.

"Monsieur Saint-Luc, I believe that is my wife you are handling so familiarly."

He was looking at her, and yet right through her, as if Ermgarde didn't exist at all.

CHAPTER

42

SHE SHOULD HAVE felt anger: Hadn't he deserted her, leaving her alone in a strange land to fight for survival? But there was only fear, its intensity striking her dumb as well as freezing her before him.

Etienne's fingers tightened spasmodically upon her waist and, had he worn a sword, it would have been drawn by now. His breath came in quick drafts against her neck.

"*She* is your wife, Seigneur?" Isabeau elbowed Anne aside, standing beside Wauter to look Ermgarde over as she waited for clarification.

"She is my wife," he spat, as if the words were bile in his throat, his eyes flitting to Saint-Luc's clinched hold on her waist.

He seemed to tremble with barely contained rage and Ermgarde shrank further against her lover, expecting to feel the back of Wauter's hand as she drew up her hands instinctively to shield her face.

Her voice sounded tremulous. "Do not dare to strike me, my lord. I have withstood humiliation enough because of you. I will not stand for that!"

"You have the gall. . . !" He took a step forward, but John's hand grasped his shoulder.

"Not here, my lord. This is not the place for dirty laundry."

" 'Tis the right place! Two years I've striven for this moment, to find her. And what do I find? This!" He cast the pair a withering glance.

"You liar!" she flung at him, her spirits returning. "You spent those two years with Alice in England, too damned tight-fisted to pay my ransom! Don't give me any piffle about striving to find me!"

"England? But I never returned—"

John broke in, feeling that things had grown too heated to

be staged before the queen and court. "Let us retire, seigneur, I beg you, and sort these differences out."

"As far as I am concerned, my lord duke, things are already sorted. I've found my wife, sorry gratification though it has given me. I shall take her back."

Three people cried "No!" with vehemence, though all for different reasons. Anne de Bois saw her lover slipping from her grasp and could not bear such an event; Etienne Saint-Luc felt certain enough of his claim upon Ermgarde's heart now to speak for them both; and Ermgarde, well, she would have said *no* to anything that Wauter decided at that moment, hating him as she did. She also did not trust her instincts, so devastated by his appearance was she at that moment.

Wauter's eyes fastened narrowly upon Etienne, voice sneering, "Ah, Monsieur Saint-Luc, so you have a tongue after all, though in your position I can see it is wise to remain mum. Tell me, is it always so misty down at Chemille? But enough talk of the weather. There is the little matter of honor to be dealt with. Not that my wife has any to defend, me thinks, but there is still mine to be satisfied."

From his gold-linked belt Wauter unhooked his riding gauntlets and tossed one down upon the tiles between himself and his wife's skirts. "We will fight for her, to the death, in single combat."

"Isn't that a little drastic?" asked John the Fearless. "Wives err all the time, my lord, and were all the husbands to fight, your country and mine would soon be without armies."

"It is proper and right," Isabeau argued, enjoying the scene immensely. "A fight is the only logical course of action."

Etienne, meanwhile, had relinquished his grip on Ermgarde and bent to pick up the gauntlet, ignoring her protest. "Don't. He will kill you!"

"He only has the advantage of size over me, cheri. As for a fight—I've never disgraced myself yet. Even when we lost at Agincourt, I still had my honor. 'Tis a matter of honor now."

"How easily you consort with those who slew your defenseless brother, my dear!" Wauter snarled over Isabeau's head, the loathing in his eyes like a stab to the heart.

"You don't know how it was . . ." she began feebly, her spirit evaporating as she realized the extent of his contempt.

Then the gauntlet hit across the cheek, stinging his swarthy face, and Etienne spat, "I accept your challenge, monsieur. A

fight to the death under the rules of chivalry, the victor to take
the lady.''

"No, I don't want that!'' Ermgarde cried out, but no one
seemed to be interested or listening.

The assembly room buzzed, and Jean-sans-Peur was already trying to decide upon a day for the event, suggesting
possible venues to Isabeau who yea-ed or nay-ed them.

"I trust you will not disappear again before this has been
resolved,'' Wauter inquired acidly, taking a sullen Anne by
the arm and patting her clasped hand fondly.

"With so amiable a companion, I'm surprised you want me
back at all.''

"It's a matter of principle, my sweet. What I shall do with
you when you're mine again is still undecided.''

"Saint-Luc, I should like a word with you,'' ordered the
duke, menacingly.

Then, before Ermgarde had time to miss his presence and
feel frighteningly alone, the queen was at her side, instructing,
"Of course you will not possibly be able to stay with your
lover at his lodgings after this, Dame Ermgarde. Someone will
be sent for your luggage and until the conflict is settled you
shall stay here. Anne, will you show the lady to the room next
to the chapel? I'm sure you'll find something to talk about.''

Gray eyes wrestled with violet ones and it was obvious that
neither would gain much pleasure from close proximity to the
other. Anne de Bois would rather have remained at Wauter's
side.

Wauter eyed the proceedings with the first twinge of humor
he had felt since entering the hall. Let her and Anne be thrown
together. 'Twould serve the cats right! He was going to find
Warwick, tour the taverns and raise hell until the town's wine
saturated his brain and he obliterated all memories of his
faithless wife.

Saint-Luc's woman, so obviously his mistress. And she'd
been with him since Agincourt. She'd been so happy with her
lot that she'd not even bothered to go through the rigmarol of
ransom. Where had she been on that foggy day when he, Lord
Thomas and Robert de la Vallée had stood beneath the walls
of the chateau? Hiding behind the walls in earshot of his desperate inquiries, laughing? And Saint-Luc had been so convincing, so sincere in his offering of hospitality!

He hadn't known the man then, and certainly didn't remember him from Agincourt. But Jean-sans-Peur had cornered him this night, and tentatively broke the news that his wife might be among them, though not alone.

The duke's words had been mere confirmation. Of course he had already guessed that she was at Chartres; Philippe de Charolais' letter had said as much. And how like Charolais to know how to strike to the heart of the enemy! When he'd begun scanning the crowd, he'd spotted her, right away, outshining all others in her gown of black and silver, some knight with golden hair cupping her breast in the most possessive of gestures! He was going to kill Saint-Luc. He'd decided it then; he was adamant about it now.

Jean-sans-Peur sat frosty-faced and impatient in his private quarters, staring at the stunned, blond-haired man. "Explain, monsieur. This night's work has placed me in an intolerable position. You are my countryman and should have my support. Yet Synford has right upon his side."

Etienne had been thinking hard all the way to the chamber and now his story was ready, foolproof against detection, he felt sure. "My lord duke, I know how this must look, but believe me, Synford is not altogether the wronged husband. In truth he did treat the Lady Ermengarde so cruelly during their years of marriage that she was glad for the peace of Chemille and never wanted to return to England. With her beauty and tender disposition 'twas not difficult to fall in love with her and do as she bid. She wanted to forget Synford, to be my wife in all senses but name. How could I deny her when I did love her so dearly?"

"Um . . . yes, well I can see that, now that you've explained. But the fact remains that I'm in a sticky position. You'll have to fight him; I can't get you out of that."

"I *shall* fight him. I wouldn't have it any other way."

"And you'd better win," said John demandingly. "The honor of Burgundy rests on your shoulders."

Ermgarde could only think that the queen was possessed of a vicious sense of humor to expect this Anne creature to settle her into new quarters.

They walked the corridors side by side, neither so much as acknowledging the presence of the other. Ermgarde shattered the stony silence by demanding an answer to a question at which she could already guess accurately enough. "What is Wauter to you?"

Anne locked her eyes ahead, a trace of bitter anger laced her words. "We are lovers, of course. And there was hope of a marriage—until *you* turned up alive and well!"

"Then I pray you'll forgive me being the cause of such disappointment!" Ermgarde said, thinking that her lecherous bastard of a husband hadn't wasted much time. First Alice, then this overdressed, pasty-faced court whore!

"This will be your room." Anne opened the door and carried the stick of candles inside, clattering them down on the nearest table. She moved toward the door, underscoring her desire to have no more of Ermgarde's company. "I forgive you nothing; neither will disappointment have the better of me for long. Wauter said himself he was undecided as to your fate, but I shall make up his mind for him. We'll be rid of you yet!"

Ermgarde barred Anne's exit; this woman was irritating her beyond measure. "And how do you think to manage that? Murder perhaps, or divorce? With Wauter's help? Foolish Anne. You don't know him as well as you think you do!"

The gray eyes narrowed in menace. In truth, she didn't know much about Wauter. He'd always managed to keep himself a stranger, the only real intimacy between them shared in the bedchamber. So her hissed threat was empty reprisal, she knew.

"I know him well enough. And, when I've finished reminding him of your amoral antics with the Chevalier Saint-Luc, I don't doubt he'll listen with interest to anything I put forward."

"Indeed? Well, mayhap then I had better warn you." Ermgarde caught her wrist and twisted it painfully as Anne made to push through the door with the last word. "Once before a female sought to win my husband by trickery. I had her locked away in a nunnery. Not so terrible a fate, you may be thinking, but I was lenient because she was family. I should not feel such compunction about using harsher methods on you!"

The murderous intent in her eyes was visible, yet Anne wondered. "Why do you want him still? You've Saint-Luc; isn't he enough?"

"I don't know that I *do* want him. Then again, why does he want me back when he has you? Think on that." She released

Anne's arm and barely gave the woman's trailing hem time to slide into the corridor before she slammed the door.

Anne's question had brought home the point only too well. Why did she want him still? Did she, in fact? God, she couldn't say. Too much had happened this night. She had felt compelled to warn off the other female, to stake a claim once more. Yet why had she done it? Some things just wouldn't admit failure. That was how it was with him. She hated him, and yet. . . .

To suddenly see him again, so handsome and arrogant, stalking through the courtiers toward her, dressed in scarlet like some Parisian executioner, sounding off in front of everyone as if *he* were the injured party. It brought back everything, all the old memories that had been suppressed but not forgotten.

Her luggage arrived soon after and there was small chance for thought as she tried to ready herself for bed among such chaos. Once in bed, drowsiness engulfed her confused mind, until sleep gave her the rest she desperately needed.

"So you've found her! Marvelous!" toasted Brodrick, but Wauter's sour face brought him up short.

"Not so marvelous. She was, literally, in the arms of another man!"

"Oh." Forboding frowns passed between Brodrick and the Earl of Warwick.

"Do you remember Saint-Luc, Brodrick? We called upon him once to inquire if he'd seen anything of her. Well he had, right enough. Plenty! The black-hearted bitch was there all the time, hiding behind the walls of her lover's chateau, while I fell into despair thinking her lost to me for ever. Hey, you," —he waved impatiently to the tavern keeper—"more drinks over here. Well, gentlemen, she'll not enjoy him much longer. I've challenged him—a fight to the death."

Brodrick sank upon his stool, perturbed. After going through so much to reach her lord in France, would she then run off with someone else? It didn't make sense to him, and it didn't fit into Ermgarde's patterns of behavior, as he summoned memories of their youth.

Warwick was enamored with the idea of combat, and mused aloud, "I wonder if the duke could find anyone for me to fight? Not in deadly earnest, of course, but with blunted weapons. I've yet to try out against a Burgundian knight, and what better opportunity could there be than this? Yes, I'll have a word with the duke. 'Twould be a suitable lead-up to the main event of the day—your clash with Saint-Luc. By and by, what's he like?''

"Young. Handsome," snorted Wauter, grudgingly.

"As a fighter, I did mean, Waut."

Synford shrugged his shoulders. "Can't rightly say. But he looks to be fit and agile, used to fighting."

"Should be quite a contest, then. Now who would be a match for me?"

He'd come here to get drunk and was making slow business of it. He shook his head, and his dark brows creased in a puzzled frown as he muttered to Brodrick, "What I don't understand was her anger. Do you know, she had the audacity to act the injured party, and after what she'd done!"

It was a matter of honor, of course, to fight Etienne Saint-Luc; the stealing of one's wife warranted such payment. But 'twas also a matter of obliterating the memory of the man's having had her. Just as the unfortunates had been turned to stone after looking directly at the Medusa, so Saint-Luc would perish for presuming to gaze on that which was Wauter's sole right to behold.

As for the Faithless One herself—he was torn on what course to take. He couldn't say what he felt for her now, but he was determined to have her back, if only to lock her up in her chamber at Synford and throw away the key.

CHAPTER

43

ERMGARDE WAS a prisoner. Oh, they might couch her status in more acceptable terms—"special guest of the queen"—but she was a prisoner nonetheless. Her meals were brought to the chamber and, if she attempted to leave, the guard at the door barred her way and asked politely what she needed.

The only thing she was sure of was that the confrontation between her husband and lover had not yet taken place. For surely she would have been informed. But why was she under arrest at all? 'Twas a drastic measure if the object was to await the deciding of her new master. And there was the irritating fact that both duke and queen had concluded that she was the guilty one, the erring wife. What yarn had Wauter spun about her to protect his own reputation?, she wondered venomously. Surely she could rely upon Etienne to put the true facts before John the Fearless, thereby clearing her good name.

The logs on the fire burned low, causing Ermgarde to huddle over the dying embers rather than bother servants at so late an hour to fetch more fuel. Soon her supper would arrive and then, fed, she could find warmth beneath the covers of her bed.

When a knock came moments later, she didn't stir, but called out absently, "I bid you enter."

"Your supper, dame."

She spun around, lethargy vanishing at the sight of Wauter on the threshold, the silver tray in his hands accenting the harsh plains of his unsmiling face in the light it cast. An expertly aimed heel shut the door with a bang.

"What do *you* want?" she hissed, anger and hatred fused to deal with him. The devil had bribed the guard. And for what purpose? She remembered Anne's threat and began to laugh contemptuously. "Do you think I'll eat from such a provider? Did Anne prepare it? A little vitriol in the chicken sauce may-

hap? Well, take it away and yourself with it. I've no mind to
be docilely poisoned!''

"Poisoned?" He laughed now, mocking her. "My dear,
I've no mind to take a corpse back with me to England."

"Then, what do you want?" she cried, the spark in his eyes
as he raked her curves answering too clearly.

He'd been thinking about her for a week now, Anne neglected as his mind became besotted once more by Ermgarde's
beauty. The urge to explore his feelings had drawn him to her
bedchamber like a thief in the night. She had no hold over him
any longer, he was sure, and this spontaneous visit was purely
for curiosity's sake, nothing more.

Her words came out, stumbling at first with rage. "And you
. . . think . . . I'd consent to having you! After what you've
done! First Alice, then with that de Bois woman. For all I
know you've just come from her bed! Nay, I say. Nay!" Her
voice rose steadily until she was shrieking, bringing consternation to Wauter's face.

Was he asking so much after two years separation? After
all, she gave it freely enough to Saint-Luc!

"Or will it be force, my lord? Your usual answer to an
unbending will. Well, I've suffered that indignity enough in
the past not to relish it from you tonight. So here, have me!
But I doubt you'll gain more pleasure from it than the other
who took what did not come his way willingly."

Wauter blinked, his arrogant mask dissolving in surprise as
Ermgarde snatched off her robe and proceeded to hoist her
shift upward, over her arms, then her head with an angry flick
of the wrists.

"There!" She cast the shift aside and stared at him un-
flinchingly, her body stiff under his gaze.

She glowed warmly in the dying fire light; a true Venus,
with long, slim legs and flat belly, full, upturned breasts and
that face and hair that were matchless. Even so he could feel
the coldness emanating from her, painfully withering the longing in him.

She didn't want him, couldn't have made it more plain, and
somehow that fact killed his urge to discover the truth. He put
the tray down on the table beside the door, not with a bang
that might betray his anger, but gently, opening the door as he
said, "Your newfound lack of modesty doth come as an
unpleasant surprise. Enjoy your supper."

Ermgarde steeled herself against the slam of the door that never came. She stared at the oaken planking, perturbed. At last she had bested him, his size as nothing against her weapon. But the victory was empty. She had never expected him to surrender, to do as she told him. In the past he would have carried on regardless, taken her and bent her to his will. If he'd but touched her once this night, 'twould have been the same. She would have fought, then yielded.

Thank heavens, then, that he had not, that her cold facade had held out. Never again would she be enslaved by a man, trapped by the longings of her own body. She could not love him again after what he had done, and there was an end to it. She *would* remain unbending and firm in her convictions.

It was late in the morning when Anne de Bois arrived in splendid turquoise-and-cream brocade. Her honey locks were framed by a reticulated headdress made of the same fabric, and laced with snowy ermine. She neither knocked nor went through the pointless ritual of greetings, her expressionless voice informing Ermgarde, "Queen Isabeau has sent me to help you make ready. The combat will be today, just after noon."

Ermgarde's face remained stony. What would have been the point in voicing her anxiety at the news to Anne? The Dame de Bois was hardly likely to give her comfort. She turned and left the room to Ermgarde.

In the process of dressing when the woman had entered, Ermgarde now dropped the gown she had selected and searched the coffer for the black velvet she'd worn the evening of Wauter's appearance. Subconsciously she knew that by dusk she would be in mourning for someone; the color would be appropriate.

The ride beside Isabeau in the queen's litter was strained but thankfully short. The tiltyard sprawled at no great distance from her residence. As both prize and the reason for the combat, Ermgarde found her station elevated for the occasion. The queen spoke to her only once, and then her voice was laced with reproach.

"I cannot for the life of me see why you set your husband aside for the likes of Saint-Luc, my dear. True, he is handsome—in that commonplace way that many courtiers are—and young. *But.* . . . One's own preferences are not shared by

everyone else, I presume. Anne de Bois was not slow to note
Lord Wauter's worth, you know.''

''I'm not ignorant as to the relationship between my husband and your lady-in-waiting, gracious lady, and need no one
to point it out to me.''

''Jean de Bourgogne will be willing your lover to win,'' said
Isabeau, waving and smiling mechanically to the crowds who
congested the streets and made the royal progress slow. ''But I
shall be more concerned that honor is triumphant, rather than
the glory of Burgundian chivalry. Who will you be backing,
dame?''

''Both of them, gracious lady, and praying all the while that
honor can be satisfied without a terrible price being exacted.''

''In truth, dame, I do not think you know who you want to
win.''

Aye, that was the way of it.

She had loved Wauter and there was still undeniably some
bond, despite his betrayal. But Etienne had been kind and he
did love her sometimes to the exclusion of all else. How could
she choose? On the one hand was a man who cared nought for
her love, who had left her to her misery in France while he
frolicked at home with Alice. On the other hand, there was a
man whom she could never love, but who nevertheless had
shielded her from much strife while never eyeing another
woman.

If she looked at the terrible problem facing her from a different angle—who didn't she want to die?—things became a
little clearer, yet no more palatable. She didn't want anyone to
die, but if a choice had to be made then let it be Etienne, dear
God, and not her beloved Wauter. She wanted *him* to live, to
go on hating him; she did not want to lose him forever. She
wanted him alive, even if she couldn't comtemplate returning
to England with him, and if that meant sacrificing Etienne,
then yes, damn it, she would live with that weighing upon her
conscience. Hate fused with love; it was difficult to separate
them. Was she becoming muddled by the two? She told herself
''no.'' 'Twas just that the capacity to truly love was no longer
hers, but she could hate with vehemence.

The tiltyard was a permanent sight for jousting practice and
the occasional tourney; its stand for the spectators was a
wooden structure built to last against any weather. Festooned
across the roof this day were the emblems of Warwick—his

bear and ragged staff, the castles and moline crosses of Synford, the grapes of Chemille and the griffon and portcullis of Bertrand de Gascoine, a captain in Burgundy's army who had answered Warwick's challenge.

The pavilions of the opponents stood at opposite ends of the field: English to the right, Burgundian to the left, green grass and list rail between them.

Ermgarde sat down and commenced fidgeting, knowing it irritated the queen and duke beside her yet unable to stop. First Warwick would fight with blunted weapons, he and de Gascoine putting on an exhibition to whet the audience's appetite for the earnest fighting to follow. Not that the Burgundian court needed such stimulation. All week they'd been talking of nothing but this confrontation. The trumpets sounded and from opposing ends of the field rode Warwick and de Gascoine. They met and nodded to each other in acknowledgment before aiming their lances in the direction of the royal box.

A knight personified, his fair face framed by curls and showing the nobleness of Galahad, Warwick found six courtly ladies vying to tie their tokens upon his lance. He basked in the glory and bestowed smiles calculated to melt their hearts, though when his gaze strayed to Ermgarde his features creased into a frown before he turned away.

Had she one friend left in the world? It would appear not. Even earlier, as she entered the lists with Queen Isabeau, Brodrick had made a detour so that he couldn't be obliged to speak to her, hurrying off in the opposite direction under the weight of horse armor he carried. There was only Etienne who would not shun her.

She watched the first charge that left both knights intact and still mounted, then turned to Isabeau. She just couldn't sit there waiting. "Gracious lady, might I be excused for a while? I must answer a call of nature."

The queen's lip tightened. "A lady should have better control over such things, dame. Oh, very well, if needs must. Off you go."

Behind the stand, away from the painstakingly formal pageantry designed for the spectator, everything was bustle and chaos. De Gascoine had broken a lance and a new one was being speedily hurried to the field, men-at-arms and servants seeming to swarm about in a frantic burst of energy.

Above, the sky was leaden, the twin towers of the cathedral disappearing into the low cloud that threatened a downpour at any moment. And beneath her feet the muddy ground chilled her to the ankles. She hoisted up the train of her gown to try to keep the sable from ruination, but by the time she reached Etienne's tent the hem and skirts were spotted.

"Etienne?" She pulled aside the silken flap colored with green and white stripes and entered, searching for him in the gloom until her eyes became accustomed.

He gave her an absent smile, his mind evidently trained upon other things, as one of his men fastened his greaves.

"What are you doing here? You should be with the queen and duke."

"I came to wish you luck."

"That was sweet of you. I feel confident, Ermgarde. I've been working down here all week with de Gascoine. The practice will stand me in good stead."

He cursed the man who knelt, having difficulty getting the poleyn of his right knee to fit. "I wish to God that Lansier were here. He could fit a harness in the blinking of an eye."

Ermgarde glanced away, a wave of guilt washing momentarily over her. She watched instead the slow progress of his dresser, feeling her presence unwanted at such a time. She supposed she shouldn't distract him longer when he was so preoccupied, and pulled back the flap of the pavilion. "I'll leave you now."

He looked up fleetingly, then down as he schooled the blundering man, and acknowledged her leave-taking absently. "Aye, off you go. No point in farewells and all that. I'll be seeing you again later, after all."

Would he? She found his confidence worrisome, and felt she should instill some wariness of his opponent in him.

"Did you know that during the Agincourt Campaign he came by the name of Sire de Morte? 'Twas bestowed upon him by the French who learned his worth upon the field the hard way."

No, it was obvious he didn't, she could tell, for his frown deepened, the blue eyes gleaming as he recognized the name. Who *hadn't* heard of the Sire de Morte? He waved aside the warning with loud bravado. "Legends have a way of failing to measure up to the reality of the people who embody them."

She had warned him. What more could she do? Perhaps,

despite his seeming recklessness, he would heed her words. Even so, was to be careful enough to keep him from being killed when Wauter came at him in earnest? Her husband would be out to kill, to avenge his honor, unless. . . .

Brodrick barred the entrance to the pavilion, his nostrils flaring in rage. "Your business here, Ermgarde Blackheart?"

"None of yours!" she hissed back stonily, inwardly injured by such words from her brother. "I come to speak with my husband. Tell him I'm here, if you please."

"I can vouch for the fact that he doesn't want to see you. He's resting before the fight."

"Tell him I am here, Brodrick!" she ordered, voice raising in pitch with anger.

"He sleeps, I say!" her brother shouted back.

Then a well-known voice began to grumble angrily within the pavilion, "Hells bells, cannot I find a moment to myself this day. First Anne, now what?"

Wauter's face appeared through the gap of the pavilion entrance at a point just above Brodrick's own. He stopped his cursing and narrowed his gaze as he recognized Ermgarde. "What do you want?"

"A word. Alone."

He lifted his brows quizzically. "Very well, but 'twill have to be quick." His eyes looked down the field, through Warwick's spectating soldiery, to where the earl was circling the Burgundian with sword drawn. "I'll have to make ready in a while for my appearance on the field. Brodrick, ensure that everything is in readiness for a hasty dressing."

" 'Tis already done, lord," stated the squire, loath to leave his place before the entrance.

"Then go check just to be sure," insisted Wauter.

The young man started off, but not before aiming one last black look at his sister.

"Such a passionate protector you have acquired," mused Ermgarde scathingly, entering the tent as Wauter stepped aside. "He suspects my reasons for coming here. No doubt doesn't put it past me to stealthily murder you so that you cannot kill Etienne."

"I wouldn't put it past you, either," Wauter told her, bluntly, standing with his legs wide planted and his arms across his chest. He was in tunic and hose, the insides of arms, backs of legs and gusset sewn over with chain mail. To her eyes he seemed to fill the octagonal pavilion.

"Well, get to the point, my dear. What brings you here? I'm surprised you managed it at all. Anne tells me the queen had been keeping you under close guard."

Ermgarde's face turned decidedly sour at the mention of the Dame de Bois, but there was no time now for recriminations. She straightened her shoulders. "I've come to ask mercy for Etienne."

"Huh! I should have known 'twould be something to do with him," he sneered, all attentiveness gone now. "If he has nerve enough, let him beg his own mercy upon the field. Only then will I listen! *Your* pleas on his behalf are wasted."

"But why must you kill him, Wauter? Wound and humiliate him if you must, but be merciful, for he is not your match."

"An unfair match or not, he deserves to die."

"I'll make a bargain with you. Spare him and I'll come back willingly to Synford with you."

"Now what sort of bargain is that? If I kill him I get you anyhow, dubious prize though you may be."

Nay, she wouldn't rise to such baiting. She must stay calm. "Aye, you'd have me back, but not willingly in such an event."

"Your opinion of yourself is somewhat inflated, my dear. I want you back because of the principle of the thing. You *belong* to me. Whether you're willing or not is of no import, seeing as how I've no mind to treat you as a wife when I get you home!"

Inexplicably, she felt wounded. It might well be that she had lost power over him. Even last night he had given in far more easily than she could ever have imagined. Had his hunger gone, along with his love? Ah, what a relief that must be for him, and she wished it was the same for herself. But even hating him passionately, still she could not conquer the incomprehensible hold his presence had over her. This she would never be able to find with another—involuntary longing, expectancy that set her knees to quivering, the feeling of detachment from everything about her when she looked into his smoldering eyes.

Wauter had been watching her features in their throes of thoughtful consternation and now he jolted her back to the present. "By and by, though, you might give me a sample of this willingness now and mayhap I shall reconsider."

He grasped the ends of the black veil that floated at Ermgarde's breast and drew her purposefully toward him. She moved as required, violet eyes shooting sparks, since she risked having coronet, pins and veil pulled painfully from her head.

"Remember, you are on trial here, so give a good account of yourself. Dear Etienne's life hangs in the balance," he jeered, face close to hers as he bent over her.

She shook her head and immediately tried to extricate herself from his arms. "Nay, not even for him can I go through with this cruelty of yours. I've changed my mind. Release me. I shall be missed and must return to the queen."

"Nay," he said simply, a large hand cupping her chin so that she couldn't reject his kiss.

She ceased to fight. Something inside her wanted to find out if he could bewitch her the same after so long. He could. His warm mouth robbed her instantly of breath, his tongue explored, his teeth bruised her lips. A hand came and rested on the back of her head, drawing her closer so that their breathes mingled and nothing but a gentle, insistent sensation lapped over her.

Ermgarde was lowered to the pavilion couch, yet was not truly aware of the fact, nor that she tugged like a mindless creature at his tunic, trying to make contact with the flesh beneath.

"No time," he moaned regretfully.

She clung to him frantically, fearing he meant to leave her. "Please!"

"I meant no time for undressing," he assured, his hands catching the hem of her gown and inching it up, fingers caressing her flesh all the while. The queen, the duke and all the court of Burgundy could have crowded in upon them at that moment, but it wouldn't have stopped him.

When her thighs and belly were exposed and he had a leg insinuated between them, Wauter turned his attention to her coronet and veil, saying "Such lethal points to its fleuron; I don't care to lose an eye, especially this day when I need all my senses."

The coronet fell to the floor and he drew his fingers through her tresses like a comb, draping the mass about her breasts so the feel of it was never far away, then he found her lips again, the magic of moments ago encompassing them both once more. His fingers found the shoulders of her gown and peeled them down to expose the breasts that were round and tautly nippled with excitement.

When he entered her, her mind reeling from his kiss, it was enough to make her convulse from head to toe as she wrapped her arms and legs about him. Each thrust that followed was like the exquisite agony of dying, drawing whimpers and moans from deep within her.

She'd almost forgotten what it could be like, could never remember it being quite like this. She was out of control, allowing him to do this to her, mindlessness personified. She'd given not a thought to anything, thank heavens, thank heavens! And now too soon she felt herself spiraling upward, a hungry, willing victim of his unleashed savagery, her tongue finding his, her loins grinding against the onslaught, cries erupting when the pleasure of his mouth upon her nipples made her writhe.

She grasped at his buttocks and pulled him deeper into her, the surer legs stiffening as warm waves passed one after the other through her, leaving her to gasp against his chest.

There was scant time to recover her strength when she felt Wauter making a relentless drive for home and arched herself against him once more, running hands over his flanks in an old remembered gesture that had always sent him quivering more quickly upon his way. He pierced her again and again, madly, his breath turning to sobs of pleasure, his loins jerking spasmodically until all was spent.

"Oh, Ermgarde." It was a cry of pleasure mingled with regret against her breast.

"Aye, I know," she murmured. Were there too many hurts to be overcome? So much had happened in the two years of separation and before.

Reality intruded.

First there was Brodrick beyond the entrance to the pavilion, calling urgently, "My lord, are you all right? The earl has beaten de Gascoine and we must make you ready."

To which Wauter gave an infuriated answer. "Of course I'm all right! Bloody fool!"

Then the hue and cry. "Dame Ermgarde of Synford! Dame Ermgarde of Synford! Where be ye?"

The couple atop the couch separated without a word and straightened their garments, minds striving frantically to adjust to the present.

Wauter straightened his hose and called to Brodrick as an afterthought, "Bring my harness and be quick about it."

Ermgarde readjusted her girdle and smoothed her disheveled hair away from her face as best she could. "I'm coming! I'm coming!" she called out as the hue and cry came again. She paused at the flap of the pavilion, the silk of its walls within her fingers, turning to behold her husband questioningly that last time. If he'd said, "Stay, let us flee this place together!" she would have gone with him, come to terms with her grudges and festering hatred, put them aside on account of what had just happened.

But her brother was at the entrance now, elbowing her aside impatiently, his arms filled with cuirass, leg harness, gauntlets and helm. Nought else could be said save, "Good luck my husband."

Wauter nodded, his habitual curtness returning as Brodrick knelt before him and expertly fastened the first leg harness in place. His amber eyes held her momentarily. "Dusk will see this thing resolved."

"Aye." She let the flap drop, giving him privacy for his hurried dressing, then stepped backward into two green-clad guards of the Burgundian court.

"Are you Dame Ermengarde of Synford?"

"I am," she admitted, falling in between them with unconscious regard for regimentality.

"Then we will escort you back to the royal stand. The queen has been worrying about you."

"There was no need. I simply became confused by all the pavilions and lost my way. I know where I am now, though."

"Even so we will see you there safely."

"As you wish."

The wind of the winter day rifled her hair, sweeping it about her face luxuriantly. It never once occurred to Ermgarde that she was minus her coronet and veil.

CHAPTER
44

ERMGARDE SLIPPED surreptitiously into her seat once more, thankful that the trumpeters and heralds diverted Queen Isabeau's attention. Behind her, smiling smugly, was Philippe of Charolais. Who would have thought one mischievous little letter could afford him such fun? His dear father was in an uproar over this whole business, knowing that a fight between Briton and Burgundian would only exacerbate already strained relations with Henry.

The Lady of Synford was feeling positively sick, and fearful lest she do something ridiculous like faint. She could feel the damp layer of clamminess that covered her forehead, shook her head gently to try to clear the buzzing in her ears. Lord, how was she to sit there and watch?

Then Isabeau swung around in her throne-like seat with obvious annoyance, her eyes accusing. "What took you so long, dame?"

"I . . . It was necessary that I go some ways off to be assured of privacy, gracious lady. And then I became somewhat confused by the route back. Luckily two helpful guards escorted me."

There was a derisive snort, disbelieving eyes fastening on Ermgarde's naked head, then Isabeau's attention returned to the field where the final blast of trumpets was bringing the knights from their respective pavilions.

"Your husband appears not to be wearing a surcoat. How odd."

"When the English fight in earnest, it has become their custom to forsake such pointless trappings as might hamper them," informed Ermgarde for the queen's enlightenment.

"It is also their custom to be a dull, colorless race," came the acid response.

Bristling at the slight, Ermgarde reminded her, "But our

326

dullness does serve us well on occasion, gracious lady. At Agincourt only the king wore a surcoat and crown so that his men might see him clearly on the battlefield and take heart. And, far from being dull, the field of gleaming steel was quite spectacular, and preferable to the eye than so many French surcoats and banners trampled in the mire."

Isabeau's lips went white with suppressed fury, the mention of Agincourt almost too much to be borne.

Philippe of Charolais bent forward, taking the side of his temporarily mute mother-by-marriage. "I did hear, from one who was at the battle, that your king did dress others in surcoats and crowns also, to cheat good French knights of the honor of slaying him!"

Ermgarde faced him boldly. "Then the man who told such a dishonorable tale was a liar, seigneur! *I* was there and can vouch that England fielded only one king and that he did fight with valor."

"Do be quiet, all of you!" ordered Jean-sans-Peur, scowling at them all. "The place of mortal combat is not suitable for such petty bickering."

Isabeau turned her ire upon him. "Guard your tongue better, duke! The Queen of France indulges in *nothing* that is petty!"

John muttered a less-than-contrite apology, turning brusquely at the approach of FitzSimmons and Saint-Luc.

The Burgundian looked splendid in his steel breast-and-back plates, draped with a green-and-white quartered surcoat, emblazoned with bunches of grapes which were his personal charges. Even his horse was dressed for the occasion in a silken caparison that bore the same design, and a gleaming steel chafron to protect his long head.

The Briton by comparison was austere—his only decoration a steel castle atop his helm, which was tucked under his left arm—the black metal of his armour gleaming like mined coal. Rogue, too, was without the beautiful white-silk caparison that Ermgarde had once stitched for him, sporting only a spiked chafron and shoulder plate that would lend protection against the head-on enemy.

The men ignored each other; no glimmer of recognition or acknowledgement passed between them as Jean-sans-Peur rose to his feet and addressed them, voice loud for the benefit of the spectators.

"On this day and, I must stress *without* my willingness, these two knights have taken the decision to fight upon a matter of personal honor. Both claim right upon their side, leaving the issue to be resolved by combat according to the ancient laws of chivalry—honor to be satisfied only by a fight to the death. I ask that they fight fairly and cleanly, and give quarter if it be asked."

"Nay, my lord duke!" cried Etienne, "A fight to the death it must be for such a prize."

What he meant, thought Ermgarde, wretchedly, was that one of them *had* to die. They couldn't both survive to claim her again. How was she to carry such a load upon her conscience?

"What say you, my Lord of Synford?" asked John.

"I say it really makes no odds to me, my lord duke. I've never, nor shall I ever, ask for quarter upon the field of true battle. Besides, 'twas I who asked that this be to the death."

"Very well, if you both insist, then let it be to the death. To your stations . . . and let the fight commence."

Momentarily she felt their eyes upon her as if they would salute the prize for which they fought, but Ermgarde kept her eyes downcast, fearing to look at either lest she dishearten the other. She could express no partiality; unlike Isabeau who called cheerily after Wauter, though wisely not loud enough for the French spectators on the other side of the list to catch. As the queen, she had a duty to appear patriotic. "My hopes are with you, English Dog!"

The knights reached their starting posts, secured their helms, lowered their visors, then accepted the gaily striped, deadly sharp lances that their squires held up to them. Satisfied that the gauntleted hand was positioned just so behind the guard, they allowed their shields to be strapped to the left forearm and were ready.

The trumpets burst forth with a high-pitched, speedily concluded fanfare, followed by the sound of thundering hooves that grew as the contenders neared the royal stand; a hundred breaths bated as they waited for the first clash, hardly daring to exhale until it was done and the damage known.

Ermgarde had closed her eyes, not wanting to look, but Isabeau jabbed her unmercifully back to awareness, as if to say, "This is your doing. Have the decency to see it through." And so she watched, wanting to shriek with terror as the lances tangled and scraped on the wood shields that first time, Wauter's splintering and breaking in half with the force of his charge against Saint-Luc.

Etienne reeled in the saddle but stayed seated, and thus, both appearing unharmed, they wheeled and returned to their stations—Wauter for a fresh lance, Etienne to regain the wind that had been knocked from him.

Thank God. Ermgarde shuddered a sigh, but remained stiff in her seat, causing Isabeau to give her a withering glance and tell her, uncomfortingly, "You'll have to gain better control of yourself, dame. I've known these things to go on for hours before the death blow was struck!"

Wauter took up the fresh lance and nodded to Brodrick to signal all was well. Aye, so far it was like tiltyard practice back at Synford. He didn't feel taxed. Still, he'd discerned that Saint-Luc had strength in his lance arm, if not the weight to put him on a par with Wauter. He shouldn't underestimate the younger man.

The next pass brought no results at all, both lances glancing harmlessly off the opposing shield. Wauter spurred Rogue back to his station, raising his visor to dash the sweat from his eyelids. 'Twas like a bathhouse inside his helm.

"Is the lance fast?"

Brodrick nodded after close inspection of the shaft. "It took no damage that last time."

Wauter looked down the field, could see Saint-Luc was ready, and set spurs to his mount, a nod of the head bringing visor down over his eyes. "Come on, old friend," he encouraged the enthusiastic Rogue. "This time."

His own breathing and the heavy plod of Rogue's hooves overshadowed all other sounds, the noise of the crowd a faint rumble within his enclosing helm. Down the field the chevalier came at him head-on, the white head of his lance camouflaged against the caparison of his horse. Wauter aimed his point at the vulnerable spot inside the shield, and readied to take the shock of contact when it came.

The roars and shrieks of the crowd signaled that something had happened, though his lance arm told him otherwise. He'd scored no direct hit, could tell by the continued inertia that sent him forward in the saddle to rest against Rogue's neck. So what—?

Of a sudden he felt himself sinking, the mounted enemy

towering over him on a snorting horse, the earth beneath him
seeming to subside with alarming speed. Wauter leapt aside
and threw away his lance, yelling up God only knew what
words of loathing at Saint-Luc.

Rogue screamed, sounding human somehow in his agony,
and Wauter drew sword from scabbard, intending to end his
distress, cursing anew when Saint-Luc wheeled his mount continually and menacingly near, drawing his flail to swing it at
Wauter over the listing rail.

Hatred for the man compounded, and he swung his sword
in a motion that sent the knight back-stepping his mount out
of range. Wauter then pierced his horse's neck and speeded
Rogue's death, unable to see him die lingeringly with the chevalier's lance buried in his upper chest.

Ermgarde sobbed. Even the queen became quiet and ceased
her taunting, thinking that the killing of horses had no place in
such an affair of honor.

Wauter shook the sadness of the moment from his mind
and concentrated his disgust and hate upon Etienne, who had
gained Wauter's side of the rail now and was bearing down
with the intention of trampling him beneath his horse's
hooves.

The Lord of Synford pulled his mace from his belt and rose
to his full height, waiting until Saint-Luc was almost upon him
before hurling the lethal weapon at the charging horse's front
legs. He'd never made war on horses, but if the Burgundian
broke the unspoken rules of chivalry with such ease. . . .

Saint-Luc's horse lurched to its knees, sending rider from
saddle as if catapulted, to land with a grunt of pain upon his
belly. Etienne struggled to his feet and mechanically drew his
sword, flexing muscles as best he could beneath the plate
to assure himself he wasn't injured. Then he stood with legs
planted wide apart for balance as Wauter came at him, taking
a surer grip on the chain of his spiked flail, which had been
tied by means of a leather thong to his left wrist. It was a sec-
ondary weapon, to be used at such times as the customary
sword proved impractical, just as Synford had used his mace
moments ago with such damnable finesse.

Swords clashed and shone dully in the winter light, the non-
rhythmic, jarring causing Ermgarde to tremble, though her
whole body was paralyzed and otherwise made not the slightest motion. Ever since Rogue had gone down, pierced by that

lance of Saint-Luc's she had retreated further into her stupor, hating this place and everyone in it. Hating her lover most of all, for erasing forever Rogue, who was so much a part of Wauter and her former life. Fearing, too, that this afternoon might obliterate her past for good and all. She didn't want Etienne to die, but neither did she want what he was striving for. She could never be his, not now. Removing Wauter wouldn't change that. 'Twould only complete the rending of her heart that the death of the old warhorse had started.

"Stop them, God, stop them," she prayed, not knowing that she did so out loud.

Isabeau caught her hand and patted it, some compassion showing as she smiled weakly. " 'Twill soon be over, me thinks."

Wauter sensed that the upper hand was his. Saint-Luc was competent with the sword, but lacked skill and experience. Still, he used his shield well and gave Wauter no opening, which heartened the French knight.

De Gascoine had said that the match could be his if he used guile to counteract the other's strength, if he could make Wauter overconfident if only for a second.

Etienne picked his moment, waiting for one of those well aimed, arcing strokes that the lord used from time to time. His shield, strapped to forearm, went skywards and took the blow, the jarring of his shoulder cast steadfastly from mind as he lowered the left arm again immediately and sent his flail hissing, with a grunt of exertion, through the air, to find Wauter unprotected in the region of his belly. Only chain-mail gave resistance.

Wauter gasped and reeled backward, the pain sending him to the threshold of unconsciousness as his back hit the ground and he twisted sideways. Christ, he hadn't expected that!

Lingering in the misty haze that precedes oblivion of the mind, fighting against it, he had reaction enough to swing around his blade and point it up at the enemy, to try to ward off Saint-Luc's advance.

Ermgarde knew that she was crying out, but she couldn't control it. Any moment now the cries would turn to screams and she feared she'd never be able to stop.

Wauter was on the ground, hurt, unable to rise in time to protect himself against Etienne; she could see it all too clearly, felt the scream rising in her throat. And then, when she

wanted her eyes to close but could not make them obey and
had to watch, Etienne pounced—to her fear-glazed eyes it
seemed he hadn't seen the sword at all—and fell onto its point.

Surprise was so acute that no one in the stand uttered a murmur.

Wauter stared up incredulously as Saint-Luc crumpled over
the point of the blade, the sword finding that vulnerable area
where breastplate ends and leg harness continues, sliding between the two and impaling him. There was a shocked gasp
from behind the visor, then the knight fell sideways.

CHAPTER
4 5

WAUTER CLIMBED laboriously to his knees, then gained his feet—the fact that he withdrew his bloody sword and sheathed it once more in its jeweled scabbard, signaled those who watched, more eloquently than words, that the Chevalier Saint-Luc was either dead already or mortally wounded. The combat was done.

Jean-sans-Peur rose to his feet, trying to soften the indignant anger from the French crowd and the jubilant cheers from Warwick and the rest of the English contingent. His speech was lost amid the noise and sudden surge of activity about him, leaving the duke to look a little foolish.

Ermgarde had been on her feet for some moments already, trying to find a way to negotiate the banner-festooned rail that fronted the royal stand. She could see Wauter swaying on his feet, the mail fringe beneath his breastplate gleaming stickily with blood where the spiked flail had caught him.

Isabeau was clinging to her arm, trying to calm the distraught girl. "He's all right, can you not see that? If he stands it can be nothing serious. Calm yourself, please dame; one must not act so before the commonalty."

"No, I must go." Ermgarde fought free of the queen's grasp and flung herself at the rail, grabbing and swinging herself over it with a swish of skirts that captured the attention of every male in the vicinity.

Brodrick had already reached her lord's side and was trying to coax him from the field with a helping hand, but Wauter shook his head. Not yet. He had to know.

She was running toward him and he watched the play of expressions upon her face, tried to gauge her mind and heart. Tears slipped down her cheeks, but for whom he couldn't say.

She looked from him to Saint-Luc, who was being lifted as gently as possible on to a stretcher, his helm removed to expose a grimacing face and blood-encrusted lips.

"Oh, God," she moaned. It tore at her insides to know she'd brought him to this, but she uttered a prayer of thanks at the same time that, as Isabeau had been quick to assure her, Wauter was all right.

She waited, wanting him to take the initiative as of old and tell her what she must do next. After all, she was his again. But he only watched her, seeming to look for something. And then Etienne moaned her name; it sounding grotesquely distorted by the blood in his throat. His hand extended to her, twitching with pain as four bearers hoisted him up.

"Ermgarde . . . Ermgarde . . ." he called in a whimper as the litter bore him away.

She looked after him, looked back to Wauter. How could she just leave him to die? Etienne was alone, while Wauter had Brodrick and Warwick to see to his hurts. Wavering with reluctance, loyalty divided, Ermgarde wished that Wauter would order her away with him, take the decision for her.

But he shook his head, removing helm and handing it to Brodrick, telling her bluntly, "*You* must choose."

"He's dying, Wauter. How can I leave him?"

Wauter put aside the anguish in her voice. He knew now, didn't he? She had made her choice. He could have ordered her away, aye, but he wanted no recriminations in the future—he would not be made to feel the villain, who had denied her comfort to a dying man.

"Then stay with him!" he shouted, cursing himself for doing so. He had meant to stay calm, abide by her wishes with civilized dignity, bow to fate—whatever it dealt him this day—with philosophical detachment. As usual, she was sending his senses reeling. "Stay and be free of me forever. These past two years I have learned to live without you well enough!"

Her heart chilled. So that was the way of it, then; what had happened earlier at the pavilion hadn't meant anything to him. It had not been the magical remedy to heal and mend she had wanted it so much to be. It appeared he cared not whether she went with him and would just as soon resume the carefree, licentious way of life that had been his since her restricting presence was removed. Very well.

She tried to keep the hurt from her voice, but it shook nevertheless. "You say I can stay. Then that is what I will do. Etienne needs me, even if you . . . you. . . ."

She looked into the uncompromising features, held the gaze of his angry eyes and her words faltered, changed into bitter crying. The noise stayed with the men even after she had taken to her heels and disappeared at the far end of the field behind Saint-Luc.

Wauter watched the spot for several moments, suppressing the ridiculous impulse to take to his heels in the same direction. 'Twouldn't have done the ache in his belly any good, for a start, and it was time, too, to realize that she was gone from him—this time forever. The end.

He set his features with studied indifference and turned to Brodrick, who was totally bewildered by the turn of events. How could his master give her away so easily after fighting so long and hard to get her back?

"I'll accept that shoulder to lean on now, Brodrick," he told the lad, the moving of one leg before the other causing his brow to furrow with pain.

Warwick was coming toward them in obvious high spirits, though his face had one brow lifted questioningly. "Was that the Lady Ermgarde I saw running off?"

"Aye."

"But she'll be leaving with you?"

"Nay, she stays behind," Wauter ground out, speaking something of a trial for him as Brodrick shouldered his weight and helped him along.

"But I thought—"

"Not now, Dick, please," breathed Wauter.

Warwick sensed it was best to leave well enough alone, and changed the subject as he obligingly took the knight's other arm and relieved the squire of some of the burden.

"I've been speaking to the duke. Tonight he's holding a banquet in our honor. It should be enjoyable, don't you think? I quite look forward to being feted, and these Burgundian women!" The lecherous grin on his face was easy enough to interpret.

"I won't be there," Wauter told him, resolutely. "As soon as I'm bandaged and Brodrick has packed our accoutrements, we're leaving. I've had enough of Chartres."

"Won't that look odd, Waut? I mean, Burgundy will be expecting you to attend, if the banquet's in your honor. Won't he take it as a slight?"

"Nay. John will be thankful that he was spared the em-

barrassment of feteing victors who've bested his own countrymen. I've some inkling as to the workings of that man's
mind.''

"Well, in that case, I think I'll pack up and come with you.
I'd feel lost at table with so many Burgundians if you were absent, not to mention outnumbered.''

"Don't cry for me. 'Tis a waste of tears and does spoil your
pretty face,'' Etienne croaked at her, each word seemingly
torn from him.

If that was what he believed, that her misery was on account
of his dying, then let it remain so. Only part of Ermgarde's
sadness was for him. The rest was for what was lost.

The surgeon had been and gone, shaking his head and suggesting the attendants leave the chevalier's armor be, for to
remove it would have caused him pointless suffering. Now she
was the only one left, going through the motions of minister-
ing to his needs, replacing saturated dressings as his life's
blood ebbed away, knowing all the time that it was useless.

"I do not understand how you let it happen. You just
walked onto his sword,'' her voice seemed to admonish in a
bewildered whisper.

"I . . . didn't see his blade. Moved in too . . . quickly . . .
too eager,'' he managed, laughing at himself, though the trace
of a chuckle set his face into an agonized mask. "Wanted you
too much. Always the same, right from . . . beginning . . .
when . . . when I found out you weren't a boy.''

She smiled along with him, turning as a chaplain stepped
through the tent flap, his face suitably solemn for the occasion.

"Get out!'' ordered the figure on the couch, with curt authority that cost him strength.

"But, my son, will you not atone for your earthly sins in
confession?'' asked the priest, horrified.

"I'll make . . . my peace with . . . Him later. My confession
now is . . . for this lady . . . none of your business . . . you . . .
carrion crow!''

The chaplain closed his bible with an indignant snap and
disappeared.

Etienne's laugh ended with a rasping cough, his hands
clutching at hers to seek comfort. "I must confess.''

She shook her head, knowing each word he spoke quickened his end.

"Nay, lie quiet and tax yourself not. Talking only causes you pain and, besides, what is there so important to tell me? You've been good to me. That is all that matters, surely?"

"But I haven't. . . . Not always been good. I want . . . your forgiveness, Ermgarde."

"You could have done nothing so terrible as to warrant forgiveness, Etienne. But if it eases you, you have it," she assured him, squeezing his hand. His words were puzzling; she supposed them the ravings of one sinking into unconsciousness.

"I never sent . . . to England for . . . your ransom!"

The poor man was obviously becoming light of senses. "But of course you did. We had the reply to it, remember?"

"I . . . penned it. Gleaned information from . . . you . . . made it up. Wanted you to stay . . . with me."

She sat back and drew her hand from his with a start, staring into his glazed blue eyes. What was he saying? It was too monstrous. He couldn't have done such a thing. The loss of blood was effecting his mind. Yes, that was it. "I don't believe you."

"He never . . . left France. He searched . . . even came to Chemille. Remember the . . . singers? Latin. . . . 'Twas he! That's why . . . why he knew me . . . called me by name. We'd met . . . before."

"No!" Ermgarde had jumped to her feet, wringing her hands wildly. "No, you couldn't have sent him from Chemille without telling him, without telling *me*! You wouldn't do that. You loved me . . . wouldn't hurt me! Say it's not true, Etienne!"

". . . because I loved you, I . . . did it."

It *was* true. She could tell by the pleading look upon his face. She slumped down on the chair, heated denial giving way to silent shock. They'd never received a ransom demand back home and Wauter had come looking for her. There had never been any dallying with Alice! He'd spent his time searching for her, probably turning to Anne de Bois only when he lost hope. And he'd come to Chemille, where she was imprisoned and she had never known, Etienne keeping her in ignorance! God, 'twas as well that he lay dying or she'd have reached for the nearest weapon!

Wauter's attitude became clear, everything fell into place—right down to the inconsequential details like Isabeau's bewilderment at Ermgarde choosing Saint-Luc in preference to her husband. But *she* had been the one chosen. He had set out deliberately and cold-bloodedly to take her for himself, had disregarded her pain and the distress his lies had brought.

Her voice was low, but it shook with rage. "How could you have done it? I loved him. Didn't that mean anything to you?"

"I loved . . . you . . . too. Could . . . not . . . let . . . you . . . go." His voice faded to an anguished whisper. His hands wavered in the air, trying to find hers, but Ermgarde shrank in repugnance. "For . . . give . . . me . . ."

Forgive him? He'd destroyed her life, her will to live. Her lips remained tightly shut and her eyes, dry of tears now, watched him with cold detachment as his eyes begged her to ease his passing.

His lips moved feebly once but no sound came forth, and soon after he was dead, the pleading eyes still fixed on her.

She went outside and summoned Etienne's attendants to take care of the corpse, then wandered from his pavilion to the tilting rail. The royal standard had been dismantled, the stand was empty and, up on their ladders, the duke's workmen were unfastening the pennons of Synford, Warwick, de Gascoine and Saint-Luc. Little remained of the recent spectacle. Even the blood was gone, a groundsman having erased the blood smears from the grass so that all stood ready for the next tourney.

What now? Her mind and body were numb. She couldn't frame thoughts, much less plans. There wasn't even a familiar face to be seen from whom she could take guidance. Wauter's pavilion was gone, along with every other hint of his presence and that of his friend, Warwick.

"He's gone without you then, I see," observed a familiar, acid voice.

Ermgarde turned and dropped a curtsy to Isabeau as the other popped her head from her curtained litter.

"Not that I blame him, though it does surprise me, knowing his feelings for you," she continued. "Thought I'd give your lover a royal send-off, but it seems I've put this poor leg of mine through a great deal of discomfort for nothing. Well, what are you going to do now, dame? I dare say I could find you a place in my household if you've a mind. What fun it would be watching you and Anne de Bois fighting like she-cats."

"Anne is still here, gracious lady?" Her ears had pricked up at mention of the lady-in-waiting, a sudden alertness breaking through her daze.

"Of course she's here. Where did you think she'd be? With your husband? Ha! If you'd truly been dead, as we believed, she might have stood a chance with him. As it is, the mere fact that you are alive is enough to insure his disinterest in all others. Would that I had such a devastating power over men."

"Nay, be thankful you do not, good queen, for it sometimes has a way of working against one's self," vowed Ermgarde.

"So, what will you do? A place at my court?"

"I think not, though I thank you. I've a mind to leave Chartres today. Might you know where I can exchange this gown and silver girdle for an outfit of boys clothes?"

"Good grief, whatever are you about?"

" 'Tis a safer way to travel."

"Yes . . . I suppose I can help, but I don't quite see. . . ."

Isabeau was still slightly bewildered as she raised a hand in farewell to the green-clad horsewoman, but had sense enough to call out a helpful hint. "Take the Normandy road!"

Ermgarde waved, then dug her heels into the horse's flanks. The Normandy road it would be, then, and by midnight—at least by dawn—she would have caught up with him. Lord, this was going to take some explaining! Pray he was in a receptive frame of mind. All she needed was a chance to speak, to tell him of Saint-Luc's terrible confession, show him the forged letter, and hope he'd understand. He would, wouldn't he? Yes, of course he would; he *had* to!

If Ermgarde could just get him to *listen*, then she felt confident he'd believe her, love her once again as he had long ago. And they could go home at last to Synford, *together*.

BESTSELLING TALES OF ROMANCE FROM JOVE

___ 0-515-08593-6   **The Rope Dancer** $6.95
by Roberta Gellis
(A Jove Trade Paperback)
The magical story of a spirited young woman and the minstrel
who awakens her to the sweet agonies of new-found love
amidst the pomp and pageantry of twelfth-century England.

___ 0-515-08637-1   **Blue Heaven, Black Night** $7.50
by Shannon Drake
(A Jove Trade Paperback)
A passionate tale of the bastard daughter of Henry II and his
fierce and loyal knight—set in England's most glorious age.

___ 0-515-08670-3   **My Lady Rogue** $3.95
by Kathryn Atwood
When the curtain falls, Ariel de Juliers Greystone, star of
the French stage, becomes England's most beautiful spy
—against Napoleon Bonaparte, Emperor of France!

___ 0-515-08932-X   **Crown of Glory** $3.95
by Rosemary Jarman
The saga of beautiful Elizabeth Woodville, who captures
the heart of Edward IV, King of England, during the bright
days of chivalry.

Available at your local bookstore or return this form to:

 JOVE
THE BERKLEY PUBLISHING GROUP, Dept. B
390 Murray Hill Parkway, East Rutherford, NJ 07073

Please send me the titles checked above. I enclose _____. Include $1.00 for postage
and handling if one book is ordered; add 25¢ per book for two or more not to exceed
$1.75. CA, IL, NJ, NY, PA, and TN residents please add sales tax. Prices subject to change
without notice and may be higher in Canada. Do not send cash.

NAME _____

ADDRESS _____

CITY _____ STATE/ZIP _____

(Allow six weeks for delivery.)   **J426**